GUARI

It Deserves to Win Top Awards...Through an amazing collection of real letters transcribed by Greene, as well as oral history, the book is filled with touching accounts of [real] lives and compelling firsthand testimonies of the Great Depression and World War II. This is one of the most spellbinding books I have ever read. I'm giving it five stars and five stars more. – Marsha Cook

Reading Pleasure...very enjoyable book to read; [the] mix of fact and fiction was seamless, also as topical now as then...Five Stars – bucknut1?

A Good Book That Gives a New View of World War II...Greene brought to life what most think of any more as just a history lesson. People lived during that time, they laughed and cried and were scared when their sons went off to war. Many mothers who have sent off their children today to fight in Iraq or Afghanistan can relate to this story...Five Stars – Wendy Siefken

I LOVED IT...I could not put it down. I even bought a copy for my mom and brother. I can't wait to read the next one. Five Stars – Marie Gaffin Brown

Guardians and Other Angels...I enjoyed the book so much, I couldn't put it down. I even bought a couple copies to give as gifts. [Greene] has an amazing talent for making the characters in the story come alive. I wanted to know more about them and could easily imagine them all in the situations she described. I loved the way she intermingled fact with fiction in using many original letters. By reading the book, I have a deeper appreciation for an era that I really didn't know a lot about and the sacrifices that families make for one another. I look forward to the next book from this author and hopefully many more to come. Five Stars – Anita M. Brown

Classic Writing...a beautifully written piece of Americana vs. love story, love of family. The author wrote with such precision and detail to everything she approached, that this journey with her...is the stuff that classics are made of. One only has to read *The Grapes of Wrath* or *Angela's Ashes*, both ranking among Pulitzer Prize winners, to appreciate

the level of care Greene took with her writing of this story, which is a walk down the ordinary, through historical details of decades, into wars and poverty, through passions and conversations, deaths, marriages, longings, and all the things that tie all of us together to make up the human condition, is the message that comes across, because Greene's story is our story, it's America's story, the World's story, and is so wonderfully told that it is my story, because in her journey we see ourselves. What is a good read if not to shine that light back in, grab hold of our real emotions, and drag us along for the ride, as if we were there?...Five Stars – Paulette Mahurin
http://www.amazon.com/s/ref=nb_sb_noss?url=search-alias%3Daps&field-keywords=paulette+mahurin+books

Like meeting old friends...This book reminded me of discovering an old chest in an attic, filled with the treasured pieces of a family's history. The walk through the years through the old letters between family members was like meeting old friends for the first time...The fictional additions fill in the blanks in the actual history, and add depth and understanding to the story...Five Stars – DeEtte Anderton

Once started, couldn't put the book down!...very well written, heartwarming, simply poignant, an enjoyable and easy read....Five Stars – Carey Street

An Important Contribution to History...while I was reading [this book], I felt like the characters were still alive and when [it] ended, I missed them. I envy the way Linda is able to put words to pen. This book will be a "family treasure", but the authentic personal letters written by the book's characters that are included in the book describe an important way of life and times in America, and Linda's superb and powerful depiction of historical events during the 1930s and 1940s also make it a "historical trasure". Anyone who likes to read heartwarming family sagas and Great Depression and World War II history that are beautifully written will love this book. Five Stars – Mary R. Brown

Love everything about this book! Beautiful book! I plan to share! I am so inspired! Thank you from the bottom of my heart!! I will recommend this story to all my friends. Five Stars – Brenda Perlin

Characters come alive...they practically jump off the page at you. This is rare in a work of history. Ms. Greene knows how to write using creative non-fiction...From all the stories I've heard from my family, she's got it down cold. Kudos to her. Five Stars – Edward Griffin "Ed Griffin"

Fascinating Story Well Told...families similar to mine...mirrored many happenings in my grandparent's home in a steel town in Western Pennsylvania during the same times...through authentic letters...family members came alive through the Great Depression and WWII. Five Stars – Margaret Hanna

An Engaging Historical Treasure...I strongly recommend this book definitely to an older audience or to young adults that are interested in Great Depression and war history. Although this novel was a very captivating one, I feel it's not diverted towards children due to the emotional, personal drama that occurs in it...Inspired by a true story...throughout the pages, the book contains many authentic letters that are written by the characters, immediately making the novel more intriguing and private to read.

Linda Lee Greene really sculpts the characters. As I was reading, I felt connected to them in some way, as if they were real people that I knew personally. I also appreciated how Greene decided to tell the story in a fictional manner, as I thought it would not have been as fascinating if it was completely non-fiction. The novel was nicely wrapped up at the end and it was finished with finality, giving me a sense of satisfaction once I completed reading. I really enjoyed this read; it truly exhausted my heart and played with my feelings...Iris Park, Allbooks Review Int. www.allbooksreviewint.com

Guardians and Other Angels...Told during the span of many decades...the mosaic picture of the two families and how their lives intertwined and shared their [authentic] personal letters with us in this outstanding novel will keep you riveted to the printed page until you find out where they wind up and what might be next...[The book] is more than just heartfelt. You can feel it in every word...when [Greene] describes how she kept vigil at the side of her dying aunt, the account reminded me of doing the same last year as I watched my sister leave this physical world, and it really brought tears to my eyes...

If you are like me, you will read *Guardians and Other Angels* in one day. I could not put it down...– Fran Lewis

Wonderful; Very Touching...I loved this book!! It moved me very deeply and touched my heart. The family spirit is strong as this story so beautifully shows. Five Stars – Vicki Osborne

Five Stars Not Enough...Sometimes a story comes along that is so much a part of a life once known and so real...that this reader didn't want it to end. That's the case in Linda Lee Greene's novel based on a true story. I stretched out the process getting to know each character and loving the way Linda Lee Greene evolved her story...Linda Lee Greene uses an Appalachian dialect for her characters that seems authentic and easy to navigate. This remarkable book reminds me of two Jeannette Walls books: *HALF BROKE HORSES* and *THE GLASS CASTLE.* The five star rating I gave *GUARDIANS AND OTHER ANGELS* is not enough. I wish I could give it more. I look forward to savoring the sequel. Five Stars – Rosalie Ungar www.nosexinsainttropez.com

Guardians and Other Angels...a saga set against the backdrop of The Great Depression and World War II, author Linda Lee Greene's prose has the texture and depth of the times she writes about. The story is reminiscent of Steinbeck's *The Grapes of Wrath* and calls those times to mind; times when young men considered themselves lucky to secure a job away from home in Oregon or California for the CCC or the WPA and made enough money to send home to feed the family; times when half-grown children were turned out to make their own way in the world and often failed; times when sudden death lurked in the shadows of freight train cars and the dark corners of hobo jungles.

This was life before we got so smart—before cell phones, television sets and reliable birth control. It is the story of four generations and how they made a mark on life in Southern Ohio during times nobody thought were good—how people stuck together and supported one another day after endless day...

This story is not lighthearted by any test, but it is one well-worth reading as it gives the reader an inside look at what many of our ancestors survived so we might follow them...Enjoy! – Diana Hannon Forrester

Hello Linda...Thank you for writing *Guardians and Other Angels*. Well written and interesting. You captured the family life...beautifully...I will impatiently wait for the next book...Thank you. – Bert Pierce

Dear Linda…Your book was one of the most spellbinding books I've ever read. I'm sure a lot of it's because of my familiarity with so much of what you wrote about, but you put me there. I mean I was literally <u>there.</u>

…I shedded some tears when Bussy died and hearing how your Mommaw grieved and suffered so.

I chuckled and my heart hurt a little at that baby girl (you) that was separated from her parents so young and the sweet little voice saying, "Up, up, becky time, toatie in da pate and milk in da guyash. "Sweet!"

…Another thing from you book I found so sweet was Bussy calling you "Tadpole". Your special bond to an uncle you never knew in life was extraordinary.

Your family captivated me. Their hard, but good life, the blizzard your Poppaw, Bob, and Arthur went through, actually feeling how tired your Mommaw was so much of the time, but still trudging on, because <u>that's</u> what you did.

So Linda, I wanted to let you know how much I enjoyed your book of love and memories. So much of it reminded me of some of my own life. Love, Carol Treadway

Also by

Linda Lee Greene

Rooster Tale
Jesus Gandhi Oma Mae Adams - Co-author

GUARDIANS AND OTHER ANGELS

A TRUE LIFE NOVEL BY
Linda Lee Greene

DeLamor Press

United States

DeLamor Press

Guardians and Other Angels

Linda Lee Greene

Copyright © Linda Lee Greene 2012, 2015

All Rights Reserved. No part of this book may be reproduced in any form by any means including reprints, excerpts, photocopies, recordings, or any future reproduction methods without the express permission of the author. Contact the author at lindaleegreene.author.artist@gmail.com to seek permission.

ISBN – 13:978-1514644645

Published in the United States by DeLamor Press

Cover painting and design by Linda Lee Greene

To view the online gallery of Linda's artwork, log onto www.gallery-llgreene.com

Dedication

This reissue of **GUARDIANS AND OTHER ANGELS** is different from the one published in 2012 in that it includes reviews of the first book, as well as the insertion of the original foreword into the Author's Note at the end of this new release. The basic story is essentially the same. At the time of the publication of the initial manuscript, my father and my brother were alive. This second edition reflects that change, as well.

My father Lee Edward Greene, 89 years of age, and my brother David Marlin Greene, 69 years of age, both of whom are featured prominently in this book, passed away within seventeen weeks of each other in 2014, two years after the release of the first edition of *Guardians and Other Angels*. I am grateful beyond words that both of them read and reread several times their own first-edition copies of it, and they loved it.

Although my parents were my inspiration for the book, I dedicated the first edition of it solely to my brother David Marlin Greene. However, this second edition is dedicated to the memory of my mother Roma Evelyn Gaffin Greene, my father Lee Edward Greene, and my brother David Marlin Greene.

Linda Lee Greene –2015

Acknowledgements

In the main this book is the product of a tradition within both my paternal and maternal families of origin, a practice of telling and retelling family stories. For the most part, at least in recent years, the ritual fell to my father Lee Edward Greene, and to my Uncle Dean Gaffin, who is the only remaining member of the family that is at the heart of this story. I couldn't have written this book if both of these remarkable men hadn't been such adroit and devoted raconteurs.

My gratitude is also extended to my maternal second cousin Freda Caplinger Proctor, and her daughter Lisa Proctor for helping me to fill in some gaps in the early life of my maternal grandmother Mary Evalena Caplinger Gaffin.

Life-long family friend Sim Workman, showing up from time to time in these pages, regaled me with tales of his own when I called on him during the course of my work on this book. In his nineties, Sim is still sharp of mind and fit of limb, and to this day, plants, tends, and harvests his enormous vegetable garden each season, a garden that supplements the diets of his neighbors, friends, and family members in Peebles, the tiny burg in Southern Ohio that is the setting of this story.

Debra Shiveley Welch, my maternal first cousin and best-selling/award-winning author of several books under her own signature, as well as the co-author of our best-selling first book *Jesus Gandhi Oma Mae Adams,* has assisted me in publishing this second edition of **GUARDIANS AND OTHER ANGELS**. We are forever-buddies and consistent helpmates.

My sister-in-law Dorothy Brown Greene met the challenge of formatting the paperback edition of the book. She is a phenomenal friend and helpmate, and I thank her from the bottom of my heart.

Finally, I must express my sincere gratitude to my maternal first cousin Mary Rosalie Gaffin Brown, the daughter of Bob Gaffin, the elder sibling of my mother. My appreciation is based on her allowing me access to, with permission to publish, our grandmother's collection of old family letters that are transcribed in this book. Absent Rosie's generosity, **GUARDIANS AND OTHER ANGELS** could not have evolved to its final version.

GUARDIANS AND OTHER ANGELS

"...You shall see rude and sturdy, experienced and wise men,
keeping to their castles, or teaming up their summer's wood,
or chopping alone in the woods,
men fuller of talk and rare adventure in the sun and wind and rain,
than a chestnut is of meat;
who were out not only in 1775 or 1812, but have been out every day of
their lives;
greater men than Homer, or Chaucer, or Shakespeare,
only they never got time to say so;
they never took to the way of writing.
Look at their fields, and imagine what they might write,
if ever they should put pen to paper.
Or what have they not written on the face of the earth already,
clearing, and burning, and scratching, and harrowing, and plowing, and
subsoiling,
in and in, and out and out, and over and over, again and again,
erasing what they had already written for the want of parchment."

-A Week on the Concord and Merrimack Rivers-
Henry David Thoreau

One

We were rocking again. In her taut arms, Mommaw held me too tightly against her quaking body, and she was crying all over me again, just like before. Those words she kept saying over and over and over, words I couldn't understand through her sobbing, but somehow knew were awful and meant I was a bad baby—I wanted those words to stop, those words that really weren't words at all but sounded more like the sad bawling of the mommy cow when her baby cow got lost that time. The creaking rocking, the tight holding, the shuddering crying—all of it made my belly feel funny and my head dizzy, but not in a good way like when Uncle Deany twirled me around and around when we played. I was scared! The rocking that made me dizzy and the holding that made it hard for me to breathe and the crying that made me know I was a bad baby, all of it scared me. I wanted Mommy, but I didn't know where Mommy was. I wanted to find Mommy, but I couldn't. I wasn't even two years old yet.

Two

I was born on the rim of a star-wound. Called crypto-explosions or astroblemes in the jargon of science, the one hundred or more star-wounds currently charted on the surface of Earth are round craters caused by meteor strikes hundreds of millions of years ago, and range in size from one-half to forty miles in diameter. The best-known star-wounds in North America are the Meteor Crater in Winslow, Arizona and at astroblemes in Indiana and Ohio.[1] As star-wounds go, mine, located in Adams County, Ohio is rather impressive by virtue of its extremely faulted and folded bedrock, which is unusual among the typically flat-layered rocks in Ohio.[2] Another unique feature of this particular star-wound is the Great Serpent effigy mound lying within its five-mile crater bed. Believed to have been constructed about 2,300 years ago, it is the largest and finest effigy mound known to man.

Radiocarbon dating shows the serpent effigy to be the earthwork of the prehistoric Adena people, one of several early mound building cultures of the indigenous nations. The most sophisticated people north of Mexico during the period of 1000 BC to AD 1500, the densest population of the Adena Indians spanned a territory from Northern Kentucky to Southern Ohio. At the place of my birth, the architects of the remarkable serpent effigy related it to the stars and moon and sun. Various alignments of it correspond to those astronomical features, suggesting that its builders were astute astronomers. Apparently, they knew how to bury their dead, as well, because artifacts discovered within contiguous burial effigies, as in the pyramids in Egypt, reveal a society that gave their departed loved ones a good send off. Those inanimate mounds, resplendent with beautiful and

---

[1] http://faculty.icc.edu/estermer/geology/box_7.htm
[2] http://www.ohiohistoryteachers.org/03/04sw07.shtml

useful items for new and exciting afterlives are suggestive of faith-based containers of the grief of the people left behind. It was a tradition whose adoption in some contemporary form might go a long way toward the healing of the spirit of modern man. I sometimes wonder if such a high ritual, designed to celebrate faith in a grand ongoing journey of the spirit, might have helped to relieve the crushing and unrelenting grief of my maternal grandmother Mary Evalena "Lena" Caplinger Gaffin, called Mommaw by her grandchildren, an unrelenting grief over her losses, especially of her son Bussy.

As the sole vessel of the grief of my grandmother, I grew up more acutely aware than most of the deaths of Dorothy and Bussy, the first- and fourth-born children, respectively, of my maternal grandparents. The facts surrounding the demise of Dorothy, having occurred just a few years shy of a century ago, and the parties most privy to those circumstances having long ago passed away, have become muddled. The surviving beliefs are that she died either at birth, the victim of a head injury caused by birthing instruments, or as a newborn, of influenza, a widespread and lethal outbreak responsible for the taking of many lives across the nation that same year. More than two decades later, when my mother was two months pregnant for me, and Bussy was seventeen, he succumbed to an illness of long duration. The life and death of Bussy still loom large and lend an air of sentimental poignancy within the collective consciousness of the family of my mother, and in some ways, are enduring central themes threading through its history, and as such, form a major element of this story.

    In the searing aftermath of the passing away of Uncle Bussy, and other taxing situations, our country doctor, old Doc Ellison, a brilliant and caring physician by all accounts, was deeply concerned over the unyielding grief of my grandmother. She grew frighteningly thin, her hands trembled, and her heart palpitated so violently that you could see it beating in her chest as if it were trying to break through her ribcage. Initially misdiagnosed with heart trouble, she was later correctly diagnosed with Graves Disease, or hyperactive thyroid, a disorder having bedeviled several of her female descendants since then, my mother, my sister Sherri, and myself, included. Aggravating my grandmother's intense psychic pain over the loss of Bussy, during the final and heartbreakingly difficult weeks of his life, her eldest child Bob was shipped overseas as a member of the Allied invading forces of North Africa during World War II. Two weeks after the burial of Bussy, as Lena was still in deep mourning and seriously ill, as well as terrified over the safety of Bob, her mother became gravely ill. While attended by my grandmother and her siblings in rotating shifts, hour by hour, day after day, and week after week, my great grandmother lingered for three months in excruciating and relentless agony whereby little or nothing could be done to relieve her pain, or to save her. Shortly thereafter, Rhoda, the youngest and beloved sister of my grandmother, was stricken suddenly with what is believed to have been a hemorrhage of her brain, killing her instantly. Determined to get his wife away from the sad memories of Bussy tied to their family home, my grandfather made a well-meaning but unfortunate decision: Even as my grandmother was still grappling with all of those losses, he moved his family to a distant farm, breaking long-standing emotional and friendship ties with supportive neighbors and friends among the country community in which they had lived for many years. It isn't any wonder that Lena was thrown into Graves Disease, a disorder often remaining benignly dormant unless and until it is triggered into activity by a person's having experienced hyper-stressive circumstances.

Subsequent to my birth in one of the bedrooms of the farmhouse, a much-anticipated birth, for I was the first grandchild on both sides of my family, my parents and I, in pursuit of better employment opportunities for my father, moved from the farm of my grandparents to Columbus, the capital city of the State of Ohio. Nestled in the foothills of the Appalachian Mountains, the farm, located in an outlying country region of the blink-and-miss-it town of Peebles in Adams County, Ohio was little more than a thirty-minute drive from the northern shore of the Ohio River. A distance of almost ninety miles north, however, separated the farm from our little apartment in Columbus.

Nineteen months after the death of Bussy, and when I was twelve months of age, although well-meaning, but obviously misguided regarding the well-being of young children, old Doc Ellison recommended to my parents that they leave me with my grandmother as a balm to soothe her losses. My parents, young and green, as well as trusting of the advice of the doctor, were unaware that the arrangement, sooner or later, was likely to bode less well for me. Therefore, they reluctantly agreed to leave me on the farm with my grandparents and the many younger brothers and sisters of my mother. Thus began a long cycle of weekly separations from my parents. They returned to Peebles from Columbus every weekend, or nearly so, and I was such a resilient child that I seemed none the less for wear from the separations. Unfortunately, their inexpert parenting skills kept them uninformed regarding emerging emotional difficulties for me created by the situation. Even had they known, it is likely my problems would have been discounted compared to my grandmother's weighty and far-reaching psychic pain and illness. Other than my stifling and terrifying nightly episodes in the lap of my grandmother as she rocked and cried, and my acute awareness of the absence of my parents, especially of my mother from whose breast I had only recently been weaned, it was a happy time for me. The effects of the separations primarily stayed in abeyance until decades later when I was faced with my own first and devastating loss–my reaction closely emulating that of my grandmother after her loss of Bussy.

GUARDIANS AND OTHER ANGELS   5

Since having spent most of the first year of my life with them, I was comfortably bound to my grandparents and their pack of rowdy children. I was in thrall of the animals on the farm, and enjoyed accompanying my grandmother while she performed her chores—a daily routine of an over-worked wife of a farmer and the mother of seven surviving children, five of whom were still at home, those five comprising the two younger sisters and the three youngest brothers of my mother. Despite the tragedies, the hardships associated with farm life, and the ravages of the Great Depression, there was an underlying quality of buoyancy to the spirits of those remarkable people. Even though I carry in my cells the unfortunate imprint of my many nights in the rocking chair with my grandmother as she cried for Bussy and Bob and her other departed loved-ones, my cells also carry the much deeper and more influential legacy of the resilience, the optimism, and the gaity of my ancestors.

The largest part of this story takes place before I was born, and before the family of my mother moved to the farm most prominent in the memories of my many cousins, my siblings, and me. It begins well over a century after the 1797 founding of Adams County, Ohio, its namesake the second President of the United States, John Adams the Elder, who was in office at the time. Notwithstanding the mysterious serpent effigy, as well as many other significant remnants of the presence of Native Americans in that place of my birth, by the time later white settlers arrived in that part of the Northwest Territory in 1791, those aboriginal architects were no longer to be found in the area. Their absence was the tragic outcome of their relentless extermination at the hands of the invading white man during the western expansion of the original thirteen colonies into what was to become the United States of America.

The parents of my father having originally hailed from West Virginia were of the Pentecostal persuasion of Protestant Christianity, or "Holy Rollers" as dubbed by skeptical, albeit fascinated, outsiders. My paternal grandfather Alderson Estep Greene, or "A. E." as referred to by my mother and many others, was a gifted and charismatic "Holy Roller" preacher, his religion at variance by several degrees of separation from the Presbyterian Virginian and Scotch-Irish settlers who finally established the area. About 1850, a small element of German people arrived in the county, the major ancestors of the father of my mother. There was but one Catholic Church in the region, forced to close its doors due to a lack of membership.[3] Never having any experience of the Catholic religion, while in Europe during World War II, Bob, the eldest of the children of my maternal grandparents, wrote glowing letters to his mother about the magnificent cathedrals he had toured there. In one letter he described as the most

---

[3] http://www.heritagepursuit.com'Adams/AdamsCI.htm

6   LINDA LEE GREENE

beautiful sight he had ever seen, a group of adolescent girls resplendent in their white communion dresses and veils, impeccably queued, and with triangulated hands before their angelic faces, their heads were bent reverently toward the sacrament each of them was about to receive.

As were the parents of my father transplants to the area, so are the prevalent white cedars, a northern species of tree that apparently migrated south in advance of a glacier thousands of years ago, the same genus of tree which is the namesake of the tiny neighborhood of Cedar Fork, the major location of this saga. Accompanying the white cedar in its southern migration were others of its northern companions, shade-and moisture-seeking trees and plants such as fir and spruce, various ferns and a plethora of rare and resolute wildflowers, plant species as integral to this narrative as are the hills and the country roads and the animals and the human beings. When I was young and so often surrounded by them, although my artist's eye took note of their beauty, I didn't know about those individuals of the plant world–their names–their little biographies, plants such as the squat miterwort, its petite snowflake-like flowers studding slim and fragile stems seeming to rise in rebellion against its cowering bed of dense maple-shaped leaves, a plant easy to miss in this Midwestern Garden of Eden, but looming grandly against the genus hepatica known by the other names of liverworts or various mosses.

Extravagantly perennial along waterways, the controversial but beautiful white magnolia-like bloodroot, hailing originally from Nova Scotia, is a tasty snack for deer, small bees and flies, but its seeds are spread and germinated by ants in a process called myrmecochory. The elaiosome, a fleshy organ on the seeds, is eaten by the ants, the seeds then becoming part of their nest debris, the debris providing a rich growing medium for the hardy plants. Producing the toxin sanguinarine which kills animal cells by blocking certain proteins, applying bloodroot to the skin may destroy the tissue and lead to the formation of a large scab called an eschar. Although historically used by Native Americans for its supposed curative properties, and as a home-remedy for skin cancer, studies have shown it to be disfiguring, painful, and ineffective in such treatments. "Folk healers" in the State of Georgia, dispensing bloodroot as a topical paste, have been arrested and charged with practicing medicine without a license and causing severe bodily harm to their unwitting patients. Despite its questionable character, the United States FDA has approved the inclusion of sanguinarine in toothpastes and mouthwashes as an antibacterial or anti-plaque agent. Bloodroot is also a popular red dye used by Native American artists and basketmakers.[4]

To calm his persistent heartburn, my father, when young, dug up the roots of the heart-shaped wild ginger, and probing below the surface of

_____

[4] http://en.wikipedia.org/wiki/Bloodroot

GUARDIANS AND OTHER ANGELS 7

the ground and scratching the roots of the plants with a fingernail, he identified their potency by the strength of their familiar "ginger" aroma. Shown to have certain microbial properties, it is used to reduce fevers, to treat coughs and sore throats, and to induce abortions. Some credence is given to the claim that it is an antidote for the consumption of tainted meats.[5]

As with many children, a favorite of mine when young was the yellow touch-me-nots, or jewelweed, shining like clusters of gems in the thick shade of forests. Seedpods suspending from stems at their maturity, when touched, burst with a pop, setting young and old alike into spasms of giggles.

As if God despaired of the sameness of this northern clime, the diversity in the geology of Adams County, carved by glacial meltwater, makes it friendly to isolated colonies of plants having migrated from the south, east, and west, as well. From the west hailed prairie plants such as prairie dock, big and little bluestem, side-oats grama grass, liatris, stonecrop, and agave, giving some areas a desert-like appearance,[6] many of those thorny or razor-sharp plants called "shin grabbers" by the locals.

Nowhere in the region is the environment more unique than in the ecosystem bounding the homes of my forebears at Cedar Fork Creek. Tucked in its matchless geological formations and botanical oddities, the area today is known as the famous Davis Memorial State Nature Preserve. The distinctive qualities of the 88-acre preserve arise from its location astride the boundary of two markedly different physiographic regions: the Ohio extension of the Bluegrass Region of Kentucky and the Interior Low Plateau Province, at one time joined to the Appalachian Plateau to the east. The coming together of the two regions created a complicated geology and a spectacular relief of Illinoian-age till and Mississippian sandstone-capped hills whose bedrock is Devonian shales and Silurian dolomite. Unlike the deep and rich soil blanketing the western stretches of Adams County, agricultural land productive in wheat, oats, corn, soybeans and tobacco, a dry and shallow soil with its unyielding bedrock at Cedar Fork bedeviled farmers and homesteaders. My paternal grandmother Eva Love Wheeling Greene, Mommaw Greene to my siblings and me, nearly broke her back, as well as her spirit, trying to coax her garden that was planted in the stubborn Cedar Fork soil into growing enough vegetables to feed her hungry children. Her neighbor, Mommaw Gaffin, in concert with Mommaw Greene, always used to say that the only way to get anything to grow on Cedar Fork was to get a lot of rain.

---

[5] http://2bnthewild.com/plants/H36.htm

[6] Ohio's Natural Heritage, Michael B. Lafferty, Editor in Chief, The Ohio Department of Science with The Ohio Department of Natural Resources, Columbus, Ohio, 1979, p, 253 – 259, chapter by Lynn Edward Elfner

8   LINDA LEE GREENE

Eons ago, the bedrock gave way in places, however. As water cascaded from hillside streams to the valleys below, it bore funnel-shaped sinkholes into the foundations of the hills, banes to farmers but booty to botanists. Noted Ohio-born botanist and geologist, E. Lucy Braun, in her writings about the area bounding Cedar Fork Creek, described mist rising from the sinkholes on hot summer days, their interiors replete with various plants "converting the sinkholes into sunken gardens in springtime."[7]

Caves are abundant along the creek, most of them belly-crawlers. Hosting many species of bats, at least nine of the eleven types found in Ohio, the larger Cedar Fork Cave is located at the foot of the Greene property. Accessible only by permit now, but when my parents and their siblings, and even my brother and I were kids, we freely played standing upright in that cave. Usually staying over-long at the Workman's place across the holler where that ornery Sim Workman taught my young paternal aunts and uncles, and my brother and me to crave his homemade cornsilk cigarettes, inevitably we came upon the cave when the light was fading from the sky. In that twilight, the bats were rousing from their daylight snooze to commence their nightly crunch on insect critters too slow or too dumb to evade their amazing echolocation, a means of tracking an object by its sound, both emitted and rebounded. As we approached the mouth of the cave, we made a lot of noise to rout the bats and send them screeching and darting in acute geometric twists and turns into the sky above us, scaring us half to death. Uneducated at the time regarding the impressive resumés of those oft-reviled flying mammals, it was much later that I learned that bats are the world's best bug-eaters, pollinators, and midwives to rainforests.[8] Had I known, I would have regarded them more sympathetically. Rolly-polly bugs swiftly wound into tight knots of self-protection as hard as pebbles as we entered the dark inner chamber of the cave, pillbugs and sowbugs and spiders and evidence of snakes nearby made our skins crawl, and our hearts thrill with the danger of it all. While at once we were terrified of the caves, we were also in awe of them—feeling a kind of reverence for them, as if on a cellular level we knew, as the Mayan culture did, that caves are *el primer templo del mundo* (the first temples of the world), and like those ancient people we accepted as true that many aspects of the cosmos began in caves, even that the sun and moon were hatched in one of those dark and mysterious and powerful wombs of Earth.[9]

---

[7] Ohio's Natural Heritage, Michael B. Lafferty, Editor in Chief, The Ohio Department of Science with The Ohio Department of Natural Resources, Columbus, Ohio, 1979, p. 253 – 259, chapter by Lynn Edward Elfner

[8] The Good, The Bat, & The Ugly, Sharon Lovejoy, Country Living Gardener, Fall 1995, p. 19

[9] American Archeology, Summer, 2011, THE MAYA'S SACRED CAVES, Photos by Bruce T. Martin, Text by James Brady, p. 13-19

This is a walker's paradise, for several recent years a favorite trek on Ohio's 1,445 mile Buckeye Trail, a designated walkway looping the state in its most scenic locations. On the way back to the log cabin where my paternal grandparents and my aunts and uncles lived before the advent of the Buckeye Trail, we kicked the old tree stump at the foot of the yard to watch the scattering of the lizards by the dozens burrowed in its rotted wood.

Well before I was born, my paternal grandfather A. E., assisted by his eldest son Bill and third-born son Lee, built the log cabin, the structure serving as a home for the family for many years. It was hard work for young Lee Greene, who six years in the future would become my father. Nevertheless, to him, its construction was as the building of a temple, as purposeful as those built by early Hebrew believers in the one God. Crudely built of stones and sticks, the reverential structures of those early Hebrew worshipers constituted faith in the protection of their God. Similarly, the log cabin meant safety and security to young Lee, qualities of life his soul yearned after and required. Foregoing most of his playtime and making acquaintances among his new neighbors, as well as exploring the intriguing terrain surrounding the log cabin, were sacrifices easily made by Lee because in so doing he was gaining his first permanent home.

The father of Lee, a man reputed to grow restless and incurious when staying put in one place for any appreciable length of time, had consistently hauled his wife and children hither and yon, ranging as far afield as Florida, and back and forth and back and forth, until Lee was fed up with journeying. Lee wanted roots—he needed roots, and the log cabin symbolized that craving of his soul. His mother and siblings were of the same mind, and A. E., yielding to the stubborn resolve of his wife to wander no more, especially to Florida, a place entirely incompatible with her nature, A. E. bought the Cedar Fork property. The purchase was a simple matter of paying back taxes on the place, a sum left outstanding by its previous owner, and filing a quitclaim deed. It was a prime piece of land owing in part to the natural and never-failing spring across the gravel road and down a steep descent into a cavernous bowl of almost otherworldly topography. It was only one among many springs of its kind throughout the region, natural pooled basins of sweet and clear and mountain-cold water sating the thirst of human beings and farm and wild animals alike. Indelible memories of my childhood are of my many treks to fetch water at that spring, a metal bucket swinging from my hand and picking my way carefully as I stepped from the gravel road and onto the flat stones placed as descending pavers to the spring, set by the hands of A. E. and his sons. My eyes took a moment to adjust to the sudden twilight shadow even though above the descent, it was still sunny bright afternoon. The cool green and mottled shade from a pageant of towering leaf-laden trees overhead dimmed the path to the spring. The slippery passageway winded among wet cliff faces, their oozing crevices garlanded with thirsty green mosses, liverworts, and ferns, the darkened course illuminated by starry petaled anemonella and hepatica and triangulated trillium, woodland plants that did best in that shady environment where they kept their feet cool and moist, against that dimness, plants radiant with a mystifying and shimmering inner light, invincible and heroic.

Thirty feet lower, I was at the edge of the creek and in golden sunshine again, the valley before me carpeted with countless species of wildflowers and their cultivators: bees, butterflies, and birds thick and busily tending their flower garden, and unbothered by my intrusion. A landscape over the ages having evolved beyond mere beauty, it revealed itself in stages: chill-halting mid-tones of autumn; striking ice-studded calligraphies of winter; fluffy pastel laces of spring, but, like none other, it came alive in myriad plays of textures and sheens and hues in summer. Irridescent dragonflies in abundance, my favorite inhabitants in that cul-de-sac dressed in towering walls of green, hovered like glowing angels above my head. Giant green grasshoppers gathered around as if in friendly greeting to me, and often one of them would light on my knee as I sat on the bank of the creek, its uneven course tinted the color of the sky. My bare feet dangling in the cool flowing water, I held the grasshopper between the index finger and thumb of my hand, and squeezed it gently, commanding of it, "Spit!" and it did, the black/brown spittle of the insect brimming to its open mouth, like the tobacco juice spit from the mouth of the father of my mother. A praying mantis, prehistoric and formidable in its make-up, stood stark still as a statue on a limb of a nearby tree, its anvil-shaped head otherwise swiveling curiously in my direction.

In the blue blue sky, a hawk floated on widespread wings and its soprano call echoed for miles and miles, taking my soaring spirit with it on a windswept and mystical journey—a brief interlude to a place of spiritual treasures known only to hawks and dragonflies and angels and others of their ken. Back up the steep hill again, my heavy bucket overfull with the cold water, it sloshed on my bare feet and legs, but most of it was still intact as I delivered it back to the log cabin where Eva Love, the mother of my father, my Mommaw Greene, patiently waited for me.

How I admired that log cabin—different than any I had ever seen, for the logs from trees on their property felled and prepared by A. E. and his sons stood vertically rather than horizontally, and the chinking between the logs was of gray clay dug from the bank at the terminus of the front of the yard. Gathering the stones and dragging them on a makeshift sled, or by a rope pulled by their horse, they fashioned the impressive chimney for the huge fireplace that dominated the main room of the home. Construction of the cabin having begun in the late fall of the year, the first snowstorm hit the area before it was completely under roof. Tarpolins were stretched across the opening in the roof, keeping dry but shivering from the bone-chilling cold, Lee and his insomniac siblings, the bunch of them burrowed under old army blankets on cots and pallets on the floor of the loft below the gaping hole.

Sometime during my early teen years, A. E. and Mommaw Greene were no longer living together. Most of their older children having followed my parents to Columbus, Mommaw Greene and her younger children, three of them near my age, moved there as well. The Cedar Fork property remained in the family, as is still the case, but the log cabin, standing empty and unattended, slowly deteriorated and crumbled decades ago. Many of the original foundation and fireplace stones are still there, scattered on the ground, giving place to the exact location of the fallen log cabin. Some of the stones have been reclaimed by several members of my family and me. Placed on bookshelves in our homes, or flower gardens in our yards, they are touchstones of our heritage, and of a bygone era well worth recalling.

Three

White settlement not only meant exterminating its aboriginal people, it also required denuding much of the Ohio land of its dense and immense primordial woodlands, "probably among the greatest forests ever to grace the earth."[10] For centuries left undisturbed, in Adams County the extensive level tracts were lush with summer-green trees, and the red, orange, and yellow foliage of autumn timberlines formed kaleidoscopic canopies, although soon-to-be-mutilated and unremembered wildernesses. The white and silver of winter freezes tracing lacey limbs of thick stands of shellbark hickories, beeches, white maples, and in some instances, white oaks boasting specimens measuring seven feet across the trunks, and "towering up royally fifty and sixty feet without a limb,"[11] climbed unencumbered the lofty foothills of the Appalachian Foothills. Along the banks of the majestic Ohio River at the southern border of the county stood the largest specimens in the area of buckeyes, of the stately oaks of many varieties, of black walnuts, of red elms, and of glowing black and sugar maples. North of the river, dense stands of mold- and moss-covered white as well as blue ash trees, gentle dogwoods, wild cherries, tuliptrees, blackgums, pawpaws, and gigantic yellow poplars, some with trunks measuring eight to ten feet in diameter, grew so densely that it was hard for a wide-shouldered man to pass through. Enormous sycamores with their ghost-white trunks akin to columns of Carrara marble elegantly fringed the borders of streams—one such known specimen was large enough for a horse to enter and turn around in, while the

---

[10] Ohio's Natural Heritage, Michael B. Lafferty, Editor in Chief, The Ohio Department of Science with The Ohio Department of Natural Resources, Columbus, Ohio, 1979, p. 5, chapter by Edward F. Hutchins

[11] Ibid p. 8 quote by Morris Schaff

GUARDIANS AND OTHER ANGELS   13

hills and knobs were densely aromatic with the mouth-watering scent of chestnuts and the soul-cleansing aromas of spruce and cedar.[12]

Lured by the siren song of the lush primeval forests having survived the ax of the early farming pioneers, the men in Adams County put ax, and later saw, to the great tree trunks, and the manic, big moneymaking harvesting of the timber took off with a mindless vengeance, and typically, without regard for the long-term environmental costs. Tannic acid bearing oaks, felled in a process called tanbarking, were valuable commodities as well, the tannin from the bark of the trees used to tan hides, and after the tannin was extracted, the remainder of the hardwood was put to use in the fashioning of furniture and other requirements of the building trades. At Cedar Mills and Marble Furnace, in examples of capitalism at its peak in that early economy, iron-forging furnaces roared, stoked by trees first burned to charcoal pellets. There was a vast market for the big trees then, the competitive environment erupting into near warfare among neighbors over them. A squabble between my paternal grandfather A. E. and a neighbor was one notable example:

The tires of his 1930 Model A Ford having worn perilously thin, A. E. thought better of driving it for the balance of the summer, unless of course, God saw fit to favor him with a mighty fortune dropping from heaven and landing in his lap some time in the near future. Summer was nearing its maturity—like a young heifer coming into her mating season, it was ripe, swollen, and nubile, and A. E. valued every moment of it. Just three months hence meant voyaging for A. E., however, in his taking up again of the nomadic lifestyle required of his ministry, and he couldn't very well journey from town to town along the eastern seaboard from the Carolinas to Central Florida on the back of a horse. As the Ford was currently placed on blocks of wood in the front yard of his log cabin in Cedar Fork, horseback was his mode of travel this evening, as it had been for far too long. New tires for the Ford were a dire necessity and some other replacements parts for it would go a long way toward easing the mind of A. E., as well.

Every nickel A. E. had earned the previous winter had gone toward purchasing the final roofing supplies for the log cabin, and although his neighbors attested to his especially inspired preaching during this latest sojourn in Cedar Fork, still the offering plate had come up piteously empty. President Roosevelt's WPA and other New Deal programs hadn't trickled down to the pocket of A. E. one tiny bit. The clippity clop of the hooves of the horse echoed on the tall cliffs bounding the creek as horse and rider crossed the rough-hewn log bridge spanning the waterway. *That man Thoreau who said 'All men live lives of quiet desperation,' weren't no preacher man 'cause if he was he'd know it ain't very quiet. All I ever hear*

---

[12] http://www.heritagepursuit.com/Adams/AdamsCI.htm

is *'Reverend Greene, my wife is down poorly agin an' I hyeard of a tonic I kin git fer her, but I ain't got no money fer it... 'er 'Reverend Greene, my boy jist keeps runnin afoul o' the law... 'er 'Reverend Greene, my girls done took up with that no account Clarkson boy agin. What kin I do, Reverend Greene?' All I kin tell 'em is ta turn ta the Good Lord... 'Put yer faith in the Good Lord,' I tell 'em jist like I do. Seems like the Good Lord is takin' His good old time leadin' me ta the new tires fer my Ford, though.*

The odor of sawdust from the nearby sawmill permeated the otherwise sweet and clear air, the scent engendering a thought in the mind of A. E. *If I jist had me some timber ta sell, I'd have enough ta git me a **new** car for the service of the Lord.* His own property having long ago been harvested of its virgin forests, he had been hard-pressed to find appropriate lumber for the building of the log cabin. From what source the elusive timber would appear was beyond the present reach of A. E., but the thought having made its way to his consciousness, it took hold and began to swell into an idea.

What man is there fer the preacher man ta turn to in times of his own troubles? I ain't got no preacher man ta worry with my problems, A. E. ruminated in his mind. *The Good Lord says ta bring all yer troubles ta Him an' there ain't no better place ta do it but the house of the Lord. Maybe I kin git the situation about the tires in my sermon tuhnight at the revival meetin'. Shorely there's some help fer me amongst all them souls.*

The regular loping stride of the horse set the probing mind of A. E. into a comfortable rhythm of thought. A. E. was an extemporaneous preacher—he didn't take notes or write out his sermons beforehand. His way was to take inspiration from the very Word of God as written in his time-worn Bible. He pulled his right leg up and laid it across the horn of the saddle. Placing his Bible on his leg, he let it flop open, as was his steadfast routine, and the pages gently fanned in the mild summer breeze. Unfailingly, and almost immediately, the yellowing sheets of the Book settled, and the eyes of A. E. were drawn to a passage on the page, as if, as was always the case, God's finger pointed to the very Words He wished A. E. to contemplate. As the horse knew the way to the church, A. E. dropped the reins and rolled his head from side to side on his neck, the vertebra popping free of the tension he perpetually held there. He felt a surge of release pass across his tight shoulders and down his spine, the healing energy relaxing and opening his mind. His eyes returning to the passage, he began to read, and in the reading, formed his sermon.

As clouds gathered in the sky, moisture-laden and low, the heavy atmosphere pressed down oppressively on the tiny church. The farmers and their families milled about in the hot yard, their gritty overalls and brogans brushed nearly clean for the occasion. The wives and the young girls in their homesewn feedsack dresses cut just a smidgen above the knees, fashioned after the dresses copied from their Sears & Roebuck and Montgomery Wards

GUARDIANS AND OTHER ANGELS   15

catalogs, shot disdainful eyes at the spirited clean-behind-the-ears-and-face-and-hands boys as they chased wildly about the dusty yard. The neighborhood dogs, released from their nightly duties of fielding the cows, gathered en masse as well at the revival meeting, but stayed apart from the human throng. Their place was behind the cover of the gravestones in the adjoining plot of ground, a spot where they clandestinely lifted their legs and peed on the etched slabs of recognition of those dearly departed personages among them, their erect tails and sniffing muzzles conducting their canine discourse in emulation of the society of human beings present there.

"Looks like we might git some rain," Farmer Wilson said to Farmer Jones.

"May be," Farmer Jones replied laconically, his face lifting to the overcast sky.

"Don't know though. My rheumatis ain't bin actin' up of late, an' it ain't never rained when my rheumatis is quiet," Farmer Wilson added, a sorrowful tone etching his deep voice.

"It's bin a summer o' threatenin' rain but we ain't got nary a drop, hardly," Farmer Gardner rejoined. He spit a stream of black tobacco juice on the ground and it pilled and shrunk rapidly, the parched earth sucking it in like a man dying of thirst in a desert. "Can't git no decent yield from yer crops hyere at Cedar Fork if it don't rain."

"We ain't agoin' ta git no relief this fall no how neither if this hyere dry spell don't let up. Jist one day it'll be hot as blue blazes n' the next 'll bring gale force wind 'n snow 'n hail, maybe. Ain't no dependin' on the weather hyere abouts," Reverend Greene offered as he strolled up to the group of farmers formed in a loose knot just outside the door of the church. "We'll ask a blessin' on the crops at service this evenin'," A. E. said as he led his people into the stuffy little church.

The delicate feet of Mrs. Hooper clipped hurriedly beside the reverend, her flushed birdlike face level with the face of A. E. They might have been two racehorses battling nose to nose for a finish line. "An' where is yer sweet wife this evenin', Reverend Greene? We ain't seen Eva Love at services of late. She ain't feelin' poorly, is she?" the woman inquired.

"We got a child with a gethered ear from swimmin' in the crik moren is good fer a body. An' the trots is runnin' through the rest of 'em. They got inta a store of green apples I put up in the cellar yisterdey, I reckon," A. E. explained as he pushed passed Mrs. Hooper and stepped up to the raised dais of the church.

As was her custom, Mrs. Hooper lowered her petite body to the spot on the front bench closest to the reverend where she was comfortably within earshot of him, and she said, "Well, I'll be sayin' a prayer fer yer children, an' remember me ta Eva Love, will ye Reverend? We shorely miss her. Ain't no body ever had a better name than yer sainted wife, Reverend

Greene. Seems like the Good Lord chose her fer her name 'cause it shorely suits her."

"Yes, Mrs. Hooper. Eva Love shorely is a good little woman, an' I'll shorely remember ye ta her."

Allowing his mind to wander during the time the people found their seats, he remembered that it was at a church service in West Virginia many years ago, a service not unlike this one, that he first laid eyes on Eva Love Wheeling. Oddly, she stood out from the others by the diminutive nature of her bearing. Excessively small in stature, her blue eyes were cast humbly to the floor. Seeming in stark contrast to the tiny package of her entire person was her chestnut hair, long strands of it streaked with red, hair that glowed like a pulsing light—a beaming light of safe harbor, a light of rescue for his lonely soul, a soul in need of the particular comfort of a loving wife and children.

The church growing quiet, A. E. pulled his mind to his present concerns. His hands behind his back, he stood erect and purposeful behind his gleaming dark lectern. He had built the lectern himself, fashioned with fine pieces of walnut from a remaining tree of the kind on his land. It was perhaps a bit grand for a humble country preacher. However, A. E. thought well of himself on the whole, for after all, he was God's missionary, the Good Lord's roving man of the road whose calling was the bringing of the light of God to His lost souls—and A. E. was diligent in that pursuit, and thought he deserved some little reward for his efforts.

That smoldering Wednesday evening grew ever hotter as bodies writhed and shouted and stamped, the Holy Spirit of the Lord seizing their sweating bodies and captured minds through the inspired message of A. E. Stumbling to the front of the church, one by one they lowered to their knees, their arms waving above their heads, their faces streaming with steaming tears, their words testimonies to their being saved for the purposes of the Lord. Wrung dry, the voice of A. E. grew hoarse as he concluded the service, and he stumbled to the lone chair sitting on the dais. It was then that each parishioner came to him, their hands and voices offered in gratitude and praise. The last person filing out of the church, A. E. looked dejectedly at the paltry collection of coins in the offeratory plate. *Where's the supply fer my new automobile Ye put in my mind ta git?* A. E. asked of his God. Heavily, he pulled to his tired and rubbery legs and walked out of the church.

His head lowered in contemplation as to where he had gone wrong for he had felt certain of God's intention of revealing to him the source of a brand new car, A. E. slowly walked to his tethered horse. "Reverend Greene," a familiar voice spoke over his left shoulder. Lowering his foot from the stirrup of the saddle, A. E. turned toward the man standing at the head of the horse. "I ain't got no money ta help ye git a car fer the Lord's work, but I got a goodly stand o' virgin timber I kin sell ye fer a fair sum if yer of a mind fer it. Seems a body kin sell it fer enough ta git that car," Farmer Newman said understatedly.

"What's yer askin' price?" A. E. replied, a smile erupting in his soul.

"Don't rightly know. Why don't ye study on it a bit an' make me a offer?"

"I'll be gittin' back ta ye after services next Wednesday night," A. E. promised. His spirit soaring, he mounted his horse as lightly as if he had sprouted the wings of an angel and had flown into the saddle.

The following two days, A. E. visited sawmills in his area comparing the going rates for various kinds of timber. His brother came through with a promise for a loan with a return of one half of a percent interest if the offer was accepted by Farmer Newman. The next Wednesday evening service comprised some of the longest hours of the life of A. E., his mind distracted by the face of Farmer Newman swimming tauntingly before his eyes. *What if he were jist foolin' me about the timber?* A. E. obsessed in his mind. *Jist look at his face—blank as a sheet. I can't read nothin' in his face!*

The service concluded, warily A. E. approached Farmer Newman and made his offer. The farmer scratched his head, squeezed the back of his neck, and then cupped his chin with his hand as he considered the offer. "Ye got yerseff a deal, Reverend Greene," he said, his hand reaching out to pump the preacher's hand.

For the first time in his life, A. E. was a real business man, and to his surprise, he thrived on it. Each day the big trees fell and made their ways to the sawmill, and the money poured in—more money than A. E. ever imagined existed in the world. He repaid the loan with interest to his brother within four weeks of the consummation of the deal with Farmer Newman and began looking around for a new automobile. His Model A decked out in new tires and some new parts, he drove it around the nearby towns in search of its replacement.

The hot days of summer passed by quickly and as the cool days of autumn approached, A. E. was in a quandary. The time for leaving on his annual winter circuit through the south was growing near, but there were still many trees to be harvested—so many that the cutting might stretch into spring. As his oldest boy Billie was away in CCC Camp, and his second oldest son Paul lived in Florida with the parents of A. E., there was nobody to put in charge of the cutting of the trees. A prayer for an answer to his dilemma was perpetually on the lips of A. E., but the voice of God remained silent on the matter.

Six weeks into the venture, on a balmy Wednesday evening in October, A. E. was already at the helm behind his lectern as the usual throng milled into the little church. Although no clue from God as to His plan for his career had been forthcoming, the man was nearer to forsaking his ministry than he had ever been, and he was considering making an announcement of the fact that very night. Gut–heart–spirit, all were as heavy as the atmosphere in the church. It was an odd and dark energy that permeated the people as they renounced their seats and stood in tight clusters around the room, their mouths whispering an incessant bee-hive drone, their hands gesticulating wildly, and eyes shooting angry daggers in the direction of the preacher. **"If ye'll all git to yer seats, we'll git ta the business of the Lord,"** A. E. suggested loudly, his throat tightening with concern. Reluctantly each parishioner found a seat, all but Farmer Newman who lagged at the threshold of the door, his usual seat at the front of the church as prominently empty as a missing tooth in an otherwise perfect set of incisors.

"What would ye know about gittin' ta the Lord's business, Reverend Greene?" Farmer Newman shouted bitterly from the door.

"Mr. Newman, if yer of a mind ta address this hyere congregation, yer welcome ta come on up ta the pulpit," a bewildered A. E. replied softly.

"I ain't of a mind ta stand beside no cheatin' and thievin' preacher in this hyere church er any other!" Farmer Newman spat in reply. Voices of the farmer's enthusiasts erupted in a loud chorus, followed by the answering shouts of his detractors.

Mrs. Hooper popped up from her seat and spun around on her tiny feet to face the rows of angry people behind her. Her face red and her lips sputtering, she screeched in ear-splitting high tones, **"Reverend Greene ain't no cheat an' he ain't no thief!"**

"People, people, please quit yer hollerin' an' please remember yer in the house of the Lord. Now what's the cause of this hyere hullabaloo?" the preacher inquired calmly.

"This hyere hullabaloo is about yer knowin' yer price ye give me fer the timber land was a cheatin' price. Ye knowed ye were facin' a fortune in that timber an' ye stole that land from me with yer paltry sum ye give me!" shouted Farmer Newman, his neck red and puffed out like a toad's.

For another month, the feud raged on in the community, resulting in much derision as neighbors took sides in the dispute. It was a community where neighbor depended on neighbor, where the lives of the people there were intertwined in basic ways, often as deeply held as among blood relatives, and that the preacher's neighbors comprised the bulk of his parishioners made the matter even worse. Upon deep reflection, and since he had already realized some profit from the transaction, A. E. decided that in the long run, it was bad blood he could ill afford. Or perhaps he just could not suffer fools gladly. In a gesture of appeasement, with most of the timber still intact, A. E. returned the land to his neighbor.

The incident however unfortunate had given the preacher his answer as to the direction the Lord required of his life. At week's end in the

GUARDIANS AND OTHER ANGELS   19

middle of November, A. E. packed up his Model A Ford and hit the road once more. As he turned south out of town toward the the home of his parents in Central Florida, his conscience seized him by the throat and engaged him in a heated interrogation:

Well, ye know Eva Love won't never go ta Florida with me no more. She hates the heat an' bugs an' bein' away from her brothers an' sisters. I'd take her an' the children if she'd go. I bought Eva Love a new cow an' she'd still have the horse if the rattlesnake didn't up an' bite it on the leg. I dug that cellar in the hill behind the kitchen good an' deep...the patatuhs an' apples 'll keep real good in there. I planted the stand o' corn an' we got a fair crop from it jist like we did the garden. Them shelves in the cellar is full of that corn an' them tomatuhs an' green beans an' peas an' berries that Eva Love an' the girls canned. The chickens 'll give 'em eggs. Lee 'll be thirteen in two weeks an' there ain't nothin' wrong with his takin' on his part. He's got the .22 an' plenty of ammunition an' he's a fair shot fer huntin' rabbits an' squirrels an' maybe even pheasants an' turkeys. Ye got ta understand that a man's got ta do what a man's got ta do. The Good Lord showed me I'm beholdin' ta the Lord above any other.

Thus ended the only brush with financial security my paternal grandfather and his growing family would ever encounter. It was also the beginning of a winter of change in the life of young Lee Greene, the fourth offspring of the preacher and his wife. It was a change that set the wheels of the universe in motion for my appearance on planet Earth in the embodied soul of Linda Lee Greene.

In current times, "of the natural resources of the county, its timber is fast becoming depleted. The portable sawmill has hastened the destruction of the finest forests in every section of the county,"[13] the tanbarking and iron forging also having long ago come to a halt. A surrogate source of wealth, for decades giant quarries have pocked the land, quarries hollowed of light-colored and porous Silurian dolomite building and paving stones unsurpassed in the world in beauty and durability. Bassic Quarry, fringing the looping gravel road of Cedar Fork, played a large role in the lives of the inhabitants of the community. A source of employment for some of the men, of forbidden adventures for the young boys and girls of the area, its mystery also spawned strange tales of its own resident ghosts and ghouls, and in my lifetime, of a guardian angel in attendance there.

---

[13] http://www.heritagepursuit.com/Adams/AdamsCI.htm

Four

The second decade of the Twentieth Century was a momentous one in history, not only marking the entrance of the United States into the First World War, but in my family, the marriage of my maternal grandparents Mary Evalena "Lena" Caplinger and Joseph "Elmer" Gaffin. She fancied herself a carpenter rather than an ingénue awaiting the favors of a man, and he, a nattily attired, Abe Lincoln-like figure with an unruly shock of new-penny hair, sang tenor in a sought-after quartet of young men, the four of them singing hymns at local church functions, popular standards at barn dances, and even at medicine shows in nearby Southern Ohio towns. A product of the poor, white Appalachian sub-culture still in existence today, Elmer had little time for recreation in his hard-working days as an extra hand at various farms in the area. Nevertheless, Sundays were days of leisure in the normal course of his life then, and on temperate afternoons following church services, Elmer enjoyed challenging his friends in horse-drawn buggy races on country roads, and sometimes when the constable was otherwise engaged, through the streets of town. Such an occasion gave rise not only to a dusty race down the main street of the town of Peebles, Ohio one bronze and crisp Sunday in the autumn of 1916, it also marked the day Elmer was overcome with a burning desire to make Lena his bride.

"I'd saw her around town an' at church a time er two. She'd be there in a bunch of other girls an' when us fellers walked apast 'em on the road, them other girls hid bashful like behind their hands—but not Lena—she'd jist look ye straight in the eye. She got her mother's spunk, but she was a little thing—purty, but young—she'd jist turned fifteen—too young fer a feller a hankerin' fer a wife. I didn't know I were hankerin' thataway 'til I laid eyes on her hikin' up her coat gittin' inta her pappy's buggy one day. I seen her ankle, an' I knowed right then and there I were agoin' ta git that little filly fer my wife someday," Elmer, called Poppaw by his grandchildren, would say, his sparkling blue eyes softening to the luster of love he felt then, and as he always would feel, for his wife. "I'd heard tell that Ot Burley was studyin' on courtin' her, but I knowed Ot Burley, an' I knowed he were courtin' other fillies—he weren't no sort fer Lena. Lena had a proper bringin' up, an' they weren't no way her mother 'ud take kindly ta Ot Burley's foolishness," proudly Poppaw said. My cousins, my brother, and I, gathered in a cluster on the floor at his feet, listened wide-eyed and spellbound as his rocker creaked contentedly in one of those endurable sounds of home, while for the umpteenth time he regaled us with one of our favorite family stories.

"Oh, pshaw, Dad. Don't talk thataway in front of the younguns," Lena, Mommaw to us, reliably interjected from her own rocking chair across the room. Her hands flying in the intricate rhythms of crochet, the pale pinks and glowing whites of the doilies she fashioned fanned out over her stomach like quivering anatomies of angel's wings, her cheeks flushing and her eyes softening in a display of feeling toward Poppaw rare for her. "That old Ot Burley weren't nobody ta me. Ye know that, Dad," she added, a furtive look passing between them, a look so telling you knew there was more to the Ot Burley story than she let on. How her blunt and roughened fingers fitted to garden hoes and pitchforks and corn knives could produce such beauties in miniature with a slim crochet hook and delicate threads was astounding. It was like watching a midget at a Steinway playing Beethoven.

The mother of Lena, Sallie Caplinger had been Sarah Huey prior to her marriage, and she wasn't long off of the boat from Ireland when she met Landon Caplinger. Great Grandma Sallie and Great Grandpa Landon enjoyed a long and happy marriage, remaining passionately in love to the end of their lives. Stories are plentiful of their public displays of affection: kissing, embracing, wrapped up in each other's arms on the davenport in the parlor, even when very old. Sallie predeceased Landon by several years, and he was never the same thereafter. I remember my great grandfather Landon—very old, very frail, and very white of hair. He lived with Mommaw and Poppaw for a while toward the end of his life. I remember nothing of Great Grandma Sallie, for, as did Bussy, she also died while my mother was pregnant for me. It was she who "wore the pants in the family," according to Mommaw, however, and the stories Mommaw told me about her mother remain so vivid to me it is as if I can hear the lilting Irish brogue of Great Grandma Sallie in my mind's ear:

"Leena! Charrrlie! Faaaye, come inta th' house now—lickity split! It's agittin' close ta bedtime. Don't meck me come out there—yer hear me now?" Sallie Caplinger, stretched on tiptoe to a full fifty-eight inches in height, her frame nearly as wide as tall in the frame of the farmhouse back door, called to her young children. In the breathless heat of that August evening in 1911, they were scampering in the pitch black yard like newborn colts just finding their legs, scampering after lightning bugs as densely alight in the yard as the band of sparkling Milky Way stars in the night sky. Captured in clear-glass Mason jars with air holes punched into their lids, the children would later place the pulsating containers on top of the dresser in the room Lena shared with her sisters, the yellow/green light of the bodies of the insects mottling the white walls of the airless room. Their phosphorescence against the luminous black of the sky beyond the open window of the room would be hypnotic, and would distract them from the stifling, sleep-robbing heat. When at long last Lena and her sisters would be fast asleep, their father would tiptoe into the room and release the bugs through its open window.

"Oh, dern it! Why do we always have ta go in the house jist when it starts ta gittin' fun," Lena pouted. She pounded her balled fist against her thigh and screwed her face into a mask of tough resolve. "When I'm growed up an' git married an' have my own house, ain't nobody agoin' ta tell me what ta do," she insisted through clenched teeth, her head jacking to a determined angle.

"Ain't nobody with a lick a sense ever wantin' ta marry a tom- boy like you, Lena," her six-year-old brother Charlie taunted her as he pressed her with a beefy hand, pushing her nearly off balance.

"Hush yer mouth, Charlie Caplinger," Lena retorted angrily. She shoved him to the ground and grabbed his Mason jar when it rolled out of his hand. In a sudden fit of pique, she twisted off the top of the jar and released the bugs into the dark night.

"I'm agoin' ta gitchu, Lena Caplinger," Charlie cried, his face dissolving into tears. Scampering to his feet, he chased her, but failed to catch her. Lena was a powerful and fast runner, faster than all of her sisters, including her older sisters, Tirza and Cora, and most of her brothers, as well.

Since her favorite playtime activities were running, climbing trees, and bedeviling the cows, the boys were more to Lena's liking as playmates. The pretty, but decidedly tom-boy, ten-year-old girl had to fight the boys off an awful lot, though—they liked to wrestle with her, for some reason. But she didn't really mind that much—she could best them in any contest, most of the time. She just got tired of it, if the truth were known. Why those boys wanted to skirmish it up with her all the time, she just didn't know, especially that old Otto Burley; he teased her all the livelong day, it seemed like. She was forced to put up with it, though, whether she liked it or not. Her mother told her she had to be nice to him since he was relations of some kind, a cousin two or three times removed. Lena couldn't bring herself to believe it, though, despite the cautions of her mother, because he was just too decrepit to belong to her family. Most of the time, she just wanted to punch him in the stomach.

GUARDIANS AND OTHER ANGELS   23

"I'm atellin' ye little ones ta git in hyere now," Sallie yelled out of the back door once more. Rhoda, the youngest of her daughters, latched onto her mother's legs like a barnacle to a pier post. As they skittered into the kitchen, the screen door smacked back against its frame with a crack as loud as a gunshot, and Lena, under the cover of the commotion her mother made over the slamming door, tripped Charlie, sending him sprawling face first to the floor.

By the time Lena was twelve, she had grown to her full height, just a smidgen over five feet tall and she was still a swift runner; not as fast as some of the boys now, but still tolerably fast, and always faster than any of the girls. She continued to prefer climbing trees and worrying the cows to dressing up dolls and playing "House" like the other girls. Her brown hair, bronzed with glistening undertones of red, and crackling hazel eyes, would find expression again in her sons, Dick and Dean, and her powerful legs, large of calf and thick of ankle, served her well then, as they would later, when hard physical work made up her days.

In teaching Lena to be a productive member of their large family, and considering the times and their particular socio-economic status, Sallie Caplinger was preparing her daughter for the only probable future available to her, that of a wife of a farmer. It was, as well, almost a foregone conclusion that she would bear several children. Having blossomed into a comely girl of fourteen, Lena was proficient in cooking, baking and sewing, and in the process, had become an adroit extra hand on their farm, itself a necessary requirement for a wife of a farmer. As she approached womanhood, Lena was in a quandary, for although she enjoyed working with the animals, and the husbandry associated with the farm, especially working with handtools and mending farm equipment, as well as building things out of wood, she disliked the chores traditionally assigned to females. Feeling ill-suited for the tasks associated with marriage and motherhood, she had begun to entertain the notion of remaining unmarried.

Old man Tate, who lived across the holler with his "simple" wife and their big batch of equally "simple" children, was a professional carpenter, and on the sly, in order to conceal it from her mother, Lena had assisted him with some carpentry projects over the last few weeks. From time to time, she also had helped her father, who was a part-time carpenter, a supplemental occupation to his duties as a farmer. Through her carpentry work with Mr. Tate and her father, like her eldest brother J. Q., she had discovered her own natural talent for the craft, her love of it smoldering steadily in her heart. In her day, however, females weren't carpenters, they were wives and mothers, or if remaining unmarried, were teachers or nurses, or companions to well-to-do battle-axes, none of which appealed to Lena. Her only option, as she saw it, was to change her appearance to emulate that of a boy, then to run away from home and find a job somewhere as a carpenter like the girl she had read about in a book one time. In reality, that was no better choice, for she would die of a broken heart at being separated from her family. She had studied on it long and hard, and out of sheer desperation, had made a momentous decision for one so young, especially considering it involved pitting her own desires against those of her mother—and nobody in their right mind ever deliberately opposed the will of Sallie Caplinger. Lena's idea was to ask old man Tate if she could openly work for him as his apprentice. Upon her inquiry, he had agreed, but only if sanctioned by her parents. The only remaining obstacle was broaching the subject with the two of them. She wasn't worried about her father who was a reasonable man she quite easily wrapped around her little finger. It was her mother who wouldn't hear of it, and Lena knew it. Every night after her sisters had gone to sleep, silently Lena slipped to her knees, and her elbows pressed to the side of the bed, she prayed fervently to Jesus to soften the heart and mind of Sallie toward her daughter's desire.

While she worked up her courage, Lena devised a scheme. *I'll go ahead an' build somethin' ta show Mother how good I am at it. Maybe she'll see the light then, an' let me be a carpenter.* A picture in a book at school gave her the idea of building a small and portable toolbox. Securing the correct wood, nails, and glue from Mr. Tate, she would use her father's tools to construct a duplicate of the toolbox in the book. Its design was simple and utilitarian, an open rectangular box with a handle spanning the top of it, but the craftsmanship would be its most impressive feature. To begin a collection of her own tools, Mr. Tate gave her a rasp and an old hammerhead missing its handle. Carefully, she whittled a hickory branch down to the right size for her hand, and after cleaning the rust off of the hammerhead, secured its new handle into place. There was a new fold-up ruler at the hardware store she had her eye on, and Mr. Ordley, the proprietor of the store, had agreed to trade her for it in exchange for her coming to his home one or two Saturday mornings to do some housecleaning for his ailing wife. In addition, her father had an old, rusted-out handsaw with a broken handle that had hung in the tool shed on the same nail for as long as she could remember. Lena had made up her mind to rescue that old handsaw as it hurt her heart to see rusted and broken tools. Yes, she would salvage that handsaw, clean it up, make a new handle for it, and hang it off of the side of her new toolbox, and when she showed all of it to her mother ....well, another prayer to Jesus was in order.

Lena devised yet another scheme. She finagled an invitation to supper for Mr. Tate the following Saturday, and when the mood was just right, she was absolutely set on springing the news on her parents while he was there to steel her resolve and to give her courage. Lena put a lot of faith in her brilliant plan, for of course, having Mr. Tate as their guest when she broke the news would make it less likely, as well that her mother would maul her right then and there in front of him and God and everybody else in attendance. Despite her determination, all through the week leading to the

GUARDIANS AND OTHER ANGELS   25

fateful evening, Lena was so nervous that she only picked at her food during mealtimes. By Saturday morning she had accomplished all of her tasks save for finishing the handle for her saw, and she didn't know how she would wangle some time to work on it among all of the chores her mother assigned to her that morning during breakfast.

Her chance to steal away to the tool shed presented itself when her parents announced to the children that they were going to town to purchase some last minute items Sallie needed for supper that evening. The gravy grew cold and congealed to a rubbery mass on Lena's plate, and the fried applies, plump and juicy when she had arranged them so prettily next to the gravy, took on the look of something more suitable for the end of a fishing line than as filler for her stomach.

At the right elbow of Lena, his nose lowered to within an inch of his plate, and his left arm encircling it as if he were guarding his food against some rival species, Lena's little brother Charlie, customarily wolfed down his meal. As he ate, he kept his eye on Lena for he sensed something was up with her, and he wanted to make sure he was in on it. Despite their sibling rivalry, Charlie secretly admired his spunky sister; he hero-worshipped her really—and she was the only one of his sisters and brothers who was fun to play with. All of his brothers were much too old to put up with him, and his sisters, all but Lena, always wanted to dress him up in big people's clothes and make him play "Father" or "Beau" when they played "House." Worse yet, on the rare occasions he would get them to play "War" or "Cowboys and Indians," they would wind bandages around his head or some other critical part of his anatomy, and make him play "Patient" while they pretended to set his broken bones or sew his spilling guts back in his belly again. But Lena! Now there was a girl worth playing with. "War" was war to her, and so was "Cowboys and Indians." The more they pretended to shoot guns and blow each other up; the more mayhem and destruction and fighting and dying, the better, as far as she was concerned. She could fix things, and make things, too. For Christmas the previous year, she had made him a wooden rifle and a matching one for herself, and darnn if they didn't look almost as real as their daddy's .22. She had promised him they would play "Soldier and Indian Scout" that morning, but the way she was acting, Charlie was afraid Lena had forgotten about their play date.

"How about another helpin' o' gravy an' fried apples, Charlie?" asked Sallie, the gravy dripping seductively from the ladle she held suspended above his empty plate. Charlie never turned down a second helping of anything, much less gravy and fried apples, and there was another piping hot biscuit right there within arm's reach tempting him with its golden brown fluffy goodness. But he thought better of it. He wanted to be ready to skeedaddle when Lena did, for heaven knew the girl was as fast as greased lightning, and there was no way Charlie could keep up with her if she didn't want him to, not unless he was right on her dress tail squalling for her to wait for him.

"No thanks, Mother," miserably Charlie replied, eyeing greedily the retracting ladle of gravy.

There's somethin' pecular agoin' on hyere, Sallie brooded in her mind. *Lena's bin pickin' at her food like a persnickety banty hen all week, an' now Charlie turned down food. Charlie ain't never passed up a opportunity ta git somethin' extra ta eat. Maybe they're aneedin' a dollup o' Castor Oil tuhnight when I put 'em ta bed.* "Better put a bottle o' Castor Oil on that grocery list, Daddy. Looks like we got us a coupla younguns aneedin' a swoller of it tuhnight," Sallie told her husband as they walked out of the back door.

Jumping to her feet, Lena stuck out her tongue at Charlie, and dashed through the house and out of the front door in order to elude the sharp eyes of her mother.

Huffing and puffing when a few minutes later he found Lena in the tool shed, Charlie asked, "Whachu doin', Lena?"

"Ain't none o' yer business, Charlie. Now go on an' play er somethin'. I'm busy," Lena replied impatiently.

"But Lena, ye said we was agoin' ta play 'Soldier and Indian Scout' this mornin'."

"I changed my mind, Charlie. I got somethin' real important ta do. I ain't got no time fer no stupid games tuhday." Guiltily Lena shifted her eyes away from the dissolving face of her little brother and added in a softer tone, "Now don't cry, Charlie. I ain't meanin' it thataway. I jist can't play right now. I got somethin' else ta do this mornin', somethin' real important, an' I would 'ppreciate it if ye'd jist go on an' play by yerseff fer awhile."

"But Lena, ye promised me."

"Charrrrlie, now ye ain't agoin' ta git me ta change my mind with yer whinin' an' pleadin'. Now skeedaddle!"

"I ain't agoin' nowhere, Lena." Stubbornly folding his pudgy arms across his beefy chest, he stood resolutely in the frame of the door, his stocky legs planted solidly. "I'll tell Mother, Lena!"

"I swear Charlie, if ye tell Mother, I'll sneak in yer room some night when yer sleepin' an' I'll pull yer toenails out one by one with these hyere pinchers," Lena warned her brother, the threat in her smoldering eyes so frightening that without a shadow of a doubt, Charlie believed she would do it. Manacingly, she waved the tool in front of his eyes, and worked them open and closed, their snapping claws like the hinged jaws of an alligator breaking beads of sweat on Charlie's brow.

"O. K., Lena. I won't tell Mother, but ye got ta tell me what yer doin' ouchere in the tool shed."

Convinced she had sufficiently terrorized Charlie into keeping her confidence, she decided to tell him her secret. "I'm agoin' ta work fer Mr.

GUARDIANS AND OTHER ANGELS   27

Tate…as a carpenter. He done told me I could, an' when he comes ta supper tuhnight, I'm agoin' ta tell Daddy and Mother. I done made me a toolbox, an' got me some tools, an' now all I got ta do is git the handle done fer my saw." Bending down, Lena reached below the workbench and extracted from its hiding place her toolbox with its cache of tools. Her face bright with accomplishment, she raised her eyes to her brother's in expectation of his approval.

"Lena, have ye gone plum crazy? Mother ain't agoin' ta let ye do no such thing, an' ye know it. Mother's agoin' ta kill ye!"

"If Mother ain't agoin' ta let me, then I might jist go ahead an' run away from home." Lena's brow puckered with concern, her chin quivered in disappointment, indeed her face registered then erased every possible emotion.

"Lena, ye can't run away! How would ye eat? Where would ye sleep?"

"Don't ye never mind about me, Charlie Caplinger. I kin take care o' myseff jist fine," replied Lena, her chin thrust forward willfully.

"But Lena. What about me? Ye'd go off an' leave me?" Bursting into tears, Charlie ran to his sister. He dropped to his knees and wrapped his arms around her legs.

"Stop yer snivelin', Charlie. Yer gittin' my dress all snotty," Lena huffed defensively. Her heart softening, however, as it always did where her brothers and sisters were concerned, she drew her hand through his dark hair soothingly, and her voice lilting with the extravagance of her suggestion, Lena added, "Maybe I'll jist take ye with me, Charlie."

"Nooooo! Lena! I don't want ta go!" Charlie wailed. His mind filling with pictures of his mother's incomparable biscuits and gravy and fried apples and pies and fried chicken, the best in the whole darnn county, Charlie was distraught with the mere idea, much less the reality, of cutting himself off from such bounty.

"O. K., Charlie. We won't run away from home. Come on, let's go in the house. I'll warm up the leftover gravy an' fried apples fer ye. There's a biscuit er two ye kin have, too." The fears of her little brother dispelled, arm in arm, Lena walked him to the house.

Other than the eldest sons, J. Q. and Curt, who were away fighting in the war, the entire family was there for supper that evening. Tirza, her husband and their baby, Cora and her new husband, Faye and Rhoda chattered gleefully around the large table. Directly across the table from Lena sat her teenage brother Clarence. Next to him was Otto Burley who had somehow wormed his way into her family as the sudden, and suspicious, as far as Lena was concerned, new best friend of Clarence. Otto winked at Lena whenever he chanced to meet her eyes, and she wished he would stop his flirting ways because it only elevated her anxiety. Woefully, Lena sat at the left elbow of Mr. Tate, and was unable to eat a bite. Charlie, on the other

28   LINDA LEE GREENE

hand, shoveled in a first, and then a second, helping of his mother's delicious food. Who knew what conditions might be like after the conflagration he anticipated that night between Lena and Sallie. His mother might be too upset to cook for a week. Jumping up and down on his seat between bites as if there were hot coals beneath his butt, his sparkling, brown eyes shifted wildly between his sister and his mother. "Charlie, quit yer fussin'," Sallie told him. *He's eatin' all right this evenin', but maybe all that fidgettin' means he's got the worms. Maybe Lena's got 'em too. She ain't et a bite agin'. She ain't hardly et nothin' all week. I best check their butts before I give 'em the Castor Oil,* the worried mind of Sallie conjectured. Scooting her chair away from the table, Sallie walked to the chair where Lena sat. "Yer lookin' awful peeked, Lena. Turn around hyere an' let me check yer forehead," Sallie instructed her daughter. Chin tucked into her chest, her hazel eyes looking up through her lashes, Lena silently implored the eyes of her mother as Sallie tested her daughter for fever. Although the heart of Lena was pounding with anxiety, her forehead was cool. The concerns of her mother allayed, Sallie returned to her chair. The suspense becoming more than he could tolerate for a moment longer, Charlie looked at his mother and started to speak. Lena quickly kicked him under the table, her mouth forming silent words of warning as her eyes threw darts at him.

It was the longest meal Lena had ever endured in the entire fourteen years of her life. Finally it was finished, right down to the very last tongue-titillating, sweet/tart crumb of Sallie's famous blackberry cobbler, and Sallie sent the men outside to lounge on the front porch while she and her older girls cleaned up the kitchen. All of the men placed a "chaw" of tobacco in their cheeks, and talked war news and weather conditions while drinking a second cup of coffee. A little disappointed that the explosion hadn't occurred at the supper table when the whole family might have jumped into the fray, Charlie lollygagged behind the frame of the screen door and tried to hide in the shadows while he fairly burst with agony over waiting for Lena to make her move. *It coulduv been a real good fight if Lena 'ud jist spoke up at supper. Boy, that Lena! She's braver 'n anybody I ever knowed,* Charlie mused in his mind. Humming lightheartedly in an effort to quell her terror, Lena pretended to sweep the porch as the men talked. A sudden lull in their conversation was her cue. It was now or never, Lena realized, and although she almost lost her words when she tried to swallow her anxiety, she approached her father boldly and told him about her apprenticing to Mr. Tate.

"What do ye mean she's awantin' ta work fer Mr. Tate as a carpenter?" Later that evening, Lena overheard the loud exclamation of her mother beyond the door that separated the kitchen from her parent's bedroom. The girl stood outside of the door, her spirit flattening as she listened. Charlie stood beside her, his pudgy paw clutching her hand.

"The girl wants ta be a carpenter, Sallie. It's in her blood. Mr. Tate tole her she can work fer him after school some days when we can spare her, an' on Saturdey mornins," Landon patiently explained in his soft-spoken manner to his effusive, and that night, his overwrought wife.

"Well Landon, there won't be no disgrace in this hyere family by no dotter o' mine agoin' ta be no carpenter. I've taut her all she'll be needin' ta know. She'll be marryin' jist like I done, and her sisters done, an' she'll be havin' her own children. That's the only life open ta her, an' yer be knowin' it same as I do, Landon," vehemently Sallie insisted to her husband. Drawers loudly scratched open, then were punched closed; doors slammed, and breaths sharply inhaled and spewed in torrential gusts, the whole house seeming to contract and expand with the fearsome energy of the ill-temper of Sallie Caplinger. Shivering in desperate sorrow as she witnessed her dream dying, Lena sank morbidly to a chair, her face inscrutable despite her pain, her stoic back ramrod straight as she stubbornly held back her tears. "Now I want yer ta tell her ta tell Mr. Tate she won't be aworkin' fer him. That's th' end of it, Landon, an' now I'll be alayin' me weary head down on me pillow an' gittin' some rest. Goodnight, husband," Sallie concluded. Wearily, Lena pulled to her feet and climbed the stairs where her tiny sliver of the feather bed she shared with her sisters, Faye and Rhoda, seemed her only remaining comfort of home. Charlie followed right behind her.

The next morning, Lena took her toolbox and all of her tools and put them out in the tool shed where she knew they would rust away or get broken or lost, but she left them there anyway. Lena buried her dream that morning, and submitting to her inevitable path in life, surrendered to the romantic attentions of Otto Burley. As in every commitment she ever made in her life, Lena gave herself wholeheartedly to him.

World War I having taken so many young men, choices of potential mates were limited for women, especially for rural women, all manner of lop-sided arrangements ensuing as a result. There is a faction of my family that believes the marriage of my grandparents to have been one of those lop-sided unions, Poppaw, deeply in love and content in their marriage, while other than in the final few years of their time together, Mommaw secretly carried a torch for Otto Burley. Poppaw liked to tell us when he was in a mood to boast of his winning Mommaw for his wife, "I was pert near sure Ot Burley was courtin' Lena, but I was like a banty rooster gittin' acquainted with a unfriendly hen…jist stay on 'er, an' soon she'll wear down. An' she did…she shorely did," proudly he added to his courtship story.

According to one legend, however, rather than becoming worn down by Poppaw, Mommaw had grown discouraged with her other beau, having seen him in a buggy with another girl one day. Rigid with unrelenting pride even then, as in her entire life, Mommaw showed Otto Burley the door, and believing him to be her only remaining choice, opened it to Poppaw. Her heart, however, as many say, remained true to her first love despite his two-timing ways, Poppaw only earning her love more than fifty years later as she helped him through the difficult, final stage of his life. If that version of their courtship and marriage is true, I'm fairly certain Poppaw never knew—truly a blessing for an exceedingly worthy man.

I'm skeptical of that version of their love story, for I feel that Mommaw did love Poppaw—a love having developed over time. I found her to be a person who loved deeply and easily, but often had difficulty showing her feelings. Tragedy had quickened caution in her heart, and love equated terrible risk to her, risk of losing the object of her love. Mourning having grown to be her most forthcoming and powerful means of expressing her love—her long cycle of mourning having its beginning with the death of Bussy on January 5, 1943, in her typical fashion, she mourned Poppaw deeply after his death, and never got over missing him during the twenty-six years spanning his death at the age of 73 and hers at 99.

Concerning Lena's realizing her true calling, her guardian angels knew what they were doing when they sent her tools to the shed to rust away—or more likely, to be used by her father and her brother J. Q. when he returned home from the war. Lena's true calling was to be the wife of a farmer and the mother of a brood of children. Nobody ever did either job better than she. Despite the backbreaking work, the hardships, the sorrows, she made the best of every minute of her new life that had its inception on April 19, 1917, the day Lena and Elmer married.

Five

It must have been the fashion in that hard little patch of Southern Ohio backcountry to give children first names that were promptly forgotten, and thereafter were called by other names instead. In the case of my maternal grandparents, as indicated before, it was their middle names by which they were known, Lena and Elmer, respectively. It is easy to accept the shortening of Mary Evalena to Lena, a fitting, although inferior name for the pretty little girl she turned out to be, but it is difficult to imagine any child being called Elmer the strapping farmer-man he grew to be—yes, but a small boy, no—it simply does not trip well across the tongue. It was a regrettable loss, that of the poetic-to-the-ear Mary Evalena, and the strong and proud sounding Joseph Elmer, and a pity, as well, that instead of having our very own Mary and Joseph, as Jesus did, we had Lena and Elmer instead, two too-weak monikers for such a stout-hearted pair. The tradition of naming names that never got used continued with the next generation. The surviving firstborn of the couple, Marlin Landon was dubbed "Bob", and then Roma Evelyn got shortened to "Ro." Lowell Eugene became known as "Bussy," and Reva Eileen was chopped to "Re." The twins Gary Lee and Mary Leah were called "Dick" and "Bette," respectively, while Joseph Dale was thereafter "Dale," and the baby, Delano Dean got tagged, "Dean." Of course! What possible other name *could* he have been called?

Owing to the bounty of the family farm of my grandparents, one of countless farms of its kind forming the bedrock of the American way of life at the time, my ancestors, in terms of having sufficient food to eat, survived the Great Depression better than did most city folks. Even though the bottom fell out of the market for the milk, eggs, corn, pork, and poultry they had formerly sold, they had their animals and garden as sources of food. Kerosene lamps provided light, and chopped wood was burned for fuel. Empty feed sacks provided the fabric Mommaw used to make most of their clothing, under-garments included. Scratchy muslin sheets, wearing and feeling like iron on your tender skin where their bulky home-sewn seams left welts on your skin, were made bearable by feather-stuffed ticking covering thin mattresses, unless, of course, the feathers, quills first, worked through the threads of the ticking and stabbed you in the rearend in the middle of the night. Mommaw's hand-made quilts sewn from pieces of old clothing, strictly utilitarian with no deliberate design, were beautiful nonetheless, and grace the beds of her granddaughters to this day. Baths in the tin washtub behind the wood-burning stove in the front room, using Mommaw's home-brewed lye soap on the skin, and the same soap and white vinegar rinses on the hair, kept skin clean, but chafed, and hair sparkling, but smelling like an Italian salad.

Upon arising, clad in one of his three pairs of white longjohns he worked in and slept in 365 days and nights a year, the stretched and gangly torso of Poppaw tortured the metal frame of the bed to near breaking, his bulk stirring a loud commotion among the ancient and challenged bedsprings. Telescoping to his full seventy-four inches, he pulled on his bib overalls and high-top brogans he wore winter and summer, no matter the temperature, whether 20 below zero or 90 in the shade, for he seemed never to take heed of the weather, be it as cold as ice, or hotter than blue blazes, or snowing to beat the band, or raining cats and dogs. His eldest daughter Roma swore she never saw him sweat, and this man was a farmer, a poor dirt farmer, who furrowed his own fields behind a two-handled plow pulled by leather reins attached to a team of sturdy workhorses, toiling the toil as torturous as a day's work in hell. He worked without stopping, from sun-up to noon when he broke for a drink of water, only his second of the day, and the middle-of-the-day meal, "dinner," they called it, and back again to the fields until near sundown. Another long pull of water and the evening's supper, as well as the rowdy conversations with his wife and children around the nine-foot-long table where they took their meals, were his only rewards. But it was enough for that clear-hearted man. It was enough.

Preceding Poppaw out of bed and even the crow of the rooster in the mornings, after her early turn at stoking with kindling the wood-burning stove in the front room in fall and winter, and the cook stove every morning all year long, Mommaw saw to her chickens and guineas and turkeys before breakfast. In winter, on thick Germanic legs no runway model would be caught dead in, her sturdy shoes crunching on the gravel lane, or barefoot any other time, Mommaw walked backwards as she fed her flock. Bundled together in her left hand, the corners of the skirt of her bib apron formed a sack for the kernels of corn she fed her fowl. Scooping her right hand into the kernels, expertly she flung them in a wide arc, and called, "Here, chicky, chick, chick...here, chicky, chick, chick." Her intent head and proud shoulders bent to her task, her body was glossed in the flat light of daybreak: sepia-toned like the pictures in the stereoscope the family amused

GUARDIANS AND OTHER ANGELS   33

themselves with in the evenings after supper—pictures of the The Empire State Building, The Statue of Liberty, The Eiffel Tower, The Acropolis, The Parthenon, places never in their wildest imaginations would they ever really see.

Nearly four decades later, when I was living in Long Island, New York with my New York-born-and-bred husband at the time, Mommaw and my mother came to visit via the first and last airplane trip Mommaw would ever take. The main agenda was the sights of Manhattan: The Empire State Building, The Statue of Liberty, the usual drill. Arriving at the foot of the Empire State Building, excitedly I said to Mommaw, "Mommaw, look up!" and I raised my arm, pointing up in the sky with my hand. Sighting along my arm and hand as if it were the barrel of a rifle, Mommaw raised and raised and raised her head, until she fell completely backwards, right into the arms of my husband. Having been shoved by more people, her ears and lungs and nerves assaulted by the noise and fumes and speed of more cars and trucks and taxis, her eyesight hemmed in by more tall buildings stuffed into one small place, and more of just about everything than she had ever seen in the entire sixty-seven years, Mommaw was saturated and worn-out by then. We never made it to the Statue of Liberty or any other place that day. Straight home is where Mommaw wanted to go. "I pert near always go ta bed with the chickens," she explained as to bed she went as soon as we walked in our front door, even though it was no more than six o'clock in the evening.

As did Mommaw, Poppaw lived his life through fixed and never-wavering morning and evening routines, a requirement in his line of work where he was bound to the rhythms of the universe and subject to his animals that lived by the same clock. Bawling cows, stressed by bulging sacks of milk, screaming morning-starved hogs, and restless straining neighing horses were his alarm clocks, his waking eyes first-falling on the mug marked "Paw" in its stained ceramic where it held court on his bedside table, its disembodied contents a set of dentures afloat in a mixture of chlorine bleach and rain water, the finger-formed false teeth pretty enough for the flawlessly fashioned face of a movie star, but incongruent to his weather- and work- and worry-wrecked features. In his size thirteens, his manure-encrusted brogans, Poppaw, like the Tinman of the Wizard of Oz who resembled one of Sinclair Lewis' "tall lean shabby structures," seemed haphazardly welded together with dented, disjointed, rusty parts. His body caped loosely within his longjohns and field-scented bib overalls, he pumped a dollop of sweet rainwater siphoned up to the washroom from the cistern at the side of the house and splashed a fresh helping of it into the communal dipper that suspended from the side of the spring-water bucket. Above the pump and the communal washpan, in the rusted-metal medicine cabinet, was his personal bottle of Bayer Aspirin tablets, and he popped a few of them into his mouth, chasing them with the first of his only three drinks of water for the day. He was a veritable camel in human form, like that animal, no doubt storing up water in some obscure part of his anatomy, a hollow leg, perhaps, or a second stomach like his cows possessed. He was as healthy as a horse, as the old saying goes, owing to his aspirins and his chlorine bleach, he submitted, and he never was sick a day in his life except for an occasional cold and once or twice the flu, until his chewing tobacco, and field- and crop-dust put him asunder with emphysema in his early seventies. We had always suspected Poppaw of being hearing challenged, as his booming voice nearly always was inappropriately loud to the setting, But, as time went by, due to his illness, he lost his voice and almost everything else of importance to him. Poppaw didn't take well to sitting on the porch and watching someone else work his fields, milk his cows, exercise his horses, and repair his fences. So one day, rather bored with his idle town life his ill health had left as his only alternative, at the age of seventy-three, unable to leave his bed, and clad in a hated pair of stiff new pajamas rather than in his beloved worn-to-soft longjohns, he turned his face to his pillow and died.

The intrusion of the future death of Poppaw was forty years in the offing, however, and in the meantime, he had business to see to, the most pressing were his cows that needed rounding up for milking.

At the farmhouse, returned from her duties in the henhouse and orchard, Mommaw, come hell or high water, or even a visit from the President of the United States of America, every morning of every year of that time in their lives, stood at the foot of the stairs and called up to her surviving firstborn daughter Roma, who was later to become my mother. "Ro! Come on now…time to get on up." Mommaw then headed to the kitchen, followed shortly thereafter by her red-headed, freckled-faced, nine-year-old daughter, a classic firstborn daughter, obedient, ever-cheerful, ever-accommodating Roma. Bussy, her six-year-old son, the love of Mommaw's life, if the truth were known, walked up to his mother and hugged her around her waist. Allowing herself a brief moment to savor the contact with her beloved son, Mommaw drew her hand through his strawberry blond hair, then bent down and patted him on his butt. Content with the start of his day, Bussy shot through the back door intent on checking his baby chickens that were snugly sheltered in a brooder in the slaughterhouse four, long, Poppaw-strides from the back door of the kitchen. Even at the age of four, audacious, saucy, her crystal blue eyes snapping wide-awake with the prospect of dominating the attention of her family for another day, her bobbed white hair fanning out as her bare flat feet twirled her in the center of the kitchen floor when stage right she entered there, Reva, the middle daughter, sang in what she wrongly fancied to be her perfectly-pitched operatic voice. The youngest daughter, sixteen-month-old Bette, whimpered and rooted at the impatient legs of her mother when Roma moved her from her hip and placed her on the floor. Having climbed out of bed a half hour earlier, and already busy on the floor pulling pots and pans out of the bottom of the tall press, Bette's twin Dick was pounding the pots and pans against one another, the crash as loud as cracking thunder, and just as jangling to Mommaw's fragile nerves. The pregnancy for the twins had been difficult, the delivery the worst she had ever endured. Her nervous system, as well as her over-taxed body, still hadn't fully recovered. How she wished she could prevent future pregnancies, but her husband was still a young and virile man, and she was unable to find it in herself to turn him away, the only sure means of birth control in those days.

At the age of thirty, although Mommaw was far from looking old, the old woman she would be was clear to see in a drawn slope to a mouth too often clenched tightly closed, and a brow pinched to tight and weary creases between her eyes. She had the haggard look of a peasant woman, hair losing its vibrant color too soon, wayward wiry strings of it springing loose from the bun at the nape of her neck. Unrelenting exposure to the sun was wreaking havoc on her formerly lovely skin, her face and neck, forearms, and hands, even her calves and feet where they showed beneath the hems of her dresses, were browned and dried to the consistency of a tanned animal hide.

For a week now, Mommaw had been working in the cornfields with Poppaw and their eleven-year-old son Bob, and a young farmhand named Arthur Billings. The teenager had shown up at their barn looking for work the week before, and Poppaw had taken him in. Two years into the Great Depression, Arthur, one of the quarter of a million displaced teenage boys and girls hoboing on the roads all across the nation, had crossed the country and back by freight train, hopping off of a train at the railroad depot in their town. Poppaw had agreed to put him up in the haymow in the barn and to feed him in exchange for his helping with the cutting and shocking of the corn. Wielding in his hand the long flat corn knife, under ordinary circumstances, it would take Poppaw, working alone, two months to cut, gather, and pile the corn into shocks, then transport it by horse and wagon to the corn cribs. Following that, the fodder had to be gathered and transported to the barn to be fed to the livestock. That year of 1931, with the aid of Arthur, Bob, and Mommaw, the crop would be brought in a few weeks sooner.

Arthur was full of stories of his adventures on the road, keeping Bob, Bussy, and Roma wide-eyed with wonder and breath bated when he related his tales to them at suppertime and on the front porch in the evenings before bedtime. Upon his appearance at the farm, the soles of his brogans were worn thin and were dotted with holes at major pressure points. He might as well have been barefoot. He had stuffed them with newspapers, a not unusual phenomenon among fully half of the population across America at that most troubling time in her history.

"Dad, did ye git a gander at the boy's brogans?" Mommaw whispered guardedly to Poppaw out on the front porch the first evening of the arrival of the teenager. She had noticed them at supper, his long, gangly legs stretched out beneath the table, his shabby boots plain to see. "It's a cryin' shame the young folks is sufferin' so nowadays. He ain't bin eatin' reg'ler fer nie on a year, I reckon, and Lord knows what he's bin eatin'. That could be our own Bob, ye know."

"I know, Mother. I'll fix the brogans fer the boy in the mornin'," Poppaw reassured his wife, reaching over and patting her hand. Hartman Gaffin, the father of Poppaw, already in his late fifties when Poppaw was born, had been a Civil War veteran of the Union Army, and a blacksmith in that conflict. At the end of the war, he returned home to Beaver Pond, a small village near Peebles, and established a successful blacksmith shop there. Upon the death of Hartman when Poppaw was a young boy, Cora Belle Purdin Gaffin, the young widow of Hartman, had kept his smithing equipment, passing it down to her sons Martin and Elmer at the appropriate time. Using those tools and salvaged leather from worn-out horse collars, discarded boots, whatever source he could scrounge, Poppaw kept the soles of the footwear of his family in relatively good condition—when they wore shoes, that is. Other than when shoes were an absolute requirement, such as going to church or to town, braving the outdoors in frigid weather, or working in conditions where thorns were a threat, stubbed toes, ripped toenails, stone bruises, gashed skin, stretched arches, sprained ankles notwithstanding, Mommaw and the children went barefoot.

"When ye take them boots off this evenin', Boy, leave 'em there in the tool shed by my smithin' equipment, an' I'll put 'em ta right fer ye in the mornin'. Don't 'spect ye'll be gittin' home ta Brooklyn in them boots worn ta thin like that," said Poppaw, eyeing Arthur appraisingly when the new farmhand walked out to the porch. The visitor had been regaling Bob and Bussy and Roma with more of his tales in the front room, and upon entering the house, Mommaw had interrupted his dissertation in order to get her children ready for bed. "Pull up a rockin' chair, an' sit fer a while," Poppaw instructed Arthur graciously. Poppaw bent to his side and picked up a canning jar he kept on the porch beside his chair. He spit a black stream of tobacco juice in the jar, a blob of it catching on his prominent chin. Sitting the jar down on the floor, he swiped the back of his hand across his chin. "I reckon ye might git a letter off ta yer kin tuhmorruh, Boy. No sense ta worryin' 'em more 'n ye have to," Poppaw suggested, inconspicuously studying the teenager for his reaction.

Arthur lowered his body to the rocking chair next to Poppaw. He exhaled a luxurious breath as he stretched out his long, thin legs, his belly full and content with the best food he had ever eaten. His trousers, worn through at the knees, revealed sharp kneecaps below milky white skin. The sixteen-year-old was pitifully thin, and he gave off an odor of sweat mingled with old dirt, *city dirt*, Poppaw noted distastefully. His hands gesticulating wildly in a display of hand talk amusing to Poppaw, Arthur replied respectfully, but gloomily, "I'll be glad ta write 'em a letter, Mistuh Gaffin,

GUARDIANS AND OTHER ANGELS   37

but I ain't guaranteein' it'll get to 'em. I had ta leave home because my old man, I mean, my fathuh lost his job. He scrabbled around tryin' ta do for his family, but most uh da time, he just stood around in da long lines like all uh da othuh men, waitin' for work dat nevuh came. We got evicted from our apartment, Mom and Dad and my two little sistuhs and me. There wasn't no school most uh da time, or if there was, me an' my sistuhs didn't go 'cause we had ta spend our time standin' in bread lines, an' scroungin' in soup kitchens. The Salvation Ahmy was da only place we had ta turn to. Dad finally just told me ta go on and leave—told me he couldn't worry about feedin' me no more. I was fouhteen yeuhs old, and he had ta tell me ta go. I don't know where dey ah now."

"Well, boy, ye do a good job fer us, we'll put ye up fer a while. Can't pay ye none 'cause we ain't got none ta give ye, but we can give ye a place ta lay yer head, an' victuals from our garden ta keep yer belly from gnawin' at yer backbone," Poppaw advised the boy. "Don't reckon it'd be advisable fer ye ta be wanderin' these hyere parts,'specially in these hyere times when things is so poorly. Thievin' is a mighty problem ta the farmers hyere abouts, and ye jist might git yerseff shot by some trigger-happy farmer who were suspectin' ye of bein' a robber. Good thing I was feelin' charitable when ye showed up at my barn, er I mighta been the farmer who'd jist as leave blowed yer head off as look at ye," Poppaw chuckled merrily, and then spit another wreaking black stream of tobacco juice in his jar.

"I'll do a good job fuh you, Mistuh Gaffin. Ain't nobody give me a chance like you done. I'll woik hard for you, Mistuh Gaffin." Gaunt and prematurely aged by too much life experience too soon, the face of Arthur flashed young and vulnerable for a moment, a beseeching look in his eyes that tugged at the heartstrings of Poppaw. The boy was tired of wandering, his soul had grown weary of begging for every meal like some no account derelict, of being filthy dirty and smelly and ragged, of being shunned by his fellow human beings, of having nothing useful to do with his life.

It had been the same in every city he had been to, Chicago, St. Louis, Seattle, and many more, droop-shouldered men, like war-wounded troops, queued in lines waiting for non-existent work, for scant food, for any handout they could take to their starving and homeless wives and children. Whatever there had been of purpose and drive was lost to them, their faces drawn with leaden concern, their waists reduced to razor thin from lack of nourishment, their dreams discouraged, their lives derailed from their natural courses. But Arthur had something to look forward to once more: a bed of straw, a nutritious breakfast, and wholesome work in the morning.

Flanking Poppaw's chair, Rex and Shep, the family dogs, were stretched out on their bellies in their accustomed spots on the floor of the porch, and both of them cracked open a lazy eyelid as they sensed the evening coming to a close. They wondered when the stranger would leave their property, and if he failed to leave, how they were going to guard their humans and animals on the farm against him all through the night. The air had cooled to a comfortable temperature for sleeping, and a sweet breeze was fresh on the ripe faces of the two visitors on the porch. Even the dogs delighted in the breeze, and raised their lethargic heads to it, and sniffed deeply. Laced within the coffers of the gentle wind was a faint odor of a skunk that had taunted the dogs earlier in the day, and Rex, tortured by the memory of it, placed a paw across his nose to shut out the tenacious noxious fumes of the scrappy animal. Taking the lull in their conversation as his cue to call an end to their visit, Poppaw noisily cleared his throat of emotion that had gathered there in response to the history the boy had related to him. "I reckon ye'd best wash up a bit in the mornin'. The missus, she puts stock in a clean feller. I reckon ye'd best be headin' on out ta the barn," Poppaw said. Telescoping to his feet, Poppaw bent down for his tobacco jar again, and spit his wad into it. Enthusiastically, Arthur jumped to his feet and headed to the barn.

The owl, an old and permanent resident of the barn, received the presence of Arthur sagely, but when she wasn't out harrying mice in her favorite field, kept her wary yellow eyes fastened onto her fellow boarder all through the night.

Morning greeted Arthur and the Gaffin family with yet another hot and cloudless day. How Mommaw yearned for the oncoming of Indian Summer with its mild, warm, and hazy weather, but it would stave off its arrival until after the first frost. While working in the cornfields, Mommaw had tried wearing long-sleeved shirts and hats and gloves and calf-high boots like the men wore, necessary elements for the wielding of the dreadful, two-foot long corn knives, the gathering and tying of the fodder into shocks, hard and heavy and skin-abrading work. In a get-up of that kind during those steamy dog days of that late October, Mommaw became overheated, and since her job was the less taxing one of helping her young son tie the shocks, she had foregone it for short-sleeved, summer-weight dresses, and sensible low-cut shoes. Already sunburned from the days before, and sweating from the fire of the cook stove where she stood cooking breakfast, she swiped her dewy forehead with her forearm, and bent forward to stretch her aching back. Distracted by the banging noise Dick made on the pots and pans, and the ear-splitting voice of Reva, Mommaw placed her favorite paring knife on the waist-high working surface of the press within convenient arm's reach of the stove. She had sliced apples with it, and a "mess" of them was stewing in a pan on the stove.

"Reee! Stop tearin' around the kitchen thataway—an' hush up! Ro, git that boy out o' them pans!" Oh, if only she could lie down in her soft feather bed for only a little while. If only she could have a whole day to herself! *Quit yer thinkin' thataway. It ain't agoin' ta happen, so study on what is, an' fergit what ain't,* silently she berated her disobedient mind.

GUARDIANS AND OTHER ANGELS   39

Responding to the harsh tone in Mommaw's voice, Bette began to wail. Mommaw bent down, gathered the toddler in her arms, and transferred her to her hip where she carried Bette the whole time she cooked the morning meal. To keep Dick out of the pans, Roma carried him on her own hip. He was a big baby, and Roma had to angle her upper body steeply to counter-balance the heavy weight of her baby brother. Mommaw disliked having to depend on Roma so much. As it had been with her own eldest sister Tirza, it worried Mommaw that her own eldest daughter was forced to bear so much of the responsibility of caring for her younger siblings. Mommaw wanted Roma to have as much childhood as she could manage for her, but unfortunately, it wasn't turning out as she hoped. After she had left the house to work in the cornfield, Mommaw knew she would worry as much about Roma being left alone to tend to Reva and Bussy and the twins as she would about being away from her little ones for so long. Roma was such a good child, and never seemed to mind doing anything asked of her. It was entirely too much to put on Roma, but there wasn't any other choice.

Breakfast consumed, Poppaw and Bob, and the new farmhand in tow, headed out of the back door. While Dick bounced impatiently on her hip, through an open window in the kitchen, Roma watched the older males in her family walk to the barn where Poppaw would hitch Roger and Babe to the buckboard, and Poppaw at the reins, the rest of them would climb on board for their two-mile trip to the cornfield.

Mommaw lowered Bette to the floor and Roma chanced placing Dick on the floor next to his twin sister. She hoped they would play quietly together for a while. The water for the dishes was boiling in a large kettle on the stove, and her hands protected by a folded dishrag, Mommaw carefully carried the steaming pot to the dishpan where it sat on the counter below the cistern pump in the washroom adjacent to the kitchen.

Roma kept busy redding up the table. "Bussy and me'll do the dishes, Mom. You go on an' git yerself ready ta go. I hear the wagon comin' up the lane."

Poppaw's loud voice rang clearly through the open windows of the kitchen, **"Whoa Roger!   Whoa Babe!"** as the chinking of the chains securing the horses to harnesses, harnesses to double tree, double tree to the wagon, came to a dusty halt. The familiar blowing of the cavernous nostrils of the horses brought a smile to Roma's face. It had come about that she got to curry the horses at the end of each working day, and she had developed a deep affection for the two animals.

"Ye ready, Mother?" Poppaw yelled toward the house. Mommaw hesitated, for a moment seriously considering sending the men off to the field without her, but she decided against it. Due to early drought conditions, the corn had come on later than it had in previous years, and they were already behind in getting it in. Reluctantly, Mommaw left the house and climbed up next to Poppaw on the seat of the wagon. **"Giddup!"** Poppaw's loud command to his team of workhorses sailed through the windows of the kitchen.

On the floor of the washroom, for once the twins played happily with each other while Roma and Bussy cleaned the dirty breakfast dishes, she washing, he drying. Though her audience had deserted her, Reva continued to sing and dance in the kitchen. After a short while, however, Roma noticed that Reva had become uncharacteristically quiet. Drying her hands on the dishrag, Roma walked into the kitchen to investigate. A red apple clutched in her pudgy hands, Reva sat on the kitchen floor humming contentedly as she tried to peel the apple with the paring knife Mommaw had left on the press next to the stove. Roma screamed, and Bette began to wail, and Dick pushed off in a dash as fast as his short legs would take him. He was headed to the unlatched front screen door. For a moment, Roma became disoriented, not knowing what to do—dash to Reva to snatch the knife out of her hands, or chase after Dick who was in danger of falling off of the edge of the porch, a good two foot drop onto hard-packed ground! Perceiving the confusion on the face of his sister, six-year-old Bussy took charge. **"Ro!"** he shouted, the sound of his voice snapping Roma out of her bewilderment. **"I'll git Dick! You git Re!"** Bussy ordered his sister.

"Gimme that knife, you little brat!" Roma insisted. Roma was quickly running out of patience with Reva, her demanding temperament, her disobedience, her bratty ways. Snatching the knife away from her little sister, Roma charged out after Bussy and Dick, catching up with them just as Bussy scooped Dick into his arms. Dick had scooted backwards down the porch steps and by the time Bussy had stopped him, he was headed across the yard to the side lane to the cornfield.

Determined to get the knife back, in a fit of temper, Reva began to chant at the top of her loud, singsong voice, **"I'm agoin' ta have it! I'm agoin' ta have it!"** While Bussy kept the twins in the washroom, Roma returned to the kitchen and held Reva by her arms when she tried to wrestle the knife out of Roma's hand.

"No Re! You can't have the knife. Yer'll put yer eye out with it!" Twisting her body away from the four-year-old girl, Roma walked across the room and placed the knife on the top shelf of the press, the highest surface in the room.

Reva continued to chant, "I'm agoin' ta have it! I'm agoin' ta have it!"

"No, you ain't agoin' ta have it, you little brat!" Roma countered Reva. "Now come on in the washroom with Bussy an' me. We have ta git the dishes done."

"No! I ain't agoin' to. I'm agoin' ta git dat knife, Wo," Reva answered defiantly.

"No, you ain't, Re. I'll whip you if you don't mind me. Now come on in hyere with us so I kin see what yer up to."

GUARDIANS AND OTHER ANGELS   41

"No! I ain't agoin' to."

"O. K., you little brat! See if I care what you do. Come on Bus, let's jist leave the little brat be," Roma said to her brother. She was feeling harried and frantic by Reva's antics, and also rushed since she wanted to have the dishes done by the time her mother returned from the cornfield. Roma also had hoped to sweep the kitchen and to do some other chores, duties her mother would be too worn out to see to when she came home.

Up since soon after daybreak, the twins grew fussy as the time for their mid-morning nap approached. "The kids er agoin' ta be carryin' on like screamin' meemies in a minute, Ro," Bussy said to his sister.

"We ain't agoin' ta git nothin' done with 'em carryin' on. Let's jist go on an' git 'em in bed. We kin jist put 'em in Mother an' Daddy's room," Roma instructed Bussy. "You git Dick, an' I'll take Bette." Out of earshot of the kitchen, Roma and Bussy failed to hear Reva scoot a chair over to the press. A few minutes later, they did hear her blood-curdling scream.

Following the doctor's orders, Reva was shut up in a dark room for over two weeks, her head kept as immobile as humanly possible without actually tying it down to the bed. There was nothing to do but wait and see if the eye would heal properly. The pain the four-year-old suffered was excruciating and unrelenting. Due to her young age, there was no available treatment for the pain other than half a Bayer Aspirin every four hours. The aspirin did nothing to relieve her agony. Hour after hour, day after day, night after night, Roma sat in the darkened room on a chair placed near the head of the bed where her little sister Reva laid. The youngster whimpered unremittingly from the pain, her body listless from its ordeal. Shaving peeled potatoes with a paring knife, one after the other when one dried up and turned black, Roma placed the potato shavings onto Reva's closed and injured eye. It was an old-time remedy for drawing out pain—but the shavings were useless—the darkened room failed to help—Reva lost the sight in her eye.

Six

Ralph Savage and Pete Whitley from across the holler had come to call on their friends Bob and Bussy Gaffin with the intention of showing their city-slicker farmhand a thing or two about living the country life. In the back pockets of their bib overalls, each of the fifteen-year-old boys proudly sported a large new packet of Red Man Chewing Tobacco.

"You reckon it'll make him sick? It did me my first time," ten-year-old Bussy stated apprehensively, his round eyes searching the eyes of the other boys. The four of them, Ralph, Pete, Bob, and Bussy had gathered at the side of the house to discuss the right-of-passage exercise they planned to conduct that afternoon for the benefit of Arthur Billings.

During the nearly four years Arthur had worked for Poppaw, he had assimilated almost effortlessly to his adopted environment. Arthur had proved to be a hard worker, and clean-cut once he had regular access to soap and water. Everybody liked him, and he was the kind of person who delighted in helping people. There were three things he refused to do, however: lose his Brooklyn dialect, learn to hunt, and to chew tobacco. Upon attaining his tenth birthday the previous month, Bussy had taken to chewing tobacco now and then, and at every opportunity since then, had regaled its charms to Arthur. "You ought ta give it a try jist wonst, Art. A body has ta learn ta chew ta be a man," Bussy would explain to Arthur. Since arriving at the farm in the autumn of 1931, Arthur had managed to elude all offers to join Poppaw and many other males of all ages in the area for a "chaw," but Bussy had become persistent about it. Arthur was actually beginning to feel foolish in the eyes of the ten-year-old boy. In order to save face, Arthur finally had relented, agreeing to give it one try.

"It ain't no matter ta me," Bob interjected in his characteristically unruffled manner to Bussy and their two friends. That time, however, he pretended a nonchalance he really didn't feel. He had grown fond of Arthur, and in truth, didn't care to see his friend get sick on chewing tobacco that day, or any other.

"It shorely will take the starch out o' him, Bus," slyly Pete replied, his lips smacking with the prospect of cutting Arthur down to size. His self-satisfied smile revealed enormous teeth amber-stained from the ever-present cud of chewing tobacco stuffed in his cheek.

"Now boys, Art's bin awful good ta us. I'd hate ta see him keel over or somethin'," Bussy replied, a nagging feeling of reticence creeping into his conscience, but leary of being ridiculed by his friends, he dared not impose any limits on the proceedings.

"Well, we best be moseyin' on out ta the barn an' gittin' ole Art," Bob said laconically. He took off with a lope, the other three boys falling in behind him.

"You see, Art, we draw a big circle in the dirt with a stick," slowly and precisely, Bussy explained to Arthur. Bussy paced out a large circle, incising the dust with a stick he had picked up on their way to the barn. He walked back to Arthur, placing one hand on his shoulder, and the other hand gesturing to Ralph. "And Ralph hyere...come hyere, Ralph...Ralph hyere, he's got some prize chewin' tobaccuh he brought all the way across't the holler...the idea is ta take a big ol' hunkin' chaw o' that chewin' tobaccuh in yer cheek...an' the rest of us 'll be doin' it right along side o' you...then we take turns spittin' ta see who kin come closest ta nailin' that chicken turd over there in the middle o' the circle. You ready, Son?" Nine years the junior of Arthur, and five years the junior of Bob and Pete and Ralph, but so big and tough for his age that he was accepted by the older boys as a peer of equal standing, Bussy had taken over the running of the initiation of Arthur Billings to the art of tobacco chewing.

Rather amused by the whole proceedings, for after all, he, Arthur Billings hailed from Brooklyn, New York where there was nothing under the sun he hadn't witnessed or been a party to. He had ridden the rails across the country and back. He had seen boys and girls alike get their legs severed at the knees, arms ripped off at shoulders, eyes gouged out, heads busted wide open due to accidents associated with hopping on and jumping off of trains. He had out-smarted "bulls" (train detectives) in every train across the land. He had been accepted into rough and ruthless groups of hobos living under bridges where nothing was sacred, and guarding your own back meant the difference between waking up alive in the morning and waking up dead. Puffed up with confidence, Arthur replied boastfully, "Why sure I'm ready, Bus. Bring 'er on!"

"Okay, Ralph. Give Art a good chaw," Bussy instructed his cohort in crime. Bussy and each of the teenagers stuffed their cheeks with their own chaws, and proceeded to chomp away.

"**Pa – ting!**" the first black streak of Bob's spittle missed the turd by a country mile. Like three torpedoes each one only a split second apart -

"**Pa – ting! Pa – ting! Pa – ting!**" Ralph and Pete and Bussy missed it handily, as well.

Then came Arthur's turn. "You kin do it, Art; I know you kin," said Bussy encouragingly. His face strained red with mighty concentration and his hands curled tightly into brawny fists, Bussy's beefy arms were bent rigidly at the elbows and his stocky body was arched forward outside the wide circle drawn in the dusty yard. Arthur held the wad inside his cheek. Just the mere contact of the ripe tobacco against the sensitive mucous membranes inside his mouth brought tears to Arthur's eyes. "Don't hold it in yer mouth, Art. You got ta give it a good chew—an' don't swaller—jist hold the spit in yer cheek fer a minute, then spit—spit with all yer might," like a handler reassuring a fighter in a boxing ring, Bussy coached Arthur enthusiastically. "Come on Art. You kin do it…I know you kin do it," Bussy coaxed Arthur once more, his arms pumping in front of him, egging the initiate on. Arthur's eyes began to stream, and he was turning a sickly shade of green—vomit green. Beginning at the base of his neck, you could see it rising as plain as day—slowly rising like mercury in a thermometer, the green crawly crud rising up his neck and over his chin and into his cheeks and drowning his eyeballs in pukey pea green. Arthur grabbed his stomach and lurched forward, bending double as he gagged. The other boys quickly jumped away from the circle to keep their bare feet from getting splattered by the copious contents of the stomach of their newfound comrade-in-arms as his vomit slopped into the dust. "He's a good ole boy. At least he give 'er a try. You got ta give 'im that much," the boys agreed among themselves. Out of respect to Arthur Billings, the four of them promptly left him there, all alone in his misery, as the code of any macho man would require, while the four of them moseyed on back to the house.

Placing his arms under his head, impatiently Bussy laid back against the feather pillow. The jolly sounds of his siblings at play outside in the yard drifted through the open window of the bedroom on a hot and sluggish breeze, a breeze so laggard it barely stirred the curtains. Sitting on the edge of the bed, Mommaw bent over Bussy, placing the inside of her wrist on the forehead of her ten-year-old son.

"Yer fever's broke. Pull up yer shirt an' let me git a look at yer belly," Mommaw instructed Bussy. He was a big strapping boy, bigger and more robust than Bob had been at his age, as he was his classmates of the same age in the one-room schoolhouse he attended with the other children in the area, as well as five of his six siblings. Bob, his eldest brother was in high school. Bussy held promise of growing to be taller than his daddy, who stood at 6'2" in his stocking feet. Carefully inspecting his belly for any signs of the measles rash, Mommaw turned Bussy over and ran her hands down his back and along the sides of his torso. "Ain't none on yer legs an' arms,

GUARDIANS AND OTHER ANGELS   45

either?" she asked, thinking in her mind how grateful she was that none of her other children had contracted the virus.

"Nary a one, Mother. Ain't been nothin' on me fer two days now. Kin I go out an' play now, Mother?" Bussy asked hopefully, his eyes pleading the worried eyes of his mother.

The squealing voice of Reva in the yard pierced the air, and sailed through the open window, hovering in a quivering mass of sound over the bed. "That girl's agoin' ta wake the baby up, an' I'm agoin' ta have to whup her," Mommaw said, irritation lacing her voice. She had just put Dale down for his nap, and was hoping to elevate her feet for a little while on the davenport in the front room. Since giving birth to Dale, by the end of her grueling days, her feet and legs had taken to swelling to the point of feeling as though they would burst.

"You ain't never laid a hand on that girl, an' you won't never. She could use a whuppin' now an' then, fer as I kin tell," Bussy commented, knowing he was speaking out of turn, but he couldn't help himself. The memory of the day she had put out her eye because of her willfulness still hurt his heart, and guilt over his part in it made him feel at once compassionate and resentful toward his sister. In the meantime, Reva had grown even more incorrigible since the blinding of her eye, and although her siblings loved her, and would fight anyone to the death to defend her, they often found her difficult to tolerate.

"Ye tend ta yer own business, Bus, an' leave Re ta me," Mommaw told her son in no uncertain terms. She knew she was overly indulgent with her middle daughter since the accident that had blinded her eye, but Mommaw was loathe to modify her methods in dealing with Reva.

Changing the emphasis back to himself, Bussy asked again, "Kin I go out, Mother?"

"Maybe in a while, after the heat has broke some. Now lay on back an' try ta git some more sleep."

"Mother," the boy pouted. "I can't sleep no more. I'm so tard o' sleepin'. I feel like Rip Van Winkle already. I'm agoin' ta sprout a big long beard in a minute," Bussy protested, his brow wrinkling in dismay, but he smiled through his pique, trying to sway his mother with his considerable charm.

Ignoring his obvious ploy, Mommaw said to him, "Do like I say, Son. Put yer head back an' rest. I'll look in on ye a while later. Dalie's stirrin'. He'll be lookin' ta feed now that Re's woke him up." Mommaw pulled wearily to her feet, in her mind yearning nostalgically for the davenport.

"You look read purty tuhday, Darlin' Mother o' mine," Bussy said to her as she walked toward the door. When she turned to look at him over her shoulder, he winked at her, and pleasure flashed in her eyes.

"Flattery ain't agoin' ta git ye out o' that bed no sooner, Son," Mommaw informed the boy, but she smiled at her son anyway, the child, since the day of his birth, who had been most attentive to her. Even as a tiny boy, he was in the habit of walking up behind her, and tapping her on the leg, would extend to her in his chunky hand a wildflower he had picked for her. As he grew older and had learned to draw and write, he made little cards for her, and left endearing notes to her on her pillow. A definite soft spot for the boy resided in the deepest region of the heart of my grandmother.

Through the thin wall separating the room where he lay and the bedroom of his parents, Bussy heard his mother cluck to his baby brother. A felty quiet descended over the rooms as Mommaw settled her baby to her breast, and concurrently the voices of her other children faded into the distance. Bussy could tell by the receding voices of his siblings that they had gone to their nearest neighbor, the Purtees, to play, and then they would head to the creek for a swim. Envy of their freedom seized him in a grip of terrible passion. Unaccustomed to being disobedient to his parents, he became alarmed at the way his body trembled with fear at what his mind was urging him to do. Regrettably, however, he was lost to the devil voice in his mind. Quickly and cautiously, Bussy climbed out of bed, pulled on his clothes, and tiptoed out of the house.

As soon as his bare feet hit the ground at the edge of the front porch, Bussy took off running like a bat out of hell. He kept on running, even though he was aware that his escape would not be long-lived, for as soon as his mother learned of what he had done, there was no doubt in his mind that she would drag him back to bed by the hair of his head. The demon in his mind owned him, however, and Bussy was powerless against its evil prompting. If his mother didn't catch him and drag him back to bed, Mrs. Purtee would. The women in the community stuck together when it came to looking out for one another's children. When his mother did find out, she would tie into him with a switch from her favorite "switch" tree out in the yard, there was no question about it. Many times he had trembled to the point of nearly peeing his pants as she marched outside with a knife and cut a switch to lay across his backside, for in his case she wasn't prone to sparing the rod like she was in Reva's.

As Bussy had been, Dale was a big baby, and Mommaw just couldn't fill him up. He was nearly seventeen months old, and still, he refused to be weaned, even though he ate his share of solid food. The nipples of her breasts were raw from his hard rooting at them, and from his biting of them with his sharp baby teeth when she tried to extract her breasts before he was content to release his hold on them. Mommaw had always been indulgent regarding leaving her babies at her breasts long beyond the time her sisters felt they should have been weaned. She enjoyed the closeness it promoted between herself and her babies, and despite her sore nipples, she was loathe to give it up. In addition, breastfeeding staved her menstrual flow

GUARDIANS AND OTHER ANGELS   47

after childbirth, and helped to space her children farther apart. She was conscious of the probability that weaning Dale would be a precursor to another pregnancy, and she just wasn't ready for it yet.

More than any of her children, other than Roma, Dale was the image of their father: redheaded and brawny. Also like Poppaw's, Dale's foghorn voice was comical in one so young. Rocking in her old rocking chair, a chair passed down to her from her own mother, Mommaw smoothed the thick and beautiful hair of her baby son with the palm of her hand, and hummed to him as he nursed. Slowly, both mother and child drifted off to sleep.

"Missus Gaffin! Missus Gaffin!" Mommaw heard a voice yelling her name. For a moment she thought she was dreaming, but the shouting continued.

"Mother! Mother! Help!" the voice of Roma screamed through the fog of her slumber. Mommaw started awake, as did the baby. Frightened by the clamor, Dale began to cry. Mommaw jumped to her feet, Dale clinging to her where he rode her hip. Mommaw darted toward the front door, and just as she came upon it, Arthur burst through the door held wide for him by Roma. In the arms of Arthur, the limp form of Bussy drooped.

"Is he breathin'?" Mommaw shouted, terror draining the blood from her brain and turning her faint with fear. She buckled at her knees, and Roma grabbed Dale just as Mommaw crumbled to the floor. Clutching onto the arm of the davenport, Mommaw held onto her consciousness, asking the question of Arthur again. "Is he breathin'?" she choked, alarm taking her voice. Her head reeling, bile rushed to her throat, and tears sprang to her eyes.

"He's passed out, Missus Gaffin. He's breathin', but it's ragged. His fever's spiked again. I ain't never felt a fever so high, an' I've felt a slew of 'em on da road. Bob's set out on Smoky ta town ta get da doctuh," Arthur explained as he hurried to the bedroom to place Bussy on the bed.

Pushing herself to her feet on wobbly legs, nevertheless Mommaw managed to rush to the bed. Bending over Bussy, she rubbed his arms briskly. When there was no response from him, she lowered her cheek to his. It was so hot she might have placed her cheek against the cook stove. Willing herself to stay calm, she spoke into his ear, "Bussy? Kin ye hear me, Son? Bussy, wake up fer Mother now. Ye kin open yer eyes now, Son." Bussy was as deathly still as if he had descended into a coma. Twisting her body to face Arthur who stood at the foot of the bed, urgently Mommaw said to him, "Art, run ta the washroom an' git me the spring water bucket an' a wet dishrag. Then run ta the barn an' git the horse liniment."

Slipping quietly into the room, Roma leaned against Mommaw, her frightened eyes spilling tears. "We were playin' hoops, Mother, an' we got too hot," Roma sniffled, her gray eyes stormy with alarm. "We run an' jumped in the crick ta cool off. Bussy got ta shiverin' real bad, an' his lips turned real blue in the water. I made him git out, an' when he did, he keeled over on the bank of the crick. I made Re run ta the barn ta git Bob an' Arthur. Dad's out plowing over by Brush Crick. He doesn't know yit."

Bussy began to mumble unintelligibly and thrash his head from side to side. The jugular veins in his neck were blue and protruding and throbbing. Mommaw panicked and yelled to her daughter, **"Roma, go ring the dinner bell ta sound out yer daddy!"** *Please Lord, please don't take my little boy—not my good little boy,* Mommaw prayed in her mind. Slipping to her knees beside the bed, her prayer was interrupted when Arthur entered the bedroom with the bucket of water.

"The boy's got pneumonia, or the worst case of bronchitis I ever run across. I'm goin' to pack his chest in mustard plasters, and rub his back with alcohol. Since we can't get ice, I want lots of cold water, the coldest you can manage. That cold spring water down yonder over yer hill you use for drinkin' will have to do. I want to keep cold compresses on the back of his neck and his knees. That fever's got to come down. Git yer children busy formin' a line to keep the cold water and cold compresses comin'," the doctor instructed Poppaw. "I want Lena to stay in here to help me rotate the compresses, and in case Bussy comes to and gets scared." Under the supervision of the doctor, the entire household worked throughout the evening carrying buckets of cold water from the spring to the house, wringing out warm compresses and submerging them in the cold water, hand over hand, slapping them into the hands of the doctor through the door of the bedroom. Six hours later, the fever had receded enough that the doctor felt the crisis was behind them. Still exhibiting a low-grade fever and seized by a racking cough, Bussy was jolted to consciousness.

The cough never went away; the labored breathing grew worse; and fighting the spiking fevers became a way of life for the Gaffin household. Little by little, the life of Bussy came to be ruled by chronic pain in his right lung and bone-crushing congestion in his head. Debilitating illness rendered him frailer and frailer, that boy who at birth had weighed eleven pounds, the largest of all the Gaffin children, and whose nickname was a derivative of the word "robust." No longer would he be the most robust boy of the Gaffin family, nor, considering the times and their meager resources, was there promise of a definitive diagnosis or treatment any time soon. Although the desperate worry generated by the illness of Bussy wore on Mommaw every day for many years to come, Bussy nearly always took it in stride, and bravely set forth to carve out a life for himself that accommodated his sickness.

GUARDIANS AND OTHER ANGELS   49

Seven

During the first half of the decade of the 1930's, "If it rains!" was the catch phrase at the top of the minds of politicians, in the reports of journalists, and on the tongues of farmers. Biting at the heels of the first year of the Great Depression, it was in 1930, in the eastern states that the drought first hit, and it lingered there until the middle of the decade. While still extremely consequential, its impact was far less catastrophic there than further west. By 1934, through a combination of the drought and misuse of the land since the time of its initial homesteading by the white man when its native soil-binding grasses were plowed under to make way for wheat fields, the Great Plains had turned into a desert, the area dubbed the "Dust Bowl" in 1935, a disaster having permanently displaced millions of people from their homes. A letter of June, 1935 from a woman in Oklahoma published in Reader's Digest magazine in part documented the devastation:

"In the dust-covered desolation of our No Man's Land here, wearing our shade hats, with handkerchiefs tied over our faces and Vaseline in our nostrils, we have been trying to rescue our home from the wind-blown dust which penetrates wherever air can go. It is almost a hopeless task, for there is rarely a day when at some time the dust clouds do not roll over. 'Visibility' approaches zero and everything is covered again with a silt-like deposit which may vary in depth from a film to actual ripples on the kitchen floor.[14]

During the drought, eastern farmers profited from the misfortunes of their western counterparts. But at the tailend of the dry spell, the Northeast and Midwest, pounded by weeks of relentless rain, suffered

---

[14]http://www.pbs.org/wgbh/amex/dustbowl/peopleevents/pandleAMEX06.html

50   LINDA LEE GREENE

catastrophic flooding, the over-flowing creeks and rivers unhindered in their unnatural courses by barren countrysides cleared of immense primevil forests by early settlers to make way for farm fields. Sucked into the slurping soggy soil, bringing farming operations to a standstill were the wheels of farm equipment, the hooves of animals, and the feet of human beings. Gardens and planted fields, like terrariums under glass, boiled and rotted in the boggy ground under a hot sun hazed by soupy air. Only impermeable weeds survived, and wended their way unchecked, strangling garden plants and corn stalks alike. Molding basements and cellars that survived caving in, toppled trees and plummeted out-buildings brought untold expenses in repairs and replacements. The many years of ravaging weather coupled with the suffering of the people caused by the Great Depression, seemed a vendetta placed against the unfortunate Americans by an angry higher being. *How could it get any worse?* But it did get worse. Incredibly, the high melodrama played on in the form of the winter of 1935-1936.

To the Sioux Nation, the December moon is the *Moon of Popping Trees,* to the Cheyenne, the *Moon When the Wolves Run Together,* and to the Creek Nation, it is the *Big Winter Moon,*[15] and the glacial December of 1935 ushered in a big winter, recording the coldest temperatures and most extreme conditions since 1884. At the very least, it seemed like a curse of the worst order for allowing oneself during that year's few halcyon days of autumn to forget the cold reality of the times. As the Great Depression raged on, the days and nights of that winter on the Gaffin farm meant much more than the standard fare of water frozen to ice in the water bucket, and an outhouse seat so gelid one dared not sit on it.

   Arthur Billings had been with the Gaffin family for four and a half years. During that time, the barn owl and he having forged a peaceful co-existence, Arthur had fashioned a corner in the haymow into comfortable quarters for himself. It held a single bed, a small dresser, a primitive twig chair, and pegs on one wall where he hung his meager changes of clothing. Although he had grown to prefer the privacy of his high-up and tiny lair, in the worst days of winter, he relented and slept in the farmhouse, either in a space made for him in the bedroom shared by all four of the Gaffin sons, or on a pallet tucked behind the wood burning stove in the front room. The night when the temperature bottomed out at twenty-two below zero on the Fahrenheit scale, nobody got any sleep, other than Dale, who was a toddler. That night the trees, like those in the Sioux territory, popped, as branches, over-laden with thick snow first sheathed in sleeves of inflexible ice, snapped off and crashed to the ground, or bared to freezing and life-robbing gale-force winds, were hurled to distant places just as if a tornado had passed

---

[15] Indian America, A Traveler's Companion, Fourth Edition, Eagle/Walking Turtle, John Muir Publications, Santa Fe, New Mexico, 2001, p. 375.

GUARDIANS AND OTHER ANGELS   51

through and had violently rearranged the landscape. The animals on the farm were the greatest concern, especially the two calves. Having recently been weaned, they had been taken from their mothers and placed in separate stalls.

To be available to Poppaw, Arthur had bivouacked in the front room of the farmhouse on a thick feather pallet on the floor behind the stove. Rex and Shep, owing to an unheard-of acquiescence on the part of Mommaw to allow the dogs in the house, snuggled up at his sides. Old Jack and Buddy, Bob's hunting dogs having joined the family in recent years, sprawled out on the floor close to Arthur, as well. Old Jack at the feet and Buddy at the head of the young man, all of the extra body heat kept the entire quintet toasty.

It had been a work-filled evening for Poppaw and Arthur, for they had pitched fresh hay onto the dirt floors of the stalls to thicken the existing cushion of hay beneath the hooves of the animals, and had boarded up draft-emitting cracks in the rough-hewn walls of the barn. In addition, they had draped the three-quarter walls between the stalls with blankets and feed sacks, all of the chores intended to protect the animals, as well as possible, from the killer cold. The hogs, huddled together in one blubbery mass in the closed shelters opening onto their pens, were less vulnerable to freezing. The chickens and other fowl, at roost high in the warmth of the haymow, or clumped together in their small, nearly airtight henhouse, would probably have a better chance of surviving. At midnight, the darkness displaced by a coal oil lantern in his hand, his face distorted by sleep-robbing worry over the horrors he feared the night had wrought, Poppaw bent down and shook the shoulder of the wide-awake Arthur. Poppaw said, "Art, we best be checkin' on them young calfs agin'. I should 've put 'em back in with their mamas. I don't know how I could 've bin so short-sighted."

"There was just too much ta do ta batten down the hatches, Mistuh Gaffin," Arthur replied kindly as he pulled to his feet. "Why don't you just stay here an' I'll go put 'em back in with their mamas?"

"'Spect I best go with ye, Art. I'm agoin' ta git Bobby ta go with us 'cause I'm afeared we got hours o' work ahead o' us out there. Bundle up better 'n ye ever done in yer life, Art. There's extra scarfs ta wrap arount yer neck 'n head hangin' on the halltree over yonder by the front door. Ye got yer good gloves with ye?"

"Yep, I got 'em on already, Mistuh Gaffin."

"Missus Gaffin is done made us some fresh coffee, an' warmed up some yeast cakes fer us. Git yerseff some while I git Bobby up." Against the roof of the house, the storm shrieked and thumped across the ribs of the tin sheets in great and thunderous poundings like a gang of screaming, heavy-footed dancers accompanied by ecstatic drummers. The ceiling timbers shook and strained, and nails in the eaves popped free, cracking as loud as pistol shots.

Double-thick stocking caps Mommaw had crocheted, lined with feather-stuffed headbands Roma and Reva had sewn together during the day,

52   LINDA LEE GREENE

sheltered the heads of Poppaw and the two teenage boys. Once their heads were entwined in scarves over the caps and headbands, only their eyes would be visible behind narrow slits in the scarves.

"There's a gale force wind kicked up out there, Boys. Ain't none of us big 'er strong enough ta withstand them winds by ourseffs. We got ta tether ourseffs tuhgether with this hyere rope, an' maybe we kin git through it thataway," Poppaw explained to nineteen-year-old Arthur and fifteen-year-old Bob. In his broad competent hands, Poppaw fingered the coiled rope nervously.

Bob's keen mind rapidly flipped through page after page of every non-fictional story he had ever read about people setting out on voyages into the icy unknown, and disappearing, or nearly so. His heart contracted in sympathy with early explorers before it was determined that the world was round, daring men who set their heads toward dark regions of the earth and seas where it was believed that the elements grew untamed and impassable by "scorching regions peopled with monsters,"[16] and bordered on a fathomless abyss at the edge of the world. Pictures in living color rose before Bob's eyes of the uncertain and perilous Fourth Century B.C. expedition of the intrepid philosopher and astronomer Pytheas. Thought to be a contemporary of Aristotle and Alexander the Great, without even the aid of a compass, to Thule, the land of the midnight sun, Pytheas set sail from Marseilles on the first polar expedition in history. Bob's nervous system cringed at the recollection of the frozen and well-preserved bodies found in archaeological expeditions in Greenland in 1921 by Paul Norlund, bodies of the lost Viking Christians from Iceland led there by the Viking seafarer, Leif Ericsson, son of Eric the Red. Without the aid of a compass or any astronomical instruments, Ericsson navigated the foggy waterways of the north "blind," following smells, colors, animal life, ocean currents, as well as the aid of crows, the birds when released, leading them to land. Over two thousand years later, Commander Peary reached the Pole after twenty years of failed attempts, and the loss of dedicated men and loyal dogs and expensive equipment, and even some of his own irreplaceable toes to frostbite.[17] All of the stories about the conquest of the North Pole flitted across the screen of Bob's mind like clips from horror films. In all its stark and ghastly details of starvation and cannibalism, the Donner party in its wagon-train quest from the eastern to the western United States during the vicious mountain winter of 1846-1847, and mired in the deep snow at the eastern summit of the Sierra Nevadas, stood out most in Bob's fertile imagination, and held him in a grip of terror.

---

[16] Man and the Conquest of the Poles, Paul-Emile Victor, Simon and Schuster, New York, 1963, p. 23
[17] Ibid, p. 13, 16, 21, 39, 43, 202.

GUARDIANS AND OTHER ANGELS   53

His heart sinking to his toes at the look of fear in the eyes of his son, his voice laced with regret, Poppaw said, "I wish ta dang I didn't need ye, Bobby, but ye got ta stay in the barn ta keep them animals from tryin' ta git back in wonst Art an' me git 'em out. I'm afeared you an' me 'er agoin' ta be exposed ta the elements fer quite a spell, Art. What we're agoin' ta do is git the animals out inta the barnyard an' git 'em movin' ta git their blood pumpin'. The movement 'll keep 'em from freezin' ta death. Rex 'n Shep 'll git 'em goin'. We'll haf ta use the cow prods on 'em, Art, 'cause they won't want ta keep movin'. Them dang dumb cows 'd jist as leave stand still an' freeze ta death. If them horses ain't too stressed already, you an' me kin ride 'em, Art."

Ten-year-old Bussy who had followed Bob down the stairs, had joined Poppaw and the two teenage boys where they conferred around the stove. Mommaw stood apart from them, her body cutting a voluptuous swath in the frame of the door of the kitchen. "I want ta go, too, Daddy," Bussy interjected, his eyes pleading the eyes of his father.

"Ye ain't agoin', Bus. That wind 'll eat ye up alive," Poppaw reasoned with his anxious son.

"Bull hockey, Daddy. I kin help a lot. I'm pert near big as Bobby, an' I'm the strongest feller on the place, 'cept maybe you an' Art," boldly, Bussy submitted.

"Ye ain't stronger 'n me, Bus," Bob shot back, annoyed by the pluck of his younger brother.

"Well, pert near, Bobby, an' someday I'll whup ye with one arm tied behind my back," Bussy returned, his chin jutting out challengingly at his older brother, his heightened emotions setting him in a spasm of coughing.

"**Bus!**" Mommaw commanded from across the room. "**Ye ain't agoin'**! Ye know yer lungs ain't agoin' ta hold up in that there weather. Ye need ta git back ta bed 'n keep warm."

"Gee whillikers!" defiantly, Bussy pouted between coughs. Stamping his foot and tightening his chin, his eyes turned dark with anger. Getting his coughing under control, his breathing grew deep and rapid as he tamped down tears of disappointment. "I swan. A feller can't do nothin' 'round hyere nohow," said Bussy dejectedly. Lowering his head, he shuffled across the room and threw himself onto the davenport.

The sympathetic eyes of Poppaw followed his brave son across the room, but he chose not to pursue the issue further. He empathized deeply with the difficulty Bussy experienced at being reduced from the heartiest of the Gaffin children to a sickly boy whose activities were compromised by chronic illness. But Poppaw had no time to devote to consoling his son. He had to get out to the barn to rescue his animals. Turning back to Arthur and Bob, Poppaw inquired of his helpers, "Are ye ready, Boys?" Art and Bob looked at each other with wide uncertain eyes, and nodded. "Okay," Poppaw said. "We'll head out the back door, with me in the lead. It ain't but a few paces ta the fence by the garden. We'll grab onta the fence, an' that 'll lead us ta the end of the yard. That open field between the yard an' the fence at the pigpen 'll be the hardest part. But wonst we git there, we got fencin' ta keep aholt of all the way ta the barn. Tie this hyere rope real tight an' secure around yer chests up under yer arms, Boys. Thataway we'll be tied tuhgether an' none o' us 'll git blowed away. Let's git goin'. Them baby cows is in real trouble. There ain't no two ways about it."

The far off screams of freezing and destitute wild animals caught in the woods, and the pitiful moans of the trees brutally thrashed by the wind, assaulted the ears of the men as they exited the back door. The farmhouse to the barn was a distance of a quarter of a mile, and the furious assault came in from the direction of the barn, forcing the men to walk against the crushing wind and blinding snow as they worked their way along the fence of the garden. Deep swells of snow, whipped up by the wind, formed boundaries as tall as their shoulders. As they strained to get through the snowdrifts, Bob wished they had snowshoes, and unarguably, a crow to lead them to their destination, like those used by the fearless Viking sea voyagers of yesteryear.

Facing into the wind, the nostrils of the three men froze, and their lungs ached from the onslaught of the frigid air they inhaled. The scarves proved inadequate as the wind bit through the cloth and singed the cheeks of Arthur and Bob, who, unlike Poppaw, were beardless. Their flesh burned beneath garments plastered to their bodies. It was as if the wind would blow them naked. Hand over hand, clutching to the fence, they made it to the foot of the yard. **"Okay, boys. Stay close ta me!"** Poppaw yelled as he prepared to lead the teenagers across the large, open expanse between the yard and the pigpen. His words were swallowed up in the whistling wind, and the boys heard nothing of what he said. Lowering his powerful upper body into the wind, his elbows bent and his hands rolled into fists of the strongest resolve, he set out across the exposed field. His eyes were tearing from the cold and brute force of the wind, and his eyelashes were stiff awnings of ice above his eyes. Arthur and Bob bent forward behind him, tethered to the rope in tandem fashion, but the wind was too strong for Bob, and he zigzagged wildly from side to side like the mad flailing of the tail of a dragon. Unable to stay on his feet, he pitched forward into the snow. Poppaw turned around, and signaled to Arthur to help him to carry Bob. Scooping up Bob, his shoulders in the frozen hands of Poppaw, and his feet in Arthur's, they got him to the fence bordering the pigpen. **"Kin ye make it the rest o' the way, Son?"** panting for his breath, Poppaw yelled, his arm encircling Bob's shoulders.

"I kin make it, Daddy," doggedly, Bob replied, his gloved hands brushing snow from his clothes. Beneath the scarves, the chafed flesh of his

GUARDIANS AND OTHER ANGELS   55

face grew hot with the humiliation at having to be carried by Poppaw and Arthur.

"We ain't got too far ta go now!" Poppaw shouted to his helpers as they closed in around him in a huddle of shared body heat. **"Let's go!"** he ordered his men, raising his arm and pointing to the barn like a military lieutenant leading his troops into battle.

In their separate stalls, the two calves bawled and wobbled precariously on their trembling legs. Bob grabbed two of the blankets from the wall separating the stalls and threw them over the backs of the calves. His hands rubbing swiftly across the back of one calf and then the other, he managed to calm them. The horses were in good enough shape to accept riders. Arthur climbed onto the back of Roger, and Poppaw rode Smoky. Whistling his orders to the dogs, Poppaw set them to herding the cows out of the barn and into the barnyard. The procedure emulated a roundup on a western ranch as Arthur and Poppaw, each at opposite ends of the barnyard, whistled and prodded the cows to keep them moving. Around and around the cows loped along, circling the barn pass after pass. At each turn in front of the large double doors of the barn where Bob, stamping up and down to keep warm, stood guard, he watched as each rider trotted by him on the steaming horses. Thirty minutes into the walk, the cows were starting to sweat, great haloes of steam emitting from their warmed-up bodies. Arthur, riding Roger, passed by the double doors of the barn, and then again, but Poppaw missed a turn. When Poppaw failed to ride by a second go around, Bob became concerned. Gesturing to Arthur to ride over to the door where he stood, Bob yelled to Arthur, **"Where's Daddy?"**

"He took off after one of the calves that strayed off. The visibility out there is down ta zero!" Arthur yelled back.

"Art, git down off the horse an' lemme have 'im. I'm agoin' ta see if I kin find Daddy," fervently, Bob instructed Arthur. He reached up and grabbed the reins next to the bit in the mouth of the horse.

"Yore Daddy would skin me alive if I let you do dat, Bob," protested Arthur, jerking on the reins of the horse to move him out of Bob's reach. Adrenalin infusing his body, in the howling wind and blinding snow, Bob took off running toward the far end of the barnyard. Arthur kicked Roger in his flanks, and tore off after Bob.

They found Poppaw, his clothing drenched and his leg twisted under him where he was slumped on the snow-covered bank of the creek holding in his lap the head of the dead calf. "He slipped an' fell inta the crik. The ice give way an' he went under. He drown'd before I could git ta him," sadly Poppaw told the boys. The rope looped around the body of the calf was still tethered to the horn of Smoky's saddle.

"Daddy, are you hurt?" Bob exclaimed, concerned about the peculiar twist of Poppaw's leg. Bob lowered to the ground and tenderly touched the leg of his father.

"I'm pert near sure my dern leg is broke, Bobby. Ye boys best git me ta the house somehow." When the three men passed by the barn with Poppaw drooped over the back of Roger, its entrance left unguarded, all of the cows had high-tailed it back inside the barn.

Miraculously the leg wasn't broken after all, but it was badly sprained, the leg and a severe case of chilblains keeping Poppaw off his feet for several days. The calf was the only loss sustained by the Gaffin family during that treacherous winter.

The new-year of 1936 brought milestones: another, and final, pregnancy for Mr. and Mrs. Joseph Elmer Gaffin, and the sixteenth birthday of their eldest child.

At the first streak of the cold dawn light, with the heel of his hand, Bussy cleaned away the frost on the window of the bedroom he shared with his three brothers. Another deep snowstorm during the night wrapped the house in its particular cocoon of silence. Sounds came muffled through it, and a bit delayed in reaching their destinations, it seemed, like bells muzzled in blankets. If he were well, he would go outside and play in the snow. He would build a big snowman, slide down their favorite sledding hill, get into snowball fights with the other kids, like his siblings would do that morning after breakfast, as he had done in all the previous winters of his life. He wondered what next summer portended for him. Would fishing and swimming also be out of the question? What about playing hoops, his favorite summertime game, where the kids ran beside metal hoops salvaged from discarded wagon wheels, and with long sticks as guides, got the hoops rolling so fast they sang, and the faster they rolled, the louder they sang? Bussy was beginning to worry about what he was going to do with himself for the rest of his life. *Tuhnight 'll be all right. We git ta make some ice cream, an' eat cake, an' celebrate Bobby's birthday. That's somethin', anyway,* forlornly Bussy said in his mind. Pulling his sweater tighter around his aching chest, Bussy laid back down in the warm bed.

The rumor was that Mommaw played the organ that sat in the front room, but nobody other than Poppaw had ever witnessed her doing so. That night she came out of the closet as an accomplished musician, the source of the gene responsible for the skill of Bob on his mandolin, no doubt, and the budding talent of Bussy, as well, when Bussy could manage a turn on the mandolin Bob hoarded as though it were God's greatest treasure. Poppaw sang, and Arthur chimed in with his pleasant baritone while he played harmony with Mommaw and Bob on his own mandolin, the only possession he had carried with him that day he had turned up at the Gaffin farm so long ago. The mandolin had belonged to his father, the only memento left of his family, with whom he hadn't had contact since he had left Brooklyn more than six years before. Roma sang, and Dick sang, and Dale sang, and Bette

GUARDIANS AND OTHER ANGELS   57

sang, and Reva, in her operatic tones, tried her darnndest to drown out everybody else.

It had been Roma's job to plan the birthday party. She had been busy for a week cutting out paper doilies and stringing popcorn to hang on the mantle behind the wood burning stove; for the yellow birthday cake with white sugar icing she made candles, baking the cake that day, the aroma blanketing the house with its mouth-watering aroma throughout the afternoon and evening. Using one of his favorite worn-at-the-elbows shirts, she had sewn a pillow cover for Bob, embroidering the word *Brother* on the front of it. The day before, what luck considering the snowstorm during the night, she had sent Arthur to town on Smoky for a box of Poppaw's favorite sugar cookies to go with their home-churned vanilla ice cream, the final, and most anticipated, activity of the party.

Arthur was going away. He was joining the CCC. He had been with the Gaffin family for nearly five years. Under President Franklin Delano Roosevelt's blanket of "New Deal" federal government programs designed to bring an end to the rampant unemployment and economic chaos gripping the country, "Roosevelt's Tree Army" had been formed two years before. Commonly known as the Civilian Conservation Corps (CCC), with that action FDR brought together two wasted resources, the young men of the nation and the land, in an attempt to save both of them. The program was a rousing success. The enrollees, over three million before it was all said and done, were eating with gusto for the first time in years, putting on much needed weight, and regaining confidence in themselves, and in their country. Through their hard work, millions of acres of federal and state lands were improved, countless bridges and roads built, incalculable spools of telephone wires strung, and the first of millions of trees planted. It was reported that in Chicago alone, the CCC was responsible for a 55% reduction in the crime rate among young men.[18]

Arthur had been eligible to enlist in the CCC for two years, but out of loyalty and obligation to Poppaw, had elected to stay on at the farm. He had long ago given up the thought of returning to Brooklyn, having never received a response to his letters to his parents. His time to settle down and make a permanent home was approaching. Therefore, he had decided to join the CCC since the majority of the camps were in western regions of the United States, and having developed a liking for California and Oregon during his former days as a freight-hopping hobo, Arthur wanted to take a look at both places again.

During his long stay with the Gaffin family, Arthur had grown close to Bob and Bussy. In many ways he had become a devout and protective big brother to the boys. Having said his teary good-byes to everyone but Bussy,

---

[18] http://www.cccalumni.org/history1.html

the evening of his departure, Arthur knocked on the bedroom door where Bussy was propped up against the pillows on the bed, weak from having suffered yet another cruel night and morning of chest-crushing coughing and fever. Even though he was feeling better, Bussy had been sleeping all day. Mommaw had wakened him to say good-bye to Arthur.

"Evenin', Bus," said Arthur awkwardly as he walked into the room. He held his mandolin in his hands, and he rotated it nervously while looking around the room as if casing it for the quickest escape route. That last good-bye was the most difficult of all for Arthur, as he had a strong feeling that if he returned for a visit someday, Bussy wouldn't be around any longer. He sensed that Bussy was dying, and he couldn't meet the boy's eyes. Arthur would take Bussy's place in that bed in a minute if he could. Words bounced around wildly in his head like Mommaw's crazy chickens all astir, and out of sheer frustration, he picked up on the topic of baseball, a favorite of both of them. Casually Arthur said, "Did I ever tell you dat I saw da "Babe" in person one time?" and they were off and running. They talked for an hour or more, Arthur having pulled up a chair next to the bed. The shadows grew long and deep as the sun slipped behind the horizon. The time approached for Arthur to leave, and he said, "Listen, Bus, I was wonderin' if you would do me a favuh?"

"Well shore, Art–anything if I kin," Bussy replied quizzically.

"Well, you know I've been carryin' dis mandolin around for a coon's age, as you would say, an' I was wonderin' if I could leave it here wit you for safe keepin'."

"But Art, that's yer daddy's mandolin. You bin protectin' that mandolin with yer very life ever since you left home. Won't you miss it powerful?" Bussy replied, his eyes wide with disbelief.

"Well, sure I'll miss it, Bus, but from what I hear about da camps, I won't have time ta play it, an' with all o' dem rough and tumble characters I'm gonna ta be bunkin' in with, it just won't be safe for me ta keep it wit me."

"Well, all right, Art. If you think you want ta leave it with me, I shorely will protect it with my life jist like you done all this time."

"It would mean a lot ta me, Bus. Well, I guess I better be hittin' da road. I want ta catch dat last freight out tonight. I'll be seein' you, Bus." Arthur uncoiled from the chair, walked over to the side of the bed, and laid the mandolin in the hands of Bussy. Turning toward the door, in three strides on his long legs he was across the small room.

"Art," came the voice of Bussy from the bed. Arthur looked over his shoulder at the boy. "I'll be seein' you–up there," Bussy said, his eyes raising in his lifted head, the index finger of his right hand pointing upward toward heaven. His eyes spilling tears, Arthur closed the door behind him.

GUARDIANS AND OTHER ANGELS   59

The following morning, there was a letter for Mommaw leaning against the back of the top shelf of the cook stove. Recognizing the handwriting on the front of the envelope, her heart crashed to the pit of her stomach, for intuitively she knew the contents of the letter. Tearing it open, her hands shook as she read:

My Dearest Darling Mother:

Don't worry about me. Art and me, we'll hop a freight and we'll be heading west. You know Art will look out for me. Some of the other boys is going with us. When we get to California, we'll join the CCC. I didn't tell you because I knew you wouldn't let me go. I have to tell them I'm seventeen. That's why we're joining up out west. It'll be harder for them to catch me in my lie way out there.

Mother, you know I would never do nothing to displease you but Mother this is an emergency. I just have to do something to help you and Daddy. Daddy's WPA work is helping but it ain't near enough. But there ain't no work for me and the boys now but CCC. I'll make it up to you my Sweetheart, and I'll never do nothing in secret against you again as long as I live. Please be my brave darling Mother and keep your chin up. I'll only be gone 3 months and I promise I'll write to you every day.

We need the money Mother. I'll pull in $30.00 a month and the biggest portion of it will come straight to you. The government set it up that way and even if it weren't set up that way I'd get the money to you any way. We need the money for Bussy's doctor care and to fix the farm equipment that's broke down. Like I said, I'll write to you every day if I can.

Your loving son Bob

P.S. I'm sorry to leave all the farm work to you Daddy but all the planting is done and I'll be home in time for most of the harvesting. I hope you have good crops.   (llg)

Another envelope was propped up against the saltshaker on the kitchen table.

Dear Kids:

I'm going out west to join the CCC. I wrote Mother a letter all about it. Ro, Re and Bette – Mother'll be needing your help even more now that I'll be gone. The new baby'll come next month so don't let Mother do nothing heavy. Ro – you do all the washing now and walking to town for the groceries. That heavy washing and walking is to hard on Mother right now. Re and Bette – you can do a lot more to keep the house clean and to help set the table and clean up the dishes.

Bus and Dick – I need you to take my place for a while and help Daddy and Mother with the chores. Daddy's going to be away at the WPA a lot now so you can help more with the milking and slopping the hogs and feeding the dogs and cows and horses. I reckon Mother can look after her chickens allright. She don't trust no one to take care of them right. Daley, you can help Mommy feed the chickens. Keep all the dogs out of Mother's eggs. Remember to keep your eyes on Rex. He's the worst of the bunch for stealing them eggs.

Bus – I need you to look after my guns. Keep them clean for me. I reckon your old enough to start hunting now so go ahead and use my Remington if you want to. But make sure you clean it ever time you use it. Daddy let me start on his little .22 rifle when I was about your age so mabe he'll let you take it out now. The squirrels 'll be gnawing on the hickory nuts pretty soon. Just remember what I showed you when I took you hunting with me and you'll get you some. Old Buddy is going to miss me Bus so look after him for me. He's learning to be a good hunting dog so take him with you when you go as he'll need the exercise and practice. Don't let him get fat like Old Jack. Old Jack could teach Buddy the ropes if he weren't so lazy.

Maybe I can bring you back a guitar from CCC Bus. I'll be seeing you soon Old Pal. And all the rest.

Your brother Bob (llg)

GUARDIANS AND OTHER ANGELS   61

Eight

Mrs. Elmer Gaffin, RR1,
Peebles, Ohio July 22, 1936

Mr. Marlin Gaffin
Rogerson, Idaho

Dear Son:- Will now answer your card received yesterday. Would of liked to write to you sooner Bobby but had no address to write too until we got your card yesterday. This leaves us all well and hope you are well. Well you sure have seen a lot of country for a boy so young and I supposed you had a nice trip. I dreamed of all kinds of dreams and imagined everything after you left. But it won't seem so long since you are only staying 3 months. Be a good boy & do everything you can to stand in good with your captain and you will be all right. Our neighbors Bruce & Maria was here Sunday evening for a while. You know he were in CCC & he said that's what you should do & thinks it's just the right place for a fellow these days. Since he can't find no job no where, he might go back in. He hasn't got on Relief yet. Harvey Thatcher is working on a farm up by Cleveland. He won't be home for 4 months, and I bet he doesn't make as much as you, and I expect works a lot harder. The Kids thinks you sure are having a fine time. Roma wishes there were camps for girls so she could see something of the world too she said. Little Dale says "Bobby is way out west." Bussy says to tell you old piggy found six little pigs. Daddy was helping dig a grave down at the cemetery for Lewis Davidson's little girl, and wasn't here to take care of old piggy and she killed two of her babies. Old Bill got down and we had to send for the truck to dispose of him. He was a good old horse to us for many a year. Everything is almost burning up here. It is so hot and dry. I don't know how we've lived through this long drought. If it doesn't rain soon, it is going to be awful hard on everything. Though it isn't as hot as it was last week, but just seems like it can't rain.

Honey I am sending you 3 dollars today as that is all I have. Will write again in two or three days and send another dollar. For you might need something. Take good care of your self and write as often as you can for I feel better if I can hear from you often. Will close with Love from Your Mother & Dad to Bobby. XXX answer soon.

P. S. Dick says to tell you old Tiger has 4 little kittens, and that the Kids are taking good care of Old Buddy. He is fat as a pig.

Mrs. Elmer Gaffin, RR1
Peebles, OhioJuly 22, 1936

Mr. Marlin Gaffin
Rogerson, Idaho

Dear Son – Will write you again tonight. It seems all I can think about is you. It doesn't seem right that you are so far away and I can't talk to you all the time like we like to do.

You were right that I wouldn't of let you go, but I can see the good of it now. I can also see where you are growing up ready to make your own decisions, and I guess I have to abide by them. Don't never keep no secret from me again, Bobby for a Mother's advice is the best advice.

Don't suppose you've heard from Art, have you? He was right smart set on seeing the Pacific again so I don't expect he would of been content staying in Idaho like the rest of you boys. I'm beholding to him for staying with you 'til you got settled in your camp. Maby someday he'll go back to New York. He was a stewing over his mother and little sisters for a while before you left. If he does go back to New York mabe he'll stop in to see us. Bussy and Daddy surely would like that. Art was a good helper to us. He's just like a part of our family. I expect I'm surprised you didn't want to go to the Pacific with Art but I'm glad you decided to stay closer to home, not that Idaho is that close but it's closer than the Pacific.

Well Bobby I expect I've run out of anything to write tonight. Daddy will look for a letter from you tomorrow as he will go to the post office. Be a good boy and be careful of any bad boys. As Ever Your Loving Mother and Dad. (llg)

GUARDIANS AND OTHER ANGELS   63

Mrs. Elmer Gaffin, RR1,
Peebles, Ohio July 23, 1936

Mr. Marlin Gaffin
Rogerson, Idaho

Dear Son:- Will write you again as Daddy is going to town from his WPA work tomorrow evening and can mail it for me. How are you? Fine I hope. We are all O. K. The Kids have gone down to the Hoffer's place to play a while tonight.

It looks like it might rain some before morning. I surely hope it does. How is it out there – is it as hot and dry as it is here? Write and tell us all about that country. We looked it up on the map and found Twin Falls. It is on the Snake River. If you are close to any water, be careful. And Bobby be careful what kinds of boys you take up with. Don't go any place with any one who drinks – as they might get you in trouble. Everyone says if you serve your 3 months out there and get an honorable discharge you can have your pick of any camp, anywhere so if you would want to join up again after you come home and take a visit you might be placed close to home. That would be a pretty good job if you was close to home. The Kids just come home. They say Virge Hoffer said Jack Houser & Sim Workman signed up today. I bet Old Sim would love to be with you out there. You two boys always was stuck at the hip. Daddy said Mr. McGlaughen told him today that his boy was making $40.00 a month now. He has been there in CCC a good while you know. t would be nice if you was where Ralph Workman is. He's so close he comes home every Saturday. But it won't take long for 3 months to pass and you have sure seen a lot of country that you would never get a chance to see any other way. I can't begrudge you that. You've been dreaming of going out west ever since I can remember. There are several boys from Peebles in the state of Wyoming and Nevada. That is just east of you and Nevada is in the desert. I suppose you got my letter I wrote you yesterday and sent you 3 dollars. Am sending you another dollar with this one. Am going to send you a stamp so you can write us a letter.

They took Fred Miller to the hospital one day last week – he wasn't expected to live when they left with him. He had typhoid fever and took some awful kind of sore mouth and it went all through him.

Roma says to look for her out there as she is going to thumb her way out to Idaho to see you. ha ha Well I will close as I haven't much more news to write just now. Answer soon and be a good boy. If I was you I wouldn't run around much till I got acquainted good and could tell which is the best boys to take up with. As ever Your Mother and Dad to Bobby.

64   LINDA LEE GREENE

Lena & Elmer Gaffin RR1,
Peebles, Ohio July 31, 1936

Mr. Marlin Gaffin
Rigerson, Idaho

Dear Son:- Was sure glad to receive your letter yesterday, but sorry to hear you hadn't received either of my letters. Bobby I hope you are still O. K. We are all well. Daddy is still working. We haven't had no rain for so long. I wish we were as lucky for rain as it is where you are. We would have some nice corn if it would only rain. It isn't quite so hot here as it was.

I am glad you like your camp, and that you have plenty to eat, and a good bed and plenty of clothes. We will try and get some one's camera and take some pictures and send you. Bobby just write whenever you take a notion and we will get it. Daddy came home from work yesterday evening and said, "I believe I will drive up to town and see if I can hear from Bobby." So he got a letter from you. We will be going up town about twice a week and once in a while I get a chance to send by someone for the mail, so you can see we will get it pretty often no matter when you write. I sent for that little oil stove, you know in the Spiegel catalogue. It is at the Railroad Depot in town now. But Daddy couldn't get it yesterday evening as it closes at 4:00. He will get it tomorrow.

Oscar Rover, that rabble rouser, is having some kind of trial tomorrow. He was drunk up town the other night and jumped on a Butler boy from Jacktown & I guess the boy beat Oscar up. I don't know whether the trial is over that or if him and Luther is having trouble again. Them two is always fighting about something. Your Uncle J. Q. is out to Mom & Dad's again from hoboing on the road. He came into your Aunt Cora's place up town on a freight. He wasn't drunk, but Cora said he was dirty as a hog. She liked to never got his clothes clean.

Rufe Young and Joe Mendenhall are having a trial tomorrow too. You know Joe's cattle got in Rufe's corn and he sued Joe for a damage and they are having a trial over it.

Write & tell us all about your work and about your trip – what states you passed through, for that is all we talk about is you. Little Dale talks about you, and we hold him up to your FFA picture and he can pick you out every time. He has got so he talks a streak. He says, "Dis is Bobby in his Future Farmer pichure." Bobby write and let me know if you got the 3 dollars I sent you and the 1 dollar after that. This is Friday. I thought I had better write this evening. Maby Dad would want to go to town early in the morning and I wouldn't have time to write then. I sent you a stamp, envelope & paper in my last letter, so you could answer right back. Will close as ever your loving Mother & Dad & Kids to Bobby. XXX

GUARDIANS AND OTHER ANGELS   65

Peebles, O. August 3, 1936

Dear Son - Will write you a short letter this evening as all has gone to bed. I expect we'll be taking your Uncle J. Q. in again for a while. He hitched hiked in from town this morning to see if he could stay with us. He took that little place of Arts in the haymow. He didn't say how long he wants to stay. You know how he just stays until he takes a notion to go off again. Poor old J. Q. never did get over what he went through in the war good enough to live normal after he got out. Won't talk about it though. He likes it out here on the farm where he can feel like he's earning his keep by helping with the chores. You know he's a master carpenter so I expect he'll be a real help to me now that your Daddy is working on the WPA and you and Art are gone and I can use his company. Your Daddy likes him too and you know Daddy never feels like J. Q. is a bother. None of us do. Old J. Q. is a right good feller to have around when he's behaving and even when he ain't he don't do like them rabble rousers do around town. Brother J. Q. is right good company for me too when he's behaving hisself. Always was, our whole lives. I expect he'll be writing you too.

Well honey I've run out of space on this little piece of paper. Daley uses all the paper he can get his hands on. He's started to draw birds and little animals. He's pretty good at it. Be sure to write soon son. You know I'm always looking for a letter from you. Your Loving Mother (llg)

Peebles, O. Aug. 8, 1936

Dear Son:- Will drop you a post card to let you know we are O. K. Hope you are the same. I got your letter telling me you got your money. Am glad you got it. Hope you are still satisfied and not home sick. We had a fine rain on the 4th & 6th. It will sure help the soy beans, and corn too. Benny Gene and Barbara are parted. I guess she caught him with another woman. Ha ha And Uncle Whitely and Beulah Austin are married. That town rabble rouser Old Eldridge has been raising Cain again. He is under a peace bond now. He is always doing some thing. Roma & Bussy has to walk to town to see if there is any Relief for us. Daddy had to work today for the WPA. My little stove come and I like it fine. Well Bobby answer soon. We love to hear from you. With lots of love, your Mother. By by. XX

August 12, 1936

Dear Son: Received your letter today. Was glad to hear from you. We got a check from your CCC work also. It was $20.00. It sure is nice you are making some money for yourself and us too, and am glad you are staying well contented. I have been awful worried about you. We heard there was a forest fire somewhere out there, but Daddy couldn't remember where it was. So I was worried until I got your letter today. Will be glad to get your pictures. Honey be careful when you are out hunting and don't get hurt. We are all O. K. yet. Will write you often letting you know how we are and you do the same. Well, I will close as Daddy & Bus & Dick is ready to go back to town. With lots of love – Mother

Peebles, Ohio Aug. 28, 1936

Mr. Marlin Gaffin
Rogerson, Idaho

Dear Son:- I will try to answer your letter. We are O. K. and hope you are the same. I have got along well and the baby is just fine. He is fat as a pig. Some thinks he looks like you and some thinks he looks like Dale. He has an awful lot of hair and about the same red color as Dale's. I guess Benny Gene is going back to CCC camp next month. I guess he and Barbara have split for good.

I guess they have Ollie & Bert up on the <u>Carpet</u> again. You know they caught Bert driving again. You know he lost his license for 6 months the last time he was carrying on in town. I guess Ollie was disturbing church. They said whatever the Preacher would say Ollie would stand at the back of the church and repeat it and then Cuss the Preacher right to his face. Isn't that a sight? So they had him arrested. I guess Ruth Purtee isn't getting no better. I am afraid she is going to make a die of it yet. The Kids have begun to think about school. Roma's starts the 8th of Sept. and the others the 14th. Little Dale will be awful lonesome when they all start to school. This is the twins first year, as you know. Bette is looking forward to it so, but Dick would just as leave stay here on the farm. I expect he'll be an ornery feller in school, fighting and carrying on. That boy's got too much energy. Wish he could give some of it to Bussy. Of course, Bussy was just like Dick in the energy department before he got sick. Bus has been feeling pretty good this summer. Maby he is outgrowed his trouble. I pray for it every night and now I'm praying for you too, son.

Mom & Dad are going to move to Mayhill. They are going to quit farming. They are too old for it, and Dad ain't well enough to farm no more.

I guess they got a pretty good raise on their government pension. I don't expect they'll move before they have their corn gathered. We are going to have some pretty good corn since we have been getting some rain, and an awful crop of soy beans. Well Bobby I expect I will have to close as I am pretty tired sitting up. I will get up about Sunday or Monday after my bed rest. Roma is taking care of me and little Dean and doing the work. We named your new baby brother Delano Dean after Mr. Roosevelt. I will close now with lots of love, Your loving Mother

Peebles, Ohio, Sept. 5, 1936

Mr. Marlin Gaffin
Rogerson, Idaho

Dear Son:- Will drop you a few lines as Daddy is going to town. We received your letter a few days ago and was glad to hear from you. We are O. K. – only colds. Hope you are well. Daddy is cutting the soy beans today, or he had Joe Mendenhall cutting them for him. They are using Archie's horses. Dad sent Bussy over to McGlaughen with our mare to get her shod as Daddy didn't have no shoes for her. Her feet were getting so sore. Well Bobby I haven't got Bruce to bring his camera out yet. He claims he will bring it today. You will be home before you get any pictures I'm afraid. The baby is all right only got an awful cold. Roma, Bussy & me all dreamed you came home last night. But maby you can get something to do around here this winter. Take good care of yourself Bobby and don't get sick. Answer soon. As ever, Your Mother & all to Bob. By by

The paucity of capital to my relatives had taken its toll, as money to repair broken down farm equipment, and to buy seeds, had long been difficult to come by. The Works Progress Administration (WPA), like the CCC, a government program designed to put men to work constructing bridges, highways and parks, provided sporatic work for Poppaw. That resource supplemented by the monthly CCC allotment from Bob began to put a dent in those problems. The money otherwise went further in rural Ohio than it would have in the highly industrialized cities of the state where fully 37% of industrial workers were without jobs. The distressing economic situation continued to be reflected all across the United States. Under the sympathetic aegis of a Democratic federal government, labor unions began to come to the fore. Their bellies hungry, and their sights set on attaining middle class status, the first major uprisings in the nation by unionizing workers demanding unparalleled job security via better pay with guaranteed increases accompanied by more far reaching benefit packages, took place in the Ohio cities of Akron and Youngstown among rubber and steel workers.[19]

It had been seven years since the onslaught of the Great Depression, and four years since the election of Franklin Delano Roosevelt, the "New Deal" president, and the namesake of the lastborn child of Mommaw and Poppaw, Delano Dean, called Dean thereafter, the boy having been born on August 21, 1936. Mommaw, having turned thirty-five on September 29th, and Poppaw, thirty-eight on December 5th that year of 1936, had brought nine children into the world, the eight still living ranging from sixteen-year-old Bob to the infant, Dean.

As Bob had promised, he was home to help with the autumn harvest. He never returned to school, although he planned to rejoin the CCC immediately following his seventeenth birthday on January 24, 1937, coincidentally a day that would go down in the annals of history as "Black Sunday."

---

[19] http://www.answers.com/topic/ohio?cat=travel

Nine

Although Mommaw had been particularly careful to keep her letters to Bob lighthearted, she and Poppaw had been heartsick from missing him while he had been at CCC camp in Idaho during the summer of 1936. However, it was Bussy who had been hardest hit by the absence of Bob, and Arthur as well, Bob, having been the most important and consistent companion of his life, and Arthur, having grown over the years in the esteem of the young boy almost to the point of veneration. His declining health gradually curtailing his playtime activities and his farm chores, therefore, more than ever before, school grew to fill in the gaps in the life of Bussy. Principally during times of inclement weather, including that winter of 1936-37, unfortunately even school was often out-of-reach for the ten-year-old boy. Long days of lying on the davenport in the front room, the heavy and painful weight of worsening infection in his lungs, as well as occasional "strange" feelings in his head, turning him weaker and more listless, Bussy lolled away his days listening to the radio, and plunking the guitar Bob had brought home to him from Idaho. The radio grew to be the most important lifeline to the outside world for Bussy, and in his typically wholehearted fashion, he set about transforming his regrettable circumstances to something valuable, both to himself in terms of his self-esteem, and to his family. While home from school, and heroically embracing the luxuries of time and solitude his illness produced, Bussy tried to make a useful place for himself in the workaday world of his family by keeping its members abreast of the weather and news reports, information he gleaned over the airwaves via their new battery-operated radio set. The five-year sojourn of Arthur Billings with the Gaffin family had turned the former city dweller's disinterest in weather into one as engaged as that of a farmer, like Poppaw, his face perpetually upturned to the sky, studying it for signs portended in cloud formations, directions and energy of winds, along with changes in temperature and humidity. For the reason that it provided unprecedented coverage of the news and weather conditions, as well as the diversion it was likely to afford the often home-bound Bussy, with money he had earned by doing work for a nearby farmer, Arthur had purchased the radio for the family before he had gone away.

Even though the economic outlook of the family temporarily changed for the better due to the CCC money from Bob and that of Poppaw's outside employment with the WPA, the anomalies in the weather continued to beleaguer them. Coupled with the persistent and pernicious economic downfall of the nation, all that was needed was a black plague or a swarming pestilence to transform the decade into a disaster of Biblical proportions for the common folks in their region. And sure enough, as if fulfilling Biblical scriptures all over again, the disaster arrived in the form of a flood to rival the one that had floated Noah's ark.

"If it rains!" no longer was the catch phrase of the population formerly choked by the long-standing drought. An abnormally warm December, 1936, combined with moderate to heavy rainfall, had been no harbinger of disaster. As rain, sleet and melting snow persisted through most of January, 1937, however, conditions that saturated soil and bloated waterways, the new lament became, "Send a boat!" The Ohio River, slowly creeping higher and higher during those warm weeks, until finally, in one of the worst weather events of the century, overflowed its banks all along the Ohio Valley, at its highest, reaching an astounding 38 feet above flood stage. From Pittsburgh to Paducah, hundreds of people lost their lives, and half a million became homeless. The devastation created 200,000 refugees in Louisville, Kentucky alone. Entire cities emptied; were blotted from the landscape, erased by the sea of water escaping the boundaries of the raging river, cities such as Dayton, Kentucky where 7,500 of its 10,000 residents were left without homes as 75% of the city was underwater, and entire city blocks of homes and other structures were washed away into the torrent of the angry river, never to be recovered again. In language that might have come directly from the Book of Revelations in the Christian Bible, "We thought it was the end of the world," stated Ruth Lyons, a popular Ohio broadcaster of the time. Lyons was associated with WLW radio in Cincinnati, where the river was 25 feet above flood stage. The biggest challenge was securing adequate, safe water for drinking and firefighting[20] as nearly a million gallons of leaking gasoline spewed from huge gasoline tanks that were ripped from their foundations causing the gasoline to mix with the snaking high water in downtown streets. Threatening to incinerate the entire western section of the city, a dangling electrical wire caused explosions and

---

[20] American History Magazine, August 2007, "The Whole World Is Listening," Chris Chandler, p. 53-59.

GUARDIANS AND OTHER ANGELS   71

a blaze that required 35 fire companies to snuff out, trucks from the Ohio cities of Dayton and Columbus included in the fire-fighting brigade.[21]

Just as on the long third weekend of November, 1963 when a shocked and bewildered American public sat transfixed in front of millions of television screens watching the assassination of their president and the proceedings attached to it, during the extended third weekend of January, 1937, Bussy, along with millions of other Americans, their ears glued to their radio sets, listened to the breathtaking news of the flood, the coverage of the life-or-death national crisis becoming the broadcast media event of its time. Until then taking a back seat to newspapers, the fledgling broadcast medium of radio, with the reporting of the flooding of the Ohio River, set a precedent for nonstop coverage of extraordinary events, emulated for the first time again in April, 1945 with the funeral of Franklin Delano Roosevelt, again in November, 1963 with the events surrounding the assassination of John F. Kennedy, and in the current century, with the 9/11 terror attacks and the Hurricane Katrina devastation. In conjunction with other stations in the broadcast area, due to an unprecedented decision to discontinue all commercial programming, the Ohio River flood emergency reporting continued over radio station WHAS in Louisville, Kentucky for more than 187 uninterrupted hours. The flood having knocked out most of the electricity, taking with it traditional emergency communication devices, radio broadcasting was called to action as the only remaining avenue for providing contact among police, fire, rescue services and the stranded public. In a coal-oil lamp lit office, relaying thousands of messages at their microphones, messages received by telephone, telegraph, ham radio and word of mouth, radio announcers braved the cold and the flood, assuming the mantle of emergency dispatchers with calls of help such as the following:

Fire patrol boats operating south of Broadway are ordered to Third and Breckenridge! All available boats are needed there at once...Milk is needed for nine babies at missing person's bureau at 1010 South Third Street...power boat, please deliver...Urgent! Fifty refugees must be moved immediately by boat from 1023 West Madison Street! This is imperative! Seven people marooned on housetop on Lower River Road...can't hold out much longer...Fifty children marooned at church. Get them out immediately![22]

His aspirins downed, his "choppers" inserted, his hat and coat donned, and his feet running as they made out across the washroom floor, Poppaw yelled over the voice of the reporter on the radio, **"Mother, where's my galoshes? I put 'em right hyere by the cook stove last night."**

---

[21] http://www.wcet.org/flood/37flood_timeline.asp
[22] American History Magazine, August 2007, "The Whole World Is Listening," Chris Chandler, p. 53-59.

72   LINDA LEE GREENE

"Dad, Bussy put 'em on last night when he went outside ta fasten that floppin' door on the toilet fer me when I was feedin' Deany. That bangin' was adrivin' me crazy an' athreatenin' ta tear the door right off o' that outhouse," the voice of Mommaw called out to Poppaw from their bedroom.

The Ohio River continues to rise at approximately 3-10 feet per hour...rain up and down the river from Pittsburgh to Louisville is continuing...Traffic across the suspension bridge connecting Covington, Kentucky with Cincinnati has for the time been suspended...The floodwaters have been closing the approaches on both sides of the river...There's a most urgent need for food, clothing, and shelter. Medical supplies are also needed.[23]

On the days he was home from school, if he was able, Bussy kept the fire going in the heating stove in the front room, and sometimes for the sake of a change of position, he huddled around the stove, his chair tilted back in a bipedal position and his brogan-clad feet propped up on the side of the hulking appliance. As Poppaw entered the front room in search of his son, he smelled the familiar odor of sizzling leather from Bussy's shoes. "Bus, that far's agoin' ta burn clean through them soles o' yer brogans. Put yer feet down, Son. Yer smellin' up the whole house," gently Poppaw told the boy. "Bus, where'd ye put my galoshes?"

The city of Dayton, Kentucky is absolutely without clothing and bedding...The Spears Hospital at Dayton had 100 patients at the time the flood reached Dayton's streets...they were taken to the Dayton, Kentucky High School. In this school in the last few days, we learn that dozens of babies have been born and several operations performed...Churches are overflowing with Dayton's refugees. There is plenty of food available, but no water. Dayton, Kentucky needs water, clothing and bedding at once.[24]

Lowering his legs to the floor, the chair dropping to its normal four-legged position and wide-eyed with disbelief at the news reports, Bussy replied to Poppaw. "Daddy, listen to what the announcer is sayin' on the radio. The Ohiuh River is drowndin' ever thing in sight, Daddy. An' its comin' thisaway. Ain't you noticed how much harder it's rainin' an' blowin' outside?"

"That's why I need my galoshes, Bus. I got ta git ta the cows an' git 'em took care of. Where the dickens ye put my galoshes, Son?"

"I reckon I left 'em out on the porch, Daddy."

"Out on the porch? Bus, them galoshes is prob'ly blowed away by now!" Storming out of the front room, his heavy footfalls shaking the rafters of the house, Poppaw slammed the back door behind him, pulled on his

---

[23] American History Magazine, August 2007, "The Whole World is Listening," Chris Chandler, p. 53-59
[24] Ibid

GUARDIANS AND OTHER ANGELS   73

galoshes, which by some miracle were still intact on the porch, and whistled for his dogs. As on every morning of every year for two decades, his cows were waiting, that morning already in their stalls, the freezing cold rain having driven them into the barn for cover. Their heavy sacks gorging with milk, their teats leaked the stuff onto the ground by the time he and his dogs reached them. Flossie, his brown Guernsey cow, his best milker, her milk so rich it turned to cream as it hit the bucket, in a fit of temper for having waited too long for him, for she tolerated being milked by no one but Poppaw, raised her long, thick, and silky tail and relieved herself, of both urine and manure, seeming to spray the total contents of her complex digestive system onto the entirety of one wall of her stall, eliciting epithets from Poppaw heard as far away as the farmhouse several hundred feet from the barn.

"Flossie's shit all over the walls o' her stall agin'," Dick snickered to Bob as the two boys sloshed through the mud of the lane to the barn to help with the milking, their hat-covered heads bent into the biting wind. When they reached their fuming father in the barn, their coats were sopping wet and their galoshes caked with mud.

By the time Roma and her younger sisters Reva and Bette pulled out of bed and sauntered lazily down the stairs to the front room, in the warm and cozy kitchen in the farmhouse, the hands of Mommaw were already wrist-deep in flour and baking powder and yeast and lard and water all thrown together in a huge mixing bowl, her strong hands kneading the dough that would become scratch biscuits. Shivering from the cold, the girls huddled with Bussy around the stove in the front room, and listened to the radio for a few minutes.

Cincinnati remains on an emergency holiday basis for the third successive day...this holiday will continue until the city can put its house in order.[25]

"Mother, Cincinnatuh is on holiday agin tuhday!" excitedly Bette yelled out to her mother as she ran into the kitchen. "Ye reckon we ain't got no school tuhday neither?"

"I reckon the school bus ain't agoin' ta attempt ta git back hyere tuhday. There ain't nothin' but knee-deep mud out there. That bus'd jist slide off the road and inta the ditch an' kin ye imagine the mess that'd be?" Mommaw replied. She lifted her forearm and wiped her dewy brow, flour dough dripping from her hand. "Best ta keep an eye on the road after breakfast. The bus might make it through, but I'd be awful surprised if it did. An' even if it makes it through, I believe I'd feel better havin' you kids hyere at home in conditions like this. If the bus makes it through, ye'll have ta signal ta the driver ta go on without ye."

---

[25] American History Magazine, August 2007, "The Whole World Is Listening," Chris Chandler, p. 53-59.

74   LINDA LEE GREENE

"Ro, Re, we ain't agoin' ta school!" Bette squealed with delight as
the two older girls walked into the kitchen. Their faces alight with bright
smiles, each girl set to work helping their mother prepare breakfast. Fresh
and warm from the bodies of Mommaw's hens, eggs she had gathered earlier
that morning from the noisy and smelly henhouse, would fry in bacon grease
in a gigantic iron skillet, the grease sizzling in wait for Reva to crack the
eggs in after the biscuits were placed into the oven. The barnyard, that
obstacle course of animal droppings and oozing rutted mud from the pelting
rain and churned up by animal hooves and wheels of wagons and plows and
other farm implements, was but a flower garden compared to that stinking
den of fluttering, feathered, female fowl Mommaw had braved entering soon
after daybreak, her hat and coat, sopping wet from the rain. Standing inside
the door of the henhouse, her garments dripping wet, the water forming a
pool on the ground at her mud-caked, boot-clad feet, she spoke to her
chickens. "Ye best keep on eye out ladies, fer if old man weather takes a
notion ta flood us out like it's doin' ever where else hyere abouts, ye best git
high up ta the trees, er better yit, ye best git ta the haymow in the barn. Ye'd
prob'ly git blowed out o' them trees in this hyere wind."

Fatty bacon from one of Bussy's hogs, having been butchered by
him and Poppaw the autumn before, the bacon, sliced thick and short,
already piping hot and curling, was tended by Roma. Presently Roma
scooped the bacon onto a plate, adding another batch to the skillet. Scratch
pancake batter, mixed to a fluffy light consistency was poured into round
circles by the precise hand of Roma, the batter spitting and cracking on the
hot lard-smeared griddle. At table the pancakes would soak-up the sugar
water syrup boiling in its own separate receptacle on the stove. To satisfy the
sweet tooth of the large family, a paraphen-sealed jar of blackberry preserves
sat on the table, the preserves canned by Mommaw and Roma the summer
before. To be smeared onto the piping hot biscuits as an accompaniment to
the preserves, fresh butter, the skim of Flossie's rich milk, and hand-churned
by the girls the day before, also held place at center stage on the table. A
small pan of oatmeal, "Daddy's Oats," as they called it, never a morning in
his life without it, he would smother in butter and sugar and Flossie's
incomparable cream. Anchoring the table at each end were large crock-
pitchers of milk, thick with cream having escaped the skimming, never the
"old blue john milk" as they called it, the fat-free milk so popular today. And
coffee, copious stove-brewed coffee, brewed in a banquet-sized pot, lasted
only halfway through breakfast, and then another pot was gulped down by
Mommaw and Poppaw and the older children. Although the school bus
failed to arrive, the morning was not spent idly, as each member of the
family set to their individual chores—all but Bussy, who, having consumed a
meager breakfast of one biscuit and a glass of milk and after tuning the radio
to WPAY in Portsmouth, stretched out on the davenport to continue listening

GUARDIANS AND OTHER ANGELS   75

to the news of the flood, one of Mommaw's colorful quilts tucked in around his perpetually chilled feet.

On this Friday, January 23, 1937, the worst fears have come true, the current flood stage reaching 70 feet, and eclipsing the previous all-time high during the 1913 flood...A Red Cross train bringing 1,600 cots, medical supplies, and food will be met with a truck...all hilltop churches and schools are overflowing with hundreds of marooned people as firemen and volunteers worked through the night...The Red Cross set up food distribution centers at Franklin Avenue and Central Presbyterian Churches...it is estimated that from 12,000 to 15,000 are homeless in Portsmouth.

As the flood of 1937 proved to be one of the worst weather events in the history of the Ohio Valley, the flooding extended to the Mississippi Valley, as well. According to the National Weather Service, 21.24 inches (156 trillion tons) of rain fell in January alone. On January 24, also the day of the seventeenth birthday of Bob, a day of crisis forevermore remembered in the annals of American history as "Black Sunday," rivers overflowed in twelve states located in the Ohio and Mississippi Valleys, inundating 12,700 square miles and affecting 75,000 homes. In all, almost 900 people were seriously injured and 250 died by drowning and flood-induced fires and explosions. No city, town, or rural community near the Ohio, Mississippi, Cumberland, Tennessee Rivers and their tributaries remained unscathed. Ohio Brush Creek, a tributary of the Ohio River, and a main waterway running through several communities in rural Adams County in Southern Ohio, including Peebles, was one example. Backwater from the flooded Ohio River into the Ohio Brush Creek was so severe a person in a rowboat could touch the bottom of the old State Route 348 Bridge that crossed Ohio Brush Creek. While the birthplace of Ulysses S. Grant in Pt. Pleasant, Ohio was submerged to its second floor, and the nearby Grant's Memorial Bridge had raging flood water reaching its upper struts, WPA workers were hastily summoned from other projects to strengthen the flood wall along the banks of the Ohio River in Portsmouth, Ohio.

The American Red Cross and the U. S. Army Corps of Engineers were heavily involved in rescue work, the new levees established upstream along the Mississippi after the flood of 1926-27 of particular concern. Rescue parties, including thousands of volunteers, highway patrolmen, and National Guardsmen fought in vain to keep the levees intact before the Corps of Engineers finally advised those people downstream to evacuate. Refugee centers (tent cities) were established throughout the flooded area, the Memphis, Tennessee fairgrounds alone housing 60,000 refugees. However, many refused to leave platforms they had hastily constructed on the rooftops of their homes, reasoning that the floodwaters would soon subside, as had been the case in former years. Exposure to the elements, hunger, and illness, pneumonia and influenza in particular, eventually sent approximately 8,000

76   LINDA LEE GREENE

people to emergency makeshift "hospitals" set up throughout the area of the flooding.[26]

For two weeks, Bussy camped out in the front room, captivated by the radio reports of the flooding, his continually chilled body cocooned within one of Mommaw's quilts. By February 5th the floodwaters had receded, the news of the flood becoming old news as Bussy's restlessness grew. It had been a year and a half since he had become ill, and no amount of doctoring had helped him. Still benefiting from a naturally robust constitution, the onslaught of a totally debilitating phase of illness was delayed. Nevertheless, he was beginning to show identifiable signs of a chronically ill young person, growing thin and repeatedly fatigued from a lack of appetite and the ravages of a persistent low-grade fever and billowing infection in his chest.

Bussy could only wait out the long days of winter until he could return to school, in the meantinme relying on his sister Reva to keep him current with his school lessons. Spring portended less dangerous weather to Bussy's health. It also brought Bob's leaving again for his second stint in the CCC, that time "just about as far as you can go," as stated by Roma in a letter she wrote to her elder brother at the camp he had gone to in Beulah, Oregon.

---

[26] http://tennesseeencyclopedia.net/imagegallery.php?EntryID=F022

Ten

At that season in what seemed the far side of Earth, as described by Bob in his letters, the world was abloom with *green grass, ripe oranges, apples, and roses.* By train for five days and five nights, Bob had traveled 3,000 miles west by what he described as the *southern route,* passing through *Indiana, Illinois, Kansas, Colorado, Wyoming, Nevada, California, and finally to Oregon* – Juntura, Oregon, in the Redwood district about eighty miles from the Idaho line. This time again Bob had company on his journey, his friends from home Gene Thomas, Tom Workman, and Tom's brother, Sim, having joined the CCC with him. Ultimately however, Sim was sent to another camp in Vale, Oregon, sixty-five miles closer to the Idaho line. Although elated by the trip, especially along the Pacific coast where, as indicated by excerpts from some of his letters to his mother, *Things are high here along the coast...you have to pay 21 to 25 cents* [a gallon] *for gasoline...the cheapest little shack you can rent will run between 20 and 30 dollars a week...the people in California think they are awful poor if they ain't worth at least $10,000.00.* Bob was reeling from the *wildness of the country...the timbered mountains nearly straight up...the rain nearly ever day...*plenty of food, and so much clothing he *didn't know what to do with them all...*by the *mountain lions, deer, wildcats, coyotes & rattlers...*by *thousands of ducks, swan, wild geese, pheasants & jack rabbits on and around the lakes & rivers...*by the great *herds of cattle & a cowboy* [who] *comes to the canteen often to buy candy & tobacco.*

A week into his stay in his bunkhouse style camp with 184 other boys from all over the United States, he had taken *3 typhoid shots, a vaccination and two tick shots* to ward against the *little black ticks on the purple sage...some of them infected with Rocky Mountain Spotted Fever.* He was already infected with gold fever, a vein of it running under Lost Creek Canyon where his foreman said they could do some *secret mining in their*

78   LINDA LEE GREENE

spare time...If we get to that place I will bring some gold home with me (smuggle it through), he promised his family in a letter.

Peebles, Ohio, April 13, 1937

Dear Brother:-Thought I would answer your letter we received yesterday. Was sure glad to hear you got to go with Tom & Gene, but I sure feel sorry for Sim having to go to another camp. If you find out Sim's address send it to me as we will write to him. We are all well I suppose. You are just about as far as you can go. I told Mother last night it looks like you could share some of your training with me. Ha ha. Will write you a letter instead of a postcard next time. Answer soon. Goodbye and good luck. XOXO Your sis Roma and all – We are going to send you the camera as soon as we take some pictures with it that we will also send to you.

CCC Co 551 Vale Oregon

Mr. Robert Gaffin – Dear Friend
    Will answer your letter received the other day. Sure glad to hear from you.
    Yes I still like this camp but not good enough to stay any longer than 6 months. Seems like I have been out hear a year already.
    Well since Dutch (died) [moonshine still operator in Peebles] *we eather have to make our own Moon or git it at old big belleys* [another still operator]. *We don't care where we get it just so it will put a man on his ear.*
    I was on a little bender last night. Me and another boy we drank two quarts of Apple Jack. I was just all in when I got to camp and by god we was short shifted. I just lay down on my bed with my clothes on and slep(t) till 11-30 this morning. You know just about how I feel now.
    Well as they are going to have chicken and ice cream I had better close before I miss dinner. So answer soon from Sim

Peebles, Ohio, April 25, 1937

Dear Son: Will drop you a few lines. This leaves us all well and hope you are the same. I thought I would write now as they are all gone except Dale, Dick & Dean. Dad is out somewhere. Roma & Reva & Bette all went down to Purtee's to visit & Bussy went away with Delbert [Workman, youngest

GUARDIANS AND OTHER ANGELS   79

brother of Sim]. *He came home with them from Sunday School. Bussy has been able to go to church regular and he runs around visiting. He's been helping Daddy some. Mabe his trouble is finally clearing up.*

The kids school was out Friday and they will be home now and I don't expect I will know whether I'm coming or going half the time. Roma's isn't out till the 28th of May. Well I reckon I will close as news is scarce. You know there never is much news on Cedar Fork. With love, Your Mother

CCC Co 551 Vale Ore.

Mr. Robert Gaffin – dear goat

Will answer your letter received the other day – always fancy getting a letter from you.How is the old world turning up that way – its turning dam slow down hear – I think it will stop the way that sun felt today.

Well how many Rookies did your camp get in this time? We got 30 and four has gone over the hill all ready and some more are gold breaking [gold bricking – going over the hill to dig for gold]. *They can't take it. I gess our ball team will come up and play at your camp the 8 of next month. Our catcher went home the other day. He was the best player we had & god we will beat your camp if I haft to play my self ha ha.*

Well I suppose we will all be riding the rail in a bout 6 weeks and that none too damn soon for me eather. We will get back just in time for squirrel hunting and plenty time for Rabbit hunting so take plenty of CC pills and don't get constipated. So answer soon from old gold break (Sim). Oh yes I sent that negative away and [will] *send you a picher like that one of Tom's as soon as I get them.*

Beset by burgeoning dust storms, nevertheless the boys in the Juntura CCC Camp kept busy, as described by Bob, *building up springs in the mountains and putting in water troughs for sheep, cattle, & range horses. In one place we are putting in troughs enough to accommodate 5 thousand sheep belonging to a sheepherder right below camp...And I seen a cowboy on a white horse riding down the side of the mountain yeasterday rounding up wild horses. And you should have seen him ride.*

Bob was eager to shoot photographs of the incomparable scenery: *the largest yellow pine forest in the world. The trees are about 200 ft high & 8 ft to 10 ft thick.* His trigger finger itchy, he wanted to hunt in those thick forests. In a letter to his mother he asked her to send him a camera and his daddy's .22 rifle.

Peebles, Ohio, May 6, 1937

Dear Son:- Will drop you a few lines tonight. We are O. K. and hope you are well. Did you get your camera? We sent it to you last Saturday. We will be looking for some pictures soon. We had a cold rain last night. We all got up about froze this morning as I had taken the heating stove down. Well Bobby if you get up there and run on to some gold, I am afraid we will never see you back here again. Ha ha

All the kids passed this year. The teacher took them to Serpent Mound. It wasn't a bit nice day. Cold & rainy. Bobby you know that boy that lived over there by Serpent Mound, Dutch Wallace, he was Guy Wallace('s) stepson. Him and that Riley man that lived down below Dad & Mom in the woods, well they was taking a load of junk to Portsmouth the other day & had a wreck and the truck got on fire & burned them both up so bad they couldn't tell one from the other. Only by the boys class ring. He would of Graduated this year. Sure was an awful thing. Well Bobby I will close as space is limited. Answer soon with love, Mother.

Peebles, Ohio, May 12, 1937

Dear Brother:

Will drop you a few lines to let you know I am O. K. and hoping you are O. K. to. I heard on the radio last week about that German airship called the Hindenburg that got blowed up. I listened to the whole thing and it raised the hairs on the back of my neck more than the first time I shot that old .22 rifle of Daddys. It just busted out in flames when it were about to land in New Jersey. It killed 36. Just burned them up to a crisp. I heard on the radio that the king got crowned in England today. You know that other one – it was his big brother I reckon, well he adicated. Mother says that means he quit. I don't reckon I'd be a quitting a awful good job like that. I amagine he made $100.00 a month maby more.

I wished I could of saw that cowboy you seen riding down that mountain Bobby. Did he look like Buck Jones? Bobby when I get well maby we could quit farming & move out there & get to be cowboys. Maby we could cowboy while we was digging that gold you got out there. Did you find any yet? Remember in our history in school about the gold rush out to the west back in the 1800s? I amagine that's how all them folks in Californa got $10,000. Well since news is scarce here on Cedar Fork, I will close for now. Your old Pal & best brother, Ha Ha – Bus (llg)

GUARDIANS AND OTHER ANGELS   81

Peebles, Ohio, May 13, 1937

*Dear Son:- Will write you a few lines to-night. How are you by this time?
We are O. K. only Bussy don't feel very good to-night. He & Dick got wet
yesterday hunting the cows and it about laid him up. We got your check too
the 11th. It was $23.00. We will send you some on what we owe you soon as
we get some bills straightened up.*

*Well will have to tell you some news. Flossy Miller & Stuart
McClellan had a fight. He hit her with a black jack & guess about knocked
her out. I guess he beat William up too. They say he is hiding from the Law.
And Ray Billings and his brother George got in to it over some whiskey. Ray
claimed George stole off him, and that ornery George just up and shot Ray
through the side. They thought at first he was shot through the liver and
wouldn't live long. But he wasen't and is getting better. They claim a belt
Ray had on is what saved his life. That is what old whiskey will cause, and
them is brothers too. You wanted to know how Buddy was. He is fat as a
pig. I don't know what he finds to eat. But he doesn't care whether he eats
at home or not. I haven't much garden out yet – just onions and lettuce and
some sweet corn planted. That patch you plowed for potatoes are coming up
good.*

*It poured down rain all day to-day and last night too. Dad isn't
quite done plowing yet and would like to get the corn planted by next week.
But I don't expect he will as all it does is pour down rain. My hens have
been dying awful. We got them some medicine today. I just got 31 left – got
3 a setting. I am afraid they will die on the nest before they hatch. Harry
Myers has started a Revival. Oh yes, Edward has lost his religion (if he ever
had any). Well I must close for this time. With Love Your Mother (answer
soon)*

Peebles, Ohio, May 28, 1937

*Dear Son:- Will answer your letter received yesterday. Was glad to receive
your pictures. You look as though you were getting enough to eat. Ha ha
and that looks like pretty country out there. Roma got Sims picture the other
day. He had a big cowboy hat on and he calls himself the "lone star
ranger." Dad and Archie are still farming together. They have the field on
grassy and that long piece up by Archie's house and the cane patch and this
piece up the road all together. Dad is done planting here at home, all except
that little strip up the hollow. Bussy is feeling better and he has been getting
tobacco ground ready today. We will have plants to set the next rain. They
have growed awful fast. I have my garden all planted only a place for late
cabbage and sweet potatoes. We sent for the fence. It is uptown. Dad is*

82   LINDA LEE GREENE

going after it tomorrow. We got fence for the hog lot too. I can't hardly write for Dean. He is on my lap trying to take my pencil and paper. He will soon be walking. He is pulling up to things and has 6 teeth.

Bobby we are sending you a dollar. Maby it will help you out untill you get paid. We will try & send you more untill you get paid. Daddy traded cars today with Walt Shoemaker. He is in the used car business now I guess. We got a 27 Ford Sedan. All good tires but once it had real good upholstery but needs paint. It is in good shape though. The Generator played out on that old Ford again and it needed a top. And God knows what else. So he just traded it off. He had to give $15 Boot [down payment] & $5 a pay till he gets it paid. I told them we would have to live on corn bread & milk till we got it paid. Ha ha We will take care of your money so you can get you a car when you come back.

Is it getting warm out there? It was awful hot here today. We have begun to need a little rain. You know we got to have a right smart rain on Cedar Fork if you raise anything. Well Bobby I guess I have told you all the news so will close and get this kid to sleep. As Ever Your Mother

Peebles, Ohio May 28, 1937

Dear Bobby, I seen your picture & you look like you sure do like them eats out there. Daddy is going to have to make the front door bigger to get you in the house when you come home. Ha ha The darn Yanks beat the Reds 3 to 2 in the ninth. It was there 24th win in a row. I shore wish I could talk to old Art about it. I don't reckon you have heard from him, have you? We ain't heard from him. I am O. K. now – been working up the dirt for the tobacco some. Well write some time soon. Bus (llg)

Peebles, Ohio, June 3, 1937

Dear Son: Will send you a quick postcard. We will send you the rifle next week. Bussy doesn't want you to sell it so Daddy said to tell you he will let you know about selling it later. [In a letter, Bob had mentioned selling the gun to Tom.] *Old Flossie found* [gave birth to] *the prettiest calf yesterday but a doggone male. Ha ha Did you get the picture of Roma and the dollar I sent you? Love, Mother*

His entire life having a passion for guns, even building them in later years, Bob and his foreman at camp, Mr. Kubli, himself a gun enthusiast, an expert hunter, and a crack shot, enriched the diet of his boys with venison, the

GUARDIANS AND OTHER ANGELS   83

bounty from their hunting excursions. Bob said in a letter: *The foreman's tent looks like a gun gallery. He has a .22 rifle, .22 Colt auto. Pistol, a 30-30 rifle, a .45 Colt & fishing outfit...The foreman & a couple of boys went out the other day & killed another yearling buck and they captured a one day old fawn & is it cute. We are going to keep it for a pet. We feed it by hand. When you hold out your hand it comes to you. It makes a noise when it's hungry like a kitten...It's been raining off & on for 2 weeks...I received the rifle and it is in good condition. Mr. Kubli the foreman, myself & Tom is going prospecting in the morning & I hope we find some gold. There is going to be a Rodeo over at Vale July the 4th. I would like to go to it, and would also like to see Sim. Tom sent home for some money too go. So would you send me $10 by registered mail? Just take it out of the money you are saving for me & I will appreciate it very much. It's going to last 3 days. There will be a sort of fair, wild horse riding, roping, bull dogging, steer riding & last but not least, the sights of it.*

Peebles, Ohio, June 28, 1937

Dear Son: Received your letter Saturday. Was glad to hear from you. Bobby you sure must be going to celebrate the 4th big aren't you? ha ha You surely ain't going to spend $10.00 in one day are you? Or do you get the whole 3 days off? Well it will be a sight you have often read about but never had the pleasure of seeing. But son you must be careful of your money. You know how some people make their living taking money off of people, and you don't know when they get it in a crowd like that will be. I am sending your money in a money order. That is the safest way to send money.

Daddy and Archie planted the field on grassy yesterday. They killed a rattlesnake on grassy Saturday. It had 7 rattles and seen a whole lot more snakes. They will have to watch this summer tending that corn. You will be surprised to receive a letter by air mail. Mr. Nicholas [at the post office] says you will get it so much sooner. So long and answer soon. Mother

Peebles, Ohio, July 3, 1937

Dear Bobby:
This letter finds me doing right fine & am hoping you are fine too. I have been thinking about you and old Sim at that carnaval at Vale today. Boy all that bull dogging & roping would be right fine to see. Maby you can

84   LINDA LEE GREENE

send me some pictures of it. Well you know I had a birthday all ready. I am 12 now. We ain't been swimming but three times. Mother won't let me go in the water any more but sometimes I go down to the creek with the kids and get splashed some. On the radio it said about that lady pilot Amelia Earhart that got lost. She was flying around the world. Can you just amagine what a adventure that would be – just to get in a airplane and just take off clear up in the sky and fly over the ocean? When I grow up that's what I am a going to do, or maby be a animal doctor. Did Mother tell you that I helped old Flossie find her bull calf? It didn't make me sick or nothing. Well, Bobby I guess I will close now. Don't forget to send me some pictures of that bull dogging and them steers. Your brother, Bus (llg)

Beulah, Oregon, July 6, 1937

Dear Mother:
         I will write you a few lines to let you know I am still O. K. and hope you are the same. I received the money OK & was glad to get it. We went to Vale & stayed 3 days and me and Tom sure had a good time. We went to the Rodeo Saturday & street carnival all combined and we met Sim on the street. We was sure glad to see each other. Me & Tom stayed at Sim's camp Saturday night. We went to the Rodeo the next day. It cost us .25 to get in Saturday & .50 to get in Sunday. They had calf roping, bare back riders, bucking horse riders, bull dogging, races, trick riding, knife throwing, and motor-cycle trick riding. The champion bull-dogger bull-dogged his steer in 10 seconds. The motor cycle trick rider took a pistol, rode the motorcycle 30 miles an hour and busted a balloon in the air. Guess how hot it was at Vale camp? It was 120. Tell Bus I will send him some pictures. XXOO Love, Bob

Peebles, Ohio, July 16, 1937

Dear Son: I will scribble you a few lines. I am glad to hear you had a good time on your trip. I sure had begun to get worried about not hearing from you. I would like to hear from you once a week anyway if it is only a card so I know you are allright.
         Bobby the white sow found [gave birth to] *an awful litter of pigs – just 3 and one that were dead. The other one will have hers I think before morning. I don't think she will find many either. Well Bobby I will close as news is scarce. Don't forget to write at least once a week. Your loving Mother*

GUARDIANS AND OTHER ANGELS   85

Peebles, Ohio, July 30, 1937

Dear Son: I will answer your letter rec'd a few days ago. We are O. K. and hope you are well. It sure is hot here and no rain. It hasen't rained here for I don't know how long and everything is just burning up. The tobacco is fired up nearly half way up the stalk. And if it doesn't rain, in just a few days there won't be any corn. As it is right where it is needing rain. You know you have to have rain on Cedar Fork if you raise anything. And we sure would have had lots of Black berries but they are just drying up on the vines. You asked about Buddy. He is still fat and I believe he is getting gray around his head. I believe he is older then we think.

The other sow found [gave birth to] *4 pigs – not much better then the other. Dad said if it don't rain pretty soon he is going to begin selling off the livestock as he won't have much feed for them. Well Bobby I will close for this time. As ever, Your Mother*
P. S. Little Daley said today: "I have a Goat out West – Bobby is feeding and salting him for me." He meant that little deer you got I reckon. Ha ha

Peebles, Ohio, August 7, 1937

Dear Son: Rec'd your letter. Was glad to hear from you. We are O. K. & hope you are the same. We had a pretty good rain yesterday. May help the tobacco but think it came to late for the corn. Sister Tirzah was here Sunday but they didn't get very much berries as the hot sun has just cooked them. I have 21 gallons put up besides Jam & Jelly. Bobby that wasn't Huckle berries the kids picked so good. It was Black berries. They won't hardly pick them now. They are tired of it. Dad has sold about all the Huckle berries he got. But we are going to can what we get from now on. There wasen't so many of them this year. Bruce & Marie has moved down below John Smalley. And Alderson Greene [my future paternal grandfather] *is back from Florida. Bussy and Dick seen Alderson's boy Lee* [my future father] *down at the creek the other day. Well Bobby must close as space is limited on this card. I will write a letter soon. XXOO Mother*

Beulah, Oregon, August 11. 1937

Dear Mother:
Will answer your letter received the other day. Has Dad hunted any squirrels yet? Are they any hickory nuts this year? I have done signed to come home, so I reckon we will be seeing you all next month. They have

86   LINDA LEE GREENE

got some new rules now. Enrolees must be between 17 to 23. No more Eastern boys sent West, that is boys from the 5th Co area which is Ohio, Kentucky, West Virginia, Virginia and Indiana. And each man must have served 1 year in CCC's to get transferred to a camp in Ohio. So we are all figuring on getting in a camp close to home about next October. I am getting my fill of the West. But I am gaining weight. When I came in I weighed 139. Now I weigh 152. Tell Bus if he wants to he can take old Buddy out and my rifle & learn to hunt squirrels if he wants to. I have an idea Buddy is getting stiff laying around with no practise. Will close for now, Your son, Bob XO

Peebles, Ohio, August 21, 1937

Dear Brother:

Will try and answer your letter rec'd the other day & was sure glad to hear from you. Yes we had a pretty good rain Thursday it is just sprinkling now. I guess you know this is Dean's [first] birthday. He is standing alone just a little once in a while. It hasn't been so very hot here this month. I think you done pretty well selling your rifle for $5. Gene surely wanted one pretty bad. Of course it is worth that. No dad hasn't hunted any squirrels yet. He is finishing up the hog fence today. We were sure glad to hear you signed to come home. We were looking for it ha – ha. It would be nice if you boys could get in camp close to home. There was [a] bunch of boys went to camp from Peebles not long ago and they come home every Saturday night. Well I reckon you are getting bigger every day ha – ha. I was surprised to hear Gene only weigh's 140 that isn't as much as Clara weighs. She took a bunch of reducing powder's but it didn't do her any good. Bobby if you come home and get a car you better be careful there was a boy over close to Jacktown just come home from CCC's and he got him a car and had a wreck the next day and he never knew what killed him. He had his little ten year old brother with him and he never got a scratch. I guess he hit loose gravel and it threw him into a tree. Arthur, Bennie and Charles had a wreck the other day I guess. They say they were driving 60 mi. an hour. It's a wonder it didn't kill them all. But I guess it didn't hurt them very bad. They all three work at Springfield now. We were talking the other day which of you boys we would rather see. Bus said "Roma would rather see Sim" and I said I guess not I would rather see Bob. Bus said he wanted to see Gene next to you. I haven't heard from Sim since the first of June. I guess he has got constipated and died ha – ha. Well I must close. XO With love Your Sister (Roma) & all.

Peebles, Ohio, September 2, 1937

Dear Son: I thought I would write to you tonight as Daddy is going to town from work tomorrow. Daddy and his crew on the WPA got transferred over on Scrub Ridge. They was over on Beach Fork one whole pay, and it costs something to get there – 25c a day. But that is better than driving our car. He says he ought not have to pay so much now to get over on Scrub Ridge as it isn't near so far.

I guess the kids will start school the day after Labor Day. We washed clothes today and canned tomatoes. Dad has to get me some cans tomorrow, hate to buy them too. They are so high but can't let the stuff go to waste. He is going to get enough roof to finish the barn too, or it will ruin his tobacco. He put the hog fence where the old one was only run it down the ditch farther which made the lot a lot larger.

I guess Sam Cooper is still in jail. His trial comes off when the Grand Jury set. I expect he will take a trip [to jail] as that isen't the first stealing he has done around town. They just got the goods on him that time. He lost his bill fold [wallet] right where he jumped out the window or that is what we heard. Of course it had his identification card in it. So I reckon they have got him good. Well I reckon I will close as news is scarce. Peg was up yesterday and had me & cut her hair. Well Bobby I will close with lots of love, Mother
P. S. The Ford runs fine & we painted it a while back. Black with orange wheels.

Peebles, Ohio, September 3, 1937

Dear Brother:

I will write you a few lines to let you know I am O K and hope you are the same. Well our school will start – week after next. We thought we would have a woman teacher but Ralph Wickerham will be our teacher and I will be glad for it to start. You know me and Dick had our birthday while you were gone. We are seven now, but Dick is still not taller than me. Roma and Bus is going on the Hill to church tonight. I sure will be glad to see you. Little Dean is getting sweeter every day and Buddy is getting fatter every day. Well I will close. Answer soon. Your sister, Bette

Peebles, Ohio, September 14, 1937

Dear Son: Will answer your letter received today. Was glad to hear you would be starting home soon. We are all O. K. The kids are going to school and Ralph is sure reforming them all, or trying too, ha ha. They will have to walk this year unless they get to ride with Ralph. Harry don't drive the bus apast here this year.

We was at Serpent Mound Labor Day. There was 1750 cars there. So you can imagine how many people were there. They had different kinds of music and speaking. The Governor of Ohio was supposed to be there but didn't show up.

Well Bobby Henry Jackson is sure in the soup. They got him Saturday night drunk & braking the speed limit. Fined him $100.00 and took his license for 6 months. They said he was going 60 miles an hour right through town. They had locked him up just a few minutes before we got there. He will have to work several pays to pay that. He still works at Cincinnati. Well Bobby I had better close as Bus & Reva are both writing & one envelope won't hold it. I suppose this will be the last one you will get & don't suppose you will be sorry. Love and hoping to hear from & see you soon. XOXO Your Mother.

Peebles, Ohio, September 14, 1937

Dear Bob:

I will try and write you a few lines to let you know I am still O. K. and hope you are the same. Me and Dad is cutting tobacco. I don't think the barn is going to hold it. We are not got all our teerpoles in yet. Old Pet [the horse] *can pull 48 big sticks at one time. I am got a nice little patch of tobacco. It is tall as Dick's head. It is not near ripe yet. It is going to make good tobacco. Ralph Wickerham is our teacher. I got a whipping the third day. The big religious Harriet Snyders little Jesus Conrad got two whippings ha ha. Dwight and Dick is coming pretty close. The old Remington is all shined up, waiting for a Super X to go into it. Old Bud and Jack is waiting to get a squack* [squirrel] *by the neck. So answer soon. Lowell* [Bussy]

P. S. I got a new box of Super X shells ready to start the last of September.

GUARDIANS AND OTHER ANGELS   89

Peebles, Ohio, September 15, 1937

Dear Bobby:
I will try and write you a few lines to let you know I am O-K and hope you are the same. Well I was glad to hear you are starting home. Well I am seeing it pretty tough at school ha ha. We was all (the) time raking Elmer Thomas but we are finding out that we have to be a little better this year. Bus got a whipping on the third day of school and boy you ought to of heard that paddle crack. I am looking for one pretty soon ha ha. Dick had to stand in the corner – little angel Conrad got a whipping too, well well. I will be glad to see you. I have to keep my crab [trap] shut this year – old man Wheeler has his nose up down here to church. I have a lot of calling downs in school but ain't got any whipping yet. Well as I have to get my lessons I will close. From Reva
P. S. I am glad you will be home when I turn 10 on my birthday in December.

Throughout 1937, and several years prior, in Germany, Adolf Hitler continued to build his power machine. Troubled by the devastation following the pro-Franco German attack on the Spanish city of Guernica, the artist Pablo Picasso painted his cubist masterpiece, *Guernica.* Japan invaded China, and Italy withdrew from the League of Nations and joined the German-Japanese pact. The year also marked the climax of Stalin's purges in Russia. John D. Rockefeller died as did George Gershwin at the age of 38. On a lighter note, influential architect, Frank Lloyd Wright completed *Falling Water* in Bear Rock, Pennsylvania; Sam Snead joined the PGA and won five tournaments; Dale Carnegie's *How to Win Friends and Influence People* sold 750,000 copies; KennethRoberts' *Northwest Passage* sold 308,000; the Academy of Arts and Sciences awarded the Oscar for best picture to *The Life of Emile Zola,* the best actor Oscar to Spencer Tracy for *Captains Courageous,* and best actress Oscar to Luise Rainer for *The Good Earth.* Bread sold for 9c/loaf; milk: 50c/gallon; eggs: 56c/dozen; automobile: $675.00; gasoline: 20c/gallon; house: $6,622.00; postage stamp: 3c/each. The average income was $1,789/year, the DOW Average: 121.[27]

---

[27] http://www.joson.com/year/wastheyear/1937.htm

Eleven

Daybreak that January morning in 1938, dim in a leaden sky, crouched reluctantly behind the dense black treetops spiking the eastern horizon, here and there a feeble ray of light piercing a chink in the bare trunks and branches. It was a leafless, winter landscape that wrapped the little homestead of the Greene family in its own private space. In his crusted foot tracks, cut into the deep snow from the night before, the collar of his coat upturned against the cold, young Lee Greene wended his way to the cow. Upon his approach, the bell around the neck of the animal clanged dully when she turned her head toward him. Her huge nostrils blew steam that veiled her bovine face for a moment, and then a steep breeze lifted the moisture and carried it away. His own breath spewed from his nose in plumes of thick mist, and raising his hands to his mouth, Lee blew on them and rubbed them together briskly to warm them, but to no avail.

"Mornin', Bessy," the boy greeted the sole cow of the family, and he patted her on her broad backside, the contact releasing a puff of gritty hair from her hide. "Let's see what you got fer me this mornin', said Lee cheerily. His milk pail suspending by its handle from his right hand, with his foot he kicked the old stump he used as a milking stool into place, sat on it, and positioned the pail beneath the hulking animal. Rubbing his hands together again, he arched forward on the stump, and reached under the cow with both of his hands. He massaged her udder, the warmth of her skin loosening the stiffness in his freezing fingers.

Despite Lee's having pulled expertly on her teats until his hands grew tired, Bessy gave only half of a pail of milk that morning, as she had the previous evening. Rising to his feet, he looked into the pail forlornly, and said, "You need more hay, don't you, Bessy? Can't give nothin' if you ain't gittin' nothin', right girl? Maybe I kin round up some feed fer you tuhday." On the ground in front of her, he threw two handfuls of hay from the meager stock of it in the small hayrack under a canopy of trees at the edge of the property. Picking up his pail, he retraced his footsteps to the log cabin. The wind rose sharply again as he approached the back door, and when he opened it, a biting gust whipped it against the wall of the cabin. Putting the pail on the cold stone floor inside the kitchen, he entered the room, turned around, and using the full weight of his body, he pushed the door shut. Stomping his frozen feet to rid them of snow, and to get his blood pumping in them again, he picked up the pail, placing it on the wide split-log ledge that formed the working station of the room, its surface housing a hodgepodge of skillets, pans and cooking utensils, as well as a pan for washing dishes. A large split-log table banked by crudely fashioned log benches comprised the eating area of the tiny space.

"Bessy ain't give us enough fer breakfast fer ever'body, Mom. Jist give me some mush with some sugar water on it, an' that'll do fer me," Lee said to his mother. She was with child again, the eighth one this time, and his pappy was gone to Intercession City, Florida, his church business there requiring his attention this winter as in every winter Lee could remember. Bill, the eldest brother of Lee was out west at a CCC camp, and Paul, the brother two years older than Lee, had always lived in Florida with their paternal grandparents. Lee hadn't even known Paul to be his brother until recently, always believing him to be a cousin or an uncle. That left Lee as the head of the household, one comprising his mother, his four younger sisters, Anna, Marie, Ada, and Mabel, his younger brother, Jake, and himself; and now, another one on the way. Like most of the young girls in their "poor" area of town, Anna and Marie had recently taken work in the homes of some "high-toned" folks in town. That eased the burden to some extent.

As was Bussy, Lee, who five years in the future would become my father, was the fourth-born child, his first-born sibling having died at birth, or shortly thereafter, just as the first-born sibling of Bussy had done. With seven other children in his family, three more to be born in the future, together with their meager resources, life was a struggle for Lee and his family.

The father of Lee, an engaging eccentric and a mesmerizing preacher, was hard pressed to support his family although the parishioners of his church reveled in their fits of religious ecstasy inspired by his preaching, and parting the moaning, sweating, and swaying bodies of their manic peers with their hands, they somehow made their ways to the front of the church, and falling to their knees at the altar of A. E., they entrusted their souls to Jesus through him. But still, the contents of the offering plate were too often inadequate. He lived a sort of half-life, never completely with his wife and children in Ohio, or with his family of birth in Florida, his commitment to his roving ministry and its requirement to be absent for several months at a time, the focus of his neighbor's curiosity.

One time when A. E. took the entire family with him to Florida, he drove them south in his 1928 Chevrolet flatbed truck, a Constantinople-type canopy rigged across the top of it, the canopy essentially a tarp stretched crossways on the arched and ribbed top. He and his wife and the latest baby in the cab, the rest of the children, bedrolls, cooking paraphernalia, clothing and whatever there was of their household they could fit in, were stashed in the back under the canopy. Another time when back in Cedar Fork again, A. E. and one of his brothers cooked up a scheme to relocate to Florida together. Securing an old Ford flatbed truck and an abandoned school bus, they bolted the frame of the bus to the truck by turning the school bus backwards, and crammed their wives and large families with their household possessions into it. Upon their return to Ohio, they ended up in Cedar Fork living in the upstairs of a log cabin with one of their church families, then in an abandoned tin schoolhouse, finally building the log cabin where they lived until I was a teenager.

A further confounding aspect of the character of A. E. was the fact of his having Anglicized his surname. The original Green became Greene at the behest of A. E., nobody ever knowing the reason for the conspicuous "e" tagged onto the end of the name. Perhaps it had to do with a hard-to-make-out relationship he had with his own family of origin, as the following story illustrates:

When a youngster, A. E., his many siblings and their cousins were playing in the yard of a brother of the father of A. E. The occasion was a Sunday gathering of the Green clan, occurring at the end of church services, as was the tradition of the family on every Sunday. Bordering the yard was an apple orchard, the limbs of the trees laden, and the ground littered, with ripe fruit. The adults, before repairing to the house, the women to prepare the midday meal, the men to the porch to discuss the issues of the day, had given a strict order to the children to resist the temptation of eating any of the apples, for doing so would ruin their appetites. Well, that is the same as sitting a box of candy in front of a starving child, and of course, one child was unable to withstand the temptation, namely A. E. The boy took one little bite of an apple. Since he had experienced them many times before, fear of the terrible consequences, if he were to be found out, overcame him. Rather than throwing the apple at a distance safe from detection, however, he foolishly dropped the bitten apple back among the other fallen apples on the ground.

The uncle of A. E., the host of the gathering, just prior to the commencement of the meal, gathered the children around the outside pump with the instruction to them to wash their hands. Although unaware of the existence of the bitten apple, while the children were washing their hands, the uncle painstakingly inspected each and every apple on the ground. Discovering a law breaker in their midst, the children were lined up in military fashion, and offered the opportunity of confessing or snitching.

GUARDIANS AND OTHER ANGELS   93

Neither having been forthcoming, while holding their mouths open, the uncle fitted the teeth marks on the apple to the upper teeth of each and every child. Having a unique configuration to his upper teeth, A. E. was caught, and soundly disciplined with a wooden paddle landing repeated and stinging poundings on his backside.

It is said that Joshua, the father of A. E., was a meek and easy-going man, a hard worker who cow-towed to his half-Cherokee, mail-order bride, Annie Lane who had a reputation as a strict disciplinarian. She was the progeny of an arm of the few remaining Cherokee Indians in the Carolinas who had managed to escape President Andrew Jackson's mandatory removal of all Native Americans of the southeast to the Oklahoma territory. Only one photograph of her survives. It is a family photo, where, although a handsome woman, but stern of face and rigid in manner, she is seated, her luxurious white-streaked hair pulled to a bun on top of her head, the bun accentuating her dark, deep-set eyes and her burnished skin, her long dress draped to the ground, a beaded necklace of a Native American style adorning her neck. Joshua, seated to her right and sporting high-top, rugged boots and casual daywear of the times, is dark–dark of hair, of eyes, of eyebrows, and long dark beard. Incongruently, A. E., a young boy, tow-headed and blue of eyes, a dead ringer for his own son Lee in years to come, stands among his several siblings, none as fair in coloring or of face as he.

It was Joshua and Annie who had been the forerunners in the evangelical involvement of the Green family. There having been a dynamic arm of it active in Pike County, Ohio where Joshua and Annie owned a farm, they became enthralled with the charismatic Christian ideology. Their commitment was genuine and total, and in order to take on the required vagabond lifestyle, they sold their farm in Pike County, living off of the proceeds of the sale as they traveled south to the headquarters of the movement in Intercession City, not far from Kissimmee, Florida.

Toward the end of the Civil War, the Union Army destroyed all railway lines between Atlanta and Savannah, and points south. Consequently, for many years thereafter, there were no connecting railway lines to cities south of Savannah. Intercession City, Florida, however, did boast a "dinky railroad," a self-contained railway system unconnected to outside lines. It supported a booming business during Prohibition as the system for supplying moonshine whiskey to outlets throughout the eastern and southeastern states, the illegal liquor picked up by trucks at designated areas along the "dinky railroad" line, and delivered to the clandestine sales outlets. The hot weather, whereby the mash of the liquor fermented much faster than in northern climates, supplemented by the "dinky railroad," gave whiskey barons the perfect environment and circumstances for making a killing. A robust town sprouted up around the illegal rotgut business: restaurants, hotels, office buildings, houses. The town went bust in a hurry when Prohibition was repealed, however.

94   LINDA LEE GREENE

A group of women, apparently somehow associated with the charismatic Christian movement, took over a section of the town after the whiskey barons abandoned it, converting it into an orphanage for children from the ages of six to eighteen. There the religious movement took hold and fluorished, thereafter becoming the home base of the Green clan, as well. Following a religious circuit up and down the midwestern and southeastern states continued as a way of life for the progeny of Joshua and Annie, A. E. and two of his brothers becoming preachers in the religion. Three other siblings of A. E. played music and sang at those religious services.

Three years prior to that winter of 1938, Lee's brother Bill got it into his head that he also would travel south, apparently seeking a better way of life with his paternal grandparents. Disappearing from the home of his parents in Ohio in the late autumn of the year, and during one of the coldest winters on record, a winter where people were freezing to death in great numbers, nothing of the whereabouts of fourteen-year-old Bill was known. Four months later, responding to a "Missing Persons" notice in a newspaper placed there by Joshua and Annie, a trucker from Macon, Georgia became the link to Bill. The man had given Bill a ride in his truck as the boy was hitchhiking through Georgia. Bill was desperately ill with malaria. He had caught it drinking mash (home-brewed beer) in the mosquito-infested swamps there.

One summer when my brother and I were youngsters, we had occasion to visit our "Green" relatives in Kissimmee. My paternal grandparents were permanently separated by then, Mommaw Greene and her younger children still established in the log cabin in Cedar Fork, Poppaw Greene, or A. E. as I thought of him in my mind, in a little shack-of-a-house on a sandy road in a rather primitive backcountry patch of stifling Northcentral Florida. I retain many memories of that long roundtrip highway excursion: the sleep-robbing heat of the place; the deceptive bleach-white sand that turned my bare feet black; the daily alfresco meals among my many great aunts, great uncles, and great grandparents known only to me theretofore through oratory legends passed down to me and my brother by our father. I remember also the ceaseless praying and everlasting conversations of the adults centered on the person of Jesus, and many other things. However, one incident stands out above all of the others:

The occasion began with a short trip to a vacant house A. E. was of a mind to purchase, and he took us one day to look it over. It was another tiny abode, clapboards of white, and risen above the sandy ground on stilts so common then in the south. Its front door opened onto a small stoop of wood with perhaps three stairs leading to the landing. The five of us: A. E., my parents, my brother and I were stuffed into our car, I with my head pushed through the window of one of the back passenger's door, gasping for air in the oppressive heat. My father braking the car to a halt, I pushed open the door and jumped out of the car onto the baking sand, my bare feet

GUARDIANS AND OTHER ANGELS   95

scorching as if I'd thrust them in a pit of burning coals. The door of the house stood ajar, welcoming my hot feet to its cooler, interior floorboards.

Leaving my companions in my wake, I took off running as fleet as a deer, and when I reached the stoop of the house, I hurdled the stairs two of a time, and deftly hopped up and onto the threshold of the door. I stopped on a dime while I got my bearings before entering the dark and airless chamber, and noticed a strange noise somewhere in the near vicinity of my right foot. **"Linda, git away from the door right now!"** rang the voice of my father from across the yard. I turned to look at my father running toward the house at a sprinters pace, a large stick in his hand, his face a mask of terror and concern. My gaze followed to the noise just inches from my foot, and there, lying in the seam of the landing and the threshold of the door was a large rattlesnake, the erect end of its tail buzzing, its fang-dominated head in the ready to strike me on my leg. My father reached it before it struck, scooping it up with the stick and flinging it into the yard. My brother David, enthralled with snakes and bugs and all manner of creepy-crawly creatures, stood by fascinated while our father chopped off the head of the snake with the blade of a shovel and I spent the balance of the day trying to retain the contents of my stomach.

I had a similar close call with yet another rattlesnake when a child. That time I jumped over it one sticky summer day as it lay cooling itself on a concrete step leading to the porch of the farmhouse on German Hill in Peebles, Ohio, the farm of my maternal grandparents. My Uncle Dean and I were playing in the yard, and I ran after him when he jumped up onto the porch to go into the house for a drink of water. My legs too short to maneuver the height, I took the steps instead, again two at a time and again a buzzing sound and a raised head of a rattlesnake ready to strike accompanied my jump to the floor of the porch. I came to no harm, and the snake was killed by Uncle Dean and his brothers. Owing to the old adage that all things come in threes, I hope my destiny is written to exclude another encounter with a rattlesnake.

The one-room, Cedar Fork schoolhouse across the holler from the little log cabin on the near side of Peach Mountain was a tolerable two-mile walk in clement weather. It was an enjoyable walk actually, if one had time to swing from a grapevine on top of a high cliff and drop into Cedar Fork Creek for a lazy dip, or stop by the Workman's place for a quick smoke of their cornsilk tobacco. But in snowdrifts as tall as thirteen-year-old Lee Greene, in threadbare clothes, thin hand-me-down coat, and barely covered feet in holey socks flopping in an old pair of secondhand shoes that were several sizes too big for him, the walk that frigid morning was worse than pure misery.

The chronically aching stomach of Lee was hollow and rumbling. His meager breakfast of cornmeal mush and sugar water was quickly wearing thin, but he had more important things than his stomach to worry about that morning. He was stewing about the paucity of milk he had drawn from their cow tethered in the yard just beyond the lean-to kitchen at the back of the tiny log cabin. The two-story structure, built by A. E., Lee, and Bill only five months before, consisted of a common, or front room on the main level, a primitive lean-to kitchen at the back, and a bedroom where Eva Love and A. E. slept, housing the only closet in the place. A rough-hewn timber ladder gained access to the upper deck, where, in an open-to-the-front loft, all of the many children slept on crude cots, or thin pads on the floor. A large ceiling-to-floor fireplace of indigenous stones in the common room on the first floor was the only source of heat in the place. Felled tree trunks supporting its roof, a porch spanned the width of the front of the log cabin.

The soil on Cedar Fork, thin, hard, and dry, a crusty layer of sediment topping bedrock of limestone, dolomite and shale, made for poor farming and gardening, posing a formidable challenge for the growing of adequate food. Squirrels, rabbits, opossums and birds, hunted and brought in by Lee, the insufficient supply of milk from the cow, and scant eggs supplied by their paltry flock of scrawny chickens in the yard, were the only sources of protein for the family. In season, a large vegetable garden and a stand of corn were coddled into fruition in the poor soil, but only if they were favored with enough rain.

His nose and eyes crusty from yet another head cold, gloveless hands thrust into the pockets of his thin coat, and his feet turning to blocks of ice, Lee trudged on to school, his white-blond head under his hat hunkered into his shoulders. Despite the fact that he might not make it through the perpetual hardships of his life, much less that cold, windy, and snowbound morning, his soul was full of dreams, his mind of intention, his body of vigor and endurance, and on the strength of pure power of will alone, and maybe some help from the man upstairs, Lee was determined that if he ever got out of his childhood alive, nothing would ever encumber him again.

The schoolhouse was dark and frigid, Lee, by design, having been the first to arrive. The door was unlocked as it always was, and Lee, halting for a few minutes to give his blood a chance to circulate again in his frozen limbs and digits, sat down on one of the benches. He would have wept if he had allowed himself to seriously consider his unfortunate circumstances— but not Lee! No, not Lee! Not the boy/man who would be my father someday. He had a chance to earn fifty cents that week, and every week for weeks to come, fifty cents for building a fire in the "Warm Morning" coal-burning, heating-stove each morning before school, and that was exactly what the sam hill he was going to do.

"Bet you wish you was back in the warm sunshine in Intercession City," Bussy said to Lee one day four weeks later during the noon-hour break in their school lessons. Due to illness, Bussy had been absent from school during most of the winter, returning at the end of February eager to resume

GUARDIANS AND OTHER ANGELS   97

his budding friendship with Lee the two boys had initiated the previous autumn. Although Lee was seven months older than Bussy, they were both in the seventh grade, Lee having been kept back one year due to an altercation with a former schoolteacher two years before. The teacher, disciplining Lee for unruly behavior of some kind, and using a wooden paddle on him, had almost beaten the boy to death, tearing one of Lee's ears loose from his head. Eva Love and A. E. had kept him out of school for that year, Lee having been in Intercession City with A. E. during that time.

"Between the 'gators, an' snakes an' skeeters an' all o' the church hullabaloo, I'd jist as soon be hyere, even if it is cold as blue blazes all the way ta May. I used ta swim with them 'gators. I git shivers thinkin' about it now. Them 'gators was in the canals, 'an canals 's ever'where down there, an' we jumped in that water ever'day, big as you please. I used ta run across't the backs o' them 'gators like they was rocks in the water. An' I was barefooted, now!" Lee said, turning his face to Bussy, his eyebrows raised in amazement, his head pumping.

"Yer shittin' me, Lee. Ain't no way you done that!" said Bussy, his face the picture of skepticism.

"I ain't shittin' you, Bus. The whole state is at sea level, an' there at Osceola County, it's peppered with lakes an' canals. Them 'gators is ever'where. An' down there, them houses is up on stilts so when them hurricanes come through, yer up high, an' boy, you want ta be as high as you can git in one o' them storms," said Lee to wide-eyed Bussy.

"Yer tellin' me you bin through a hurricane, Lee?" Bussy replied, his mouth agape in astonished disbelief.

"Tore right through my pappy's yard. Took ever'thing in its path. The wind took yer breath away. It weren't one o' them hurricanes with enough water ta git up ta the floor 'cause the house were on stilts, but it were the powerfulest storm I ever seen," said Lee, raising his right hand to swear to the truth of it.

"You've bin through a hurricane, an' you lived ta tell it. I'll be dern," Bussy mused, shaking his head and pursing his lips in utter amazement.

"An' that ain't all," continued Lee. He was on a roll and he wasn't about to stop now that he had a captive audience. "We used ta crawl around under them houses. Gee God, there was rattlers an' coral snakes an' ever' manner of bugs you kin imagine. They was them little brown spiders. Them brown spiders 'll jist as leave sting you ta death as look at you. An' there was tarantulas!" Lee said, raising his voice for impact, but he was interrupted by a disbelieving Bussy.

"Wait a minute, Lee," Bussy said, placing his hand on Lee's arm. "You mean ta tell me you crawled around under them houses with them big ole spiders with the long stingy tails on 'em? Them is poisonous, ain't they?"

Bussy inquired, his lips curling in disgust, and his hands clutching the edge of the bench. His knuckles turned white, and he visibly shivered.

"Them is scorpions. Them ain't in Florida. Arizona an' the desert country around them parts is where them are. No, buddy, you ain't never want ta tangle with no scorpion. Tarantulas is them big ole hairy spiders with the long legs. They git as big as a growed man's hand, jist about, maybe more."

"You saw them tarantulas, Lee?"

"We played with 'em, Bus. They'll make you a good pet if yer of a mind fer it. They don't hardly bite you, an' if they do, it won't kill you; you'll jist swell up a little where they bit you. Them suckers kin live ta be forty years old," Lee said, his head shaking in disbelief as his mind flashed with pictures of some of the dangerous things he had done. "The Good Lord looks after little kids an' drunks, I reckon," said Lee with a chuckle.

"Forty years old, Lee? Why a horse don't hardly live ta forty years old."

"Well, them tarantulas lives up ta forty years old."

Suddenly feeling as if he needed to regain some ground in the conversation, and so as not to be outdone, Bussy said to Lee, "I had a 'coon fer a pet wonst. I got him trained jist good as a dog."

"Well, we got a tree out in front of our log cabin that's got a million lizards in it."

"Well, we got the biggest mud dauber's nest in the whole dern county hangin' out in our barn."

"Well, we got black wider spiders in the walls of our log cabin."

"Boys!" the voice of Mr. Wickerham, the schoolteacher, broke into their exchange. "I'm glad to see you boys have got yerseffs so nicely reacquainted, but don't you think you should be about eatin' yer dinners? We have to git back to readin', writin', and 'rithmetic some time today." Lee and Bussy raised their eyes to the teacher, and then scanned the faces of their classmates. Twenty pairs of expectant eyes were glued onto them, and everybody burst into laughter, including Mr. Wickerham. Bussy started to laugh, and Lee to giggle uncontrollably. Lee's face turned red, and he beat his hand on the table. Laughter came easily to Lee. He was always laughing and joking about something, and Bussy liked that about him. As had Arthur Billings entertained the Gaffin family with his tales, Lee had told Bussy yarn after yarn about his adventures while traveling with his large family, as well as while living in Florida. Lee seemed exotic to Bussy, just as Arthur had been. Lee had been to places and done things Bussy feared he never would get to experience, although Lee considered his adventures unsought by-products of a very unstable childhood rather than glamorous. He would have traded all of his adventures in a minute for the warm home and full belly and indulgent parents of Bussy. In addition to the jolly personality of Lee, Bussy liked that Lee played the guitar and sang, and Bussy was trying to get up his nerve to invite Lee to come to his house to play some music with him. Since becoming too frail to indulge in the rough and tumble play of childhood, Bussy had turned to the mandolin Arthur Billings had left in his safe keeping, and the guitar Bob had given him, as well as the harmonica his Uncle J. Q. had left behind for him. Through his many idle hours at home while ill, he had developed into a good musician. Every time he attempted to broach the subject with Lee of jamming with him at his home, however, he was deterred by Lee's advising him that he had to rush home to take care of some domestic chore, the cow being of latest concern to Lee. "That dad blamed cow ain't givin' but a samplin' of milk of late. I reckon she's goin' dry." Picking up the conversation again, Lee whispered to Bussy in order to keep the teacher and the other children from overhearing what he said. Privacy was difficult to come by as all of the children shared the long table they used as a substitute for individual desks. Lee propped his elbows on the table and dropped his head into his hands, his long hair, straight and yellow as new corn silk, tumbling over his hands.

"You got any other cows, Lee?" Bussy asked sympathetically, although he knew they had only one cow. Everyone in the area was privy to the facts of the hard lifestyle of the Greene family.

"Nary a one. My pap got 'er real cheap before he left last fall. The farmer he got 'er from prob'ly knowed right then 'n there she were worthless as tits on a boar hog. Our other cow got inta some green corn an' got tainted, an' died. We couldn't even eat her meat 'cause we didn't git to her in time ta bleed her out," forlornly Lee explained to his friend. He was too proud to admit to Bussy that the cow couldn't give adequate milk because she wasn't getting enough to eat.

There wasn't anybody in the acquaintance of the Gaffin family who was well off, especially in that time of the Great Depression, but Bussy figured that Lee and his family were just about the poorest people he had ever known. For the reason that Lee never had any food to eat during the noon hour break, Bussy had begun asking his mother to put extra food in his dinner pail to share with his schoolmate.

"I got fried chicken an' cornbread tuhday, Lee," Bussy offered generously, hoping the food would help his friend to get his mind off of the unproductive cow. Opening wide his dinner pail, Bussy invited Lee to join him. Since Bob and Arthur had gone away, Bussy desperately needed a new and very special friend, and he hoped Lee was the one. Bussy placed an elbow on the table, and laid the side of his perpetually aching head in his hand. Feeling envious of his appetite, Bussy watched Lee eat. *There ain't no sense o' Mother even packin' dinner fer me no more, so I'll jist keep agivin' it ta Lee. Now if I kin jist figger a way ta git him ta take that coat o' mine I don't use no more, an' them old gloves. The coat is old, and the gloves 'er holey in a finger 'er two, but they're better'n what he's got 'cause he ain't got none,* Bussy ruminated in his mind as Lee took his fill of the fried chicken and cornbread Mommaw had packed that morning for Bussy and his new best friend.

"Oh Mom, I don't want ta put on one them ol' onion plasters," Bussy appealed to Mommaw. He pushed away from her where she sat on the side of the bed, and the quick movement set him into a spasm of coughing—a deep rasping cough, the kind of cough that caused Mommaw to fear that he wouldn't catch his breath again. She pulled his frail and helpless body across her lap and pounded him on his back as she had done countless times before. It was the only thing that would dislodge the phlegm that collected in suffocating clumps in his bronchial tubes.

"Bussy honey, I know ye don't like the ol' onion plaster, but it helps ye breathe. Please son, it'll ease my mind."

"Mom, Lee told me yisterdey he'd come ta see me after school tuhday an' I don't want ta have ta be in bed while he's hyere. That onion plaster 'll keep me laid up an' stinkin' like somethin' that up 'n died an' turned to rot," Bussy said, his brown eyes pleading and brimming with tears.

"Well land sakes, I ain't got no say in it long as ye got it in yer mind ta see Lee. But soon as he leaves, I'm puttin' it on ye. An' don't git briggity an' be pluckin' on the mandolin an' guitar. An' keep that harmonica out o' yer mouth. That'll set ye ta coughin' quicker 'n anything."

"I ain't agoin' ta do nothin' but talk, Mom, an' prob'ly laugh some. That Lee tells some funny stories an' jokes."

"Ye've took a real shine ta that boy, ain' ye, Son?"

"I ain't liked nobody since Art the way I do Lee. He's a right good an' smart feller, Mom, an' you know how yer always tellin' us kids ta only take up with good folks. Well, he's a good n', awright."

When Mommaw left the room, Bussy reached for the mandolin propped against the leg of the bedside table and laid it across his aching chest. He strummed it softly a couple of strokes then placed it back in its designated spot next to his bed. He hadn't told his mother that he no longer owned the harmonica. In an impetuous move so typical of Bussy, one that he had come to regret as he so often did, he had initiated a trade with a friend at school, the terms: the harmonica for his friend's pocket knife. The novelty of the knife having soon worn off, now he sorely missed the harmonica because it had become almost an extension of his arm, so readily had he taken to it, carrying it with him everywhere, and playing it at every possible opportunity.

GUARDIANS AND OTHER ANGELS   101

Twelve

January, 1939

Dear Mother,
        Will write to let you know I am O. K. I would of wrote sooner But couldn't. I am going to Oregon, Co. number – C.C.C. Co. [1534], Marshfield, Ore. M. G. [Marlin "Bob" Gaffin]

Peebles, Ohio, Jan. 18, 1939
Dear Son: Will ans. your two cards received yesterday and sure was glad to get them for we didn't know what on earth had become of you. They had me some worried for a while. Jim Hoop and some more claimed you were all going to Hawaiian Islands to military training. And then it came over the Radio that Roosevelt said he wasn't going to put any CCC boys in training...first [you] *hear one thing and another...Well I don't care so long as you are in the U. S. A. and well. We are all O. K. and sure are having some winter. Has been a snow on for about a week, and snowing again to-day. We had to call the fertilizer man for Old Pet* [the horse] *yesterday. She got down again and we couldn't get her up. You know that morning you left, after Roma got up she went out to see about her and she was up and on the other side of the barn eating fodder. But she didn't come out of it this time. Dad got his tobacco away but hasn't got the returns from it yet. He had 366 lb...Roma is home the rest of the week. They closed school untill next week so many was sick. She said 101 were absent yesterday. Well I will have to quit there isn't much news on Cedar Fork. Ans. soon & tell us how you like your camp & how much winter you are having. With love Mother & all*
P. S. Deany says Bobby is in (CC tamp) ha ha.

102   LINDA LEE GREENE

Jan 25, 1939
CCC Camp Sitkum, Ore.

Dear Mother & all:
Will answer the letter received yeasterday, and was glad to hear you were all well. I am here for six months. There are no more 3 month terms. I would stay longer than six months here but the fire season starts the 1ˢᵗ of July and we leave here about the 20ᵗʰ of June. I don't mind a common fire, but they are fighting fire 5 days out of every week after the 1ˢᵗ of July. The timber is very heavy here & many get burnt up, because of burning trees that fall. We are 50 mi (miles) from the coast...We are going to the coast pretty soon. We get transportation & board for 25c each. I got a tooth pulled about a week ago & my jaw bone hurt for a week. I was working in the rock quarry but started to cutting timber today. The foreman said I was the best hand he had. Ha – Ha. The kinds of wood are: fir – pine – cedar, Redwood, Myrtle Wood & Cottonwood. The trees are covered with moss & mistletoe. All the rock's & trees in the forest is covered with it, because we have so much rain. The woods too looks like a jungle. The bunches of ferns are 6 feet high. A nice country but too much rain. The heavy rain's are caused by the ocean. It stood waist high on the ground in places last year. They have had 40 in(ches) less this year than last...How is the old ford making out? Tell dad he better watch that loose rod. I was 19 yeasterday but they think I'm 20 – Ha-Ha. Does old bud miss me? It seldom snow's or freezes here. But it rain's 3 days out of every week. I will have to close for it is about bed-time. With love, Marlin. [Bob]

Peebles, Ohio, February 2, 1939

Dear Son: Will answer your letter received Tuesday. Was glad to hear from you. Hope you(r) jaw is getting all right. I just allowed you would have to have some teeth pulled. Roma has been having the tooth ache. She had to stay home yesterday on account of it, and she didn't go today on account of the funeral for George Johnson...Bussy is feeling a lot better. We had to take Bussy to the Dr. again January 30th. He had taken some cold and spit some more blood that morning. So we thought we had better take him up again. The Dr. told me to put him to bed until he got over this cold and keep him home from school for a while. His head is still in a pretty bad shape. He is feeling pretty good this morning. I expect I will have a time keeping him in bed. I suppose you have received my letter telling you about George's death. Wasn't that awful(?) This sure was an awful day for a funeral. It has rained just about all day and So muddy you go in over your shoes almost. They could not get into the cemetery with cars. So Will Purtee

GUARDIANS AND OTHER ANGELS 103

hauled poor old George with the mules & sled from the road. He sure did look nice just like he was smiling. Mrs. Johnson went home with Claudie & Earl tonight. I tell you it sure looks lonesome down there. And I think we will miss him more than anyone as he and Mrs. Johnson came up just every few nights. Well, Bobby I guess you must be in a pretty wild country. But I bet it is pretty. It will be nice if you can get transferred back here in 6 mo. or 5 mo. as it will soon be a month since you left. But if you can't why just come home and we will try and make out some way with the house [they are building a new house]. *It has been so bad Daddy hasn't got much done to the logs yet and Bussy can't help now. I guess he* [Daddy] *is going to get a one man saw and finish them. A truck couldn't begin to get in here now. But he is going to get them ready So when it freezes up again they can come in and get them.*

They have a new Dr. in town. He is a physician & surgeon too his name is La Neave. An odd name. I don't think Old Buddy has begun to miss you much yet. And the old Ford is still O. K. Well Bobby I will close so answer soon with love Your Mother.

Sitkum, Oregon, Feb 5, 1939

Dear Mother:

Will answer your letter I received yeasterday and was sure sorry to hear of George's death. I suppose it is our loss and God's gain...We will sure miss him chopping wood, hunting and comeing up to call on us of a night. But we all have too go sometime. I knowed he had heart trouble years ago. That's the reason he would have to stop every once in a while to rest, while chopping wood. You say he died on the night of the 31st? We had a sad like show on that night. It was about 12:00 so I reckon it was about 3:00 in the morning in Ohio. And as I went to bed something just told me something was happening back home. And I couldn't hardly wait till I got a letter from you. I got Bus letter the other day. He can write a pretty good letter. I got 6$ pay-day. I paid 2$ for a wooden locker. We have to pay 35c for shows, laundry 25c and fire building 25c. We have 12 shows a month, so it's worth 25c a month. It is raining here today. I(t) rains at least 5 days out of every week. But it will quit raining in April. I've just worked ½ day on K. P. & a half day yeasterday for a feller for $1.00.

Is it very cold back there now(?) You'll have to keep Bus in, he may get pneumonia. I'm going to take the pneumonia shot soon. Say! Tell dad if he see's Vernon Frost tell him to write his boy. He is in the same camp I am, sleeps 2 bunk's below me. I don't think he got 1 letter from home. And Denver Shupert is here with me. He was in Idaho with me in "36. Has Dad got another horse yet(?)   I sawed up some logs the other day that would make 600 FT to the log.

We are going too have a dance here Saturday.   There's some real purty Indian girls & they come to the dances.   I'm a purty good dancer so I'm going to be a dancing with them, and some white girls I reckon.

Our camp rated 2nd best in the District.   Oh yes!   Jim Cramer is here too.   He was in the same barracks I was in Co 2505.   Well I reckon I'll have too close.   Running short of news.   (answer soon)   With love, Marlin L. Gaffin [Bob]

February 10, 1939

Dear Son: Will scribble you a few lines as the kids are sending you some valentines.   We are OK and I guess Bussy is better.   The Dr. gave him a shot & sent some of his spit to Columbus & it came back O. K. didn't show any T.B.   The Dr. said he had the worst head trouble he ever seen for a child his age.   He thinks he can have him cured by warm weather.   Hope you are O. K.   It does nothing but rain here & I never saw the like since the winter of '37.   It has either rained or snowed every [day] *since George was buried...We got your check the 6th it was $17.00.   I suppose you got your pay too.*

They sent Howard [nephew of Mommaw] *home gave him a medical discharge on account of his neck.   You know he had scarlet fever after he went out there* [to CCC camp] *and I suppose it settled in his neck.   You know he had it hurt once.   Well Bobby I will have to quit for this time as I am washing* [doing laundry] *& it will soon be mail time...Answer soon.   I got a card from Mother she said for you to write to her & send her your address & she would write to you her address is Peebles, R R 2.   With love, Mother*

Peebles, Ohio, Feb. 16, 1939

Dear Brother;

We rec'd your letter and were sure glad to hear from you.   You can type pretty good to not have any more experience than you've had.   Just keep on practicing and you will get to be pretty good.   I'll tell you how to correct some things that you didn't have right.   Don't put a period between any ones given name and family name, and don't put a period between the names of town or city and the state.   Put a comma.   Do it like this: Mr. Marlin L. Gaffin C. C. C. Co. 1539 Sitkum, Oregon.   I can do pretty well in Typing now, of course, I've had 6 mos. of practice...Bobby if you don't be careful

GUARDIANS AND OTHER ANGELS 105

you will sink in that mud out there and never get out. It will be as bad as in the "Three Stoog(e)s" comedy when the concrete dried on Curlie's feet. Ha – ha. Well it's not been much better here lately.

Bob did you read Zane Grey's story "Wild Horse Mesa?" I read it just about a week ago. I think I will try making up a poem about the wild horse in it. His name is Panquitch.

Bobby I will have to close as I have said just about all of anything I know of. Write me a letter the next time. Answer soon with love, Your sis, Roma

I guess you can see where I have been correcting mistakes. I think I made about 1,000,000,000,000,000 if you can read how many that is. Ha

Peebles,Ohio, Feb.17, 1939

Dear Brother

I am writing to you to tell you that I am ok and hope you are the same. Old Track is still growing and Old Buddy is ok. They gave George,s pup to Charlie McFarland. Old Peet came back last Saturday and brought John,s dog with him. They came after them Sunday. The other dog led all right, But They had to drag old Pete to The car. We miss George very much. I did not get to see him because I was sick and couldn't go out. Bussy did not get to see him either. Bussy is getting better. He has to go to the Doctor once every week. Deany is learning to talk better. The Cow we got from Evert has got a black heifer calf. Daddy and mother has been sawing the logs. Old bird [the horse] is ok. Mother said she would write some the next time. I would like to be out there where you are and see some of them big trees...I will close four I am run out of news. Answer soon. Your brother Dick

February 24, 1939

Dear Marlin thought I would try to answer your letter(.) Was sure glad to hear from you and to no you was well and liked your camp(.) Well we either of us are not well but up and around good enough for old people. I suppose I got a letter from your mother said they were all well(.) Well is has been awful cold here(,) was 12 Below Zero yesterday morning but is 39 above this morning(.) I could tell it was warmer in the night(.) Well I hope it will stay warm(.) No daddy has not had toothache this winter he got 3 out they was the ones that hurt him the worst(.) They is lots of flew all a round here and – & chicken pox with it(.)..They is a sale to morrow(.) We are thinking of going to it to buy ous a cow if she suits us(.) We sold ours last fall and have not had a cow this winter(.) Daddy did not think I was able to milk this

106   LINDA LEE GREENE

winter(.) Well I hope the snow will go off to day(.) It is melting fast(.) I don't like snow(.) When are you going to come home(?) You must come up when you come home(.) I did not no your address as I would of sent you a Valentine(.) You must take care of your self and not get sick out there for you are far from home(.)...Charlie and Gladys has moved Back to the old man Compton(')s. Charlie is going to Build a new house as the old man is for him(.) You ought to see Charlie(')s little girl(.) She is so pretty and sweet as she can be(.) Her hair is curly as it can be(.) Well I don't know much more to write to interest you and it is about Mail time so be good and take care of your self and Write to Granma(.) I will answer so no more for this time from your grandmother and grandfather [Caplinger/parents of Mommaw] *to our grand son Marlin Gaffin. Good bye and write*

*Marlin L. Gaffin
C.C.C. co 1534
Sitkum, Oregon*

*Dear Mother:
        Will write you a few lines to let you know I am O.K. and hope all of you are all well...We went to the ocean Saturday, and reilly seen something. It was worth a hundred dollars to see it. Big waves as high as a house which wholed clear to the beach. The ocean roars like thunder all the time. And there is always a breeze. So I guess I've gone far west as I can get...It is raining here today and will rain most of the night...Well since another fellow wants the typewriter I'll have to close. Answer soon. With the best of luck, Your son, Marlin L. Gaffin.* [Bob]

*Peebles, Ohio
Mar. 2, 1939*

Dear Son: Received your letter and was glad to hear from you. We are all well but colds. And Dale has had a gathered ear. It has broke now and is running so I suppose it will be all right now. Bussy is still getting better I guess. You can't tell much about him though. He is going to go back to school Monday. Ralph [Wickerham, the school teacher] *has been asking when he is coming back. So I am going to send him and see how he stands it...We have a lot of the logs sawed and Dad has several drug out. I had to lay off to-day & wash* [do laundry]*. Maby we will get done soon.
        Well Bobby I suppose you have Bussy(')s card by now telling you about Old Buddy(.) He hasen't come back yet. I don't know whether he is*

GUARDIANS AND OTHER ANGELS 107

*just out running around after some dog or whether some body has stole him.
There is a new dog catcher. He might of picked him up some place. Archie
claims he seen him last week, out close to Ova Tollers. Dad went to town
yesterday & asked about & no one had seen him that new him. We got their
tags the first of the year. Well theres no use to worry about him. Roma just
caved when she found out. Bus wrote you about it. Said she* [Roma] *was
going to write & tell you he had come home. Well I must close & get busy(.)
answer soon With Love Mother & all Be careful & don't get hurt working
in the woods. I sure would of liked to had your trip to the ocean. By By*

Peebles, Ohio. Mar. 9, 1939

*Dear Son: Will answer your letter received yesterday...We are all well now.
But Dad has had the flu, and was sick a few days. But is better now. He is
getting tobacco bed wood up to-day. We are doing pretty good on the logs*
[for the new house]*we are going to finish them up when he gets the tobacco
beds sowed...It is right pretty here to-day, But I expect it is just a good sign
of some rough weather. I got your check yesterday. I think I have enough to
buy the roof now. This check was $22.00. I will take good care of it all.
Dad & Mother & Charlie* [youngest brother of Mommaw] *were down
Tuesday. She said she had got 2 letters from you. Charlie said he would
give anything if he could take a trip like you have. He said he guessed he got
married to soon. Ha Ha. Well Bobby there is sure lots of sickness around.
Mrs. Johnson is down sick now. She has Bronchial pneumonia. The new
Dr. is doctoring her. You can't tell much about a person when they get as
old as her. She hasen't been well since George died.*
        *Bobby you know that fellow that owned that Grocery truck that
came past here every week(?) He dropped dead last Monday morning at his
home in West Union & Verna Nicholas is dead. And Blane Lewis's wife's
sister & her man got killed Tuesday in a car wreck. Well Bobby poor Old
Buddy has never come home. I don't no what could of happened to him. My
Dad said maby a car hit him out on the state road because you know he was
so hard of hearing. You know he couldn't hardly hear us call him when he
would be in the barn. I don't want you to worry about him because it won't
do any good & he was old & would soon of had to go anyway. Dad isen't
going to try to get another horse. He & Everett are going to splice up* [share
horses]*; you know, Earl took Old Bill* [the Johnson horse]. *Everett told Dad
he could have his mare to drag out the biggest logs. Well Bobby excuse this
fine paper I have to write on – just what I can find. With Love Mother
answer soon.*

Everett & Earl have both got saved since George died and Everett is looking to get layed off any day. They are sure cutting them off the WPA here now. They claim it will be all shot by June. Well By By XOXO

Mr. Marlin L. Gaffin
C.C.C. co1534
Sitkum, Oregon

Dear Mother:
I'll answer your letter received today and was glad to hear from you. I'm sorry to hear that old Buddy had never come back. He has probably just now missed me, and went on the hunt of me and something happened to him. But theres no use to worry about him, he wouldn't of been much use though for squirrels in A year or two, because it takes A dog with good ears for squirrels. But of course I'd sure hate to loose him.
I'm glad to here you've got enough money all ready to buy the roof, you can take the next to [two] for windows and things. And the other's [checks] ought to get the tongue-groove flooring. Well my head is about well now, it wasn't so bad. I am running a stone crusher now...Well since news is scarce and they are going to have A show I'll close till the next time, so answer soon –
With love, your son, Marlin L. Gaffin***

***notes on the back of the envelope in the hand of my grandmother:

Roof.	*32.00*
Windows.	*16.00*
Flooring.	*27.00*
Nails.	*5.00*
	80.80

Peebles, Ohio
March. 10. 1939

Dear Bob,
Will try to answer your letter rec'd yesterday and am very glad it wasn't you that got killed with dynamite. Dad's been sick with the flu and about had pneumonia but he(')s all right now. You wrote and asked about Track a while ago, but I forgot to tell you about her, she's bigger than old Buddy and can out run any dog around here, her and Everett's dogs jumped

up a rabbit Sunday morning and she out run all of them, old Drum quit and Everett's airdale run a snag through it's thigh, She goe's through brush like a fox she run the rabbit till that evening, Track looks just like her mother(;) her ears and head is a light tan and She's lighter than she was. Dad bought two ton of alfalfa hay from George Moore (T)uesday, Earl Johnson run over my big red rooster and killed him, and Dad bought me a big Bramey and we brought him home and he jumped right on Dean. Bob, Holt Whitley moved in where Emment Oxley lived and weve got some mean boys on Cedar Fork. Well Bob it wont seem like home when you get back. Bob it was some of Sims relatives run off from West Virginia and came to Sims house. The(y) chased them all around here and couldn't catch them and they sneaked in to Sims and here was there parents waiting. Well they throwed their shoes away and they made them make up Sims old rough road bare footed, the old man and woman their parents threatened throwing Sim and Elzie in Jale and Sim told them to go ahead and throw. Well I must close as it's about bedtime. Your brother, Bus ha. ha.

Sitkum, Oregon
Mar. 25, 1939

Dear Folks:
Will answer your card rec'd today and was sure glad to hear from you. Is the flu still going around back there? I've had it for about 4 day's but am getting better now. It has been regular summer weather here for about 2 weeks. I think the dust from the rock crusher is what caused me to get sick. We do a lot of blasting, and the burnt powder and dust is pretty hard on a fellow if he breathes it. I'm sorry to hear that old Buddy has never come back. Somebody might of done away with him, or he might have been stold, so I suppose I'll just have to forget about him. What did Bus think about having his ear lanced? I think he's got some disease of the head, and of course it would effect his ear's, nose, tonsils and maybe his eyes. Say, tell Bus if he takes good care of my gun's, he can have the rifle. I know how he'll feel to own the rifle, because I remember how I felt the first one I had. And write and tell me Tom & Sim's address.

I sure hate to hear that Old Buddy hasn't come back, he probably down on Turkey Creek if he didn't get run over. And tell Bussy to keep Track pretty close, Because so(me)body might take A notion to steel her. Well I suppose dad will be plowing pretty soon, I reckon I'll get back in time to help him out, I hope. Is he going to put out any corn on Blane this year? I hope he does because we could reilly raise some corn outnthere. I suppose old jersey [their best milking cow] *was fresh a long time ago? Well I reckon*

110   LINDA LEE GREENE

I'll have to close because the whistle is blowing for us to come sign the payroll. Your son, Marlin L. Gaffin [Bob]

Sitkum. Ore
Apr.1, 1939

Dear Mother:
Will answer your letter and was glad to find everybody well. The sun is still shining bright out here & it gets pretty hot along about noon. I'm not working on the stone-crusher now, because the superintendent picked out 20 of us boy's to go over to McKinley to help their boys plant pine slips. We planted Thur & Fri and planted about 20,000. We have got about 240,000 to plant yet, and it will take us from 7 to 10 day's yet...Say, we are planting trees in the burn't over areas. There are thousand's of acres of forest burn't too the ground, & we can see the ocean from where we are working. Denver said he was coming home in June & Wallace sure is home sick. He's night guard. To tell you the truth I don't know whether I'll come home or stay. I would like to get a car, and again I hate the thought of fighting forest fires. But maybe I'll come home & help build the house & come in to [CCC's] next spring. I've been thinking about getting a loging job when I get back If we get another horse. I feel like I could build the house in two weeks myself If I had the lumber. Haha
I guess Roma was 16 the 29th, the years sure fly...Well we are celebrating the 6th year of the C.C.(C.)'s tomorrow with contests and games, so I'll have to sign off and get ready for a big day.
Your son, Marlin

Sitkum, Ore Apr. 7, 1939

Dear folks:
I will write you a few lines too let you know I a(m) still O. K. and am still setting out trees. We will get done Wednesday because we've just got 80,000 left to set out...We all went to the Pacific again today, and I took two roll's of films. I've not got my pictures back yet, but when I do I'll send part of them to you.
Say, I sure seen some sights today. I seen sea-biscuits, clams, sticking on rocks by the million's and star fish. The sea was pretty high today, because it was windy, and it seam's as though I can still hear it roaring. I've got me a clam and a poke of granite sand. I suppose dad has started too plowing by now, and is thinking of makinga garden. Has he got

GUARDIANS AND OTHER ANGELS 111

all the logs out yet? The fruit trees are bloomed out here, and they are sure pretty.

Well I suppose school will be out pretty soon. Is Bus going to school now? I've forgot to ask about all the other kids, are they all well? And I reckon Bus will be fishing some soon, won't he? I sure use to have some times fishing, but them day's are gone forever, as Sim says. Well it is getting kind of late, so I'd better close. I have to get up pretty early in the morning. So (Adios) till the next time. Your Son, Marlin L. Gaffin [Bob]

Peebles, Ohio Apr.17, 1939

Dear Son. Will answer your letter. How are you by this time(?) We are all well but Dad, he can't hardly go. You know he has had something like flu and seems like he can't get over it. He just coughs his head off. I told him maby he had the whooping cough ha. ha. You know he never had it. Well it has rained here ever since Friday morning day & night and this is Monday(;) just let up today about noon. It just simply poured and just about drowned us out in this old house. It sure was a flood, bridges washed out and a little bit of everything. I'll bet the [Ohio] *river is up some. Well Bobby I will close and let Gary* [Dick] *& Reva write some. Ans soon as ever Mother*

Dear Brother I will write you a few lines to let you know that I am ok and hope you are the same. I got past to the forth grade. Mary [Bette] *got a dresser set. All of the school got past to the next grade but Paul S. had to stay in the same grade. So I will have to close Your Brother Dick*

Dear Brother,

We are all well except Daddy he hasn't been well for about three weeks. None of us went to school every day but Bette. She got a little dresser set for going every day...As space is limited I will have to close. Your sis, Reva

112   LINDA LEE GREENE

> Middle Fork Guard Sta
> Remote, Ore
> Apr.17, 1939

Dear Folks:
        I will write & let you know I am still O. K.   I & 5 other boys are transferred to the side [spike] *camp.   My address now is (Middle Fork Guard Station, Remote, Oregon.)*
        This is a nice place here and we get fed like King's, unless we happen to get low on supplies.   We are just like one big family here.   There are twelve of us, and 6 more coming in Sat.   We are on the State Highway 17 mi from Myrtle Point.   We went there last night.   This spike camp is about like the one in Eastern Ore.
        Did you get my pictures?   I weigh 170 now and have gained 1 in. (inch) in heighth.   Has dad got all the logs out yet?   Well I don't suppose it will be long till you have a new house.   I reckon I can feel that I helped out that much.
        I don't reckon old Buddy has came back yet, has he?   And I'll bet Bus is proud of old Track by now.   Well the Rook(ies) came in Saturday.   We got a hundred of them...all from Indiana.   So I suppose it will be pretty much work done over there now.   We [are] *building a fire trail here, back* [to] *the Mt's. about 9 mi.   There is different kind of wood here than over at Sitkum. There is Red fir, Balsam fir, White Cedar, Yellow pine, Loria, Myrtel Wood & I was sure surprised when I seen White Oak in the forest.   We have a good Foreman.   His name is Saunder's.   I don't know whether he's relation to Sundown Saunders or not.   Ha. Ha. and he sure likes to fish.   We can have gun's here, so I might get me an 8 shot pay-day for $6.44.   And I think I'll get me a cowboy hat & shirt before I leave here.   Has Bus shot his rifle any yet(?)   The deer's are just thick around here.   We seen two bucks today. Well I'd better close, it's about chow time.   With love, Your son, Marlin P.S. (Don't forget the Address.)*

> Peebles, Ohio, R. R. 1
> April 23, 1939

Dear Brother,
        Will try scribbling you a few lines today in answer to your letter which we rec'd yesterday.
        It sure is hot here.   This is the prettiest day that we've had this year. And the best part of it is that this is Sunday.   It has been bad on Sunday for the last 3 or 4 weeks.

Clifford, Chloia, Wilma, Charlie, Lowell [Bussy] *and I went to town again last night. Chloia, Clifford, Lowell, and Charlie went to church, but Wilma & I stayed in town. We're too good to go to church, as you know. Ha ha. I think that we all will go to town next Saturday night, and to Grandma's on Sun., that is, if it is pretty weather.*

Oh yes, Clifford wanted to trade Bus a coon dog for the rifle, but Dad soon put a stop to it anyhow, but you know how Bus is. He would just about trade his eyes for something different. He thinks a lot of the rifle.

I gave him a good fountain pen not long ago and he traded it to Salvador Jones last night for an old knife. Can you beat that? He sure is fickle. Listen at this, when Bus got your last letter he came in yelling, "Oh! Mommie, Bobbie is a highway patrolman." Can you beat that?

Well I must close now. With Love, Your Sis, Roma

May 2, 1939
Dear sis & all:

I'll drop you a few lines this evening in answer to your letter rec'd today. I am still here at spike camp and getting along fine. We worked on the telephone line last week and I was the climber. I am still sore. I got [a] letter from Denver yeasterday and he said he was getting to hate the camp more every day. I suppose he is getting home-sick. We had to go to main camp Mon & Tues. for fire practise. We roamed around all [the] time in the timber with them telling us how to fight fire till I could fight it in my sleep...Well Sis I'd better close and write mom a few lines. Your Brother, MG
Dear Mom:

I'll write you a line or two while I'm at it. How much lumber do you think Dad will have when it's sawed? I hope he has plenty. Has he planted any yet or plowed much? I suppose I'll get there in time to help him with everything.

How is all the kid's by this time? I suppose their glad to be out of school. I'm glad they passed...Have you put out any garden yet? The fruit trees are all bloomed out here and every one is plowing. This is a pretty good farming country. Well I suppose I'd better close. With love, Your son, Marlin Gaffin (answer soon)

Peebles, Ohio May 3, 39

Dear Son will drop you a few lines this morning. Hope you are O. K. We are all well as common. I don't think Bussy is much better. He coughs &

spits awful yet. I don't think Dr. Ellison is doing him much good. Maby he will out grow that trouble(.) I hope so anyway. My Dad had some kind of a spell last Monday-week. He started to Louden and felt it coming on him and started back home & he finally got down and crawled nearly a mile. Pearl Chambers heard him hollering for help & went and found him & took him home. He isen't a bit well yet. I guess he won't start walking out soon again by himself. It sure is queer weather here. There was a big frost here this morning. I am afraid it is going to kill all of the fruit yet. We planted a patch of potatoes yesterday & I am going to put out my onions this evening. I have 33 little chix(.) This is sure hard weather on them. Elmer & Everett are plowing up Elmer Matheny bottoms. They have them about done. George Moore has hauled two loads of logs. He said he would get them all out right away now. I hope so anyway but we couldn't start it now if we had them all ready it is so cold but suppose it will warm up soon. Well Bobby I must close as it is about time for the mail. ans. soon & take good care of yourself. As ever Your Mother by by

Middle Fork Guard Sta.
Remote, Ore.

Dear Mother:

I'll answer your letter rec'd yeasterday and was glad to hear that you are all well. I am still getting along fine. We have been having pretty weather here. We are building road's now. I am running the grader. So I reckon I'll learn all about one. I worked on It some last week getting It fixed up for the job today.

Well I am surprised to hear that you had a frost back there this late in the year. How much corn is Dad going to raise on the bottoms? Did Grandpa look very bad when you seen him last? Well I hope he never has anymore strokes.

I'll have to write to them [grandparents] soon. Well they brought a paper around today and I don't know whether to sign it or not. It has to do with: In case an enrollee get's a dishonorable discharge he is not boarded by the Gov't or in other words he has to take care of his self. Or if he can get a job and wait till the troop train runs(,) he can ride free. Of course I don't expect to get a bad one [discharge]. But I want to read the rule in the book of rules and regulations before I sign it. The boy I was in camp with in Co 2505 is here at spike camp now. He runs the tractor. His name is Karl Cramer...This company is getting worse every day. All the old boys are going home. It is getting to much like the army. I signed to come home about a week ago. The foreman here is not so bad for a guy fresh from college. We get along good. We scrub every morning. The boys take turns and I am barracks leader. What an honor. Ha – Ha. Well I'll have to close

GUARDIANS AND OTHER ANGELS 115

and shave. Excuse my writing. I don't [write] *enough to keep in practice.
With love, Your son, Marlin* [Bob]

Peebles High School, May 15, 1939

Dear Bob,

*Will try to drop you a few lines this evening as I haven't much to
do. School will be out Friday and I sure will be glad. I'm getting tired of it.
We have our tests tomorrow and Wednesday and no school at all Thursday
and a half day Friday. I suppose it will be out by the time you get this letter.
I suppose you are counting the days until you can come home too, ar(e)n't
you?*

There is a revival going on down here. Alderson Greene [father of
Lee Greene] *is holding it. That little Lee Greene is getting cuter everyday.
Him & Bus spends a lot of time together playing music mostly. Lee ain't
going back to school next year. Says he has to go to work. He ain't old
enough yet for CCC. We are well and hope this letter finds you O. K. Bus is
a lot better, but he let his* [juice] *harp fall in the well the other day and boy
did it make him mad.*

*Donald Austin has a banjo to trade or sell and Bus is wanting it.
Don told him that he might trade it for the rifle, but Dad said that Bus
couldn't trade it* [the rifle] *off because you gave it to him. Bob I imagine you
are wondering why Sim hasn't answered your letter yet. He said that he just
despised to write letters. He said that he would tell you all the news. He
said to tell you, hello and that he would be glad when you came home. Well
Bob I had better close as my madula oblongata is exhausted. Answer soon
and be good and* don't *sell your mandolin.*

Your sis, Roma

Peebles Ohio. May 18. 39

*Dear Son - Will answer your letter rec'd yesterday. Was glad to hear from
you and to get the pictures...Hope you are still O. K. We are all well. Dad
is getting ground ready to plant corn. The truck just brought the fertilizer
awhile ago. We have planted 100 lb of potatoes and going to plant another
100 lb as soon as it rains for we can't get the ground in good enough shape
untill it does. They are early potatoes and then we are going to plant 200 lbs
for late ones. I have 54 little chix and 12 hens a setting. I am going to try to
raise some chickens this year and have one hen on duck eggs...We are going
to have to get after George Moore I reckon. He hasen't hauled any logs for*

116   LINDA LEE GREENE

several days. He said he would get them all out this mo. So I think he will have to get busy...Well I suppose you will be leaving out there in about another mo. I expect you will be home before we get the house started. We was out home 2 weeks ago last Sunday. Dad dosen't look bad at all. But he is getting awful feeble. And Mom had a sick spell just a little while before Dad had that spell. But they are both better now.***

You asked how much corn Dad was going to raise over on Elmer Matheney's. I think him & Everett plowed up about 10 of them [acres]. *They haven't planted any yet. No one around here has. Not out along the road even. It wouldn't come up if it was planted it is so cold nights. I looked at my sweet corn in the garden this morning and it is just like it was when I planted it. Roma's school will be out tomorrow and I guess she will be glad. Well Bobby I must close as it is about mail time. With love, Mother answer soon*

***At this date the father and mother of Mommaw were 76 and 71 years of age respectively.

Middle Fork Guard Sta.
Remote, Ore. 5/19/39

Dear Mother:
Will answer your letter rec'd a few days ago. Was glad to hear from you. I would of answered sooner, but have been out fighting fire for the last 5 days. It covered 300 acres and there was 75 boys on it. Them five days were the hardest work I ever done. They seemed like 5 weeks...Well I suppose the carpenter will get started [on the building of the house] *pretty soon. Maybe I'll get home in time to help with it. I bet Bus is sure proud of the rabbit. Has Dad an(d) Bus trained old Track any yet? Well I reckon we will have to just forget about Buddy. I don't believe I'll ever find a squirrel dog just like him. Nor any as fast as him. But I'll look for him, in case he was stole.*
Well I suppose I'll have to close...So best of luck and answer soon.
Your loving son, Marlin Gaffin [Bob]

Peebles Ohio May 27, 1939

Dear Son: Will now try and answer your letter. Hope you are still O. K. We are all well. I hope you don't have to fight any more fire(s) for it is hard work and dangerous too. We are having some hot weather now. Elmer &

GUARDIANS AND OTHER ANGELS 117

Everett will finish planting corn Monday. I guess they have all of our(s) out, and his, and now they are getting Elmer Matheney's bottoms ready. You asked if they are going to raise any tobacco this year. We are going to put in the Acre by the barn and he is putting in that piece back of Mrs. Johnson's toilet...Mrs. Johnson has got her pension I guess. She has received one check. No the carpenter hasen't started [building the house]. *Moore hasen't all the logs sawed yet. He said he would have them all sawed and hauled out here by June 15th. Bobby(,) Quint* [brother of Mommaw] *is here. He came walking in here last Tuesday. We wants to help on the house. He says he will work for $1.00 a day & his board of course(.) We have already spoke for Randall. But I suppose they both could work & get done that much quicker. Quint will be allright if we can just keep him from getting* [into mischief]. *I feel awful sorry for him. He just works all the time doing something. Works in the garden, help(s) milk, cuts wood and just keeps hunting any thing he can find to do. He says he wants to try and do enough to earn his board. He had walked hunting* [for] *work till his feet was covered with blisters. Said if we couldn't give him a job on the house he was just going down to the poor house. Of course we have enough* [help with building of the new house] *the way it is, but you know we just can't turn him out, or won't as long as he behaves himself. Of course he don't want pay for only when he is working on the house. I bet you will be home before we get started.*

Well Bobby I must close as it is nearly mail & dinner time. Answer soon. With love, Your Mother

Remote, Ore.
June 15, 1939

Dear Mother:

(Will) answer your letter rec'd yeasterday & was glad to hear from you and to find you all well. I am still O.K. I heard from Denver the other day and he and Wallace are sure glad to get to come home...Well I'm starting back across I reckon about the 22nd, the same time that Denver & Wallace leaves. I suppose we will see each other on the train. There being lots of work to do I suppose I'll get there in time to help out. Has Moore got all the logs sawed yet? Well I hate to close but it is work time. (answer soon) Your Son, Marlin [Bob]

118   LINDA LEE GREENE

Peebles Ohio June 16, 1939

Marlin Gaffin
Remote, Oregon

Dear Bobby:
Received your letter yesterday was glad to hear you were O.K. We are O.K. only I am so tired I can hardly see. Just got through dropping an acre of beans. Us & Everett put in our bottom in soup beans & Pinto's. It sure is hot here. Bobby I am sending you what will be left out of a $5 dollar bill after I get the money order & stamp. I am going to send it air mail so you will get it sooner. Wilma got a letter from Denver saying he was starting home yesterday. But he surely must be wrong for he went the same time you did. If you did start home yesterday you won't get this money in time. But I hope you do. Moore is hauling out more logs today. He haulded & sawed 3 loads for us and didn't make half enough stuff and we had to cut a lot more & now will have to cut a lot more for him. He says it ain't turning out much on account of it being such small stuff. I reckon he is giving us our share of it. Well Bobby I will close as it is nearly time for the mail. I guess this is the last letter I will get to write you so by by untill we see you. As ever your Mother
P.S. Oh yes Sim & Ted signed up for camp yesterday but they won't get to go until October. They didn't want to go very bad now anyhow. You know they just about have to do something for money to keep the rest [of the family going] *on.*

Thirteen

Music grew to be ever more crucial in the lives of Bussy and Lee. It was their means of surviving the difficulties of their lives. Bob and Bill, the older brothers of Bussy and Lee, were home from CCC, and they joined the jam sessions organized by the two younger boys, in winter, held on almost every Saturday night in the front room of the farmhouse of my maternal grandparents, and out on the front porch in warm weather. On cold evenings, the room, toasty from the stately woodburning stove, the windows shining from the light of kerosene lamps supplementing the one electric table lamp, the plump davenport and roomy lounge chairs, their arms and backs adorned with the colorful and intricate doilies crocheted by the skilled hands of Mommaw, put everyone at ease. On warm evenings, flies swarmed in and out of open windows and doors, in the kitchen and bedrooms suspending strips of sticky and malodorous fly papers pinned to the ceilings were textured black with the carcasses of the insects. Unceasingly, dusty millers and their fuzzy-winged counterparts fluttered around the clear glass chimneys of the kerosene lamps. No matter the season, the mood was gay as each member of the family from Poppaw to three-year-old Dean, as well as friends, packed the room to standing room only capacity. Denver Whitley on master guitar and vocals; Robie Dameron on the master guitar; Sim Workman on the guitar and vocals; Merle Dameron on guitar and vocals; Bussy Gaffin on mandolin and guitar; Bob Gaffin on mandolin and guitar; Bill Greene on vocals, and Lee Greene on guitar and vocals, music became the salvation for those boys, their songs a varied selection. There wasn't a dry eye in the house at the closing of the heart-felt rendition of the song *Two Little Boys* as performed by Lee, its words weaving a story of two brothers growing up together and going off to war, and while in battle, one brother is killed, but his brother pulls him up onto his horse and removes his body from the conflict. Until his late eighties, my father Lee sang the song for us:

There were two little boys, had two little toys, each was a wooden horse.
Gaily they played, each summer day, both were warriors of course.
One little chap, had quite a mis-hap, he broke off his horse's head.
Cried for his toy, then wept with joy, when his young comrade said,
"Do you think I would leave you crying, when there's room on my horse for
you?
Climb up here Jack, and let's be going, we're off to the ranks of blue.
When we grow up we'll both be soldiers, then our horses they won't be toys,
And then perhaps we'll remember, when we were two little boys."
Long years had passed, and war came at last, and gaily they marched away.
Cannons roared loud, amidst the mad crowd,
Wounded and dying Jack lay.
There rings a loud cry, as a horse dashes by, out of the ranks of blue,
Gallops away, to where Jack lay, and a voice rings loud and true.
"Do you think I would leave you dying, when there's room on my horse for
two?
Climb up here Jack, and let's be going, we're off to the ranks of blue.
You say Jack that I'm all atremble,
Perhaps its this battle's noise,
and then perhaps I remember, when we were two little boys."

Their ethnic favorite, *Danny Boy,* again sung by Lee, his pleasant baritone voice strained to hit the high notes. Country ballads, patriotic, and folk songs comprised their repertoire.

As that rag-tag company of country boys and their faithful audiences turned to music as their solace, so did the rest of the nation. By the end of the decade, the Great Depression was in its tenth year, and people had had enough of the hardship songs such as *"Brother Can You Spare a Dime?"* The pendulum, although subtly for most common folks, was beginning to swing back to better times, literally swing with the big bands of Duke Ellington, Benny Goodman, Tommy Dorsey and Glenn Miller. Broadway produced some of its most enduring musicals, with the brothers George and Ira Gershwin's *Strike Up the Band, Girl Crazy, Of Thee I Sing, Porgy and Bess;* Cole Porter's *Anything Goes, Jubilee, Red Hot and Blue,* and the immortal music of Irving Berlin and Johnny Mercer.

With fully 80% of the population owning a radio, it was at its zenith. On tap were Jack Benny, Fred Allen, George Burns and Gracie Allen, *Amos and Andy, Fibber McGee and Molly* and the soap, *Our Gal Friday.* The population listened to *The Lone Ranger, The Green Hornet,* FDR's *Fireside Chats,* Edward R. Morrow's news broadcasts, the Hindenburg crash, and Orson Welle's broadcast of H. G. Wells *War of the Worlds,* a fictional enactment responsible for putting a million listeners in a panic for fear of an actual Martian invasion of planet Earth. Television, featuring

GUARDIANS AND OTHER ANGELS 121

flickering black and white images on a five-inch screen made its debut in the 1939 New York World's Fair, and in an exhibit at that same World's Fair, General Motors demonstrated an outrageous future seven-lane, cross-country, highway system. The world had been introduced to the book, *Gone With the Wind*, and it had been made into a movie classic. Disney created *Snow White and the Seven Dwarfs,* his first feature length cartoon; Hollywood's Golden Age brought us Greta Garbo, Clark Gable, Bette Davis, W. C. Fields, and the singing/dancing, curly-headed moppet Shirley Temple. The Parker Brothers put the game *Monopoly* into millions of our homes; Lou Gehrig and Joe DiMaggio were every boy's heroes and every girl's heartthrobs. We read new literary works by F. Scott Fitzgerald, Ernest Hemingway, John Steinbeck, Richard Wright, and Erskine Caldwell. Ogden Nash delighted us with his light verse; Dr. Seuss popped and Dale Carnegie swaggered onto the scene. Jackson Pollock, Willem de Kooning, Grant Wood, John Steuart Curry, Thomas Hart Benton, Georgia O'Keeffe and Picasso painted everything under the sun from drips of paint on giant canvasses, to a farmer and his wife with a pitchfork, to skulls of steers in the desert of the American Southwest and giant pistils in enormous purple flowers, to colossal murals on walls. Mount Rushmore was completed, as was Frank Lloyd Wright's Falling Waters. The Golden Gate Bridge, The Empire State Building, The Chrysler Building, Rockefeller Center and The Lincoln Tunnel were opened for business. The National Gallery in Washington, D. C. was endowed by Andrew Mellon; the first jet engine was built; Mildred Babe Didrikson and Jesse Owens made sports history; Karl Menninger made strides in the field of mental illness; Richard E. Byrd explored Antarctica; Will Rogers philosophized and Walter Winchell gossiped to us on the radio; Amelia Earhart was lost somewhere over a fathomless ocean.[28] In London, King George VI and Queen Elizabeth were crowned. Fascism was rearing its ugly head in Europe, and mega-dreams of encroachment on the best parts of the world were filling the heads of the Japanese. Albert Einstein wrote a letter to President Franklin Delano Roosevelt about the atomic bomb.

By 1940, Lee Greene had given up going to school; he needed to go to work instead. He plowed fields and howed gardens, cut weeds, and mended fencerows for farmers in Adams and neighboring counties. In Cincinnati, he was employed in a casket factory as a material handler moving the items necessary for casket construction from the bulk area to the welders, carpenters, and painters.

Seventeen-year-old Roma Gaffin had graduated from high school, and was doing domestic work for her Aunt Faye, and occasionally for other women of the town.

---

[28] http://www.geocities.com/bettye_sutton/greatdepression.html?200730

122   LINDA LEE GREENE

Lee and Roma were smitten with each other by then, Roma saying of Lee that for her it was love at first sight of the "ten-year-old, dreamy, blue-eyed, toe-haired, giggly boy," at church years before even though she had dated other boys until Lee grew old enough to finally pay romantic attention to her. Mommaw, however, was vehemently opposed to the budding love affair of the two young people who, three years later, would become my parents. She didn't mince her words to Roma about her fears concerning Lee, fears that he might turn out to be a "vagabond" like his pappy. And besides, they both were so young. Mommaw wanted more for Roma than for her to marry at a very young age, and to begin the process of family-making too soon, as had been her own lot in life.

Lee always was a small person, as a grown man standing at 5' 7", and at his heaviest, weighing no more than 155 pounds. At fifteen, he was lucky to tip the scales at 120. To Roma, Mommaw disparagingly referred to him as "Little Lee" or "Honey Boy," and when she was in an especially strong fit of pique over the situation, with acid tongue and twisted mouth, she referred to him as "Itty Bitty Boy."

"It ain't that I don't appreciate Lee. A body can't help but like the cute little feller with his friendly 'n laughin' ways. An' I guess he kin tell more jokes 'n anybody I ever knowed. I jist don't want him sniffin' 'round one o' my girls," Mommaw would confide to Poppaw at night in the privacy of their bedroom.

"Mother, I don't 'spect yer helpin' the situation none. Nature's done set it in motion, an' there ain't nothin' nobody kin do now," Poppaw would reply, attempting to mollify his wife.

One Saturday afternoon in the early spring of 1940, in preparation for Sunday supper of fried chicken, mashed potatoes and gravy, corn, her famous "Light Bread" and two or three pies, Mommaw instructed Roma when the girl, drying her magnificent red hair with a towel, walked into the kitchen, "Ro, run on down ta the hen house an' catch that big old red hen. I want ta fry 'er up fer supper tamarruh before she gits too big an' tough ta eat. Just bring her on up ta the slaughterhouse 'til I git time ta kill 'er first thing tamarruh mornin'." Her heart sinking, for she had just finished her bath in the big round tin tub she had dragged into the downstairs bedroom of her parents, patiently filling it with several buckets of water she had heated on the cook stove, Roma issued a sound conveying annoyance to Mommaw. Along with the other boys, Lee was coming to jam with Bussy, as usual, but also to clandestinely court Roma. Risking the filth of the hen house and its yard failed to bode well for her toilette.

In response to the annoyed sound that Roma had risked making, Mommaw spat, "Don't ye be sassin' me, Girlie. Don't ye be thinkin' yer'll be sneakin' off with 'Itty Bitty Boy' tuhnight. I know why ye been soakin' in that tub 'til yer skin is puckered ta resemblin' a prune." To punctuate her authority over Roma, Mommaw rolled up her sopping dishrag into a long coil, and snapped the end of it just shy of the backside of the girl.

"Mom, can't Bob git the hen?" Roma remonstrated with her immovable mother, her voice whining as she quickly maneuvered out of harm's way of the stinging tip of the dishrag. Countless times over the years, Roma had nursed nasty red welts on the cheeks of her rearend raised by the lashing tongues of Mommaw's coiled wet dishrags, and she certainly didn't relish receiving more of them. "Bob's milkin' with yer daddy. Now quit yer moonin' over 'Honey Boy,' an' git yerseff ta roundin' up that hen before I go out in the yard an' cut me a switch ta lay ta yer backside."

Reva, overhearing the exchange between her mother and her older sister, sauntered into the kitchen from the front room. Her eyes sweeping sympathetically over the dejected face of Roma, Reva interjected her opinion of the situation in her precise manner of speaking. Somehow she had learned to speak sans the countrified dialect of her family. "Mother, can't you see that Ro is all cleaned up?" Reva stated, sweeping an elegantly manicured hand in the direction of her sister.

"Hush yer mouth, Miss Prissy Face. Ye ain't never done yer share 'round hyere, so maybe you should go an' git the hen," retorted Mommaw, her arms akimbo on her hips, her head wagging sarcastically. A raised eyebrow and compressed lips on the face of Mommaw made it clear to Reva that Mommaw was rapidly outgrowing her tendency for letting Reva off so lightly all of the time.

"All right! All right, Mother!" replied Reva sheepishly, raising her hands in defeat as she realized she had just about stepped into something she would rather avoid, namely some chicken shit. She also had been primping all afternoon in anticipation of the arrival of the boys that evening, especially Jim Dameron. "I didn't mean to interrupt," she said, swallowing her words and turning on her heels as she tucked her chin to her chest. Reva hurriedly returned to her book in the front room.

"Mom, Reva's all dressed an' readin' a book in the front room an' my hair's still wet. Why *can't* she go an' git the hen?" Roma inquired of her mother, her eyes and her voice laced with hurt at the unfairness of the attitude of their mother.

Her face crimson with rage, Mommaw turned her back to Roma, the set of her shoulders conveying her determined intention of sabotaging in any way at her disposal the efforts of Roma to prepare herself for Lee. Throwing up her arms, her hands balling into tight angry fists, Mommaw bellowed, **"I told ye ta go git that hen!"** Her eyes pooling in tears, Roma laid down her towel, walked across the floor of the kitchen, and thrust open the back door. As Roma took off for the hen house, the screen door banged sharply against its frame.

124   LINDA LEE GREENE

Ten minutes before the first thrum of the guitar of Denver Whitley by which all of the other boys tuned-up their own instruments, a diminutive brunette eased her way through the crowd. A progeny of Cedar Fork/Peebles, Ohio, as were the others in the close room, the lithe girl of eighteen slithered close to the chair where Bob sat. Standing demurely within arm's reach of his face, with dark sultry eyes, she darted glances full of meaning at his crystal blue eyes when he raised them to hers. Dorothy Boldman, or Dot as she was known, like her friends Roma and Reva Gaffin, was gleamier of hair, shinier of face, and starchier of dress than anyone had ever seen her. It was apparent that she too had spent the afternoon polishing for the evening. The alluring aroma of the perfumed powder on her glowing skin wafted seductively to Bob's nose, and his senses swam as his heart thudded in his chest, and his vision burst into sparks in front of his eyes.

The last ripple of the tuning up exercises erupted into the full-bodied and melodious chords of the high-pitched ringing of the mandolins, and the tripping magical notes of the strings of the guitars of the Dameron brothers. Lee, strumming the rhythm on his guitar, broke into song, the other boys joining him in harmony—all but Bob, whose throat clenched closed with the sudden and overwhelming emotion of everlasting love for Dorothy Boldman, and it remained too tight to squeeze out as much as one note of any of the songs performed so magnificently that warm and luscious evening.

Despite his involvement in music and with his large group of friends, his infrequent treks into the woods to hunt with his favorite dog and gun, and his intermittent chores on the farm, given the deteriorating state of his health, life was growing considerably more difficult for Bussy. He was beginning to suspect that his future life would always be significantly different than those of his brothers and friends, different not merely by virtue of his chronic ill health, and the loneliness of his unique situation in the history of his family and among his peers, but also because he was finding his way where there were no mentors or clues or paths to follow. Although the possibility often troubled Mommaw and Poppaw, the prospect of an imminent death never seriously concerned Bussy, but by all accounts, he did suffer the disappointment of a soul whose aspirations would remain unfulfilled, aspirations fashioned by a soul that by every aspect and virtue had come into the world prepared for a long, illustrious, and eventful life. By nature Bussy was attracted to high adventure and great challenges far beyond the assets of his neighborhood. As time passed and reality sat in, however, he was careful to keep his prolific imagination reigned in and his desires limited, for intuitively he seemed to know that his life would never reach far beyond the borders of the farm, and someday perhaps, no further than his bed. For the sakes of his parents and siblings, though, he presented a stoic demeanor, and it would have taken an insightful outsider to see that beneath the charming exterior, the ready wit, the affable manner that put people at their ease, immense anxiety roiled within him, and it was made more acute by its so seldom having an appropriate outlet. Since he suspected that he would never leave it, he exercised genuine care and paid close attention to the workings and business of the farm and its animals, since early childhood showing a particular interest in the chickens. During the torturous years of his painful and debilitating illness, and under the stresses and strains of his life as a result of it, Bussy had developed a hot and quick temper given an opportunity for it to be unleashed. He also craved novelty, an expected symptom of a young person so often a shut in, his impulsivity reliably leading to feelings of regret. These characteristics of Bussy were best illustrated in his relationship with his favorite fighting or stag rooster, Tarzan by name:

Never in the history of the world of chickens had a rooster been more deserving of its name. A big gray game rooster, a veteran of 62 kills, Tarzan took on all comers: the stag roosters of the Whitley boys across the holler, and those of the other neighbors so bold as to challenge the champion game rooster of all time in that area. Not only was he Tarzan, he was also Joe Louis and Joe DiMaggio all rolled up in one infamous feather-bound package. Like the literary Tarzan with his animal sense, his proud bearing, his resonating call, and his role as alpha male, the game cock owned all of the female fowls and dominated all of the other males in the chicken yard. He was the Joe Louis of his territory who, like the world champion boxer, was built for his role, an aggressive heavy weight with a hard-hitting and lightning fast punch and big feet sporting enormous and steely-strong needle-sharp spikes on his heels—no other contender ever stood a chance against him. This was no dud-heeled crossbreed; this was a thoroughbred. And like that other thoroughbred master of his game, baseball great Joe DiMaggio, this rooster with his accurate eye, his cunning, and his good looks, was the envy of all of the other animals in the barnyard, as well as the rival boys and men of the district who aspired to ownership of the preeminent fighting cock in the annals of cock warfare. The prestige Bussy derived from Tarzan was enormous. It was perhaps the high point of the life of the teenager.

One brilliant October day, four months after the ninth birthday of his youngest sister Bette, and her twin Dick, as well as his own fifteenth birthday, Bussy proudly surveyed the impressive chicken kingdom he had diligently and patiently coddled into existence, and Tarzan was the pride and glory of the entire enterprise. In addition to being the champion fighter of the farm and beyond, Tarzan was a prolific breeder, his progeny a superior strain of hens with their baby chicks, and of handsome, haughty and tough young roosters in their own rights. Like all heirs apparent of all kingdoms everywhere throughout time, they lusted after their old man's power and

126   LINDA LEE GREENE

lived to dethrone him. Nobody's fool was this lord of his domain, however, and Tarzan kept a sharp and wary eye on his scheming and adversarial sons.

As the young rooster princes grew into their mighty manhoods, many incidences of mayhem had erupted in the chicken yard. Since they knew that none of them had yet developed enough individually to conquer their sire, they ganged up on him, three and four of them as a group. With his keen instincts for sizing up his opponents, Tarzan knew he could handle two of the strong pretenders at a time, but three and four was risky business. With each challenge by the group, Tarzan allowed the youngsters to have some fun with him, and feathers would fly. Squawking and crowing, glancing thrusts of their phallic heels would ensue, but then Tarzan would walk away, himself, nor his sons, none the worse for wear.

A great conflict pertaining to the situation had grown within the breast of Bussy. Tarzan had become the alter ego of the frail and pale teenager, a prized, four-pound package of macho masculinity of a kind Bussy aspired to for himself, but feared he would never attain. On the other hand, Bussy's affection for his brave young rooster sons pulled equally as hard at his heartstrings. A critical state of affairs had arisen, requiring Bussy to spend an inordinate amount of time in the chicken yard policing the situation.

The chicken yard comprised the main chicken house and several smaller coops surrounding it, the yard extending into the apple and peach orchard where the flock preferred to spend the bulk of its time, roosting in the trees, and on the ground where Bussy's feathered friends scavenged insects drawn there by the fallen fruit. To facilitate his guard duties, Bussy had placed several tree stumps all around the area for the purpose of providing seating for himself and the rest of the family, as well as friends who stopped by. Due to Tarzan's refusal to kill any of his challenging sons, a rumor had begun to circulate around the neighborhood that he was showing signs of having lost his nerve, this momentous turn of events drawing the boys and the men of the area to the chicken yard of the Gaffin farm on a regular basis. Their wads of chewing tobacco in their bronzed cheeks, or cigarettes dangling from their sunburned lips, they openly speculated on the situation. "Do you think he's jist playin' it smart, Bus?" Denver Whitley asked one day.

"I reckon, Den. I can't hardly think he's turned coward," Bussy replied, his head shaking and his face turning grim. "But maybe. He's gittin' old, an' maybe he's tard o' fightin'."

Bussy's most frequent companions beneath the fruit trees, however, were his little sister Bette and his youngest brother Dean. "I fink dat big ol' wed woostowh's mad at Tawzan, Bus," five-year-old Dean said to his big brother one earth-shattering day, his pudgy finger pointing up to a fat branch of an apple tree where the most aggressive challenger roosted, his head belligerently following the movements of Tarzan who strutted proudly among his hen-harem on the ground.

"I know, Deany. I'm tryin' ta keep him up in the tree an' away from Tarzan an' I'm tryin' ta keep Tarzan down hyere close ta me where I kin keep a eye on him. That big red's the worst ta wantin' ta fight Tarzan. He ain't brave enough yit ta do it by hisself but he kin make some awful trouble if he's a mind to," Bussy replied confidently, unaware that the big red was indeed ready to chance a challenge to Tarzan.

"I kin pway my mandowin, Bus an' maybe dat'll keep 'em fwom gittin' mad," Dean offered. On his chubby short legs he walked to one of the tree stumps and sat on it, the mandolin held lovingly in his arms.

"That'd be right nice, Deany," Bussy said. Bette sat on the stump nearest her little brother, her brown eyes darting anxiously around the yard. She was especially concerned about the safety of the many fuzzy and yellow baby chickens gaily pecking the ground beneath the group of trees centered in the chicken yard. On the frequent occasions that Bussy was too sick to tend to his chickens, Bette would fill in for him, and during his times of relative health, she acted as a capable and regular assistant to the boy. As a result, Bette's affection for the chickens nearly rivaled Bussy's, especially the mother hens and their babies. She barely tolerated the roosters, however, all of that testosterone induced posturing all of the time being at odds with her shy and quiet nature.

"Kin you play 'Old MacDonald', Deany?" Bette suggested, her eyes skipping to the eyes of Bussy, a look of mutual pride in the musical aptitude of their little brother swelling in the breasts of the older siblings.

"I weckon!" the little boy replied enthusiastically, his hazel eyes alight with the musical notes of the song already skipping merrily in his brain.

Just as the small fingers of the young boy began to caress the strings of the instrument, a billowing cloud of dust floated up from the gravel road leading to the farm, the dust a tandem exhaust of a conveyance of a visitor. A ramshackle buggy led by two long-in-the-tooth and haggard horses, the whole rickety affair managed by a raggedy old man at the helm, came to a rattling halt at the approach of the road nearest the orchard. The sides of the buggy was littered with suspending pots and pans, each one dented and blackened with much use, with various hand tools, ropes and wires, and other useful paraphernalia, and its closed interior was stacked to its ceiling with folds of both new and old blankets, articles of clothing and shoes, small pieces of household furnishings such as tables, footstools, lamps, dishware, and even a toy or two. The buggy, in harmony with the over-taxed horses, seemed to sigh with relief at the interlude in their work, the horses, calling into service their swishing tails, lazily brushed away huge horseflies that buzzed and bit their swayed-in backs. The visitor, a peddler who regularly

128   LINDA LEE GREENE

called on Mommaw and Poppaw, as on all of the farmers in the district, yelled out to the children, **"Yer mother 'n father at home?"**

"Deany, go an' git Mother," Bette said, remembering that Mommaw, as was the usual case, was looking forward to the visit of the peddler. She enjoyed picking through his merchandise, and occasionally found something she could use.

Dean took off running toward the house, and just as he cleared the grove of trees, the big red rooster jumped from the branch of the apple tree and sailed to a wrathful stop mere inches from the head of Tarzan. Swiftly the big red jumped in the air at a height above Tarzan, a spike of his large claw hacking the eye of the older rooster. It was a deep and serious wound, drawing copious blood to the surface of the skin of Tarzan, drops of it pooling to the dirt. This time Tarzan retaliated, for he was fighting for his life, and with a magnificent leap in the air, he lashed out with one of his matchless spikes and slashed the throat of the big red, the razor sharp incision trailing down viciously through the breast of the young bird. The red rooster flopped to his side, the scent of the kill stirring two of the other young roosters to a frenzied state, and they hopped onto Tarzan's back. A fight to the death sprang up, the three roosters thrashing around the yard. Several baby chicks, their mournful and frightened peeps ringing ineffectually in the noise of the commotion, ran blindly for safety, but they were caught, captive beneath the bodies of the fighting birds. As the spikes of the three roosters lashed out to one another, several baby chicks became victims of the battle. Angry mother hens, like female tigers avenging their dead young, jumped into the fray, their beaks pecking at the eyes of the mad roosters.

Her face wet with tears and her voice staccato cries of anger and sorrow, Bette ran to the dead baby chickens and scooped them up in a pouch she made with the skirt of her dress. His commands to the birds to stop fighting falling on deaf ears, and braving serious injury to himself, Bussy hurled his body into the fracas. Bending at his waist, deftly he grabbed one of the legs of Tarzan and pulled him free of the other fighters.

"Hyere!" Bussy said to the peddler, his arm thrust toward the man, the squawking rooster flailing wildly, his wings flapping in a feeble attempt to extricate himself from Bussy's hand. "Hyere, take him," Bussy repeated. "I'll sell 'im ta you real cheap."

"But Bus, are ye shore? This hyere's Tarzan, yer champion game cock. Ain't no cock like 'im in the whole county. Yer'll never git another 'n like 'im," the peddler remonstrated with the red-faced teenager.

"I don't want 'im no more. Ain't no rooster o' mine agoin' ta kill my baby chicks. Gimme thirty cents fer 'im an' he's yers," Bussy replied stubbornly.

"Awright Bus, but ye know I kin sell 'im fer some big money, don't ye?"

GUARDIANS AND OTHER ANGELS 129

"I don't care what you do with 'im. Jist git 'im away from this hyere farm."

Two days later, Bussy realized his mistake, a mistake resulting from that impulsive streak in the boy, that red hot temper. The peddler was correct in that Bussy never had another game cock of the likes of the magnificent Tarzan.

As a palliative to his broken heart over his loss of Tarzan, as indicated in the following postcard from his friend James Louderback, like his two older siblings, Bob and Roma, Bussy allowed himself the luxury of entertaining the sweet promises of love, however illusive he feared them to be for himself. His romantic interest in girls extended to the persons of a neighbor Ruth Hoffer, and Anna Greene, one of the younger sisters of his friend Lee:

Dear Bus.

I will drop you a card as I am thinking of you. How are you? I am not feeling so well as my legs and arms hurts so bad. I am plowing as Dad hasen't been able to work a bit. He feels worse than he did over there. [Apparently James and his family had recently moved from Cedar Fork to Blue Creek.] *How are you geting along in school? I have got three teachers at my school. Roma said that Ruth Hoffer had a fellow named James D. I bet it made you mad. Do you like Anna Green(e) yet? You no them little pigs that we had? We sold them and* [in] *about two day(s) the barn* [of the buyers] *got on fire and burnt down and burnt the pigs up. Ans soon. James Louderback*

Fourteen

The jam sessions grew more and more infrequent as the members of the makeshift country band almost en masse migrated away from Cedar Fork in search of work and other opportunities nonexistent in that region. The master guitarist of the group, Denver Whitley joined the CCC and was sent to Dayton, Washington, his letters to Bob descriptive of his life there. Bob and his cousin Ralph along with a small contingent of their friends traveled southwest of their home, ending up in Blanchester, Ohio where they found work. The deteriorating health of Bussy was often the spine of the copious correspondence among family and friends as related in the following letters:

D. D. Whitley
CCC Co 545
Dayton, Washington
Feb. 1, 1941

Mr. Marlin Gaffin
Peebles, Ohio R #1

Dear Friend
Just a few lines to let you no how I am getting along. I am sure out here in the west this time, but I don't like it so well yet. It will be ok after I stay a couple of weeks, I hope. I sure miss my guitar and all of our jam sessions. I am going to get it [the guitar] *sent to me here. Maybe I can get some boys together and play sometimes. I wonder how Lee and Roma is, and Bus is specially. Tell them I said hello and I will be seeing them sometime, I reckon.*
Well how is everything on Seader [Cedar] *Fork? Ralph Jones and Loyd went to Idaho. Glenn Thatcher came with me. He seams to be making it all right for the first time* [his first tour in CCC]. *I expect me and him both*

GUARDIANS AND OTHER ANGELS 131

[will] *be heading that way* [home] *in June, but a fellow never likes it so well for a while. They are talking about moving the camp to California in April. I am sure it would be all right with me any day they get ready...Well, write and tell me all the news. Hoping to hear from you soon. Denver*

D. D. Whitley
CCC Co 545
Dayton, Washington
March 11, 1941

Mr. Marlin Gaffin
Peebles, Ohio R #1

Dear Friend
 Will try to answer your letter received a few days ago. Was sure glad to hear from you. It makes me feel a lot better when I get a letter from back there. Boy, I am telling you that the CCC are getting lousy any more. They get worse every day. It is getting just like the army, but I don't care what they do. If the rest of the boys can take it, I can to.
 Well how is the world serving you? The weather is nice out here. It is a pretty mild climate out here. It never gets very cold. Its just about like it was in Oregon but theres no timber here where we are. But there is plenty of it about ten miles from here. We are only a ½ mile from town. We go when we get ready. We never have bed check at night. You know that healps a lot. Well I cant think of much to write so I will sign off for this time. Answer soon. Denver

Blanchester, Ohio, R #1
Wed., Apr. 23, 1941
Dear Mother:
 I will write you a few lines to let you know I am O. K. and hope you are all right. How is Bus by this time? I hope he is better.
 We sure had a time coming up here. We done all right till we got on the other side of Fayetteville. We had tire trouble and didn't get here until 9:30. I went to work Monday morning. But Ralph hasn't got on yet. I guess I kind of put the wheels to turning. They couldn't work unless they had a truck driver and the men couldn't get to work unless I hauled them. Ha. I am driving a 39 Chevrolet truck.
 When I went to work the boss asked me if I could drive a truck and I said sure I could. He asked me if I could handle the tractors and I said I

132   LINDA LEE GREENE

could, so I went to work. Ha – Ha. Well a fellow has to tell a <u>few</u> [lies] once in a while. But I operated them like an old hand and kind of fooled them. Ha. They [operating the trucks and tractors] *just seemed to come natural to me or something. Well it is late an(d) I'll have to close. So answer soon. Your son, "Bob"*

Wednesday, April 23, 1941

Dear Son. Just a few lines to let you know about Bussy. I think he is a little better this morning. He still coughs pretty hard. How are you? And are you getting any work? Roma went out to Faye's [sister of Mommaw] *Monday evening to work. We had a pretty good frost here yesterday morning. The Dr. was here to see Bussy Monday night at 10:30. He is coming back today. I will let you know about him again soon. With love, Mother*

Thursday, April 24, 1941

Dear Son: Just a few lines to say we can't see much change in Bussy. The Dr. was here yesterday. Told us he [Bussy] *had pneumonia. He* [the doctor] *is coming back tomorrow. Bobby maby you had better try and come home this Sunday if you can. Bussy wants you too.* [He] *said for you to bring the guitar. But he couldn't play it if he had it he is so weak. Of course he thinks he can. He woke me up last night & said he wanted you to come home this Sunday. So come if you can. Love Mother*

Thursday evening, Apr. 24, 1941

Hello Bobby: Bussy is a whole lot better this evening. So I thought I had better let you know about him. I wrote you a card telling you, you ought to come home Sun. since he wanted you to. But since he is so much better, why you needn't to unless you just want too, for you had so much trouble going up Sunday. I sure was glad to hear you had a job. And I suppose you would rather had that job than any other. Bussy's fever has broke and he is sure a lot better. This evening is the first that he has wanted anything to eat. So I will keep letting you hear from him. Mom

Thursday Morning, May 1, 1941

Dear Son. Just a few lines to let you know Bussy is getting along fine now. He got up [from bed] *last Monday. He is pretty weak yet. How are you? The rest of us are O. K. Roma is still out to Faye's. Are you coming home Sunday? I have been looking for a letter from you all week. Wiseman's are moving down here on the Ott Smalley place today. They traded their property in town for the farm. Bussy went to church last night with the kids. He said he seen Glenn Thatcher there. I don't know why he is home so soon. You know he went with Denver* [(Whitley) to CCC Camp]. *Love, Mother*

Friday, May 2, 1941

Dear Mom:

I will write you a few lines to let you know I am all right an(d) hope every body is fine. How is Bussy? I hope he is well. I got a letter from Dorothy yeasterday an(d) was sure glad to hear from her. I am still at my job. But it is pretty tough. The dust is awful. I might get a job in Cin'ti [Cincinnati] *pretty soon. Ralph is working in Cin'ti. He is making 40c an hour. He said he thought I could make 90c. He said there was 100's of jobs. Carpenter work especially. J. Q.* [brother of Mommaw] *could get a job in a minute making 90c per hr. Cin'ti is only 30 mi. from here. 25 mi. to where Ralph works. Well Mom I'll try and be down this Sat. I may get there if it don't take all my wages for patching* [innertubes for tires on the car]. *Ha. I got me a new battery $3.25 on the old one. The boss got it for me. But something is wrong with my generator and I've not much time to work on it. I am still driving trucks, tractors and whatnot. Ha. Well Mom I persuaded John* [(Lilly) with whom Bob is rooming] *to buy a car. So help me he got a 31 Chev* [Chevrolet] *coach for $35.00 a real buy. Car's are cheap here. Well I'll be seeing everyone. Your son, Bob*

Friday, May 10, 1941

Dear Son: Just a few lines in answer to your card. This leaves us O. K. Hope you are all right. I suppose you are working every day. Dad is getting ready to plant corn. We sure are needing rain bad. We have been cleaning house. We have both the upstairs rooms cleaned. I suppose you will be home tomorrow night. I think Hannah [Smalley] *got a card from Everett* [Smalley] *saying you all would be home. Lee* [Greene] *worked for Everett*

134 LINDA LEE GREENE

two days this week [doing farm work while Everett worked in Cincinnati at another job]. *Must close and get to work. With lots of love, Mother*

Peebles, Ohio May 29, 1941

Dear Son.
   We received your card yesterday. You sure made good time going back. Sorry to hear you got layed off. Of course it will be allright if you get another job soon. They have the toilet done and will finish the well today [for the new house]. *It sure is going to be nice. And is it hot today. Dad is getting tobacco ground ready and Roma is staying with Mrs. Smalley this week. Well Bobby I will quit as it is about mail time. Answer soon. With Love, Mother*

Having subtly grown moment by moment by tautly strung and fastly held controls on the parts of both the parents and their chronically ill children, the overly-protective and co-dependent natures of the relationships often are not easily negotiated by children who wish to loosen the deep-seated restrictions of these bonds. To all outward appearances, the children delicately bend to the wills of their assiduous parents, but all the while beneath the surface, it is the sick children to whose wills the boundaries are most closely attuned. As on the parts of parents in similar circumstances now as then, Mommaw's fear of Bussy's budding independence as he approached the age of sixteen, that turning point when he expected to begin his transformation into adulthood by getting his driver's license, was unyielding, but compared to the determination of Bussy, it had found its master.

   That Bob and most of the other boys in their group had left town in pursuit of greater employment opportunities, or in some cases, having joined the CCC, Bussy's grasp of the extent of his isolation and his sense of uselessness grew to be as dangerous to his spirit as the chronic infection he carried in his lungs was to his body. Due to his ill health, Bussy was unable to seek employment, or to go very far afield for any purpose, again putting him in the position of searching his soul for something constructive to do with his life.

   At the supper table one evening a month before his sixteenth birthday, her internal dialogue a restless counterpoise to the lively conversation of her husband and children regarding Bussy's chances of passing the driver's test, Mommaw announced shrilly, "I ain't give my permission fer Bussy ta git his driver's license. Now Dad, ye know I got feelin's that's holdin' me back from lettin' Bus git his license. I don't rightly know why yer talkin' like I ain't got them feelin's."

GUARDIANS AND OTHER ANGELS 135

"Mother, now jist settle down a little. We're only talkin' about the test. There ain't a body at this hyere table don't know yer feelin's about it," Poppaw replied cordially, being very careful to keep his voice at a friendly tone.

Her back stiffening and her eyes leveling pointedly at the eyes of her husband where he sat at the opposite end of the table, Mommaw retorted, "Elmer, I know what yer doin'. Yer afraid to drive that old rattle trap of a car we got, that 'new fangled machine,' as ye call it, an' ye jist can't wait ta give that job over ta Bus. If it weren't Bus it'd be somebody else."

"Now Mother!" Poppaw shot back, his normally loud voice rising considerably in volume, his hand springing in protest into the air.

"Don't ye 'Now Mother' me, Elmer," Mommaw came back sharply, her own hand wagging back and forth in front of her face. "I ain't been married ta ye fer more 'n twenty-five years for nothin'. I know what's goin' on in that head o' yers."

His chin lowered to his chest, Bussy threw up his hands and covered his ears, his sharp elbows peaking through the fabric of the sleeves of his denim shirt. Both so delicately atuned to his every movement and nuance since that fateful day of the onslaught of his sickness, Mommaw and Poppaw grew silent as mummies, their faces turned to their son, their eyes sweeping over him worriedly. "It ain't the rattle trap car! It ain't Daddy's hatin' ta drive! It's them spells that 'er worryin' you, Mom," Bussy said, his voice nearly inaudible. Removing his hands from his ears, he turned to face his mother. "Ain't it, Mom? Ain't it?"

Lowering her eyes, her hands nervously wringing the hem of her apron, Mommaw replied, "But, Bus, what if.....?"

"Mom, I ain't had one o' them spells fer months now. I ain't blanked out 'er even got dizzy fer I can't remember how long," Bussy reasoned with his mother.

Fishing a handkerchief from the pocket of her bib apron, Mommaw wiped her moist face with it. The evening was very warm. She was still hot from standing over the cookstove, as well, and now her nerves were stretched to breaking. Red-faced and her eyes pooling with tears, Mommaw said imploringly, "Bus, they've been other times when we thought them spells had quit an' they come back agin. What if one o' 'em comes on when yer drivin'?"

"Mom, I got ta git somethin' ta do. I can't lay around hyere no more jist all the time. I know when I'm feelin' poorly I can't do nothin' else, but the rest of the time, I need a job, like all the other boys got. I know I can't go away like the rest of the boys, but I need somethin' ta do, Mom. Drivin' is easy, an' I kin do it jist about any time, an' jist like Bobby, I like them machines. I kin tell when one of them spells in comin' on, an' I promise, Mom, I won't drive then."

Reluctantly pulling her brimming eyes away from her tormented son, Mommaw turned her face to her husband's, the eyes of Poppaw softening in compassion for his wife. A few moments passing by, the silence at the table having grown palpable, Mommaw and Poppaw nodded their heads in assent to each other, barely discernible movements of acceptance marking their lips. Mommaw reached over to Bussy where he sat next to her, her hand cupping his chin. Raising his face to hers, she studied his begging eyes.

She understood full well his emotional agony, his growing need to contribute to his family, to counterbalance in some meaningful way the burden he felt he placed on them, especially his parents. Oh, how she sometimes rued those delicate choices parents must make regarding their children. In that moment, she realized for the first time that it was beyond her control, all of it was, really. In her mind, she said yet another prayer of protection for her second-born son, the child of her heart since the moment of his birth. Inhaling deeply, she held her breath while she argued with God one more time, then releasing the breath, an exhalation of defeat, then acceptance, she said to Bussy, "O. K., Son," her lips compressing into an unwelcome compromise for what she hoped was best for her beloved child.

Subsequent to the turn of his sixteenth birthday and having easily passed his driver's test, Bussy found the new purpose in life he had anticipated. He became the designated driver for the family when he was able, enthusiastically motoring into town on errands for Mommaw and Poppaw, driving them to church, and to visits with their extended family members and friends strewn all over the county.

His male friends all having gone, Bussy was surrounded by females. As males have been carting females around since the beginning of time, on their backs, in carts, on horsebacks, by horses and buggies, on bicycles, on modern-day motor-powered conveyances, Bussy found himself chauffeuring all of the girls of the neighborhood, picking them up hither and depositing them yon, all over the countryside in the 1927 Ford Sedan owned by his parents. Bussy enjoyed that part of his life immensely. I can see him in my mind's eye delighting in the ceaseless chatter and narcissistic fluff of those girls just as if they were a run of his beloved chickens.

I called my Aunt Anna Greene-Armstrong recently to tell of her of the postcard to Bussy from James Louderback, the contents indicating that Bussy had discussed her in an amorous way with his friend James. My eighty-plus-year-old Aunt Anna giggled girlishly, and said, "Lord, I never knew that. You know, it surprises me that Bussy had those kinds of feelings because he was so sickly. Mrs. Gaffin (my maternal grandmother) used to talk to Mom (my paternal grandmother) a lot about Bussy. You know Mrs. Gaffin took care of him all of the time. He was such an invalid the biggest part of his life after he got sick. During his bad times, she had to take care of him just like he was a little baby, bathe him and all. Mrs. Gaffin told Mom

GUARDIANS AND OTHER ANGELS 137

that he never developed through puberty like normal. He never got hair on his face or body, or even his pubic area like normal boys do during that time, and I guess his body down there stayed just like a young boy's too. That old sickness did that to him."

It isn't any wonder that Bussy occasionally erupted into fits of temper as he did that day he traded Tarzan to the peddler, but according to family legend, he showed his temper rarely.

Thursday, July 17, 1941

Dear Son: Just a few lines in answer to your card. We are O. K. and hope you are the same. Dad is cutting his oats today. Roma came home last night. Suppose you will be home soon. It is sure hot here but expect it is worse down there. [Bob is working in Cincinnati and living at 247 Pike Street, Cincinnati, Ohio]. *I suppose we will be seeing you soon. Love Mother*

"The Precious Jewel"
Way down in the hills of old Adams County,
There in the grave lies the girl that I favored.
When a girl of sixteen we courted each other,
Those were the happiest days of my life.
But the angles (angels) called her for a jewel in heaven,
To sit with the rest on that beautiful throne.
A jewel on earth, a jewel in heaven.
They've broken my heart,
And left me to roam.
Now I'm alone in this world,
Of its trials and troubles,
No one else to fore and above.
But I'll always think of that jewel that left me,
Till we meet on the banks
Of that beautiful shore.
May the angles (angels) have pease (peace)
God bless her in heaven,
They've broken my heart,
And left me to roam.
Thursday, July 24, 1941
Marlin L. Gaffin [Bob]

At the time of the writing of the above poem, the relationship between Bob and Dorothy/Dot had grown from mere flirtation to an actual romance. It is natural to conclude that the inspiration for the poem was based on an earlier romance between Bob and an Adams County girl, although nothing is

138 LINDA LEE GREENE

mentioned of such a girl in his letters or in family lore. There is another possibility. Among the letters of Bob, found in the effects of Mommaw upon her death, is a mysterious postcard addressed to her from him. The face of the postcard features a sepia-toned photograph of the Oregon Coast Highway, and although the message is undated, it had to have been written in 1939 while he was in CCC Camp in Oregon. In addition, there is no postage stamp on it, indicating that it was never actually sent through the mail. In my reading of his letters, I have discovered that the boys in the CCC Camps played practical jokes on one another. This postcard could be the product of a practical joke, or it also might reflect a true situation that Bob was fearful of bringing to the light of day to his family. The postcard reads:

Dear Mother & all,
I am married to an Indian girl. She is a very pretty girl even though she is an Indian. We are going to live at Remote & I am going to teach Remote School. They all think I'm a smart guy out here. Especially the Indians. I told them that I graduated from the Ohio State University last yr. That is why I'm getting the (   ). With much love, Marlin & Whispering Winds

The allusion in the poem to the girl's being an Adams County girl might have been a cover-up for Whispering Winds. However, a third, and most probable inspiration for the poem was the prolific imagination, as well as the dreamy nature of Bob. At heart he was a romantic, and his was a soul of a writer, although, other than in letters, he failed to fulfill that calling.

August 12, 1941

Dear Son: I am sending your classification card [Local Board No 1, Selective Service For Adams County, West Union, Ohio]. *It came today. And they put you in 1ˢᵗ class. That is what I was looking for. Maby your examination will change the class. I hope so. It says you must show this card to your employer, and if you want an appeal, you will have to send it in within 5 days from the date on the card* [August 8, 1941]. *And that won't even give you time, as it was mailed Fri. and we didn't get it untill today* [Monday]. *So I don't know what to tell you about it. I am going to send them your address down there* [his Cincinnati, Ohio address]. *Hope you got down there O. K. It sure is hot today. I wish it would rain. Well I will close. Answer soon. Your Mother*

GUARDIANS AND OTHER ANGELS 139

Sept. 25, 1941

Dear Bob,
Will try to ans, your card to say hello. We're all well except Dad. He's
better tho. He's had such a cold. He worked for Geo. S. yesterday. I would
write to Lee if I knew his address. [Lee is also working in Cincinnati]. *I*
suppose you'll all come home [for the weekend]. *Tell Lee I said hello & to*
be good. Well Bob I must close I guess. I'm so nervous I can hardly write.
[My guess is that Roma is nervous because she is missing Lee]. *Expect you*
can tell it can't you? Well Bob I'll be seeing you. With love, Your sis, Roma
by. by.

Sunday night, September 30, 1941

Dear Mother: Will drop you a few lines before I turn in to let you know I am
here O. K. We got here at 10:30. Boy, I sure hated to leave this time.
Worse than ever. I guess I am still a home boy after all. And of course
there's another reason too, it's Dot. Well a guy has a time in this old world,
don't he? Was there much of a crowd at church? Did Dot come back to
church? She said she didn't know whether she would or not. And Mom I
forgot to ask Dad where he got the heifer. It sure is a beauty. It should
make a good cow, I hope. Well Mom since space is limited I'll close. So I'll
see you all. And be good. Your loving son, Bob XO

Oct. 1, 1941

Dear Son. We rec'd your card yesterday. Glad you got down there in time
to get some sleep. We are O. K. I guess. I helped Dad cut corn yesterday
morning, and it about got me. I was so sore I could hardly get out of bed
this morning. Ha-ha. It is raining here to-day. It will help the corn as it
was so dry [we] *couldn't hardly cut it. It was to bad about Lee getting fired.*
I suppose you know about it by now. Bussy took the car to town yesterday
[to be repaired]. *They said they would have it done by Friday. Yes Dot came*
back to church. Bussy brought us home then went back and took them up on
the hill to the school house I guess. Don't suppose Bill [Greene/brother of
Lee] *will get his car now since Lee lost his job just because he was too*
young. [Bill and Lee were planning to share the cost of purchasing a car].
Well must close. With Love, Mother

Nov. 10, 1941

Dear Mom. Will drop you a few lines this morning to let you know I got here [from a weekend trip home] *O. K. but a little late. I am going down on the job in a little bit. I am going to see Edwards this evening* [about getting deferred]. *I hope I can get defered. It would mean a lot to all of us. Boy it sure is cold here in Cincinnati, seems colder here than down home there. Say Mom write a card and let me know how all of you are sometime this week. Did Bus get back home O. K.?* [after driving Bob to the bus depot] *Well Mom I'll have to close for now and write Dot a card. So I'll be seeing all of you. As ever, Bob*

"Why don't you come back to me?"
The sun is gone, the moon is here.
The star's are shining through,
And every night I see that moon,
It make's me think of you.
Why don't you come back to me?
Why did you ever roam?
Sweetheart, since you left me,
I'm heartbroken, sad, and alone.
If you'll only but give me a chance,
I promise to always be true.
For there is no face,
That can take your place.
I love you sweetheart, I do,
Since you've been gone away from here,
I'm lonesome as can be.
Nov. 11, 1941 – M. L. G. [Marlin L. "Bob" Gaffin]

One week to the day of the date of Bob's poem of love gained and love lost, a form from the U. S. Government Printing Office arrived in the mail. It informed him that he had been selected for training and service under the Selective Training and Service Act of 1940, and that he would be inducted into the Army on or about December 1, 1941. A subsequent letter arrived telling him to bring hand baggage only with a pair of strong comfortable shoes; extra suit of under clothing; three extra pairs of socks; two face and two bath towels; a comb; a toothbrush; soap; toothpaste; razor and shaving soap.

A letter of December 1, 1941 addressed to my grandmother notified her that Bob had been accepted for military service and sent to the Reception Center at Fort Thomas, Kentucky.

GUARDIANS AND OTHER ANGELS 141

Fifteen

Dec. 4, 1941

Dear Son. Received your card yesterday. Well I just knew you would pass that last exam, but was hoping you wouldn't. I guess I will just have to make the best of it. We are all well and hope you are O. K. I told Roma I was going to write you today. Expect you will be gone from Ft. Thomas when this gets there. Dad is stripping tobacco today for Archie. It is trying to rain here today. I got a card from the War Department yesterday too. They said they would keep me informed where you were at. Write us as soon as you get settled, and then we can write to you again. So good by and be good. Love Mother. We haven't seen Dorothy. Suppose she is O. K.

Ft. Thomas, Ky.
Dec. 4, 1941

Dear Mother:
Will write you this evening to let you know I am O K and hope you and everyone are well. Well, I'm in the army now as the slogan goes, and its not so bad so far. Of course we haven't had any actual training yet. I sure hated to leave civilian life, but we can't help it. Some of the boy's are leaving out tomorrow. Some to Texas, Va., Missouri, and every where. I don't know where I'll go yet. I hope I go to Virginia. We can't have our choice of where we go. I seen the Sergeant about it. Oh yes, I was over to see Bill & Ralph last night [in Cincinnati]. We went to a show. It cost them 40c. A high price one. But it just cost me 20c. Soldiers are half price. I told them I might be back tonight. We will probably leave here before

Monday. If you want to write, go ahead. If I am not here, it will be forwarded on to me at my appointed camp.

     Boy we have sure got to keep spic & span here. No dirt in the Army. But I always liked to keep that way in civilian life, and we have got some nice uniform's to. Only they gave me my shoes a size to big. They say they do that so when you are on long marches, you will have plenty of foot space [for swollen feet]. *Ha-Ha and how!*

     Well, my arm is sure sore tonight. I took a shot and a vaccination today. We haven't done any work out side of scrubbing the floor's and ourselves. We drilled a little the first day. I kind of like to drill, and believe I can just about go through all the positions myself. [We] *just drilled about 2 hrs. Maybe I'll get buy. I will try to get back in the spring Mom. If I get in Va, I might be home before then. I hope they get us out of here soon and in the field. I'm getting tired of lying around. Well Mom I'd better close and write Dot. So I'll be seeing you all, and tell everyone hello for me, and <u>keep your chin up</u>. I'm sending a picture Mom; it's not very good. I had it taken where I had them other pictures taken in Cincinnati. If you write, my present address is:*

Pvt. Marlin L. Gaffin
<u>Co</u> *D Receiving Battalion,*
Ft. Thomas, Ky.   As ever, Your loving son, Bob XOX
Put it [his photograph] *with Dot's on the organ Mom*

                                    Sunday Eve. Dec. 7, 1941

Dear Bob,

Will try to answer your letter rec'd yesterday. Were sure glad to hear from you. Sure hope you like army life because it won't be so tough on you then. Dorothy and Clarine just left, Bob. They came over & stayed all day with us. Dot showed us the picture you sent her. They were pretty good, but not as good as you. ha. ha. Lee was here today too, but him & Bus went home with Sim. Lee sure hated to see you go of course, he didn't say so to you. We went to town last night & about froze. Its pretty cold here today & sure is going to be cold tonite too. We're going to try to get you something nice for Christmas. Mom was talking to Howard last nite and he told her to tell you if you got in the Detachment Corps you wouldn't have to do any guard duty or K. P. Mom said she thought that was the name.

     Alderson [(Greene) father of Lee, Bill and Anna] *said he hated to see you go awful bad too. I guess every body did Bob. Of course we've just got to grin & bear it. It's happening to millions of families all over the U. S. We're just one in millions. Bob I got a new frame for that picture of Lee & I*

and put yours & Dots in the red frame...I bet you're wondering why Mom didn't write, but she asked me to write in her place because she was so nervous. The kids all said hello. Of course we can't all write if we did we would have to send them in a coffee sack or something. Ha. ha.
Junior B. has a cigarette paper, a chewing gum paper & some other things including the old rag you shined your shoes with to remember you by. He sure thinks you're "it" doesn't he? Well Bob I guess I'll have to close as space is limited. Be good & ans. real soon. Take good care of yourself. Lots of love, Roma & all

President Franklin Delano Roosevelt, in his address to Congress said, *Yesterday, December 7, 1941 – a date which will live in infamy – the United States of America was suddenly and deliberately attacked by naval and air forces of the Empire of Japan.*[29] In the *Fireside Chat* on the radio where he talked to the nation about the Declaration of War with Japan subsequent to the bombing of Pearl Harbor, in part he said:

MY FELLOW AMERICANS:
The sudden criminal attacks perpetrated by the Japanese in the Pacific provide the climax of a decade of international immorality.

Powerful and resourceful gangsters have banded together to make war upon the whole human race. Their challenge has now been flung at the United States of America. The Japanese have treacherously violated a long-standing peace with us. Many American soldiers and sailors have been killed by enemy action. American ships have been sunk; American airplanes have been destroyed.

The Congress and the people of the United States have accepted that challenge.

Together with other free peoples, we are now fighting to maintain our right to live among our world neighbors in freedom, in common decency, without fear of assault.[30]

---

[29]http://www.millercenter.virginia.edu/scripps/digitalarchive/speeches/ spe_1941_1208_roose...
[30]http://franklincollege.edu/pwp/bgaskins/EDE226/Franklin_Delano_ Roosevelt.html

144   LINDA LEE GREENE

Monday Morning, Dec. 8, 1941

Dear Son. I will try to write you some this morning. I was so nervous yesterday I just couldn't write and not much better this morning. But the children are all gone and I am here alone so maby I can write some. Bobby we heard down at church last night that war had been declared. It sure does worry me. I just can't help it. They tell me if I don't be careful I'll go crazy. But I don't know. They surely can't take you though untill they get you trained. Of course I know that I am just one Mother in thousands. We will just have to trust in God. Of course you know that we are praying for you, and that will help you along. Herman preached last night. He surely is a good man. Well Bobby you didn't say what they fed you. But I suppose you have enough to eat and a good place to sleep. If this country is in war now I expect they will call all those boys back that they let come home, won't they? Roma told you what Howard said. I think that is the word he used (Detachment) Corps. I think he said it was in the Infantry. Berlin & Irene said that Bill told them you sure was a fine looking soldier (Ha ha). Well Bobby I will have to close as it is almost mail time. So write often and we will too. There are so many people wanting to write to you when you get settled I don't know how you will answer them all. So Good by a(nd) good luck and R(em)ember Mother as always [is] always thinking of you and loves you. So as always Your loving Mother & all

Ft. Thomas Ky.
December 9, 1941

Dear Mom & all:
        I will answer your letter I rec'd today and was more than glad to hear from you and Roma. I got a X'mas card from Clarine & a letter from Dot to Mom. I sure like to hear from everyone. I guess it's our only mean's of communication.   Well Mom I guess we are in a war again.   Japan declared war on the U. S. Sunday eve. at 1:30. Followed by the bombing of Guam, Honolulu and other U. S. property in the Pacific.   104 American soldiers were killed & a U. S. ship sunk with 350 on board. Germany the kingpin has taken action against America and is Declaring war. Roosevelt is Declaring war on Japan. Plane's and ship's of the U. S. were rushed to the danger point at once, and enemy plane's were reported over the West Coast last night at 5:30 A. M. The citizens blacked out San Francisco. No bombs were dropped. My guess is they [the Japanese or the Germans] were taking picture's, drawing map's and fixing for a future attack. I hope I'm wrong. We are being issued the strictest of order's here, to be ready to leave here for camp anytime.   Maybe a week or in the next 10 minutes.   All

furlough's have been canceled, until further order's. All reserves discharged were ordered to report to their draft board's at once. I could run on & on Mom telling of things that took place in the last 48 hr's. I'll maybe get to see everyone in 6 mo. Mom. I hope before then. But it may be yr's. But it takes the <u>courage</u> and <u>unfaltering faith</u> of the pioneer Mom to face such a crisis as this. So have courage Mom as we of the Army have and we will pull through. God is our shephard. So we will have to do the best we can. Tell Roma I was glad to hear from her, and tell everyone Hello for me. And that I will write to everyone when I get settled. And I appreciate your prayer's Mom a lot. Don't worry to much. I can take care of myself. Oh yes, about Bill [Greene]. I guess he is doing pretty good now. I was over there Sunday all day, and as soon as war was declared he wanted to come with me. So he came over Sun. night & enlisted. He won't be examined until the last of the week. Don't tell Eva or Alderson [(Greene) – my paternal grandparents] yet. It will worry them. And Bobbie Mendenhall is here in the same barracks with me & Woodrow W. Hoop of Peebles. Well I'll close for now Mom. Wishing all of you luck. So answer soon. XO Your loving Son, Bob.

Unlike Uncle Bob who remained on the east coast for the duration of his training, my uncle Bill Greene was sent to boot camp in California. While still in training there, Bill was in an automobile accident, his injuries so extensive that he spent several weeks in a hospital-rehabilitation center in that state. Although he went on to serve his full four-year tour in the Army, his compromised health as a result of his injuries kept him stateside serving in an administrative capacity in California for the entirety of the war.

Thursday night, Dec. 11, 1941

Dear Son: Will try to answer your letter received today. Was glad to hear from you. We are all well and hope you are O. K. I expect you are getting tired of Fort Thomas by this time. But the longer you stay there the farther you will be away from fighting and that is some consolation. Have you had to take any more shots? I bet you will be glad when they are all taken. Roma is out at Fayes. She has been out there all week. Faye is down at the farm selling Xmas trees and Roma has to keep house out there. I got a letter from her [Roma] today. She said they were having fresh meat as one of Howards big sows got run over and killed on the road. Said one of their cows died Sunday night. We sure was surprised Tuesday when Billy came in and told us he had enlisted. Will you and him be together? I hope so. We was over at Ed Workman's Tuesday to hear Roosevelt's speech. It sure was plain over the Radio. He is a nice talker. My I sure wish they get them all whipped by Spring anyway before you get into it. We heard today they had taken the Texas boys to the [Pacific] *Islands. You know they have been in training a year. I don't know whether it is so* [true] *or not. I just wonder if Howard* [husband of Faye, the youngest sister of Mommaw] *has been called back. I haven't seen any of them. I guess Mom has been sick again. She never wrote me anything about it. I guess she thinks I have enough trouble as it is. Harl(e)y & Edna* [(Ward) - aunt and uncle of Lee Greene] *changed their minds about going to Florida. They said they didn't like to be so close to the coast since war had been declared. It has been awful cold here today, and still is cold tonight. Tom and his wife was up last night and he came up again tonight to buy a dozen eggs. Well Bobby I must close. Answer soon and let us hear from you often. I just watch the mail box and I never set down to eat without thinking of you and wonder what you are eating. So good by and be a good boy. As ever your loving Mother XOXO*

A second card from the War Department of the United States of America, addressed to my maternal grandparents, dated December 12, 1941, informed them that Bob would be assigned to AF, Replacement Training Center in Fort Knox, Kentucky

Ft. Thomas, Ky.
Dec. 16, 1941

Dear Mother:

Will answer your letter I received tonight and was sure glad to hear from you again and to find all of you well. I guess this finds me the same. It's been a nice day here today. Of course it freezes up at night though. But we've got plenty of clothes to keep [us] *warm. We got combat suit's today. They are lined with wool. They make us wear to much sometimes and we about burn up. We have got about $100 worth of stuff issued to us now. Army things are high. They say a soldier can be issued $l,000.00 worth of equipment, counting clothes, guns, tent's, trucks & everything. That is a lot of money if a fellow would destroy all of it. That's the reason they make us keep such good care of it.*

Boy we seen a day of it today. We marched a long way through the mud to study some tank's and trucks. It's hard to keep in step in mud [while] *marching. But it will make a man of me. Haha. I tore down a machine gun this evening and put it back together. It wasn't so hard since I like to fool with gun's. It was a .30 cal. water-cooled Browning. It shoots 380 times a minute. Just like a jack hammer running. We will get to the .45 auto. pistol & the rifle and .50 cal. Machine gun later. You see this is more of a training school. I think I'll get to drive either a truck or a half track armored car.*

They [the half track] *are a combination of a truck & a tank. Wheels in front and clee tracks behind. They have a "White" motor and shift like a "Chev"* [Chevrolet] *truck.* [He drew a diagram of the shifting directions] *Excuse the illustration Ha ha, but allowed Bus might want to see how a "Chev" truck or a Clee-track armored car shifted. Well Mom the war looks tough. But as I told Dot in my letter awhile ago keep your chin's up and* <u>courage</u> *is the order of the day. I hate to fight. But if I have to I'll fight for all that's dear to me. And thats America, you people and Dot. Tell all of them* [the kids] *hello, and Dad. How is Bus? I wrote Tom W., Quint & Lee & Estie Hughes the other day. I have to write to Grandma, Cora* [an older sister of Mommaw] *and everyone else soon. I'm sorry Grandma is sick. Well Mom I will close for now. I'll be seein all of you sometime. So be good. Tell Everett hello, and to write. Your loving son, Bob XOXO Im allowed to get some X'mas cards* [to send out]. *But they don't sell them here, and I can't get to town yet. Oh yes I get plenty to eat Mom.*

Ft. Knox, Kentucky, Thursday, 12/18/41

Dear Folks: Will answer your letter rec'd today. This leaves me O. K. all but a sore arm. I got a typhoid shot a while ago. We have about six more to take. The cards were sure nice Mom and thanks a lot for them. I sure appreciate Dot's buying you the handkerchief's. Don't worry about getting me a present Mom. I thank you just the same. I answered a card from Dot yeasterday. She said she sent me a package Saturday, but I haven't got it yet. I(t) must have got lost in the mail. Well Mom this makes about 7 cards and 2 letters I've wrote this wk. So I put my spare time in pretty good Ha ha. Oh yes Mom, I think the Nazi's are pretty well on the run. They can't last. So I'll close. Will write a letter next time. So love to all. Bob XO

Ft. Knox, Kentucky
Dec. 19, 41

Dear Sister: Will write to let you know I am O. K. and hope you are well. I received your package today Roma and was glad too get it. It is sure nice. The towel set and the stationary both. I would of liked to get you and everyone a present. But you know how it is sometimes. We won't get paid any at all until the tenth of January. I would like to get a present for Dot for her birthday in January, but I may not get to. It comes on the ninth, if I'm not mistaken.

148   LINDA LEE GREENE

I got a package from Dot today to Roma. A pocketbook and a set of hankerchiefs with the initial "B" in the corner. I(t) was sure nice. I guess she still likes me a right smart. Ha-ha. I would sure love to see her. I would sure like to see all of you for that matter. But you know how hard it is for Dot & I to stay away from eachother. If something would happen to her or anything, I wouldn't want to come through the war very bad. I don't mean that I wouldn't want to see all of you at home, but you know what I mean Sis. I don't think I'll be in actual combat. Say, I got a Xmas card from Uncle Quint [brother of Mommaw] *today to. He told me if I had to fight, to shoot straight and make every one* [shot] *count. Ha Ha. Say Ro, if I'd had $20 I could of come home 4 days Xmas. But I haven't the $20. So I'll have to wait till some other time I suppose. I may get home in the spring. How are you and Lee getting along by this time? As well as usual I hope. Back to the subject. Ha Ha. I'll save some Dinero if I can and then maybe I can come home. I can get a round trip ticket from here to Peebles and back for about $6.50. That's awful reasonable. But the boys had to have $20 a piece for maintainance they* [the Army] *said. Of course that was just an old army gag to keep the whole company from wanting furlough's. You know 20's are scarce in the army. But the Sarg. told me if I wanted one* [a pass] *later on, to get me a ticket* [I'd have] *to borrow a 20 from some one for a minute to show the Lieut. and I could get by. Ha. Ha. Well sis write and tell me the new's, and I'll do my best to come* [home] *before I leave for God know's where and Tell everyone hello an(d) tell Lee to write. Kiss Dot for me will you? Ha Ha, and Mom too. So be good. Your Loving Brother, Bob XOXO*

Rookie Arithmetic

1. *Take your age and double it.*
2. *Then add five.*
3. *Multiply by fifty.*
4. *Add the age of your girl friend.*
5. *Add the no. (number) of days in the year.*
6. *Subtract 615.*

The last two figures should be your age.
The last two his or (her's)
Thus:
21 + 21= 42 + 5 = 47 . 47 x 50 = 2350.
2350 + 19 = 2369 . 2369 + 365 = 2734.
2734 – 615 = 21 (mine) 19 (Dot's)
Excuse my writing Sis. Im nervous about one thing [or] *another, two.*

GUARDIANS AND OTHER ANGELS 149

Saturday, Dec. 20, 1941

Dear Son. Rec'd your letter yesterday. Was glad to hear from you. We are O. K. and hope you are well. This sure is a pretty day. The kids have been out and got their Xmas tree. Dad is stripping tobacco. Have you heard from Billie [Greene]? Roma & Reva both have got a letter from him. Roma is still out at Faye's. She will be home tonight I guess. We was reading in the paper what all the soldiers would have for Xmas dinner. I just wonder if you will have all that. Will write you a letter soon. It is about mail time. So this will be all for this time. May God Bless and keep you. Love Mother. Ans soon

Tuesday, Dec. 23, 1941

Dear Son: Will drop you a few lines this morning. Hope you are well. We are all well except Bussy. He isn't very well. I had him to the Dr. Sat. again. You know how he is sometimes can't hardly drag. Bobby I sent you a package yesterday and Roma sent you one last week. Did you get them? And Dorothy sent you one a good bit ago. I just wondered if you got them. Well it sure is warm here and raining. Surely is a bleak looking Xmas. Roma is out at Fayes again. She is coming home tomorrow night. Bobby I got a letter yesterday from the Ft. Knox chaplain. He surely writes a nice letter. Clarine & Ruth were here all day Sunday. They said Dorothy was worried because she didn't hear from you last week. I told them you wrote to her the same day you wrote to me & I got mine Friday. She got one from you yesterday though. So you know she feels better. Must close ans. soon. Love Mother

Tuesday night, Dec. 23, 1941

Dear Son: Will write to you tonight, if I did write you a card this morning. I know you will be glad to get it just the same. I was in such a hurry this morning. I only had time to write a card. I was in a hurry to get down to school, as they were having a Xmas play, and this was treat day too. They had a good play and this teacher gave them an awful nice treat. Ruth Hoffer was Santa Claus ha ha, or I guess it is Ruth Whitley or ought to be if it isnen't ha ha. But she done very well. All of Boldman(s) [Dorothy's family] were there except John [the father of Dorothy/Dot]. Then we all went to town this afternoon to get their treat up there. There sure was a crowd up there. I saw Dorothy up there and gave her a box of handkerchiefs. They

150   LINDA LEE GREENE

were all up there. Junior gave Dean a nice sponge ball for Xmas. Nona [mother of Dorothy/Dot] *told me they mailed you a cake yesterday. We can't understand why you are not getting your packages. Dorothy was worrying about it. Said she was so sure you would get it when she sent it. Roma said she insured the package she sent you. And Dad & I sent you one yesterday. The card I got from you today was mailed the 19th and it never got here until today the 23rd. I guess everything is slow at Xmas time.*

Well Bobby they say the Russians are just cleaning up on the Germans and [the] *U. S. on the Japs, and that is sure good news. Although, I sure feel sorry for the poor soldiers. They say them poor German soldiers are freezing to death by the thousands. That is awful. I sure hope its over by spring at the farthest. I saw Denver Ward up town today, and several more soldiers. You said you might see us all in Feb. Do you think you can get a furlough by then? I hope so. Lee was asking me if I had got your insurance papers & I told him I haden't. He said they had got Bill's allready. You ought to see about it Bobby. You know if you should get hurt or anything they would have to take care of you. But of course you know Bobby that we surely don't want anything like that to happen. I want you to come home as good or better than when you left. I don't know how I would stand it if it would be otherwise. But I surely am hoping and praying for the best. Well Bobby I must close hoping to hear from you soon. Oh yes, Bussy seems to be feeling better tonight. He drove us to town today. Him & Reva are down at Toms and of course he drove them. So good by and God Bless you. Love Mother.*

Ft. Knox, Kentucky
Dec. 24, 1941

Dear Mother:

Will write to let you know I am well and hope you are all the same. I received your package today and was glad to get It. I guess Santa Claus has come to me after all. Ha Ha. I got a package from Roma, Mom. She sent a stationary pack and a towel set. I got a package from Dot too. She sent me a box of hankerchief's and a nice pocket-book. All of the presents I've got are sure nice Mom, and that (B)ugler [a brand of loose cigarette tobacco] *will come in handy. I can't get it here at the canteen. I have been smoking (N)orth (S)tate* [a brand of loose cigarette tobacco], *since I came here. Boy, we sure have been having some weather here. It rained all day yeasterday and most of the night last night. This place look's like a young river. I'm not on duty today. I don't guess we will have much to do till after Christmas. I may get to take three or four day's off in January Mom. I hope I do any how. For when we get our basic training in here (3 mo.) we may be*

sent anywhere in the states, or to any of their possessions. We may eaven be sent to the Hawaiian Islands or the Phillipine's. The German's are kind of getting the worst end of it now Mom. They are being driven back on the 1000 mi. front [of the USSR]. And the U. S. A. F. brought down 30 planes the other day. Jap's if I'm not mistaken. And they destroyed several sub's. Winston Chruchill has came to the U. S. to discuss a plan of Hitler's early defeat the world over. I hope they get something definite worked out pretty soon. Hitler has taken supreme command of the German Army. I don't think this thing can go on over a year or 2. Well to get back to more civilized things. Ha. You said something about what we would have for Xmas dinner. We decorated the mess hall all up yeasterday, and put up a tree and trimmed it. We are going to have turkey, pie, cake, and all the trimmings at dinner Xmas. So I guess we'll have enough to eat. Well I was issued more clothes Mom. I've now got a locker, bed clothes, overcoat, raincoat, two wool uniforms, 2 suntan shirts & tie, 3 wool suits, underwear, 3 of cotton, 2 pr shoes, 1 pr overshoes, 6 pr socks, 1 combat suit, 1 pr gloves, 1 tent, 1 haversack, 1 first aid kit, 1 shell belt, 1 canteen, a mess kit, and toilet articles. Whew. Well I guess I'll have enough to run me and there's more to come. Tell the kid's, dad and all "A Merry Xmas and a Happy New Year"! So be good. Till we meet again. XOXO Your loving son, Bob.
P. S. Did Tom and Archie get mail from me? Tell Bus to take care of himself. ByBy.

Although he told his family he had borrowed the money, in truth Bob sold the cake, the stationery, the towel set, and other Christmas gifts he had received. In that way he raised the $20.00 required of him by the Army to get a four-day pass, and he went home for Christmas, surprising his family. As his younger brother Bussy's new fighting rooster Ranger, named after the Lone Ranger, Bussy's favorite radio character, coaxed the sun to rising with his ringing five-note greeting, and the cows bawled in the field as if in welcome to him, the gravel on the road leading to the farm of his parents crunched beneath Bob's boots. At that hour only his mother would be up, his father and his many brothers and sisters still would be sleeping. He adjusted the small duffel bag slung over the shoulder of his new Army-issued wool overcoat, and bent down to straighten the creases in the immaculate wool trousers of his spiffy new uniform.

His mother had been right, it was bleak in Southern, Ohio. There was an eerie mist hovering over the land, a fuzzy band of fog like a shimmering boa hugging the neck of the earth. As far as the eye could reach, dense bare trees, their feet cloaked in the mist, seemed lonely and unsupported, their jagged and raw heads, unprotected, piercing the top of the mist. The silver conditions of the morning seemed to mirror a shift that was occurring in Bob's spirit—an aloneness he was coming to know all too well; clear colors and details formerly sharp and contrasting, fading to gray and merging, transforming everything, often to unrecognizable states, a wary feeling of exposure to an ineradicably new life, where, not only his surroundings, but he was becoming unfamiliar to himself.

It had been difficult for him to articulate the specifics of the issues that were needling him, and part of the problem was directly tied to the impossibility of finding that voice in the environment where he was being trained to be a killing machine. Although in the beginning he had spoken with such bravado about being ready to go to any lengths to protect his country and family, as well as Dot, the girl he loved, as the reality of his being involved in the actual fighting approached, methods of killing and maiming and destroying nobody on the outside of it could possibly anticipate or comprehend, his sense of purpose was becoming blurred, like that foggy landscape.

Bob had naively played with the idea that he had a kind of affinity with the ways and means of war, for as a backcountry boy he was familiar with the natural cycles of birth and death of the animals on the farm, surrounding forests, and countryside. He had euthanized sick animals, shot hogs in the head in preparation for slaughter, and he knew guns, the feel of them in his hands, their kick against his shoulder, the real damage they did to animate and inantimate objects alike. Guns had long been a hobby for him, actually. In his creative mind, he had even begun to design guns. As a matter of fact, in his spare time at the training camp in Ft. Knox, Kentucky where he was stationed, he had made some rudimentary sketches of a canny little gun he planned to someday fashion out of a Zippo cigarette lighter. Hunting had been nearly a daily activity for him since his adolescence, and he was learning that his experience in that regard gave him a decided advantage over many of the other boys at Ft. Knox, town and city boys whose experience with guns extended no further than toy guns, or perhaps Bee Bee guns, boys who had never held real guns in their hands, or tracked down living prey in their sights, and once positioned in the crosshairs, squeezing the trigger, and killing that prey. But that nagging voice inside of him was urging him to pay attention to the fact that killing an animal was a whole other matter than bringing a human being to its death. Despite the fact of his believing in the necessity of the war, for after all Japan had attacked the United States, and Germany had aggressed against his country as well, his being away from Ft. Knox for only a few hours now had helped him to see that he was wrestling with that moral dilemma, the first and most serious moral dilemma of his life.

His was a tender society that believed in goodwill toward all people. He had been taught that "Thou Shalt Not Kill" his fellow man, and it constituted a basic tenet of his very soul. *How am I going to kill another human being?* he worried as he sauntered in his usual loping fashion toward the farmhouse. He decided he would try to find time to talk to his favorite preacher Harley Ward about it before he returned to camp. Perhaps the man of God could help lift the mantle of confusion weighing so heavily on Bob's soul.

Barely glowing from the moisture-streaked window closest to the cookstove in the kitchen of the farmhouse, was a sole low light. In the thick mist, a plume of white smoke billowed delicately, charging the air with the scent of wood smoke, a scent of home, and sparks in the smoke twinkled like stardust shooting from the chimney at the top of the peaked roof. As he neared the back of the farmhouse, he took note of its slick, moisture-sodden clapboards. It was a house weeping from the melting icicles along its eves, weeping like those damp and lonely trees, weeping like the boggy fields, as if in an act of complicity, they collectively wept, as if the whole of nature and his home grieved an unapprehended and ill-omened fortune laying in wait for him, his family, his girl, his country, laying in wait like the hidden land mines he would encounter on the beaches of Southern, Italy in the not too distant future. Shuddering like a threatened animal in the few minutes that passed, he worked at shaking off his paranoia as he entered the perpetually unlocked back door that opened to the kitchen.

At the cookstove, her back to him, his mother stood in the arc of light from a kerosene lamp, her body noticeably weary as she bent to her duties of stoking her cookstove with her poker. At the sound of his footfalls that she knew so well, but dared not believe were real, and visibly shaking with fear that they would prove to be products of her imagination, she turned to him. Her empty hand flew to her mouth to stifle her cry, and tears spilled from her eyes.

The changes in his mother in just a few weeks took his breath away. It was as if the changes in him were manifestly reflected in her, as if by some means of osmosis beyond the natural connection between parent and child, his experiences and fears and bewilderments also were hers, only exaggerated and accelerated. She seemed already to have endured what he was facing; she seemed to have already passed through, and had been permanently altered by, the ravages of war—the superhuman demands on ones body and heart and mind and conscience; the depleted stores of psychological reserves; the lifetime of recurring night terrors. In her rote movements as she had bent to stoke her stove, in her turning to him, and in her covering of her quivering mouth, a rigid, choking anxiety afflicted her.

He lowered his duffel bag to the linoleum-clad floor while concurrently she dropped her poker with a crash. That emptying of their hands was the prelude to the opening of their arms. As she swayed weakly in his embrace, Bob's dilemma was erased from his mind. In that moment, his conscience split into two expedient parts, and in a reversal of roles, he became her personal protector. He knew then that to keep his mother safe, he would kill their enemies, and without hesitation, if not with relish, at least with the automatic precision of the professional soldier he was learning to be, and as grievous as they might be, he would live with whatever consequences his choice quickened in him.

Ft. Knox, Kentucky
Dec. 29, [1941], Monday night

Dear Folks:
    Will write you tonight to let you know I am O. K. and hope all of you are still well. I made it here pretty good Mom. I got here at 1:20 this morning. So I made it better than I thought I would. I got to Cincinnati about 9:00 and took a bus to Louisville and got out of the bus a(nd) took a taxicab to here. It brought me right up to the door. I rode the bus to Cincinnati with Thiere Nelson. He is here in Knox. He's an instructor in tank mechanics. He's stationed here permanent. He said he worked on the assembly line where they made tank's before he was drafted into the Army. Say if the Sargeant told me right today we won't go out of the U. S. He talked like we would either go to California or Arkansas. Of course that will be bad enough, but not like going across the water. It sure has been cold here today. I've been studying and practicing on a real gun today Mom. A .45 Colt 6 gun. I would sure like to own the one I used. I could of got one in West Union just like it one time for $10. But I hope I don't have much use for it. I got a card from Bill today. He said he hadn't even drilled any yet. He said he would be moved about the 15th of January. He don't know where to yet of course. His address is: Pvt. William E. Greene, CoF Ft. Benjamin Harrison, Indiana.
    Say Mom, did Dot stay very long Sunday night? I hoped she would stay all night. I sure hated to leave all of you there. Mom, I would of liked to take leave of all of you, Mom, but I had to get out Mom. I didn't even say anything to Dad when I left. Tell him I am awful sorry. Don't worry to much Mom. I know it's tough. But we've got it to face. You looked older Mom than you did the last time I saw you. So be brave, Mom and trust in God, which is the only man that can stop this war. I don't have to be a Christian to be talking this way. But I guess you know me. So be hopeful and look on a brighter side. Where there's life, there's hope. So I'll be seeing you. Tell all hello. Your loving son, Bob XOXO

GUARDIANS AND OTHER ANGELS 155

Sixteen

By 1942, Ohio was playing a key role in America's *Arsenal of Democracy* during World War II. Throughout the conflict, about one million of her workers produced goods for the war effort, primarily in aircraft, armaments, and shipbuilding, in large part, the war production pulling Ohio, as well as the rest of the country, out of the Great Depression. Some 23,000 among the 839,000 Ohioans who served in the armed forces gave their lives for the cause.[31]

As Bob prepared to make that ultimate sacrifice, if such should be his fate, he began what he and millions of men and women of the armed services would think of as very lonely double lives, in their letters retaining their connections to what should have been the natural courses of their lives, and if they were fortunate, would someday be again. In their workaday worlds, however, they encountered unaccountable existences in any setting other than the implausibly surreal, existences hectic with unsuspected and unsought associations, and for reasons of security and esprit de corps, remaining undivulged to outsiders, yet personally enumerated, and therefore made all too real in countless, essential details of the instruments and ingredients of warfare.

Although their agonizing displacements were made more bearable by their being simultaneously shared by millions of others, and officially endorsed by most of the rest of the world, like so many others as well, Bob's situation was made ever more thorny by his having fallen truly and unalterably in love with a girl back home. His commitment and the endorsement of his cause notwithstanding, Bob survived by clinging to the hope of one day returning home to Dot.

---

[31] http://www.answers.com/topic/ohio?cat=travel

156   LINDA LEE GREENE

Although, while in active military service, other than when the war was approaching its end, Bob was tight-lipped about his fighting experiences, his preserved letters, sent from Africa where he was involved in the fighting against the German General Rommel, as well as while serving in Europe, are replete with his observations of the people and places he encountered. The following story was a personal recounting by Bob upon his return to the states, one of those items that no doubt would not have survived the scrutiny of censors whose job it was to ensure that letters sent back home by Allied troops met all security standards which included being vague about their locations:

Bob was a person of extreme handsomeness with blond hair and blue eyes, fitting perfectly Hollywood's image of a German soldier in all of the movies made about both of the World Wars. While the "mopping up" exercises in Berlin were being put in place at the end of the war, he was there. One day as he walked the war-torn streets of Berlin, alone and with a heavy heart at all of the destruction, upon entering a commercial area comprised of formerly pristine cabarets and shops of various kinds, he spotted an ornate sign designed in accordance with an old craft guild emblem. Above the door of one of the shops, the sign hung askance from a curved wrought iron arm, its center carved in deep relief from the wood of an ash tree felled centuries before, the carvings of celery, carrots, a tomato, and a pear, the whole of it painted in rich colors, and surrounding the words **LEBENSMITTEL GAFFIN** (Gaffin's small general grocery). Taken aback by the appearance of his own surname on the sign, not a common name anywhere, as far as he knew, the matter struck him as more than coincidental. It warranted investigation.

Intent on encountering the obviously German bearer of their shared surname, he prepared to enter the lebensmittel. Suddenly, however, a middle-aged Frau burst through the door of the place, arms flailing in the air, her face shining with ecstatic happiness. "Mein liebschen, mein liebschen (My dear, my dear)," she shouted. Upon her approach, she grabbed him, and gathering my stunned Uncle Bob into her eager arms, peppered his face with copious kisses. She babbled on and on in German, a language he failed to understand, the situation rendering him dumb with incomprehension. Eventually, and with great effort, managing to extricate himself from her clutches, and aided by her hand gestures and the spattering of German words he had picked up while there, he was able to discern that she thought him to be her own son having returned from the war, and aware of the Allied occupation of his city, was disguising himself in a uniform of an American soldier. In service to his undercover status, she thought as well that he was pretending not to understand his native language.

Intrigued beyond believing, he allowed himself to be ushered by the Frau into the lebensmittel. The once showpiece quality of the market, perfectly organized and artistically arranged meats and cheeses in cases with glistening glass fronts, beaming shelves of an assortment of breads, was still in evidence despite its then half empty cases and shelves due to rationing. The Frau led Bob through a curtain of sumptuous damask spanning a doorway opening onto the back of the building, the portion serving as her apartment. There, hanging upon the wall above a miniscule fireplace was a large and elaborately framed photograph of a man, the man in the picture an exact replica of Uncle Bob, closer in appearance to my uncle than would be an identical twin, the twin in the picture, attired in a German Nazi SS uniform.

At first aghast, and then perplexed, and determined to get a closer look, he pulled the photograph from the nail on the wall where it hung. Upon closer inspection, the resemblance between Uncle Bob and the man in the picture was uncanny. Pressured by a lack of time, he was forced, although reluctantly, to immediately leave, never again having had the opportunity of seeing what he believed to be his newly discovered German relatives. He was never to meet, or to learn, whether or not the man in the photograph had survived the fighting. Thereafter, Uncle Bob, for the remainder of his life, prayed that if the German soldier in the photograph had died in the war, that it had not been his bullet that had claimed him.

October, 1942

Dear Mother,

Please pass along my congratulations to the happy couple. Its about time Ro and Lee tied the knot. I wish I could of been there. I hope to get the happy news soon that I'll be a uncle for the first time. But not to soon, I hope. I enjoyed Ro's jolly description of their Belling ceremony after the marriage services in her letter to me. I laughed at Lee's funny comment when someone asked him what they would do now. "Oh, just go pick some corn!" It sounds just like Lee. Ive come to know Lee real good over these years and he is a good fellow Mom. He'll do our family proud, you mark my words and they'll make a good marriage because they are meant for eachother just like me and Dot. Sometimes I worry that me and Dot should of got married before I left but I didn't want to saddle her with a baby maybe with me being away and not knowing what the future has in store for me. Not that I think anything bad is going to happen to me because it won't. Don't you worry about me Mom.

My training is completed for a special mission and Im now officially a soldier in the 3rd Infantry Division of this man's Army. We are called the "Rock of the Marne" a motto earned by the Division during World War I. You and Dad remember that battle at the Marne River along the road to Paris when the last great attack of the German Army took place. Flanking units had retreated but our Division Commander Major General Joseph Dickman told our French allies, "Nous Resterons La – We Shall Remain

158   LINDA LEE GREENE

Here," and it has been our motto ever since. The 3rd Division held on during that fighting and threw the enemy back across the Marne River. It made an Allied offensive possible. General "Black Jack" Pershing called the performance of the Division that day "one of the most brilliant pages in our military annals."[32]

Soon we will sail on a across the sea to some far away place to fight. Its a top secret mission and Im not permitted to tell you where Im going and what Im doing. Someday I'll tell you all about it.

I pray for you and our family everyday and I know you pray for me.

Your Loving Son Bob (llg)

Since the bombing of Pearl Harbor by Japan in December, 1941, the American public followed its country's retaliation against that aggressor primarily through radio broadcasts, newspaper stories, and newsreels in movie theaters. Although regularly reported in those media outlets, of far less concern to the common people of the United States of America was the war waging in Europe since 1939 by the theretofore unlikely alliance of Russia, China, Great Britain and other Allied nations against Germany and its Axis cohorts. While the countries of Western Europe consistently fell to Germany and its Axis partners, and by mid 1942 the Russian oil fields in the Caucasus were also tottering against a formidable German advance, President of the United States Franklin Delano Roosevelt was gravely concerned that a weakened Russia would also capitulate and be forced to sign a separate peace with Germany and thereby join the Axis surge, a course designed to conquer the whole of the world, and ultimately the resource-rich Americas.

Despite public opinion polls favoring limiting his country's involvement in the European war to the providing of aid, Roosevelt sent fighting men to the Allied effort. The entry of the United States into the European Theater of the war had its beginning with Operation Torch, an invasion intended to gain a foothold in French North Africa, a region of the continent under German control since its conquering of France early in the war. Germany's puppet regime in those areas of North Africa was known as the "Vichy French." American troops having embarked on transport ships, the landing was accomplished in November, 1942 in the cities of Oran and Algiers in Algeria, and Bob and his 3rd Army's "secret mission," Casablanca in Morocco. These were key positions whereby the Straits of Gibraltar would be sealed off by American forces, thereby denying naval access to the Mediterranean by the enemy. Possession of the Mediterranean was crucial in that it was a port of entry to the rich oil fields of Egypt. Three days of intense

---

[32] http://www.warfoto.com/3rdsociety/History.htm

GUARDIANS AND OTHER ANGELS 159

fighting resulted in the capitulation of the Vichy French, and at their surrender, they joined forces with the Americans.[33]

Christmas, 1942

Dear Mother ,
          Merry Christmas Mom and Dad and All. How I wish I could hold you in my arms now and kiss your beautiful face Mom. Please tell Dad how I miss him and wish I could be there to help with the work. If only I could be there for you during this time when Bussy's health is getting worse. Tell him to hold on and I will be home soon and then we can have our jam sessions again and go hunt us down some squirrels.
          You probably heard on the radio of our successful campaign in Morocco and Algeria. It will make all of the difference in our victory in this war. The Nazis can't hold much longer now. Im alive and well and so excited that I will be an uncle in August of next year. Please tell Ro to take care of herself and protect that little Tadpole in her belly.
Your Loving Son Bob (llg)

The 3rd Infantry Division moved east to lend support to the British forces at the Mareth Line in Tunisia, a fortified stronghold initially built by the French, but having been captured and held by German and Italian troops.[34] While Bob and his comrades in arms were waging a battle against the German General Erwin Rommel in Tunisia, back home, his brother Bussy was waging his own battle against an infection intent on taking his life.

---

[33] http://www.warfoto.com/3rdsociety/History.htm
[34] http://findarticles.com/p/articles/mi_qa3723/is_200311/ai_n9312796

160   LINDA LEE GREENE

Seventeen

A series of descriptive passages in letters spanning 1942 from Mommaw to Bob regarding the progression of Bussy's illness convey the concerns of a baffled and worried mother. She wrote:

> ...*I don't know what to think about him* [Bussy] *Bob. Dr. Ellison said the clinic Dr. would probably be at West Union about the last of this month. If they send him away* [to a clinic in Columbus specializing in diseases of the lungs] *I am going to try and help you get a furlough. Looks like they ought to let you come home to see him before he goes away...I took him uptown to get him some new clothes for he oughtn't to go to Columbus without some new clothes. He's dropped so much weight that what he's got just hangs on him and they ain't fit to be seen in no-more. The little feller could hardly drag hisself into the store. I was just going to get them for him but he wanted to go. He got two pairs of pants and two shirts, and some socks. I reckon he can do with his shoes. He'll be in bed most of the time...Honest sometimes I think he has stomach ulcers. He gets rid of about a pint of puss every night, and where on earth is all that coming from? And* [he gets rid of] *about that much during the day...We have never heard from the x-ray. But suppose we will know when we go to West Union as they are going to show it to the clinic Dr...*

On the evening of December 15, 1942, Mommaw and Bussy were sitting at the table eating their dinner when Bussy took a turn for the worse. He seemed to suffer the symptoms of a stroke, and experienced five more of the episodes shortly thereafter resulting in unrelenting and bone crushing headaches, as well as paralysis on one side of his body. As Christmas approached, a pall fell upon the Gaffin household as Mommaw and Poppaw made the decision to move Bussy into town to be nearer his doctor.

GUARDIANS AND OTHER ANGELS 161

Mommaw's sister Cora opened her home in Peebles to Mommaw and Bussy, and a busy schedule of nursing him through his bouts of high fevers, chest and head pain, and coughing up of puss and blood ensued. Nothing had ever come of the idea of sending him to the clinic in Columbus as the doctor of the clinic in West Union advised my grandparents that nothing more could be done for Bussy.

As the days passed of the holiday season of 1942, Bussy Gaffin was still confined to his bed at the home of his Aunt Cora. His valiant eight year battle with lung disease had shaped his once robust body into a concave web of skin over bones, his sharp collarbones drawn forward, his shoulders hunched as if in a protective embrace of his crushingly painful chest. Shallow, fetid breath, tainted by the raging infection in his lungs, whistled through teeth bared by his drawn lips, drawn in perpetual grimaces of unrelieved pain, his eyes hollow as if his soul had already absented his worn-out body.

Her worries over the rapid decline in Bussy's condition since the onslaught of winter, and the safety of Bob, as well as her concerns over the lasting quality of the marriage between Roma and Lee, had shrunk Mommaw to a rack of skin and bones, and in that regard, she resembled Bussy. Having placed a chair next to his bed, she sat day after day, hour after hour with Bussy, taking her scant meals in his room: crumbled cornbread in a glass of milk, a piece of "Light Bread" smeared with raspberry preserves, a cup of coffee. Bussy had given up solid food, his only nourishment a glass of diluted milk now and then, or a dish of vanilla pudding.

Visitors had come calling on Mommaw and Bussy that morning, the Reverend Harley Ward and his wife Edna, an uncle and aunt of Lee Greene's. They had heard of the sudden decline in Bussy's health. To escape the glacial winters of their Midwest home, for several years they had wintered in Arizona. Their mission that day had been to offer to take Mommaw and Bussy with them on their drive to the Southwest, their departure planned for two days hence, the hope being that the warmer, drier climate would be helpful to Bussy.

Fitfully, Bussy had slept through most of the morning, and when he woke, his eyes fell upon the expectant face of Mommaw. "Ye look like the cat that swallered the canary, Mom," with difficulty Bussy whispered. Speaking had become problematical for him, it hurt his esophagus, and it took almost more effort than he could muster.

"Edna and Harley Ward come by this mornin'. Ye know how they go ta Arizona ever' winter? Well, they want me 'n you ta go with 'em this time. The weather there'll be good fer ye. It'll mean leavin' in two days." Mommaw studied the face of her son hopefully.

"Not be home fer Christmas, Mom?" Bussy asked, his tortured face a mask of concern.

162   LINDA LEE GREENE

"Can't be helped, Son, if that's what we decide ta do." She reached out her hand and took his in her own, the gesture her plea to him to agree to taking the trip.

Bussy turned his face away from his mother, his mind projecting into the future. Knowing it to be his last Christmas, he wanted to be with his entire family, his parents, his many siblings. Anyway, Bussy knew that no trip to anywhere then would save him. Turning his face back to his mother, he swept his eyes lovingly over her strained face, the face he had most loved since the day he was born. For a brief moment, he regretted that love—regretted that it would be the only great love he would ever know—regretted that he would never know what she felt—the love of a parent for ones child, of a spouse for ones life partner. Squeezing her hand, he whispered finally, "Maybe next winter, Mom, when I'm feelin' a little better. I don't think I'm up fer that kind o' travelin' right now."

Lee Greene had taken a job as a general laborer at Wright Patterson Field in Dayton, Ohio, the home of the Enola Gay, the airplane that would drop the atomic bomb on Japan in 1945, the action that would bring the beginning of the end to the war. However, in those early days of the war, in service to the effort, as with other airports across the land, Ohioans were scrambling to beef up Wright Patterson Field, building new runways, office buildings, and new housing for the workers. For the first time in her life venturing beyond the borders of Adams County, Roma joined her groom there, the first home of the couple in a streetcar having been converted into a tiny apartment. It was located in Xenia near Dayton. It would remain the favorite home of my mother until the day of her death.

During the first decade and a half of the marriage of my parents, every weekend and every holiday, as well as the largest part of every summer for me and my brother David meant, "going down home to the farm." That routine continued unwaveringly until the summer of 1953 when I turned ten years of age. That was the summer my mother was big with child for my sister Sherri. David and I stayed home that summer, and every summer thereafter. The Christmas of 1942, however, found Lee and Roma at home on the farm, Roma spending most of her days helping Mommaw care for Bussy at the home of Aunt Cora.

"You should see my little apartment, Bus. It's all done up with real nice furniture put in it by our landlord, an' there's the purtiest little white curtains on the windas," excitedly Roma said to her brother Bussy. He was lying in his bed, propped up with pillows at his back against the headboard. His emaciated body beneath a bleached muslin sheet was a landscape of reedy white sticks and slight rises. In readying him for their Christmas Eve celebration, Roma had given him a washpan bath, and had just finished combing his hair.

GUARDIANS AND OTHER ANGELS 163

"I wish I could see it, Ro," Bussy whispered, his voice labored and thin. The bath had worn him out, as life was wearing him out—he just wanted to go to sleep.

"Soon as it warms up some, an' yer on yer feet agin, we'll come an' git you an' you can stay with us fer awhile," Roma replied. Efficiently, she bent over her brother and tucked his sheet around his hips. "Yer lookin' peeked like yer wantin' ta go ta sleep for awhile. You want me ta scoot you down some so you kin sleep, Bus?"

"In a minute, Ro. First I want ta listen ta that little Tadpole in yer belly."

"You can't hear nothin' yet, Bus. It ain't no bigger 'n the end o' yer finger. It won't start movin' an' makin' noise fer a coupla months, prob'ly."

Aware that he wouldn't be around in two months, Bussy replied to his sister, "I don't care. I want ta listen ta it now."

Roma helped Bussy scoot over to the edge of the bed, and she positioned her abdomen next to his ear. Wrapping her arms around the head of her beloved brother, she stroked his hair and held him against her body while he listened. "Yer right. All I hear is yer stomach gurglin'. That little Tadpole in there is goin' ta take my place," Bussy said as he pulled away. Roma helped him lie deep in the bed, pulling the sheet up over his bony shoulders. His skin was hot with fever, and clammy again with his perspiration. Bussy was instantly asleep. Standing over him, Roma placed both of her palms on her abdomen, rivers of tears streaking her cheeks as she turned to exit the bedroom of her brother.

Saturday, January 2, 1943 brought more visitors. Poppaw with Dale and Dean arrived, the two youngest children of the family hovering uneasily in the room of their older brother. With labored breath Bussy said, "I got somethin' fer you, Deany. I bin savin' it fer yer seventh birthday but I 'spect I'll give it to you now. It's over hyere under my pillah. Come over hyere an' you kin git it." The little boy approached the bed apprehensively, his hand snaking beneath the pillow. "You got it, Deany?"

"It's just a old tobaccer pouch, Bus. What's in it?"

"Open it up, Deany."

Dean pulled open the strings of the pouch and looked inside. "It's pennies, Bus. How many you got in there?"

"Jist thirty, I think," Bussy replied. "You better put 'em in yer pocket so you won't lose 'em."

Dean put the bag of pennies in his pocket, his hand brushing against his new pocket knife. He pulled it out and held it in his hand.

"What you got there, Deany?" Bussy inquired.

"Oh jist a old pocket knife I got fer Christmas," Dean replied. He pulled the blade out of its housing to show it to Bussy and stuck it between the frame and springs of the bed to straighten it. Suddenly the tip of the blade snapped off.

164   LINDA LEE GREENE

"You best be careful 'o that knife, Deany 'er yer'll put yer eye out with it like Re done when she was little," Bussy instructed Dean.

Nine-year-old Dale, who hovered apprehensively at the threshold of the door of the room spoke up in his man-sized voice. "Don't worry none, Bus. I'll look out fer Deany."

"Daley, come on over hyere to the bed, kin you, Son?" Bussy asked weaklly.

"I reckon," Dale replied. His quivering chin tucked into his neck, the boy slowly sauntered to the bedside of his brother.

"I guess yer big enough ta take care 'o my map fer me, Daley. Bette 'n Dick'll look after my chickens an' roosters an' hogs, but yer the only one ta take care 'o my map. Kin you do it fer me, Daley?"

"I reckon, Bus," the boy replied, his hand jumping to his eyes to brush away his tears.

"You got ta listen ta the radio ever night an' read Bob's letters real good. Then yer'll know where ta draw the line on the map ta show where Bob is. Mommy kin help you if you need it."

"I reckon I kin do it, Bus," Dale said.

"I reckon you kin too, Daley," Bussy said, his scratchy voice weak with fatigue. "I reckon I'll go ta sleep now. I'll see you sometime, Brothers."

Peebles, Ohio   Jan. 10, 1943

Dear Son:

It is with a sad and aching heart [but] *I am going to write to you. I have studied and thought what is best to do. But this is the only way I can see. Son, poor little Bussy left us on Jan. 5 at Cora's house. I am so lonesome & nervous. I was constantly by his side for 3 weeks. He passed away just 3 weeks from the day he took bad. He & I was sitting at the table eating our dinner on Dec. 15, when I just happened to look at him & seen something was wrong with him. His face & head was jerking awful. I ran around to him & asked what was wrong. He coulden't talk. It only lasted a short time. When he got over it he said, "Oh Mom. It is just this old disease getting the best of me." We had the Dr. He* [the doctor] *said he could do nothing. He* [Bussy] *had 5 of those spells then took an awful headache. We took him to the hospital. They said there was a clot on his brain. It was on the right side but made his left arm & leg useless. He woulden't stay in the hospital. I took him to Cora's as they told me it would be allright since they could do nothing. Said all I could do was keep his head packed in Ice, rest & quiet. We were at Cora's a week, and the last few days he seemed so much better. I thought he was going to get well, and could soon take him home, as I wrote and told you. Don't know if you ever got the letter or not. But the suffering I guess was to much for his heart & then you know what a condition he was in any way. Son, he took it all so patient. Just prayed all the time almost. He wanted Herman* [Tolle, the preacher]. *He told him he*

GUARDIANS AND OTHER ANGELS 165

was ready to go. Oh son how he prayed for all you boys. It would wring your heart. The last words I heard him say was, "Tell them all to meet me." His mind was so on Sim [Workman, their friend who was also in the Army fighting in North Africa] *somehow. Said "Mommy, I feel sorry for Sim. He diden't have a Mother to tell him about Jesus like I have." Although you know Sim has a good mother. He* [Bussy] *would put his arms around me and say "I love you Mommy." I don't know whether I can ever stand this or not, but Son, put your trust in Jesus. Ask him every day to take care of you. Bussy would say "Mommy, don't worry about Bob. He is coming back." But the Lord can cut us all off any time. So don't forget to pray if it is only to yourself. Poor little Bussy is in a better home but I miss him so. He was always here with me. I can never stay here alone anymore. Well Son I can't write more but can only say put your trust in God and we will all be living on for happier days some where. Answer if you can.   With so much love, Mother.*
P.S.   This is Mon. morning. I forgot to say the rest of us is well. Son, I hope you are well. Try and not to grieve to much only live to meet Bussy. I feel a little better this morn(ing). Some think I shoulden't of let you know. But I coulden't of lived a lie & write to you like everything was allright, and then probably some one else would of said something about it when they would write to you. All we can say is Gods will must be done. By by. XOXOX

February 5, 1943
Dear Mother and Dad,
Your letter about Bussy's passing only reached me today. It was dated Jan. 10 and you told me he died on Jan. 5. All this time he's been gone and I didn't know it. The mail is so slow to get here overseas. My chest is so tight with awful emotion and my hand is trembling so hard with my grief I can hardly write. Oh Mom and Dad what will we do without our Bussy?
He was my beloved brother but also my best friend. I'll never have another like him. Now I'll never meet and get to know the girl he would have married or hold the children he should have had in my arms.
Mom and Dad I don't have the words to say how sorry I am for the loss of your beloved child. Our only consolation is that his suffering is over now and he's in a better place. How I wish I could wrap my arms around you this very minute. Don't worry about me because I can take care of myself and we'll all be with eachother someday.
Your beloved son Bob (llg)

In 1889, Paul Vuillemin, a student of Louis Pasteur's, coined the word *antibiosis*, by combining Gr. anti, "against"; bios, "life," the new word meaning a process by which life can be used to destroy life. *Antibiotic, a*

166   LINDA LEE GREENE

derivative of *antibiosis*, is a chemical substance produced by one organism that is destructive to another. With the growing acceptance of the germ theory of disease whereby bacteria and other microbes were deemed to be the causation of a variety of ailments, scientists in the late 1800's began to search for agents that would kill the disease-causing bacteria.

Sir Alexander Fleming, a Scottish physician, and later to become a Nobel Prize winner in Physiology and Medicine, early in his medical career, became interested in the natural bacterial action of the blood and in antiseptics, continuing his studies while serving throughout World War I as a captain in the Army Medical Corps, and later while a professor at St. Mary's Medical School in London, England. Although originally noted by a French medical student, Ernest Duchesne in 1896, it was in 1928 while at St. Mary's and working on influenza virus that Fleming rediscovered penicillin. He observed that a blue-green mould had developed accidentally on a staphylococcus culture plate, and that the mould had created a bacteria-free circle around itself. Further experiments by him resulted in his discovery of an active substance he named penicillin,[35] after the Penicillium mould.

The importance of the discovery by Fleming was not understood until 1939 when Dr. Howard Florey, also a future Nobel laureate, and three colleagues at Oxford University began intensive research resulting in demonstrating the ability of penicillin to kill infectious bacteria. As the war with Germany drained the resources of Great Britain, the scientists turned to the Peoria Lab in the United States for help. Florey and his colleague, Norman Heatley, on July 9, 1941 arrived in the United States carrying a very valuable package: a tiny supply of penicillin. The target was to grow large quantities of the powdery substance as quickly as possible, and after many elaborate methods were tested, ironically it was from a mouldy cantaloupe in a Peoria, Illinois market that led to the production of the largest amount of penicillin.

By November 18, 1941 the scientists had increased the yield of the penicillin to ten times the amount initially carried into Peoria Lab. In 1943, penicillin was shown to be the most effective antibacterial agent to date, and the required clinical trials were underway. And although it was available for the Allied soldiers wounded on June 6, 1944, D-Day,[36] it came too late for Bussy Gaffin, who died shortly after the clinical trials for the drug had begun. It is believed it would have saved his life.

The day following Bussy's funeral as Roma was stripping his bed and turning the mattress, she found an envelope tucked between the mattress and bed springs. Across the face of the envelope in Bussy's nearly illegible hand

---

[35] http://nobelprize.org/nobel_prizes/medicine/laureates/1945/fleming-bio.html

[36] http://inventors.about.com/od/pstartinventions/a/Penicillin.htm?p=1

was written the word "Tadpole." Roma opened it. Bussy had placed a five-dollar bill inside of it. That "Tadpole" was me.

Eighteen

I found a drawing I did of my mother when I was ten –
She would have been thirty then –
It was a nude.
She was lying on her side,
Her head supported by her hand,
And wavey strands of her hair cascaded her shoulders, covering one eye.
She was long and slender with a waist so small as to cause her hip to rise
like a gentle mountain,
And she was white all over except for the color of her hair and the matching
triangle of color where her legs came together and covered the home I knew
before I was born.
Her breasts were small and round and far apart –
A space wide between where I laid my head before I was weaned.
I found this drawing just the other day, as I was packing and sorting to go
away,
And I wondered what model I'd used for this nude –
I'd never seen my mother that way before that day –
And although the caption read "Roma Greene," I soon knew,
The woman in the picture was really me, as I saw myself to be someday –
And I was only ten, then –
Linda Lee Greene

I was born with many weaknesses, believe me, physically and otherwise, but by way of compensation, I suppose, I am blessed with the ability to write a sentence or two, with an eye that shoots photographs that speak to you, that paints pictures people want to hang on their walls, that recognizes just the perfect elements to gather together for a beautiful and well-functioning physical environment. By the age of eight, I was the official letter writer for

GUARDIANS AND OTHER ANGELS 169

my family, was rearranging all of the furniture in the homes of everybody who would permit it, was drawing like a champ, and in my perpetually grubby little hands, was the Brownie camera owned by my parents, black and white film rolled up inside of it.

Dispersed among the many members of my family, in drawers and boxes and photo albums, are copious black and white photographs taken by me mainly during the decade of the 1950's. There are photos of Mommaw and Poppaw, all of my aunts and uncles, my early cousins, my parents and my siblings. As is common among firstborn children, as I am, and as is revealed in the poem at the opening of this chapter, written by me when I was her age in the sketch, to a great extent, I identified with my mother. I especially loved taking photographs of her. There are two of my mother that often come to mind when I think of her, taken during a huge snowstorm one winter very early in the decade. In the one, she is sitting in a chair on the back porch of our old Victorian house on West Second Avenue in Columbus, Ohio. Her legs are crossed, and she is wearing her new full-length fur coat. I don't remember the type of its fur; it wasn't a mink, I assure you, but it was as dark, and seemed to me at the time, as well as to her, to be as luxurious as a mink. The coloration of the coat was spectacular against her deep red hair and her milky skin. I had her place her hands beneath the collar of the coat, and then raise it to hug it high around her jaws. I shot the photograph, the deep white snow in the foreground, and the backdrop of the white house, framing perfectly the high contrast of the black and white image of my mother in its center.

In the second photograph, she is standing on the same back porch, her body framed by the pillars and roof of the porch. She is leaning against one of the pillars. She is wearing trousers, and a sweater, the white of her brassiere showing through the loose weave of the garment. I got down low and beneath her at an appropriate distance, and shot up, the effect elongating even more her already long and slender body.

If the movie director John Ford had ever seen my mother when she was a young woman, he would have scooped her up for his films in a second. A statuesque redhead with a deep and glossy wave over one of her slanted, gray eyes, her "Chinky eyes," she called them, and cheekbones you could ski off of, she took your breath away. And her name was Roma—Roma, no less. My God, what a name! It was the name Mommaw found in a book when she was pregnant for her, and even though there wasn't a drop of Italian blood in her, she did justice to that name. But to Poppaw, she was Maimal. Nobody ever knew where that one came from, or its meaning, but you could tell it was something special by the tender sound of his voice and the gentle look in his eyes when he said it. It was his affectionate name for all of his daughters and granddaughters and great-granddaughters, up to a certain age, but until the day he died, Roma was his only enduring Maimal, and she was a woman with grandchildren by then.

Roma was *his* daughter. It seems to happen in every family, that out-of-the-ordinary rapport between two individuals, existent between parent and child, or between siblings, or cousins—any combination, really. Poppaw and Roma championed each other, and in that way, protected each other—from Mommaw, who was hard on the two of them in a way she was hard on nobody else. In fact, while Roma felt that Mommaw withheld her love and approval from her, she spoiled the rest of her children, and made no bones about the fact that she preferred her boys to her girls. Reva, outrageous and seeming to have been dropped in their midst from a spaceship from an alien planet, and Bette, with needs far beyond the scope and resources of her unsophisticated and poor parents, were always too much for Mommaw, and as a result were left to their own devices most of the time. But Mommaw never left Roma alone. She demanded things of her firstborn daughter, expected things of her she didn't expect of her other children. It wasn't that Roma resented her extra responsibilities; she rather enjoyed them, really. She loved her family. Family was everything to her. She understood that as the eldest female, her mother was forced to depend on her in ways she didn't her other children. It was that Mommaw expressed herself in such a perfunctory manner to Roma that it came across as unappreciative, and although, in the end, Roma benefited from all of those higher expectations, I don't think she ever quite forgave Mommaw for her failure in showing the tenderness to Roma that she needed so badly.

Not only were both of my parents knockouts in the looks department, they each were blessed with that divine sweet madness in the head that rendered life with them unfailingly interesting, and the following are delightful cases in point:

One of the most enchanting features of the farm was its peach and apple orchard. Roma, who at the time was a teenager, completely disregarding the fact that green apples gave her the "runs," and convincing herself that she would get away with it that time I suppose, in a fit of gluttony, set about one hot summer morning to stuff her belly full of the sweet green teasers. Predictably, later in the day, she found herself in dire need of visiting the "path" as this family called their outhouse, whereupon she sat, for long intervals of time, for several visits in a row. This was back in the time before fluffy white "Charmin" or any other machine-perforated roll-perfectly-into-your-hand toilet paper came on the scene; these were the days of pages from magazines, newspapers; the Sears & Roebuck catalog was an especial favorite. And when paper products ran out, corncobs would do. This particular day, Sears & Roebuck were on duty, and Roma, having gone through a good portion of the catalog, pulled up her underwear, and confident her ordeal was finally behind her, pun intended, proceeded to walk to the back door of the house, the door opening onto the kitchen. She lighted into her piled-up kitchen chores, working away uninterrupted for an hour or

GUARDIANS AND OTHER ANGELS 171

more, enjoying that peculiar euphoria that comes to one with the release of all of the toxins in ones body.

At length, she realized that the house was unusually quiet, a phenomenon never occurring in that filled-to-human-capacity household. Taking a mere glancing note of it, she continued to sweep away, when out of the distance she thought she heard what sounded like a snicker. She hesitated for a moment, listened, but when all was quiet again, she fell back into the rhythm of her swishing broom. But suddenly, there it was again—a snicker, then two, then three. She realized she had company in the room. She turned to look, and there they all were, all nine members of her family, snickering and pointing at her backside. Horrified, she realized what was the matter, and twisting her head to get a gander at her backside, like a dog chasing its own tail, Roma took off spinning around and around in the middle of the kitchen, howling like a dog, and flapping her hand at the offending article protruding from her underwear. In her haste to vacate the outhouse, the tail of her dress had caught in the waistband of her bloomers, and with it, the Sears & Roebuck page also had fastened itself there, the page waving like a flag flapping in the breeze, and ironically hailing its colorful advertisement of a supply of women's under panties.

Another delightful feature of the farm was the tin roof on the farmhouse. I hail from a family of drinkers—coffee that is, and no bladder, no matter how healthy, could make it through the night without emptying itself of the copious cups of coffee consumed by that family in the course of a day and an evening. As the children grew older and married, and had their own children, still, we all returned to the farm each weekend. It was like a family reunion every Saturday and Sunday. The second floor of the farmhouse had two bedrooms, one small room at the head of the stairs containing one full-size bed, and through a connecting door, was another room, long and wide and stuffed to capacity with more full-size beds lining its sides in dormitory fashion. Through a hole cut into the floor, the pipe from the wood-burning stove in the front room below, like a lone pillar at the end of the room, extended up the full height of the room, and terminated to the outside through another hole in the tin roof.

Almost as if we had ordered it for our own pleasure, it rained nearly every Saturday night, it seemed. The females in attendance, the wives of Bob and Dick and Dale and Dean: Louise, Betty, Patty and Nellie, respectively, my cousin, Rosie, my mother and me, were typically assigned the dormitory room. Aunt Re and Aunt Bette, and their families, seemed never to make it back to the farm in those days. The men slept in other places all over the house: the full-size bed in the adjoining room, the full-size bed in the downstairs guest room, the davenport, the lounge chairs, the floor, wherever there was a flat and level surface. My aunts and cousin Rosie, as well as my mother and I would lie in bed and gossip and giggle, but silence would ensue when the rain came, that unequalled sound of the patter of the rain on the tin roof lolling us to sleep.

Predictably, at about midnight, the coffee made its presence known in every bladder in the house, the men stumbling to the backyard, and lining up in a row, watered the grass right along with the rain. If the weather wasn't so cold "it would freeze the tits off of a boar hog," my brother and our male cousins, usually slept in the hayloft out in the barn, therefore we failed to be privy to their bladder relieving routine. In conditions of hearty rain or snow, the walk to the outhouse for the females was the equivalent of Stephen King's "Green Mile," so we opted for the front porch instead. Following Mom, who was the oldest, as well as the ringleader in everything we did, like ducklings falling in behind their mother, we all repaired to the front porch: Louise, Betty, Patty, Nellie, Rosie, Roma, and I, all seven of us, one after the other. Our nighties pulled up around our waists, legs spread just precisely, feet planted at just the right angle for perfect balance, as well as to ensure the splash didn't soil our legs and bare feet, we squatted, and let loose. "Psssss – psssss – psssss – psssss – psssss – psssss – psssss," the pee flowed in seven rivers across the pitched width of the porch. Manufactured toilet paper had found its way into use at the farmhouse by then, and Mom, who had remembered to snatch up a roll on our trek to our destination, at the finish, passed the roll down the line. Wiping accomplished, thumbs and index fingers pinching the barest top fibers of our soiled wads of tissues, the white flags of tissues dangling from our outstretched hands like diapers hanging from a clothesline, again, we fell in behind Mom as we made our way back through the door and to the kitchen, where we delicately tossed our tissues in the trashcan. To the pump to wash our hands, still in formation behind Mom, we then followed her single file up the stairs, and back to bed. In some ways, those days were the happiest of my life. Never again have I found that kind of closeness and utter acceptance.

The walk to the outhouse on the Gaffin farm paled by comparison to the one at the log cabin on the Greene's place, as it was across the gravel road from the cabin, and down a steep hill. The pee was trickling down your leg by the time you got there. Talk about a long walk fraught with fright—you cannot begin to imagine. It was dark out there—spooky dark—the blackest black darknes—the kind of darkness whereby if you held up your hand to within an inch of the end of your nose, you **COULD NOT** see your hand. It was the kind of darkness your eyes **NEVER** adjusted to. And you **NEVER,** I mean, **NEVER** went to the outhouse alone. It was so dark, and you were so terrified you couldn't talk because you had swallowed your voice, so the only way you knew you weren't alone was by listening to the breathing of your fellow trekker to the outhouse.

My brother and I split our weekends and summers between the farm and the log cabin, our time at the log cabin being especially fun for us since the two youngest siblings of my father were very close to our own ages.

GUARDIANS AND OTHER ANGELS 173

Mary and Kenny, the youngest sister and the youngest brother of Dad are only six days and two years my senior, respectively. Our hot and sticky summer evenings before bed were spent out on the front porch listening to ghost stories and "token messages" as related to us by our paternal grandmother Eva Love. Every animal cry in the night was a token message of an impending disaster or death, or a ghost coming to get us. To bed we would go, literally shaking with terror, and I would crawl under one of the scratchy wool Army blankets, pulling it up tightly over my head. And I would sweat and quake with fear all night long under that blanket, and you can bet your bottom dollar, I held my pee until the following morning.

Mom and Dad retired in 1987, she from her job as a cook for the Southwestern City Schools, a suburban school district bordering Columbus, he from the Anheuser Busch Brewing Company where he had alternated between working as a brew-master and a maintenance worker. Until his death on March 29, 2014, the pension Dad received from his long tenure at Anheuser Busch provided him with a very nice retirement.

Within a week of Dad's retirement ceremony, they had moved to their little lakeside cottage in Hawthorne, Florida, a lifelong dream finally come true, a dream they had toiled and scrimped and saved for all of their married life. The couple had done quite well for themselves considering that Dad had only received an eighth grade education, and that when they first left the farm and moved to the city, neither of them knew how to operate a telephone.

Leaving behind their suburban home outside of Columbus, a home they, and Mom and Dad's brothers, had built with their own hands, they generously signed over the house to me and my two sisters Sherri and Susan. And they never looked back. They transformed their North Central Florida cottage into a tropical paradise. Roma flower gardened, painted, decorated, swept, shined, shopped, cooked; Lee vegetable gardened, cut, cleared, dug, scraped, hauled, each of them loving every minute of the freedom neither of them, ever in their lives, had had a minute of for themselves. My parents were workers, the kind of guests who pitched in while they were visiting. Two weeks before her cancer was discovered, racked with pain in her back brought on by the tumor, she spent a week with my sister Susan, helping her clean up and move into her new home in Crystal Beach, Florida. Mom worked like a man; she was groomed for it—honed to it—hardened by it from picking and hanging tobacco; harvesting and shucking corn; cutting and pitching and bailing hay in the fields of her girlhood home on the farm— by milking and feeding and watering, birthing and tending its livestock—by nailing, sawing, painting, cleaning, sweeping its house, its out buildings—by washing, ironing, sewing, mending, and cooking for its people. And she went toe-to-toe with Lee when they were building their house in Grove City near Columbus, an intended pun considering the following story:

174   LINDA LEE GREENE

Having grown up going barefoot on the farm, wearing shoes, to Mom, was antithetical to her nature. Although the soles and heels of her feet were hardened almost to leather, and her toenails were so tough they were lethal weapons, she was always injuring her feet: stepping on thorns, stubbing toes, ripping toenails, developing corns and bunions and spurs, ingrown toenails, hang nails. She waged a constant battle with her feet. But still, the stubborn Roma refused to wear shoes. On the construction site of their house, she stepped on nails and screws, punctured her skin with wood splinters, dropped boards and tools on her unprotected feet, but still, the stubborn Roma refused to wear shoes. Her bare feet were the source of a constant and raging battle between her and Lee. My father would get so frustrated with her that he would just raise his hands in total amazement and dismay. But still, my mother refused to wear shoes.

"Oh, Roma. Why don't you jist put on some shoes?" Dad would lament each time she injured a foot or a toe. And then he would walk away, shaking his head and cursing under his breath. But still, she refused to wear shoes.

Spread eagle across the peak of the rooftop of the house they were building, her set-aside shoes, as usual, thrown to the ground below, bare feet shining in the bright summer sun, Mom worked merrily away nailing shingle to rooftop, shingle to rooftop, one on top of the other, row after row after row, when down below at ground level where Lee was installing a window, he   heard   her   loud,   sustained,   blood   curdling   scream, **"LEEEEEEEEEEEEEEEEEEEEEEEEEE!!! OH MY GOD—HELP ME!!!!!!!! LEEEEEEEEEEEEEEEEEEEEEEEEEE!!!** Up the ladder he flew in a flash, and there he found her, slumped forward, weeping and in excruciating pain, both hands bloody from cradling her spurting foot. She had nailed her big toe to the plywood decking of the roof, hitting it with her heavy roofing hammer built to drive the nail home with one powerful whack. Between her wails, Lee begged her once more, "Roma honey, why don't you jist put on some shoes when yer doin' this kind o' work?" But still, the stubborn Roma refused to wear shoes, and barefoot and bandaged toe, she worked toe-to-toe with Lee again, as soon as she was able.

The matter of where to place the kitchen in their new home was also a bone of contention between Roma and Lee. Since the house sat on a sloping lot, the back wall of the basement opening onto the back yard, and departing entirely from the original floor plan, as well as adjustments in the budget any revisions would require, Mom decided she wanted the kitchen placed in the basement rather than on the first floor. She wanted the luxury of walking out onto her back patio and spacious back yard from her kitchen whenever she darn well pleased without having to descend the stairs in order to do so. It didn't matter to her that the dining room, livingroom, and the only bathroom in the place at the time, were on the first floor. The stubborn Roma wanted her kitchen to be in the basement. After going around and

GUARDIANS AND OTHER ANGELS   175

around about it, Lee finally capitulated, as he always had to do to have peace in the family, and he put her kitchen in the basement. Years later, racked with pain from chronic arthritis in her knees caused by the dampness and the hardness of the concrete floor of the basement, and I imagine, by descending those stairs a hundred or more times a day, she saw the light. She had Dad install a new kitchen on the main level of the house in the exact spot designated for it on the original floor plan.

As soon as Dad had completed building her original kitchen in the basement, the following little argument between them ensued: "I jist never did understand why the hot water spigot is on the left an' the cold is on the right. It jist is ridiculous ta me because if yer holdin' a big old heavy pot in her right hand, which most people is right handed, right?....then it appears ta me the cold water ought a be on the left so you kin turn it on with yer left hand when you want ta fill the pot up, right?" Mom would point out to Dad. Dad would just sigh because he knew what was coming. And on and on she reasoned, day after day, week after week.

"Okay, okay!" Dad retorted finally, again throwing up his hands in defeat. "I'll change the dern pipes so you kin have yer cold water spigot on the left. This was back in the days of galvanized and copper pipes and blowtorches and threading tools and heavy pipe wrenches—there was no such thing as easy-to-install PVC plumbing pipes back then. He took weeks between his heavy working schedule at the brewery to make the change, then sat back, patiently waiting for her to eat her words. It didn't take long. She just needed to scald her hands, and have the hands of her children scalded a few times, to realize her mistake. But Dad just left it that way—we never had proper plumbing in that house until he built the new kitchen on the first floor.

One day, my parents came to help me tear out an old bathroom in the basement of the house I had just purchased. Our plan was to carry all of it out to the back alley to be picked up by the trash collectors. As soon as Mom spied the toilet, an antique of an interesting configuration, I knew what she had on her mind. Half jokingly, but knowing my mother as I did, it also was a warning, and I said to her, "Now, Mom, next time I come to your house, I don't want to see that toilet in your back yard with petunias billowing out of it." The following week when I went for a visit, there it was, big as you please, the antique toilet positioned in a place of honor at the edge of the patio floor, and planted in flowing purple petunias.

Two weeks before Mom died, my daughter Elizabeth and I drove to Florida to see her. My sisters Sherri and Susan were there, as well, as were my brother David and his wife Dorothy. Mom had been ill for more than six months, having gone through the whole chemo- and radiation-therapy routine. There was nothing else to do, but she was holding on far beyond the time she should have gone. And she was suffering so. As soon as I got there, Mom got me busy rearranging things for her in her bedroom. The clutter was making her nervous, she told me. She wanted me to box up things and put them away. And of course, I did. One day, she called me over to her bed, and she said to me, "Linnie, I can't leave yer daddy. What will he do without me?" I knew right then that she was holding on for him. I left the room, and went to my brother and his wife. I told them what Mom had said to me. "We have to make some decisions about Dad's future. She won't allow herself to go until she is satisfied about his living situation after she is gone," I said to them. David and Dorothy made the decision to move in with Dad right then and there, and they were with him until the day of his death, twenty-two years later. "I don't have the courage to tell her she can go, David," I said to my brother.

"I'll do it, Lin," David said to me, rubbing my hand as I cried. He stood up from the sofa, and walked to the bedroom of our mother. He kneeled down on the floor next to Mom's bed, and taking her hand into his, he told her of their plans, and that it was all right for her to go now. It was the bravest thing I have ever seen anybody do. She died only a few days later.

When Mom died, Mommaw was in a nursing home. Mommaw was eighty-nine at the time, having had a stroke that had left her rapidly descending into dementia. She had already lost four of the children she and Poppaw had brought into the world: Dorothy, Bussy, Bette and Reva. By the time of the death of my mother, the mental faculties of Mommaw were already so compromised that she was unaware that Mom had been ill, and we didn't tell her in the event she might understand and the strain of it would be too much for her. Mommaw no longer recognized any of us other than her youngest son Dean, and his wife Nellie, and even then, not always. Having received word of the passing of my mother, Dean drove to the nursing home that morning to be with Mommaw, not to tell her of the death of her firstborn girl, but just to be there with her.

At the funeral a few days later, Dean pulled me aside, an astonished look on his face. "Lin, I have somethin' ta tell you. It's the derndest thing," Uncle Dean said to me. "I drove ta the nursing home ta be with Mom after you called me about Ro. When I walked in, Mom recognized me fer the first time in a long time. And she said ta me, 'I seen Ro this mornin', Deany. She was sittin' right there on the side of my bed, big as ye please, aswingin' her legs an' alaughin' jist like Ro does.'"

In Hawthorne, Florida, late the night before, a few moments after her loving and beloved caretaker Dorothy, the wife of my brother, had given her a dose of morphine to ease her pain, Mom said to Dorothy, "I jist want ta go ta sleep so bad, Dorothy."

"Well, Maah," Dorothy replied in her Texas drawl, "why don't you just go ahead and do that."

My mother closed her eyes and peacefully slipped away, the bedroom lamp flickering, and the grandfather clock stopping, marking the

GUARDIANS AND OTHER ANGELS 177

exact time Mom died. The clock is still set to that time. That just goes to show how strong and willful and stubborn that redheaded powerhouse of a woman was. When she left, she knocked out the electricity, for a moment or two. When Uncle Dean told me what Mommaw had said to him, I wasn't surprised by his words. For many months, Mom had been deeply concerned about the welfare of her mother in the nursing home, and her inability to be with her mother on a regular basis. That Mom's spirit sailed to her mother first thing upon shedding its cumbersome and useless body was just the kind of thing my mother would do.

Mom came visiting me the morning following her death, right after she had satisfied herself that Mommaw was all right, according to the timing I have been able to put together. She came to me in the form of an angel at my window. I had moved into my new home in Columbus the day before, the morning of the evening my mother had died. My east-facing front door received the morning sun, and its being June 29th, 1992, the sun had been bright all that week. The door was pierced with a small, frosted glass window with a design etched into it, the etched lines clear, and if someone wanted to look in, the clear lines made it possible. I had received the call about the death of my mother sometime around midnight, if I remember correctly, resulting in my being up the rest of the night. Of course, I was unable to sleep after that. In addition, I had many calls to make.

I became paranoid about the exposed window in my door, and went searching for a piece of fabric I could temporarily put over it. Among my vast collection of fabrics, I found a blue one in an abstract design, and as it was too large for the opening, I folded it a couple of times, and taped it over the window. The following morning, the bright sunshine streamed through the window in my door, and there within the fabric, as a result of the way it was folded against the etched lines in the glass, was formed the perfect outline of an angel. Instantly, I recognized it to be my mother. I left it there for several months, and during those months, every sunny morning my angel-mother came to me.

My sister-in-law Dorothy, who still lives at the lakeside compound in Hawthorne, insists that Mom haunts the place. There is a particular glass jar having been used by Mom as a storage container for dried beans that gets moved around mysteriously. Since the death of my mother, Dorothy has continued to use the jar for the same purpose. However, whenever Dorothy moves the jar to any place other than that designated for it by my mother when she was mistress of the lakeside cottage of my parents, it gets moved right back to its original setting. The men swear upon pain of death that they never have touched the bean jar, and we believe them.

It is the same way with a little trinket given to my sister Susan by Mom. It is a penguin crumb eater, and when Mom gave it to Susan, Mom decided it looked best at a certain position on a particular shelf on the corner cabinet in the kitchen of my sister. As with the bean jar, if it gets placed anywhere other than that exact place on that shelf, mysteriously, it gets moved right back to the place Mom wants it to be.

My nephew Leland, the son of David and Dorothy, has been awakened in the middle of the night with Mom warming his cold feet with her hands. My niece Samantha, the daughter of my sister Sherri, was in a serious automobile accident several years ago when she fell asleep at the wheel, and praying to my mother, her grandmother, for help, was taken by her to a safe place.

My father, only eighteen years of age, and anxious to try his luck in the big city, soon after the death of Bussy, moved his bride to Columbus, the capital city of Ohio. He went to work for a company whose business was cleaning soot and ashes out of furnaces in residences, and he also worked at a fruit stand in the North Market there. My father, through a good portion of his working career, held down more than one job at a time. As my mother approached time to deliver me, he took her back to the farm where she wouldn't be alone during the day. He stayed in Columbus, traveling to Peebles on weekends. I was born there, in the farmhouse, delivered by the same doctor who had ministered to Bussy through the entirety of his illness. When I was three weeks old, Dad, having been called up to the Navy, left to take his training at the Great Lakes boot camp in Michigan. His stay there didn't last long. Having suffered with a chronic stomach problem for several years, the diet, especially the daily ration of beans, rendered him too ill to continue his military commitment. Six weeks into his training, he was given an honorable medical discharge.

Back home, Mom and Dad were down to their last dollar, and since they were without an automobile then, having sold it when Dad left for boot camp, and while Mom and I stayed on at the farm, Dad hitchhiked to Columbus in search of work, then hitchhiked back again on weekends. It being the boom days of the war production, it didn't take long for him to find a job, and purchase a cheap car. However, until he received his first paycheck and rented a room, clandestinely, after dark, he sneaked up onto the back porches of residences in the neighborhood and slept on the swings that were so popular back then.

When my father prospered enough to have us join him, we took a tiny third-story apartment on High Street, the main north and south thoroughfare bisecting downtown Columbus. My parents lived in that apartment until my brother David was born in April of 1945. Shortly thereafter, they bought their first home, a tiny Cape Cod located in the Westside of Columbus. They paid cash for it: nine brand new one hundred dollar bills. We hadn't lived there long when Dad decided he didn't like the way the house sat on the property. He wanted to move it. Vernie, the husband of Marie, a sister of my father, was in the heavy equipment business: bulldozers and other earth-moving equipment of all kinds. Dad commissioned Vernie to move the house back on the property maybe twenty or twenty-five feet, at the most.

Dad had learned a thing or two from his father A. E., and like A. E., Dad liked to reconfigure automobiles. One time he did a reconfiguration his pappy would have envied. Dad bought two '55 Plymouths, neither of them in good enough shape to drive. Taking a page from his pappy, with a blowtorch, he cut each car in half, and welding the two best halves together, had a perfectly functioning car. Luckily, they both were green in color, but the scorched pathway bisecting the middle of the car, never got painted. My brother drove that car for a long time, lowering it to make it into a hotrod, despite the fact that it contained only a 25 HP motor.

Another time, Dad got hold of an old '51 Nash Metropolitan convertible that he converted into a hardtop. Fashioning gray sheet metal into a roof for it, he riveted the top onto the frame of the car with huge bolts. Back in the days when my brother and I were teenagers, it was the fashion for our friends and us to hang out at local drive-in restaurants in Columbus, the kind of place where a carhop secured a tray onto the door of your car, then took your order, and delivered your food to you whereby you ate it from the tray through the open window of the door. Well, of course, those drive-ins were the places all of the boys showed off their cars. All evening long, around and around the parking lot, like a carousel in constant motion, the cars paraded for all to see. Mom loved to drive that Nash reconfigured hardtop, and one Saturday evening, having to fetch David and me at the house of a friend near our favorite drive-in where all of our friends hung out, Mom decided she would give them a gander at our new gray-sheet-metal-topped car. My brother, in the back seat yelled out to Mom, **"No, Mom…please don't do it! Please don't do it!"** But she did, laughing as if she were demented, while my brother, completely mortified, flattened himself to the floor of the back seat.

One day in the hot summer of 1944, as I approached my first birthday, and prior to my living with my maternal grandparents, my mother opened the windows of the apartment on High Street in Columbus. There were no screens. The head of the bed of my parents was placed just below their bedroom window. My mother and I were playing together on the bed, when suddenly I dropped out of the third-story window. Darting her hand after me, Mom caught me by the tail of my dress, scooping her free arm under me, breaking my fall. If the fabric of my dress had failed to hold, that would have been the end of me.

180   LINDA LEE GREENE

Nineteen

The former days of the music-filled rooms of the Gaffin house were no more. The music went out of their lives when Bussy died and upon the overseas deployment of Bob. Even the melody of the bells around the necks of the cows seemed perpetually muted; the morning music of the cock's crow; the weirdly harmonious cacophony of the chatter and clatter and clucking of the chickens; the home-welcoming barking of the dogs, all for a while were muffled beneath a blanket of grief. The transatlantic correspondence between Bob and Mommaw was her only refuge when her world became too crushing and grim…that, and her caretaking of me.

It had been two years and three months since Bussy had died, and I was twenty months old. I had been with my grandparents for seven months, and as the doctor deemed it still necessary, I was to remain with them for many months to come. On the radio we had heard the news about the push of the American troops across the Rhine to invade the heartland of Germany. An end to the war in Europe seemed imminent, but as a letter hadn't arrived from Uncle Bob for more than two weeks, Mommaw was frantic with worry. I was feeling despondent because my mother and my newborn brother David had gone back to Columbus a few days before. As had I, my brother had been born in the farmhouse of my grandparents, but the time had arrived for Mom and David to return to my father in the city.

At daybreak on the last day of April of 1945, I heard Poppaw yell at his dogs, Rex and Shep, **"Let's go get the cows."** It was the task of the dogs to dash to the far field where the herd had hold up for the night, round them up, and corral the best milkers into their separate stalls in the barn. The others were steered to designated spots among the huge cow-pods and horse droppings lying in wait in the barnyard. The massive piles of manure, some crusty from the day before, and the new ones wet and warm and steaming, but whether old or new, each one was coiled like a rattlesnake poised to lay waste our ill-fated feet. The task of Poppaw in those predawn hours, his only respite in the long day ahead of him, was to plunge his hand into his ever-present pouch of chewing tobacco where it resided in his hip pocket, and to treat himself to his morning "chaw" while he reckoned with the omens of the day, signs understood only by farmers, forecasts inscribed in the sky and air and dewy blades of grass as he trudged ancient foot-worn paths leading to his cattle. Other than a nagging suspicion that his landlord was cheating him in their sharecropping transactions, worrying about Bob, and of course, missing Bussy, Poppaw was a man constitutionally content with his life. He was profoundly awed by the jewel of the crescent moon still visible in the new-day sky, the music of the dawn-rising birds hovering in newly-leafed trees, their songs mingling with the spring morning sounds of his wife and awakening children back in the farmhouse, with Flossie's bawling welcome, her special greeting to him every morning. Scents of brewing coffee and baking biscuits mingling with the odors of earth and hay and manure and smoke and tobacco and warm milk spewing onto the ground from the dripping sack of Flossie, coiled into his head and made him dizzy with the wonderment of his life, and its abundant blessings. Ah yes, yet another blessing, his one and only sip of the day of the smooth and icy-cold water from interior wall of the natural mountain spring, the spring a never-ending cascade into the man-made catch-basin, the receptacle the drinking place of his animals, the water of the spring when captured in a bucket, the source of drinking and cooking water for his family.

As in all of the mornings before and after my arrival, while my aunts and uncles still slept, and while Poppaw was out with his dogs rounding up the cows for the morning milking, Mommaw went to the henhouse to gather eggs for breakfast. The routine hadn't changed except that then I accompanied Mommaw to the henhouse. One particular morning, however, I had delayed the departure of my grandparents with many questions, for, as never before in my experience, Poppaw was taking one of his hunting guns with him. During the night, a fox had raided the henhouse, and Poppaw explained to me that he would carry the gun with him at all times until he cornered, and killed, the fox.

While peeking tentatively around the outside edge of the ajar door of the henhouse, I waited for Mommaw while she gathered the eggs inside the nearly derelict building. It was malodorous to the extreme, even worse than the barnyard, and the chickens frightened me, especially the roosting hens. Like any good mother, they were protective of their eggs, and loathed giving them up to Mommaw. When she put her hand beneath their bodies to retrieve their eggs, the hens fluffed their feathers, seeming to inflate themselves grotesquely to twice their normal sizes. Low in their throats, they growled at Mommaw, like Rex the dog did at strangers who approached our property. Like shelves in a library, their nests were on racks stacked row above row on all four sides of the structure, the long boards forming the

182   LINDA LEE GREENE

fascias of the racks disgustingly coated white with the encrusted droppings of the chickens. Countless feathers were impaled in the chicken-wire coverings on the windows, and the feathers fluttered furiously when Mommaw entered the building. Sometimes one or two of the chickens would grow hysterical upon Mommaw's invasions of their nests, and flop around insanely, trying to fly on their ineffectual wings. They darted around like out-of-control Kamakazi pilots, crashing into the walls and the ceiling of the structure, setting in a swirl, feathers and chicken poop and dust, causing me to cough when rarely I braved entering the place. A riled Mommaw never failed to yell at the top of her lungs, **"Oh, jist settle down, won't ye, ye crazy birds! I ain't agoin' ta hurt ye none!"**

The eggs, some brown, some white, some speckled, bundled into the satchel formed by the skirt of the apron Mommaw wore, crashed to the ground that morning and broke into two dozen oozing yellow masses when the nervous hands of Mommaw flew to her terrified face upon the loud discharge of the hunting gun. She stumbled and fell to her knees, and I ran to her, crying and pulling on her hand. "Mommaw, get up. Get up," I begged. Her face streaked with tears, she pulled to her feet, and carried me back to the farmhouse. Later in the day, I protested vehemently to Poppaw as boldly I watched him skin the dead fox. He hung the beautiful red hide, its hair the color of my mother's, on a nail in the smokehouse. "A present for Bob when he gits home from the war," Poppaw told me. Somehow that made it all right for me.

Despondency had turned Mommaw quieter in the company of her fellows. She seemed to move by rote through her days; she had grown lean of body and gaunt of face and a distant look in her eyes was haunting. If she could get by with it, she conversed as seldom and as briefly as possible to everyone but me during that time. I had become her replacement for Bussy. I was the only person she wanted in her life, then. Except for the nightly rocking and crying, I reveled in the attention, and since her greatest and only pleasure was telling me little stories about our family, I took full advantage of her in that regard.

"Mommaw, did I weawy walk da furst time even before I had one birfday?" I asked her for the hundredth time.

"You came into this old world awalkin' and atalkin', Honey," Mommaw told me once again, and as attested to by everyone else in the family, by the time I was nine months old, I actually was walking like a trooper, and talking a blue streak. Once we returned to the kitchen from the henhouse, Mommaw returned to it to get a replacement batch of eggs. With the assistance of her eighteen-year-old daughter Reva, and fifteen-year-old daughter Bette, Mommaw prepared breakfast. The eggs were stacked five levels high on a round serving plate at their finish, their crispy edges swimming in bacon grease. Accompanying the plate of eggs was an enormous tray, crosshatched by row upon row of thickly sliced bacon,

GUARDIANS AND OTHER ANGELS 183

butchered by Poppaw from one of our hogs, the browned slices of bacon curled up on their edges like fallen leaves in autumn. If my mother had been there, she would have seen to the biscuits, otherwise Mommaw did it. It was my favorite part of the breakfast preparations. I watched transfixed as Mommaw stirred the dough in the big crock she tucked under her left arm like a football running back protecting his ball. The sound of her fork scraping the sides of the bowl as she stirred the dough was a confident sound, the sound of an expert craftsperson at work on what she did best. She never missed a beat. One dip of her hand in the flour bin magically produced the precise amount of white flour she needed, and like stardust falling from the sky, she sifted it through her fingers and sprinkled it onto her baking board. With the residue left on her hand, she coated the length of the smooth rolling pin. The slight tick, tick, tick of the rolling pin against its handles, the muffled bump, bump, bump of the rolling pin against the baking board as she wielded the instrument in her deft hands, pass after pass across the biscuit batter, at first a large flour-dusted lump of dough like Mount Vesuvius rising from its sea, then little by little, the dough stretched and stretched to a nearly flattened disc of dough I always worried would spring a bubble in its middle, and tear. But not to worry, without fail, at the finish it was always the perfect thickness, smooth and bubble-free. My favorite part of all, however, was when she cut the biscuits into perfect circles with the dusted rim of the dented tin cup she kept in the flour bin specifically for that purpose. Then onto the baking pan they would go, nudged into rows, aligned flawlessly by the knuckles of her curled right hand. It was a thing of beauty to watch Mommaw bake her biscuits, her light bread, her yeast cakes, her pies and cobblers and cakes. She could have made a good living at it in any fine restaurant in New York City, or anywhere.

I was forming complete sentences by then, and thereafter, it became my task to announce breakfast to the sleeping boys in the upstairs bedrooms. Standing at the foot of the stairs, in full voice and puffed up with the importance of my assignment, each morning I called out in all of my blond-headed blue-eyed ebullience, "Up, up, bekey (breakfast) time. Totie (Post Toasties) in da pate (plate) and milk in the goyosh (glass)." I had elected to forego the eggs and bacon in favor of cereal and milk, and in my young mind, concluded that my uncles should follow suit.

That very morning there had been yet another episode between Mommaw and her middle daughter Reva, "Aunt Re" to me. She was my favorite aunt by far among my many aunts, both once and twice removed, on the maternal and paternal sides of my family. Even though my mother always insisted that Aunt Re was the favorite daughter of Mommaw, at the same time, she was a trial to Mommaw. A blue-eyed natural blond, she had the pale and luminous beauty of leading ladies of the golden age of Hollywood, and she was funny, as well as loads of fun. She was the only person alive, it seemed, who could tease a smile out of Mommaw. Aunt Re liked to "primp" in the mirror above the dresser in the upstairs bedroom she shared with her younger sister, her primping sessions all too often delaying her appearance in the kitchen to see to her allotted, and most critical, morning chores.

"**Reee – VA!**" the accent on the second syllable of her name, Mommaw yelled up the stairs to her for the third time that morning. "**Quit that primpin' an' git down hyere an' help yer sister fry up them eggs...Reee – VA! Do ye hear me?**"

"Yes, Mother," floated the unhurried and melodious voice of Aunt Re down the stairs.

"**Don't ye 'Yes, Mother' me, young lady. I'll git me a switch an' come up there in a minute.**"

"Yes, Mother," the voice of Aunt Re rang prettily through the rooms. But still she failed to appear. I was mesmerized by her pluck, and I loved her all the more for it, for among all of her children, Aunt Re was the only one with the courage to defy Mommaw. Not that I was of a mind that defying Mommaw was the thing to do, it was just that Aunt Re actually did it that captured me so. To me, Aunt Re had turned exotic and dangerous right before my eyes during those months, exotic and dangerous in a way I also would aspire to be someday, although, at the time, I failed to comprehend the components of my attraction to her. It was just an instinctual thing then. We were kindred souls, having found each other among a multitude of other souls under the same roof. And on top of it, I was very proud of looking like her, an opinion held by many. Aunt Re and I shared a special bond until the day she died.

The commonly held view of my looking like Aunt Re failed to go over very well with my mother, who, until Aunt Re became terminally ill over forty years in the future, experienced mixed feelings toward her younger sister. That Aunt Re was the favorite daughter of Mommaw, had been a bitter pill for Mom to swallow. My mother, as the oldest surviving daughter, and typical of a child occupying her place in the order of the births of her siblings, was the obedient daughter, the noble daughter, the surrogate mother/daughter, the helpmate/daughter, the daughter deserving of the tenderness Mommaw showered on Aunt Re, but withheld from Mom. In addition, Aunt Re was an incorrigible flirt, and according to Mom, there had been instances where Aunt Re had acted inappropriately around some boyfriends of my mother's. When anybody advanced the notion of my looking like Aunt Re, Mom never failed to offer her succinct correction, "She looks like her daddy." And Mom was right. I do resemble Dad much more than I do Aunt Re.

Another few minutes passing with Aunt Re still failing to appear in the kitchen, Mommaw huffed and puffed in a rage, and stormed up the stairs. A few minutes later, Mommaw pulled the girl down the stairs by the hair of her head while she screeched and flailed her arms in vehement protest.

GUARDIANS AND OTHER ANGELS   185

Aunt Re was one of the great screamers of all time, a component of what I can only describe in layman's terms as a sort of hysterical side to her personality, the hysteria manifesting in troubling ways throughout her life. The most incredible example of it occurred over a number of years while she was experiencing menopause, when, with her own long fingernails, or tweezers, she painstakingly plucked out every hair by tiny hair on the front of her head, as well as on her eyebrows and eyelashes. I adhere to the opinion that the root of her "primping," of the hysteria, of her indistinct boundaries with the opposite sex, and of her mutilation practices, was the tragic accident at the tender age of four when she blinded one of her eyes with a knife, the "dead" eye remaining in its shriveled socket until she was a young woman in her twenties, at that time finally having it removed, and an ocular prosthesis put in place. What young teenage girl, at the time of her life when she is more preoccupied with the inadequacies of her personal appearance, real or imagined, than at any other time, could have survived her situation without "primping" excessively? More than likely, her sessions in front of her mirror were spent trying to camouflage her distorted, colorless eye, or to enhance her other features to compensate for it, a most frustrating and time-consuming affair, I would imagine. That she was otherwise so beautiful made it even more heartbreaking, in a way. Years later, she told me horror stories about how cruel her peers, and even perfect strangers, had often been to her, saying dreadful things to her about her spoiled eye, sometimes going as far as to shun her as if she were a leper.

The prosthetic eye, although a tremendous improvement, had its downside, as well. A fixed black pupil centering a crystal blue iris, the inactivity of the pupil was disconcerting to many people, and often, the sclera, even with the most scrupulous hygiene, became inflamed and oozed, requiring constant attention. She was forever swiping it with handkerchiefs, and later tissues, to keep it clean, and the persistent trauma of the wiping of the delicate tissue around her eye rendered it red and chafed nearly consistently.

When Aunt Re died, she was nine years younger than I am now. I was at home taking a nap in the afternoon of that day. I had curled up on my favorite napping place, a soft and pliable leather loveseat I kept in my bedroom, a private area where I read, wrote, and did paperwork. The back cushions of the loveseat conformed in such a way that it gathered in wrinkles all across the face of them. Due to circumstances beyond her control, as well as unfortunate choices she had made in her life, Aunt Re was a woman tragically and deeply alone in her last years, basically. She had been terminally ill with cancer for several months, and in those final days of her life, was in a facility whose purpose it was to provide hospice care to dying patients. As I napped, my body was turned toward the interior of the loveseat, its back cushion mere inches from my face. I awoke gasping for my breath, startled by something I was unable to immediately identify. When I opened my eyes, perfectly formed within the wrinkles of the cushion, as if the Hand of God had sculpted it there for me to see, was the face of Aunt Re, etched there to the smallest detail, even to the sloping eyebrow above her bad eye. I knew with a knowing beyond all knowing that Aunt Re was calling me to her, calling me because she was facing her final hours alone, and she wanted me there with her. I telephoned Debra, the oldest of the three children of Aunt Re, and arranged to rendezvous with her in the reception area of the facility within the hour, offering to enter the room of Aunt Re with her. Aunt Re's youngest daughter Amy arrived soon thereafter.

As we walked in the door of her room, Aunt Re called out to me in a way consistent with someone whose soul is deeply burdened. She seemed to visibly relax, however, as if she felt safe then in what she deemed to be my capable hands. I approached the bed, and when I bent to kiss her on her cheek, she whispered in my ear, "Linnie, I've never been baptized. Please help me get baptized. And please, Linnie, please wash my hair. I want to die with clean hair." Countless times over the years, I had washed and styled her beautiful and wavy blond hair. I, the artist in our family, did her make-up, too, on special occasions, and with my pencils and eye shadows and mascara, mustering every drawing skill at my command, endeavored to balance the distorted eyelid and its equally distorted eyebrow with its mate. She wore one of those special head coverings provided to female cancer patients who have lost their hair due to chemo- and radiation-therapy. Since her treatments had been discontinued several weeks before, her hair had begun to grow again, forming a not-unattractive cap of snow-white hair on her head, by then having reached a length of about two inches.

Feeling reassured by the vigil of Debra at the side of Aunt Re, as well as other members of the family who had drifted in, Amy and I left the room in search of a chaplain, and once found, arranged with him for her baptism to occur within the hour. Although she was sinking fast, she was still lucid when the chaplain arrived soon thereafter, and performed the ceremony for her.

Never before had I kept vigil over a dying person. The experienced impressed on me how antithetical the dying process appears to be to the human body, or perhaps more precisely, to the human spirit, given the merest opportunity of holding onto life. As the hours ticked by, her breathing became shallower and shallower, her breaths spaced further and further apart, as if she were dying in incremental parts, as if as one part died, perhaps a foot or her spleen or her pancreas, less breath was required to sustain the remaining body. The breaths were so widely spaced apart that the next and the next and the next seemed as miracles to me—it was incomprehensible to me that she could have remained alive during the interminable spaces between those breaths.

I seemed to cross into that river of consciousness where Aunt Re and I, and whatever force conducts existence, merged as One. In that way it was not unlike the act of love when the engagement between the lovers is so complete that all boundaries dissolve and time and space drop away and the lovers enter the Now. I go there often when I paint, when the piece emerges fluently almost despite myself, or when I write a passage that sings the praises of the written word and later I wonder from what source the words had come—surely not just from me! During those times I wonder what miracle had led me there—what elements had arranged themselves so precisely as to take me into the very heart of existence where past and future, life and death are One—are Now. In that instance, it was the miracle of the embodied soul of Aunt Re that led me there.

I had things to say to Aunt Re. By that time, she had slipped into a deep coma, and gave no indication that she could hear me, or to grasp the meaning of my words, therefore I spoke to her in my mind with the assurance that my spirit was at one with hers, and that she comprehended my words. I bared my soul to her and asked her forgiveness for my failure to keep her with me for the duration of her illness. Upon her initial release from the hospital after her disease was first diagnosed, I did take her home with me for a period of time, but my own dire and complicated circumstances at the time made it necessary for me to contact Debra for the purpose of making other arrangements for Aunt Re. When I advised Aunt Re that other arrangements had to be made for her, she said to me, "But why, Linnie? Is it because I've lost my hair? Is it because you can't stand to look at me?" It was for my failure to keep her with me, a decision I will regret for as long as I live, that I asked Aunt Re to forgive me.

Her last breath came forth with a kind of popping sound, like a balloon or bubblegum popping. I failed to recognize it as being her last breath, as, by then, I had grown accustomed to the long spaces between her breaths. I held my own breath, waiting and waiting for her next breath. It never came.

When Aunt Re died, I was so sheathed in that cocoon of consciousness with her spirit, that I was unaware of the presence of others. And somehow, someway, suddenly nobody else *was* there, and I was actually alone with Aunt Re. It seemed fitting to me that it should be that way, in the final analysis. Aware of the Buddhist belief that the spirit takes many hours to depart the body, I bent over her and held her in my arms as I would a baby, her face mere inches from mine. I wanted her to see my face there in front of her spiritual eyes—and something else, some inward prompting urged me to bear witness to the totality of her dying as I had her living.

With the force of the final release of her body, simultaneously with her last breath, her prosthetic eye was pushed out of its socket, and it deposited itself in the hollow place below the socket of her eye and the top of her cheekbone. Pulling myself away from her, gently, I lowered her head to the pillow. I stared transfixed at the prosthetic eye, stubbornly clinging there to her cheekbone, staring back at me as I stared at it. Strange thoughts flit through ones mind during such times. My first reaction was panic. *My God!* I thought to myself. *I have to get that damn eye back in its socket. Aunt Re would be mortified at having anyone see her with an empty eye socket.* But then, reason settled into my mind, and I realized, in or out, the location of the eye was mute at that point. Morbidity had its turn with me next. *Maybe someone will want to keep it as a memento*, I suggested to myself, and immediately sickened with the idea of such a thing. Finally, rage overcame me—rage at that damn eye, and all that it represented—all of the pain and suffering Aunt Re had encountered in her life directly connected at their very cores with her blind eye, I believed. Quickly, I pinched that damn eye between my thumb and index finger, and tossed it in the wastebasket, the ping of the glass eye against the metal of the receptacle, like a high-pitched ding of a triangle in an orchestra, sending a vibration of sound through the room. On the day she was given her terminal diagnosis, I visited her in the hospital. A woman morbidly unhappy for reasons far beyond her terminal diagnosis, her only words to me were, "Life isn't all it's cracked up to be, anyway." I imagined that at that moment the spirit of Aunt Re rose on the wave of the sound of her glass eye hitting the metal wastebasket, and she rode that vibration to a peaceful place, finally.

I removed the covering on her head, and washed her face and hair with a soapy washcloth. The final rinse completed, I threw the head covering and the washcloth in the wastebasket, and for the last time, combed the hair of my favorite aunt as I had done so many times before.

I straightened her gown, as well, although it was very difficult, as she was extremely heavy from retaining fluids due to her kidneys having shut down. I marveled at her legs: no broken blood vessels, no cellulite, no flabby muscles. Her legs put mine to shame, and I was nearly seventeen years her junior. But the deep scars on her hip and lower torso were still there. She had been eight months pregnant for Debra. She had been wearing a flowing nylon dress with a full skirt that blew in the heavy breeze. She had been burning trash in a barrel in her back yard. She didn't know she was on fire until a screaming neighbor bore down on her with a blanket in his hands. She lived, as did Debra. It was a miracle.

The hands and forearms of Aunt Re had also been badly burned, but not a scar was visible upon them. That was due to another miracle. Betty Newton Gaffin, petite and frail, the woman who was the wife of my Uncle Dick, had been born with a neurological disorder presenting itself as epilepsy, although nobody ever named it as such back in those days. She used to tell a story about something that had happened to her when a little girl. One day as Betty was alone and playing on the elevated front porch of the house where she, her brother, and their father lived, her mother having died two years before, Betty went into a seizure. She awakened from the seizure unharmed, and rather than lying on the floor of the porch as normally would be the case, she was being held in the arms of the spirit of her mother. Her mother whispered a secret in her ear, then walked her to the back of the house where her father was doing yard work. Subsequent to her burning accident, Aunt Betty visited Aunt Re in the hospital, who, like a mummy, was wrapped in bandages from her breastbone to her knees. Aunt Betty peeled back the bandages on the arms and hands of Aunt Re, and taking them in her own hand, one by one, blew on them while waving her free hand back and forth over the burned areas. As she performed the ritual, she repeated the secret prayer her mother had whispered in her ear that morning when she was a little girl. The burns healed almost immediately, never leaving the slightest hint of a scar. I saw Aunt Betty perform similar miracles several times on other people. Never did she reveal the secret words, no matter the promptings on the part of anyone, explaining that if she did reveal them, she would lose her power to help people.

Oh, how different life would have been for Aunt Re if not for the accident of the blinding of her eye with that knife when she was four years of age. I often wonder about fate, as most people do, about how it never fails to prove itself to be so elegantly precise, like the greatest ballet ever performed. My only comfort is that Aunt Re had to have been destined to show up at the dance with a blinded, distorted eye, and monstrous burn scars on her otherwise beautiful body. Surely her soul had arranged all of it as a means of experiencing the lessons it needed to learn in its "Aunt Re" phase of its evolution. Otherwise, none of it makes any sense at all to me.

It wasn't until my writing of this book that I realized what a profound experience my ministering to Aunt Re after her death had been. I did it because I loved her; I loved her in spite of her exasperating, even her enraging side, to the point of where involvement with her was actually painful at times, especially if you genuinely cared about her. In addition, Aunt Re was unforgettable in the ways of all great characters. While writing my first novel, Aunt Re was fodder for parts of that story, such juicy tidbits as the fact that she was an accident waiting to happen behind the wheel of a car, for the most part tied to her compromised eyesight, and a certain penchant toward a lack of common sense. She was extremely smart in other ways, however; was a good writer and poet. By the time she stopped driving, I think she had gone through every insurance carrier known to man. I'm sure she was on permanent retainer to nearly every auto body repair shop in town. Always, I mean always, there was another part of her car-of-the-day missing: a headlight, a side view mirror, a fender. One time she drove around for months with a missing driver's side door. And always she carried in her car, a huge flashlight, not for the purposes of using in emergencies, but as a **substitute** for headlights—many times she did this. It was Aunt Re, as I attributed to a character in the book who actually held up traffic when she got out of her car with the intention of duking it out with the man in the car behind her because he was blowing his horn at her when she stalled her car. Stalling her car; running out of gas; burning up engines due a lack of oil; driving around on balled tires were common behaviors for Aunt Re.

Breakfast gave Poppaw and the boys another opportunity to monopolize the conversation with "farm talk." Concern over a sick animal, a broken blade of the plough, the lack of, or excess of rain, all were discussed enthusiastically among them, the fog-horn voice of Uncle Dale, who himself would be a farmer in his day, even louder than Poppaw's, whose stentorian voice was rarely bested in any arena. Uncle Dick winked at me through breakfast, and fidgeted. He found it impossible to sit still for any length of time, unless, of course, he was monopolizing the attention of a female of his species. Then he would wait all day, or weeks, or however long it took him to win the object of his affections. He was the wild one of the bunch, to this day, his escapades throughout his life providing ample fodder for conversations among those of us who knew him.

After breakfast, Uncle Dean, "My Neenie," I called him, the youngest in the family, and seven years my senior, who also has spent the larger part of his life as a very successful farmer, never failed to pull me up onto his shoulders and carry me out to the barn where I imagined I helped with the morning milking of the cows. I was fascinated with the large sacks, the pink and pendulous udders of the cows. As Poppaw and the boys expertly massaged the lower portions of the sacks, then pulled on the udders of the cows with their strong hands to cause the milk to flow, I loved the rhythmical sound of the hard spray of the milk hitting the bottoms and sides of the metal pails. Sitting on a low stool at the left elbow of Uncle Dean while he milked his allotted number of cows, I stretched open my mouth to him like a baby bird while he squirted a long steady stream of the hot and cream-laced milk down my throat, the excess splashing on my cheeks and chin, the run-off soiling my sweater. Upon my fill, Old Yaller and Old Gray or just Cat, three of the large pack of cats who never had any real names, and whose job it was to keep the mice and rats at bay on the farm, stood up on their hind legs and boxed one another out of the way to get to the stream of milk Uncle Dean aimed in their directions.

Later in the day, when Aunt Re, Aunt Bette and the boys returned home from school, it was playtime for me. Positioning themselves in a triangular formation in the living room in front of the davenport, every one of those afternoons, my three uncles tossed me like a ball to one another, and then threw me onto the davenport. I screamed with glee, and yelled, "Do it again," as I pulled to my pudgy legs and jumped back into the arms of Uncle Dick.

"Okay, Squirt, here goes," Uncle Dick called to me as he tossed me to Uncle Dale, Uncle Dale to Uncle Dean, and back to the davenport to start the round all over again.

GUARDIANS AND OTHER ANGELS 191

As, like Mommaw and Poppaw, the sun gave up working for the day in our corner of the world, and retired behind the lazy hills reclining all across the broad horizon, it was then that the gloom of death-revisited settled in upon the household once more. Our nightly ritual never varied. Riding Mommaw's hip, she carried to the room where I slept. While the bedtime stories of other children were of "Snow White and the Seven Dwarfs" and "Cinderella," mine were of Uncle Bussy and Uncle Bob.

On the wall, within eyeshot of my bed, was a photograph of Uncle Bussy, a grainy black and white enlargement of his face and upper torso picked out of a family photograph taken when he was about eleven. Riding my grandmother's hip, always she carried me to the photograph where it hung on the wall. He had been a good-looking fair-haired pale-skinned boy, and like my mother, his nose and cheeks were dusted with freckles, his station in life clearly evident in his bib overalls. It was like one of those portraits where the eyes follow you all around the room, and although some children might have been frightened by it, it called to me, instead.

"Mommy says dat Uncle Bussy called me 'Tadpole' 'cause I was in Mommy's tummy when he knew me," I reminded my grandmother, my pudgy index finger tracing the cheek of the young boy in the photograph. The man he would never become was unmistakable in the outline of the jaw, although not quite angular, was on the verge of being, like a flower halfway between budding and full bloom.

"My land, yes, Honey. He tried so hard ta hold on so he could see you. Poor Little Bussy," my grandmother replied, her voice breaking, her great intake of breath tamping down the nagging voice of her great loss.

"I wish Uncle Bussy could know me, Mommaw. He wooks so sad in da pichure. I could pway wiff him, and make him feel bettuh."

"He was jist so sick, Honey."

"Is Uncle Bussy in Heaven, Mommaw, wike Mommy says?"

"He surely is, Honey."

"Can people come back home fwom Heaven, ever, Mommaw?"

"He surely would want to, if he could, 'specially ta see you."

"And, dis is Uncle Bobby," I pointed to a photograph on another wall in my bedroom, a photograph of a young man in a military uniform, sporting a handsomeness so blond and well put together as to be the envy of any movie idol. Mommaw carried me over to the photograph, my brow wrinkling seriously. "Uncle Bobby is fighting dat bad man in...I can't 'member dat pwace, Mommaw."

"Uncle Bobby is fightin' a bad man named Hitler in a place called Germany. Hitler is the leader o' them German people, an' we 'er fightin' them 'cause they do bad things," Mommaw patiently explained, speaking to me as if I were an adult, as she always did.

"Uncle Dickie spanked Wex dis morning. Wex got in da henhouse. He ate some eggs after dat fox weave."

"I know, Honey. Uncle Dickie had ta learn the dog that it's bad ta eat them eggs. That's kind o' like what Uncle Bobby is doin' over there in Germany, but not exactly."

"Is Gewmany weawy, weawy fawr away, Mommaw, wike Heaven?"

"Germany is away over on the other side of the world, but not as far as Heaven."

"Why did Uncle Bussy go to Heaven, Mommaw?"

"Because he went out ta play."

"You wet me go out to pway, and I don't go to Heaven."

"Uncle Bussy got real sick outside. When people git real sick sometimes they go ta Heaven."

"You made bad wike Wex, Mommaw. You forgot to tell Uncle Bussy no when he went outside, wight?"

"No, not exactly, but I shoulda stayed right there in the room with him."

"Did Uncle Dickie spank you for being bad wike he did Wex?"

"God spanked me, Honey."

"Did it weawy weawy hurt when God spanked you, Mommaw?"

"Yes, Honey. It really really hurt, an' it still hurts mighty powerful."

"But when I go out to pway, I won't get sick 'cause Uncle Dickie says I'm weawy weawy stwong. Uncle Dickie says dat Uncle Bobby is vewy big and stwong. And he wuns weal fast wike Old Smoky."

"He runs pert near as fast as that old horse."

"He can wun home to us, den, if dat bad man twies to hurt him."

"The Good Lord awillin', he will, Honey."

The nightly "visit" to the photographs of Uncle Bussy and Uncle Bob completed, Mommaw carried me to the living room, where the old rocking chair sat in wait. And the rocking and the holding and the crying on the part of Mommaw commenced anew. After I had fallen to sleep, carefully she carried me to my bed in the downstairs room nearest to the bedroom she shared with Poppaw.

My mind fixated upon the idea of Uncle Bussy finding his way home to be with me, one dark and still night, after all of us had gone to sleep, I woke to a sound I imagined to be Uncle Bussy coming home through the back door in the kitchen. *Maybe he's hungwy. Maybe in Heaven, God doesn't feed his people Mommaw's wight bwead,* I thought to myself. *Maybe Heaven people can't see bery well,* and determined to help Uncle Bussy find Mommaw's loaf of light bread resting on the sideboard beneath the larded cloth she had placed over it after supper, I climbed off of the bed to go find him. At first disoriented, I wandered through the downstairs rooms, my tiny bare feet pattering across the worn linoleum floors, and into the kitchen, once I found my bearings. But the kitchen was bare; Uncle Bussy wasn't there, after all, and suddenly, it was oh so full of dark shadows of ghostlike figures gripping me in fear of their black gloom. They, as I, seemed to me to be looking for someone they couldn't find. Next to the cloth-covered loaf of Mommaw's bread on the sideboard, a knife lay. My mouth watering from the smell of the bread, I thought a bite of it would make me feel less frightened, and maybe sharing it with the ghosts would make them friendlier to me. Pulling a chair over to the sideboard, I hiked myself up and on to it, and took the knife in my hand. The knife, much too heavy and unwieldy in my small hand, the bread wouldn't cut for me the way it did for Mommaw. I became despondent, and lonely again, lonely for Uncle Bussy, who would never get to know me if he couldn't find his way out of Heaven and come home to me; lonely for Aunt Dorothy, whom nobody ever seemed to know anything about; lonely for my father, who was working so hard in the big city that like Uncle Bussy, he couldn't come home to me every night, either; but most of all, I was really lonesome for my mother. *Maybe if I put my eye out wiff da knife da way Aunt We did when she was a wittle girl, Mommy will come and get me,* I pouted to myself in my mind. *Maybe if I stick it in my heart and die wike Aunt Dorfy and Uncle Bussy did, and go to Heaven where dey are, maybe dey can take me to Mommy,* my thoughts continued.

"**Linnie! Lordy, Lordy, what are ye adoin' in hyere in the dark with that old knife in yer hand?**" Mommaw screamed as she grabbed the knife away from me. I saw her clearly in the moonlight streaming into the room, the shadows from the tree outside the window next to the stove, flitting across her contorted face like wings of startled black birds.

Considering my close relationship with the family of my mother, it is easy to understand the comfort my parents felt with their decision to leave me with my grandparents during that time. Although they returned to the farm nearly every weekend, the heartbreak of their separation from me etched upon their faces, their heartbreak notwithstanding, at the insistence of the doctor whose authority nobody at that time had the wherewithal to question, still my parents left me there with my grieving grandmother—mrocking in that creaking chair, wrapped in the arms of her quaking body while she cried, finally only taking me home with them as I approached my second birthday. The therapy of my presence brought Mommaw out of the shock of the death of her beloved son. And, although on the one hand, my time there engendered in me an abiding and deep love and an appreciation for my elders and my roots, the effects of being nightly deluged with that depth of despair, as well as being separated from my mother at such an impressionable and vulnerable time in my life, have bedeviled me ever since, manifesting in a penchant toward mourning over-long, and a fear of abandonment.

Eight years after the death of my own mother, and in the days following the burial of Mommaw at the age of ninety-nine, among Mommaw's personal effects were found letters received by her during my many months with her as a toddler, letters written in the familiar hand of my mother. The letters, replete with words written by Mom describing her love for me, and her utter agony at being away from me during those early months of my childhood, were my own balm that soothed a loss I had sustained fifty-six years before; my loss: the surety of the commitment inherent in genuine love, an aspect of love I have distrusted since that time. When I read those letters written by my young mother, I shed tears amassed inside of me during the whole of those many decades. At last, I read the words I had so desperately needed to hear from my mother way back then, but never had.

Twenty

Overhead, their wide-swept dusty wings caught on invisible drafts of warm air, silent and deadly persistent, the turkey vultures circled. It was a common sight in that country, an Ohio land teeming with wildlife, teeming as well with domestic animals on the farms of the parents of Dick and their neighbors. Usually Dick paid scant heed of the sky or of buzzards, unlike his father and older siblings who kept wary, yet watchful eyes on the sky, for its caprice determined the quality of their lives. And the scavenger birds, well, they too often were the markers of a hog or a cow or a horse having come up missing. That day, however, the buzzards seemed an omen, one portending an unenviable future for Dick, and the birds, in agitated and impatient readiness to swoop down upon their carrion, magnified the apprehension of the boy. His long, sensitive fingers, in order to satisfy a passionate and inquisitive inclination of mind were incessantly tracing human skin, animal fur, tree bark, rock flesh, those fingers curiously upturned and flattened at their terminal digits like the heads of cobras catching scents in the air, now quivered with alarm, and now were bleeding around their nail beds, those fingernails that had been nearly ripped away from his flesh as he let loose his tentative hold and dropped from the two-story window frame he had clung to for several minutes, minutes longer and more frantic than any ever in time during his clumsy escape from the hardware store he and his younger brother Dale had vandalized. Was the carrion the hungry birds coveted his own bloody flesh?

Dick shivered and plunged his hands deep behind the ripped chest piece of his seen-better-days bib overalls and racked his brain for just the right prayer to a God he had theretofore ignored. His mind, that territory where personal preference had always won out over the negotiations in his conscience, negotiations between the sacred and the profane, came up empty this time. He eased back against the bole of a large tree whose girth and dense foliage provided him adequate coverage and allowed himself the more practical device of surveying his surroundings and, therefore, weighing his alternatives. Panting air, he was tempted to withdraw his hands from their hiding places inside his overalls and massage his calf muscles, which, although miraculously having remained uninjured in his fall, were strained and buzzing with burning pain, pain from his long and pushing run from the scene of the crime. He thought better of it, however, in case it was he the buzzards were tracking. Having lived and worked all of his life on a farm, and as strong as a mule and as fleet as a horse, he, therefore, under normal conditions could work or run all day without stopping. The circumstances of his escaping the hardware store though, had placed mental stresses on him he had never encountered. He felt depleted, empty in a way he never could have imagined. He was sure his legs were beyond their working capacity, and as for his brain, well, it was as blank as a white sheet donned by some of his neighbors when they assembled for their Ku Klux Klan meetings.

Lordy, what if the constable gits up a posse o' them Klan fellers ta hunt me down? Dick fearfully speculated in his mind. On many pitchblack nights, while carefully remaining out of sight behind the cover of dense bushes, he and his brothers had spied on some of those meetings, their goings-on scaring the boys witless. Since he was intimately acquainted with some members of the Klan, and therefore privy to the location of their clandestine, late-at-night meetings, Lee Greene, the husband of his sister Roma had led the brothers to the meetings. Their late night jaunts to spy on the Klan had taken place in the years before anybody ever suspected Lee would someday tie the knot with Roma. Every whipstitch there were rumors about people the Klan deemed as undesirables, people who had come up missing at their hands. One story abounded about a trio of black men they had hog-tied and skinned alive, the Klan then tanning their hides and making harness straps for their teams of horses out of them. *No siree bob, I don't want them fellers after me,* the shaky thoughts of Dick persisted.

A red fox squirrel, its bright pelt the exact color of his brother Dale's hair, charged through the branches of the tree, setting limbs and leaves aquiver. As if it were the king of the forest, bravely, and as it turned out, foolishly, it established itself on a fat branch of the sheltering tree, a location within striking distance of the head of the boy. The rodent, angry and vociferous in its ire, like a host bedeviled by an unwelcome and over-staying guest, ineptly barked its demands at him, its graceful, fuzzy tail nervously conducting its tirade. Trying to turn a deaf ear to the quarrelsome squirrel, Dick retreated to his thoughts again.

Please Lord, let Dale git away! a prayer for the protection of his little brother was the only one he could muster to a God he normally deemed questionable, and he turned his wet face to his bicep to wipe away his tears. Irked now by the pesky animal, and braving exposing his bloody hands to the buzzards, petulantly he spat at the squirrel, "Oh, hush up!" and like a

GUARDIANS AND OTHER ANGELS 197

striking cobra, pulled a hand out of the bib of his overalls, scooped up a heavy stone, and hurled it at the head of the scrappy squirrel. A crack of skull preceded the dusty dump of the squirrel to the ground. The animal, at any other time, would be sought-after prey for dinner, and instinctively Dick fished his knife out of the pocket of his overalls in ready to skin it, but he thought better of it. Although he knew that eventually it would become of paramount importance to him again, food, for the moment, and for the first time in his nearly fifteen years, was the last thing on the mind of Dick, and he put the knife away.

His twin sister Bette and he were middle children among their other six siblings, his eldest sister Roma insisting that Dick was the meanest kid who had ever drawn breath. She still hadn't forgiven him for stealing and eating, in the critical hours before the ceremony, all of her wedding candy, a rare and extravagant treat for the poor, dirt-farming family and their equally impoverished guests. His stomach, unused to the confection, had rebelled in kind. Between his gasps and moans later in the day, "Serves you right, you little varmint," Roma had whispered to him beyond the outhouse door, the occurrence souring him on sweets for the remainder of his life.

Not long after their marriage, Roma and her groom Lee Greene, seeking more favorable climes, had left Peebles, and the couple now lived in Columbus. They had two children by then, me and their newborn son David. Dick would give anything to find a way of high-tailing it to Columbus right then and there, a theretofore abominable thing to his country-bound soul, but a sacrifice he now would gladly make in order to escape the wrath of old Ed Hopkins, the owner of the hardware store. And the consequences to be wrought on him by Constable Will Branson and his cohorts, was nothing to savor, in any case, as well. In that back woods and culturally backwards burg of Peebles, Ohio, nestled within a sleepy and remote crotch of Midwest hills, the seldom-used, but nonetheless important business of crime-solving was hard to come by for enthusiastic purveyors of law and order. The dreary, monotonous, and reliable fare of raiding clandestine rot-gut stills and chasing thieves of someone's prized coon dogs was as far as the underbelly of life ever got there. No doubt about it, the bored-to-tears lawman was chomping at the bit with the prospect of getting his sweaty paws around Dick's and his brother Dale's very vulnerable, stuck-out necks. Dick didn't care as much about his own neck as he did Dale's. Although Dale had temporarily fallen from grace when he had concocted the scheme of vandalizing the hardware store, Dick still believed his brother, at his core, to be a much more worthwhile person than he could ever hope of being. To the mind of Dick, if anyone in their family had a chance of amounting to something special, it would be Dale, and Dick was protective to a fault of that potential in his brother.

In addition to owning the hardware store and the gristmill, old Ed Hopkins was the owner of the farm rented by my maternal grandparents.

198   LINDA LEE GREENE

Their farm rental agreement consisted of an equal sharecropping deal with Ed Hopkins, a questionable agreement, one often seeming to the tenant farmers as purposely designed for the camouflaging of dubious accounting practices favoring the pocketbook of the old man. One such recent and shady contrivance by Ed Hopkins resulted in spawning Dale's idea of getting even with him by the vandalizing of his hardware store, initially just outrageously vengeful scheming neither of the brothers really took seriously. As the wrath of Poppaw grew toward their landlord, however, the more the pot steeped on the idea of vandalizing the hardware store, until the lid blew, and Dick, changing roles with Dale, found himself actually initiating the caper, and leading his brother into it. It was an ill-conceived and ill-fated affair having set Dick to flight into the dense forest of the Appalachian foothills bordering their farm. Dick was unaware that eleven-year-old Dale had run home and buried himself deep in the hot and scratchy, bug-infested straw of the hayloft. Both boys were oblivious to the fact, as well, that the bright, copper-penny hair of Dale was responsible for revealing the identity of the brothers to the two eyewitnesses to the crime.

That the boys were amateur criminals was evident by the details of the episode. Taking place in broad daylight late one Sunday morning when the brothers had felt sure all of the inhabitants of the town still would be in church, they forgot to consider those few who failed to adhere to the principles of the Bible as zealously set forth and supposedly practiced by the religious trade in that portion of the world. Until then, Dale had lived an exemplary existence as the appeaser between his erratic and eccentric older brother Dick, and his precocious, little brother Dean.

The misdemeanors committed by Dick up until then had been confined to episodes by scale and consequences not much more malignant than his stealing of the wedding candy of his sister, misdemeanors, as well, such as his daily skirmishes in the yard outside their one-room schoolhouse where he felt honor-bound to straighten out every bully, or any other challenger of school age and beyond, in the area. The skirmishes, although often instigated by others, were inevitably blamed on Dick. Trouble just had a way of attaching itself to the boy. One young fellow, mild of manner, but tough almost beyond measure with whom Dick felt fortunate to have avoided confrontation, was Lee Greene, who before marrying Roma, was a former classmate and friend of Dick's and of his deceased brother Bussy. Prior to the pairing of the couple, Lee had spent time in a CCC camp at Rock Bridge Camp, near Logan, Ohio. A camp set up for the purpose of reclaiming the land and stopping erosion by the clearing of dead brush, trees and rocks, Lee had made $36.00 per month in a rated position as a second cook, the usual pay being $30.00 per month for non-rated duties. For the first time in his life having appropriate clothing, nourishing food, and adequate shelter in the barracks of the camp, Lee experienced for the first time, as well, the donning of boxing gloves. A talented, bantamweight fighter, Lee

GUARDIANS AND OTHER ANGELS   199

had bested all contenders save for a "scrappy, street-smart little feller from Toledo who beat the tar out of me ever time," as Lee explained it to his spellbound friends. Dick wasn't about to test his fighting skills against Lee, no matter the provocation. Besides, he genuinely liked Lee, better than any other fellow.

Teasing girls to the point of hysteria was also one of the favorite and maddening preoccupations of Dick, his devilment extending to any available female, including his schoolteacher Peggy Sue Heatley. The enduring romance of Dick with the females of his species blessed any and all females, short, tall, skinny, fat, cross-eyed, toothless, it didn't matter to him. To Dick, all females were beautiful and worthwhile, and throughout his lifetime, he demonstrated his considerable appreciation to a staggering number of them. The pilfering of the dentures of his grandmother and the scaring of Miss Heatley half to death with them one morning as he smiled his usual flirty greeting to her, his huge double rows of uppers and lowers resembling the dental structure of a shark, failed to go over as well with the teacher as he had intended.

Since the age of ten, having had nightly wet dreams about the teacher, he crooned her name to Dale incessantly. "Peggy Sue—Peggy Sue, it sounds so sexy an' makes her seem younger than she is. Not that I have a thing against older women, now. I shorely do appreciate all o' that experience they like ta learn me," Dick would tell Dale. Dick's eyes flashed with mischief, and he would draw his hands up to his mouth and snicker lasciviously behind them as if he had secrets he was dying to tell, but wouldn't. The most fascinating thing about Miss Heatley was that she had the largest bosoms Dick had ever seen, and he had spent an inordinate amount of time devising a plan whereby he might touch the breasts of Miss Heatley. For weeks having carefully considered his options, he happened upon the idea of somehow scaring her to the point of where she might fall, possibly even swoon, into his eager waiting arms. But, the lady had failed to swoon when he flashed his double rows of incisors at her, the desperate plot he had concocted as his means of fondling her breasts. To make matters worse, in his overly-anticipated expectation of her fall, in his lightning fast manner, Dick had jumped behind her, adeptly slipping his arms beneath her armpits, and as skillfully as Don Juan on his best day, cupped each of her voluminous breasts in his pawing and dewing palms. The lady screamed, and followed her decidedly unladylike expletive with an elbow to the solar plexus of our young and hopeful lover, the force of the blow ejaculating the dentures in his mouth smack dab into the back of the skull of Miss Heatley. A sharp kick of her heavily-shod foot at the seat of his pants punctuated his hurried escape to the door, a door closed to him for the balance of the school term.

Within the uncouth space of bewitching, smoldering, and shadowy eyes, and a boyishly, crooked smile, and clad in grimy overalls, the whole of him wrapped in effusive backwoods ways, the disparate parts of Dick amazingly and flawlessly settled into an extremely attractive package. His charmingly misfit ways rendering him ready for anything, extraordinary things, those things unfortunately never came to pass other than in risky ways. But, even with the jeopardy he embodied, those of us who knew him and loved him weren't ready to let him go when his time came, and we never have, really. He and his twin sister Bette were decidedly of the same windswept and nonconforming spirit, a spirit drawn to a life beyond acceptable boundaries as prescribed by their place and time. Having been bored with real life, and craving excitement, when their natural lives failed to provide the excitement, they created it. Even as they were a pair of human beings inhabited by the same spirit, at their cores the manifestations of that spirit in their separate souls couldn't have been more unalike. Whereas the conditions of her life shaped Bette in opposite ways, Dick was blessed with that lightness of being that we all are attracted to but too often repress in ourselves. He had that openness, that sense of delight in the new and novel conditions of life. Although he was deeply flawed by "normal" standards, his flaws came across as confusedly touching to us in mysterious places within ourselves beyond naming. Perhaps it was his lover-boy qualities: his gender, his good looks, his charisma, his sex appeal, his wit that prejudiced us in his favor and made us forgive him of everything. We forgave him as we would never forgive either Bette or Reva, or any female held to unfair double standards prevalent in our culture.

Toward the end of his life, Dick told me, "I've wasted my life dreamin' o' what could be, an' missin' what was right there in front o' my eyes." He said this more as advice to me, and less as a lament over his own life. Despite his words, I think at his core, even then as he was waging a war with his own death, he failed to understand why he had to leave his life feeling it to be so profoundly unfinished. His mechanical, daily routine of 8 to 5 factory work, the domestic requirements of adoring wife and beautiful daughter, of his prize chickens and fighting cocks, none of it was enough for Dick. If he could have had one grand adventure, one nobly grand adventure, just one, maybe he really could have settled in and accepted his life, but he was like Willa Cather's, Claude Wheeler: he was an "idealist without a big enough ideal to cling to."

I wish I had been wiser then—that day he said those words to me. I would have told him the truth about myself so that he would have known he had a kindred spirit right there within arm's reach. Not that I condoned all of his behaviors any more than I did my own then, but I wish I had at least been able to let him know I understood his struggle. His is a soul whose work is far from finished==the world will see that soul again—and perhaps again and again, until its spirit is satisfied.

Although failing to rise to the heights coveted for him by Dick, not another incident in the life of his cohort in the crime, his younger brother

Dale thereafter would mar a scrupulous and nearly perfectly-lived life of devoted husband and father, as well as farmer. A year or two after the death of his wife, Dale paid me one of the great compliments of my life. He was confiding to me his desire to find another female companion, and he said to me, "I'd like ta meet someone like you, Lin." I was profoundly touched and typically speechless at his admiring words. Shortly after Dale's death, I had a dream that I was attending the wake prior to his funeral. I stood among my relatives and friends gazing at the reclined figure in the casket at the head of the room, the body of my deceased Uncle Dale. An odd feeling nudged me to glance over my left shoulder, and as I did so, the figure of Uncle Dale, that redheaded, little boy having grown into his man-sized voice, stood within arm's reach of me. There he stood, tall – erect – imposing, his bearing jovial and larger than life, as usual. He looked at my astonished face, a mischievous twinkle sparking in his eyes. A broad smile rearranging his rugged, asymmetrical features into a landscape of even planes and gentle rises, he said to me, "Fooled you, didn't I?!"

Like Dick, like all of us with a mystical bent of mind, Dale also, in his way, lamented his loss of that special wisdom of childhood, that sense of the ecstatic Oneness with all of Creation. Despite Dick's far-reaching ideas of him, Dale, from his beginnings had fewer possibilities in life placed before him—he was less handsome than Dick, less charismatic, less sexy, less witty, less dreamy, and due to his narrower options, he escaped that hollow wandering, "the sickness of infinitude" in the words of Kierkegaard, that afflicted Dick. Fortune had smiled on Dale in that early in his life he happened upon the adventure presented to him through communion with his own true being. He took the interior journey rather than the outer one, the only true journey if one is to find ones way. Perhaps Dale did rise to the ambitions laid down for him by Dick, after all, for he had mastered that poignant emptiness, that formless longing. This is what Dick was trying to say to me that day. He was telling me he'd had a glimpse of the greater journey within himself—his own nobly grand adventure right there behind his eyes all of the time, and because he didn't have a clue as to its presence, he'd missed most of it while out wandering other landscapes, landscapes barren and cold and lacking that for which he'd yearned.

Miss Heatley had responded negatively to that restlessness, that untamed and untamable side of Dick. Unlike so many of us, especially females, she, for whatever reasons, was inured to the urgently, over-abundant, Dick. The incident with Miss Heatley, who in addition to being the schoolteacher, also owned and published the local newspaper where Roma worked as a reporter at the time, had become just one more item in a long list of comparable escapades responsible for the feeding of the life-long love/hate feelings of Roma for her ornery brother.

202   LINDA LEE GREENE

There was no turning back. The moment he had broken into that hardware store, Dick had entered another world, a world far beyond the walls of that building, of the geographical lines of that town, of the chambers of his prolific imagination. *I'll hop a freight. I'll live on the road like Arthur Billings did,* Dick said in his mind. Having been so young when Arthur had worked for Mommaw and Poppaw, and remembering little of their former farmhand, Arthur lived within the memory of Dick in stories told to him by Bussy. Pulling to his feet, Dick brushed his hands on the legs of his overalls, took a deep breath, and set to running again. He headed for Brush Creek and a train trestle spanning it a good forty-five minute run from where he had stopped.

Half of an hour later, his weakening legs seeming to have failed to get him any closer to Brush Creek, Dick was gasping with fear and fatigue. He pulled up abruptly, crumbled to the ground, and crawled under the shelter of a clump of trees. The sun was swiftly lying down behind distant hills, and with it pulled a brisk wind across the land. Although he was overheated from his run, only moments later, the chill of the wind seeped into his bones. Curling into a ball, he hugged his knees, and chattered from the chill, from his painful going, and from the dread of the sudden unknown quality of his life. The open terrain, shrouded in its dimming mantle of night, was teeming with life, the life-sounds of sleepy, crooning birds; drowsy, humming insects; creepy, chittering bats loosed from their caves along nearby Brush Creek. A howling, mongrel dog and an eerily, lonely hoot owl, added their voices to the cacophony, but none of it was much company for an entire lifetime, as no doubt would be the case for a life lived on the run.

It grew noticeably colder as dusk approached, lowering over the clear, April day a gauzy curtain of gray, a gray as somber as the mood of the nation at the recent passing of their beloved president Franklin Delano Roosevelt. FDR had been president for as long as Dick could remember, and he had been like a second father to Dick, as to all young Americans. Inside the sleeves of his denim shirt, the hairs on his arms turned prickly with gooseflesh as his body quivered in a spasm of cold and fatigue. Longingly Dick thought about his coat hanging on a peg inside the back door of the warm kitchen in the farmhouse. His stomach cramped with hunger. There had never been a day in his life when cold and hunger had failed to be easily relieved, but now he was hungry and cold and tired, and he didn't know what he was going to do about it. His cold, his hunger, his fatigue, his sudden loneliness instilling second thoughts in his mind about taking on the life of a hobo as had Arthur Billings, his mind raced with the consequences of his actions. If he went home, he would be apprehended and probably sent to the Boys Industrial School, a benign name for prison for young offenders. If he continued to run, well, God only knew what would become of him.

In letters to him from Bob, his older bother described the life of war he and his comrades endured, brutal challenges on rough seas, in the

GUARDIANS AND OTHER ANGELS 203

trenches, on enemy infested beaches, in forests, or mountains of alien places such as Africa, Sicily, Italy, France, Austria, Germany. No matter the cold, or heat, or gale force winds, or drenching rain, or blinding snow, or stinging sleet, always, always there was clenching hunger and crushing fatigue. To shield them from undo worry, Bob and Dick had made a pact between themselves to keep the descriptive letters secret from Mommaw and Poppaw. In a safe place in the barn, Dick hid the letters, but always he carried the latest one on his person until a new one arrived. Looking around and listening intently to make sure his pursuers were not upon him, Dick pulled the envelope from the pocket of his overalls. Unfolding the letter, he held it in his trembling hands. Squinting in the low light, he read:

April, 1945

Hello Brother,

As night fell in the Alps in Southern Germany in our push against the Nazi horde it was so cold the air froze in our nostrils and we thought our lungs would bust. During the day we had moved swiftly to cut the Germans off from their mountain stronghold and we was successful in that effort but it left us with nagging fatigue and hunger and cold like I never knowed. These mountains here ain't gentle and softly green underfoot like ours at home. The terrain of these mountains is a rock bed and our attempts to dig foxholes made only little furrows that wouldn't hide a rabbit or a squirrel. That left us with only trees and boulders for camouflage. We had to sleep setting up with a buddy at our backs and we supported eachother that way. We kept our rifles acrossed our laps and our fingers froze to the triggers.

By now you and all Americans have probably heard of the bravery of my fellow 3rd Army comrade in arms Second Lt. Audie Murphy. He personally killed fifty Germans in the woods near Holtzwihr, France in a fight where there was six German tanks and infantry support for the tanks. I wrote and told you about our hard and dangerous advance across France under the command of "Old Blood and Guts" General S. George Patton, Jr. During our advance to Bastogne there was a beating wind that whorled white with a blanketing snow. The snow turned to tiny ice particles that stung our faces like buckshot and stabbed our eyes and smothered us so we couldn't breathe right. It was so dense that the fellows and armored equipment up front or behind me was only ghost figures that most times I couldn't see. The tanks and half-tracks whipped back and forth on the icy ground and slid dangerously on the hillsides. When we found a road, they got stuck in deep mud where the road was rutted from when the Nazis had passed through before we got there. The foot soldiers got the worst of it. They wrapped their boots in their extra clothes but still their feet was as numb as stumps from the freezing and wet snow. We are fighting against German tanks and roadblocks everywhere. Machine guns and snipers nests hit us at every bend in the terrain and every cluster of rocks. And they are hold up in every window in every structure in every town it seems. Sometimes they swarm us like flies. There are so many acts of bravery on the parts of our boys. So many more than can ever be acknowledged. Every fighting man deserves a Medal of Honor.

Keep your heart young and gay for the next few years, brother because another war might come along that will take your innocence away before you are ready for it. I was lucky because I was twenty-one before I got called up and my stints in CCC helped me get use to being away from home. But there are boys here only a year or two older than you. They took so many young men right out of the CCC camps, you know. They are kids no more than sixteen and seventeen who like me had lied to get in CCC. I hear them young kids crying in the trenches and in their sleep at night.

We're bringing them damn Nazis to their knees. They can't hold on much longer and God willing I'll be seeing you soon.

Your brother, Bob (llg)

"At least they ain't no sniper shootin' at me, not yit anyway, an' they ain't agoin' ta be, not if I git ta that freight on time," said Dick aloud to himself. Quickly, he folded the letter back into its envelope, stuffing it in his pocket. He shot to his feet, and took off running.

Finally reaching Brush Creek, for a moment he sat at its edge. While gulping air, he removed his high-top brogans and socks. Stuffing the socks in the shoes, he tied the laces together and hung the shoes around his neck. Popping to his bare feet, and to camouflage his scent from the dogs the constable would put into the chase after him, he kept to the shallow edge of the water as he ran.

The creek was swollen and running hard and fast from spring rains and run-off from the hundreds of small tributaries feeding into it. Even in the low light, the grass was green and lush, the trees and bushes shivering in tender buds and petals. The profound affection Dick felt for his homeland tempted him to stop and roll around in the green grass, to cradle his head against a boulder, and to dream, as he so often did, but he dared not give in to temptation this time.

"Slow down, Son!" a voice called out. Dick stopped, doubling over with a sharp pain in his side from running so long and hard, and he fell on his backside into the water. "Where do you think yer goin'?" the voice came again. Believing it to be the constable, Dick panicked, and beat the water with his hands in anger. There was no time to lose, so he jumped to his feet, and dashed off again. **"You heard me, Dick. Stop! Stop! Stop!"** the voice bounced off of the tall cliff walls bordering the sides of the creek.

It ain't the constable, the voice in the mind of Dick said, and he came to an abrupt halt again. Thrusting his arms up into the air, he revolved around and around, his eyes frantically scanning the craggy faces of the cliffs. He recognized the voice...it couldn't be anyone else. **"Bus?"** Dick called out hysterically. His hands jamming to his head, he pulled his hair frenetically. "It can't be you...yer...yer d---." He recalled the incident involving their Grandmother Sallie who had died shortly after the death of Bussy. She had gotten blood poisoning in her foot from stepping on a rusty nail. The infection spread. At her bedside she had told Mommaw that Bussy was there to take her to heaven, and that he was sitting on the end of her bed, but that his weight was hurting her sore foot. "Lena, move the boy fer me, will you, please?" Grandma Sallie had requested of Mommaw, and then she had slipped away.

I'm goin' ta die! Dick shouted in his mind. *That's why Bussy's hyere. He's hyere to take me with him like he done Grandma.* He began to cry, and his legs having gone rubbery pulled him down into the water at the edge of the creek. Raising his legs, he rested his elbows on his knees, his hands cupping his ears.

"Go home, Son," calmly the voice came again. Dick lowered his hands from his ears, his head jerking back and forth, his breath panting through his opened mouth as his eyes searched the area again. The voice spoke once more. "You ain't goin' ta hop no freight an' live on the road. Think about what yer doin', Son, what yer doin' ta Mom. Ain't she got enough on her already? Mourning herself ta death over losin' me, an' worryin' about Bob, an' losin' her sister an' her mother jist almost right after losin' me, an' now even losin' you if you take off thisaway. You got ta go back home an' face the music, Son. Mom an' Dad can't take this. You think losin' his children don't hurt Dad like it does Mom, but believe me, it does. You got ta go home."

"But, Bus," his face pinched with dread, his voice convulsed with resistance, Dick protested, "If I go home, I'll git sent off ta B.I.S. That's prison, Bus."

"I know, Son, but you kin do it. Now, go home, 'cause if you keep runnin' now, runnin' 'll be all you kin do fer the rest o' yer life."

"No! I ain't goin' home, an' I don't believe yer hyere. Yer not real. This is my mind playin' a dirty trick on me," Dick rejoined, his face screwed in anger. In the distance, the familiar whistle of the train carried on the wind, the lure of that whistle smothering any logic from any voice anywhere, whether real or imagined. Dick jumped to his feet, and hopping like a kangaroo, thrust on his shoes.

If I follow Brush Crik, I won't git there in time. I gotta risk crossin' the road, an' skirtin' the quarry, Dick alleged in his mind. It was open country, even moreso since he and his friend Charlie Copley and his little brother Dean had set the sage and shin grabbers surrounding the quarry on fire the summer before. It had been a huge fire, threatening to spread to nearby forests, but miraculously, it had stayed contained to the dry grasses

206   LINDA LEE GREENE

around the quarry. Nobody had ever found out it was they who had been the culprits.

Squatting behind a bush at the boundary of the gravel road, Dick scanned the road in both directions before attempting to cross it. Beyond a dogleg in the road, he saw the unbroken plume of dust signaling the approach of a vehicle. The loud, intrepid crunch of hard, rubber tires filled with disastrous intention for him was acoustical in his ears, those tires ringing out his future, holding the whole of time in their circular boundaries. He dashed across the road.

"**I seen him!**" a man shouted. In tandem with the voice of the man was the metallic slamming of two doors of the vehicle, the cocking of three rifles. "**Split up! Virgil, you head ta the south…Walt, you go thataway. We got him surrounded. He can't git by us now.**"

Having slid feet first beneath a clump of cedar trees, Dick rolled into a ball, his head between his knees, his hands clamped around the back of his head. He stilled his breathing.

"**There he is, yonder–under them trees!**"

Jackknifing to his feet, Dick sprinted toward the quarry. Its nearest edge to his position was the shortest route to the adjacent fringe of a dense forest.

"**Git him!**" a voice called out. A volley of bullets thrashed into the dirt around Dick's feet. His arms pumping, his head thrust forward, his legs tore across the open field. Turning his head over his shoulder to get a fix on his pursuers, the toe of his boot caught on a small stub of a fallen sapling. Dick tumbled face first to the ground, his legs dangling helplessly over the edge of the quarry. His furious feet clambering ineptly for purchase, one hand holding frantically onto the stub of the sapling, the weight of his body pulled it loose from its tentative hold in the dirt. In a blaze of red sparks in front of his eyes, sparks of terror, for Dick could not swim, he slid into the bloated blades of the black water of the quarry.

His heart fluttering wildly, his blood gorging his neck and face, Dick tossed his head back and forth madly, his open mouth swallowing, then spewing the water, swallowing, spewing, swallowing, spewing, his thrashing arms and legs pulling him down, down, down into the heavy, deep water. Too terrified to look at the water, like a small child avoiding something frightful, he stilled his arms and legs and closed his eyes, his childish mind willing his awful fate to vanish. His arms relaxed and outspread at his sides, his head peacefully lolling back on his neck, his brain slipping into the freedom of unconsciousness, Dick sank into the cavernous depth of the murky water.

Suddenly, Dick's head popped to the surface, his mouth coughing grimy water, his arms and legs flailing like mad again, the arm of a strong and determined swimmer wrapped around his chest, pulling him to the edge of the quarry. "**Gosh dang, Dick. Quit yer flailin'**" the voice yelled out at him. **"I never could learn you ta swim nary a lick,"** the voice shouted. As he lay on the ground beside the quarry, Bussy's face peered through a tiny window of Dick's consciousness. It was the last thing Dick saw before he passed out.

Twenty-one

Shaking Reva's foot, his voice hoarse with sadness, Poppaw whispered, "Re, wake up. Wake up, Maimal." Rolling her head away from Poppaw where he bent over the bed, she opened her eyes to look out of the window. Through the thin curtains, she could see that it was still dark outside. Turning to face Poppaw, she raised her head off of the pillow, her eyebrows formed into a question. "It's Mother. I woke up from the sound of her wailin' agin," Poppaw said to Reva, his broad and rough hands slamming to his face to cover the onslaught of his tears. "I don't know what I'm agoin' ta do no more, Re," Poppaw sobbed uncontrollably, his brawny shoulders shaking

"Give me a minute to get dressed, Daddy, and I'll go with you to get her," softly Reva replied. She sat up in bed, and put her arms around her father. "You go on downstairs and wait for me on the davenport."

"We can't go off an' leave the baby by herself, an' I don't want ta wake her up," Poppaw said to his daughter as he pulled out of her arms. He swiped his wet face with the heels of his hands.

"I'll bring Bette down with me. She can crawl into bed with Linnie. And the boys are here. We can see the house from the cemetery, so everything will be all right, Daddy," reassuringly Reva said to Poppaw. Having gotten out of bed, she stood next to her father, and wrapped her arm around his waist. "Now, go on downstairs. We'll be there in a minute."

It was an hour before sunrise and the chickens in the henhouse were already beginning to fuss. Shep and Rex fell in beside Reva and Poppaw as they walked across the dew-soaked yard. "No Shep. Ye stay behind an' look after Linnie. We won't be but a little while. Come on, Rex, lead the way," Poppaw ordered his faithful German Shephard dogs. In the light of the half moon, beyond the gravel road and up the rise that opened to the cemetery, the lines of tombstones were clearly visible from the house, the slumped figure of Mommaw beside the grave of Bussy, a dark form in the distance.

GUARDIANS AND OTHER ANGELS 209

Father and daughter walked in the half moonlight, Reva holding the elbow of her father. He turned his face to her, and she could smell the familiar sweet scent of his chewing tobacco, the pleasant man-smell of his work. "Re, I bin wantin' ta talk ta ye some more about what ye got planned fer when ye graduate. It's starin' us in the face. Lordy, Lordy, where does the time go?"

"Daddy, I've made up my mind to go to Columbus, after all. Ro and Lee said I can come and stay with them while I attend that secretarial school." Like a lantern alight in the night, the moonlight glowed on Reva's white-blond hair.

"Well, that's good, Re. When 'er ye thinkin' o' leavin'?"

"Not until the middle of July, I think Daddy. I'll look for a job as soon as I get there. School starts in September."

As Poppaw listened to his daughter, his eyes studied the sky, and his nose sniffed the air, the weather, like a flowing river, the undercurrent of all other matters of their lives. "Ye got my blessin', daughter. Don't 'spect there's much in the way o' secretary work fer ye 'round hyere. We'll be missin' ye, Re."

Reva placed her cheek against the muscular arm of Poppaw. "I'll miss you too, Daddy."

"Well, I done made up my mind about somethin', an' I don't know how ta tell Mother. I done bought that farm up at German Hill. It's a better farm than this one, an' it's got electric in ever room, even in the barn. Ta git it, I had ta use the money we bin savin' fer a tractor," Poppaw explained, his face turning toward the horizon, his eyes taking on a misty quality as if he saw himself astride a brand new and shiny red tractor. Turning his head back toward Reva, he said, "Mother an' me looked at that farm jist a short while before Bussy took his last bad spell, but I ain't had the heart fer movin' with all the heartbreak an' trouble befallin' us of late. But I got ta git Mother away from this place. She kin see Bussy's grave from our kitchen winduh, an' ye know how she stands there an' cries. Mother's agoin' ta waste away, an' I ain't never agoin' ta git her back if I let things go on thisaway."

Although in principle she agreed with everything Poppaw was saying, Reva knew that Mommaw would refuse to accept moving so far away from the cemetery. Reva shook her head, intending to make a protest to Poppaw, but he held up his hand to stop her. "I want you an' Bette an' Dale an' Dean ta start packin' tamorruh when ye git home from school. Dick wouldabin a real help ta me, but he ain't hyere. I'll put him ta work real good soon as he gits home from B.I.S. Don't say nothin' ta Mother. I'll tell 'er when we git her back ta the house."

Poppaw's voice grew quiet as he and Reva approached Mommaw where she sat on the ground, her body bent over the grave of her son. She was so still that they caught their breaths in dread that she had also passed on, but as they came closer, she commenced to rock and whimper again.

"Come on, Mother," Poppaw said to her gently, reaching down and placing his hands on her shoulders. Snaking his hands beneath her armpits, he tugged on her until he set her onto her reluctant feet. She swayed weakly, and fell against her husband.

"No…no…Dad. I can't leave Bussy hyere in the dark night all by hisseff. I can't do it, Dad," Mommaw wailed, lifting her pleading face to him in the dawning light. The slopes and planes of her face had grown exaggerated with her grief. It was nearly inhuman in its anguish, its pain. She raised her arms to the shoulders of her husband, and resting them heavily there, buried her face in his chest. "No, Dad, I can't leave him hyere in the dark all alone." It had been the same every night since the death of Bussy, every night the family had gone to bed hoping it would be the last night that Mommaw would go to the cemetery to be with Bussy, but it had been many months, and still it continued.

"Come on, Mother. Ye can't stay out hyere," Poppaw said to his wife. He placed his hands on her arms, and tenderly pulled her to his side. Holding her closely, he wrapped his arms around her shoulders. "Jist lean on me, Mother. Re an' me, we come ta take ye back ta the house."

Quietly entering the front door of the house, Poppaw walked Mommaw into their bedroom, and he sat her on the edge of their bed. He placed his hand beneath her chin, raising her face to his. Poppaw said to his wife, "Lena, I done made up my mind, an' I went an' bought that farm over at German Hill. It ain't bin no good hyere fer a long while with old Ed Hopkin's cheatin' us ever time we turn around, an' since Dickie and Dalie's trouble with him, it's got even worse. An' I ain't agoin' ta permit ye ta keep agoin' over ta Bussy's grave no more thisaway." Poppaw saw the body of Mommaw stiffen with resistance, her face harden in cold immobility, but he squeezed his hands into tight fists of resolve. His feet planted determinedly in front of her, he said to her again, "I done made up my mind, Mother. Ye kin argie with me all ye want, but I done made up my mind."

Twenty-two

The farmhouse on German Hill was consistent with its counterpart at Cedar Fork in that the same grainy photograph of Bussy held its place of honor on a wall in the front room. And as at Cedar Fork, the new farmhouse seemed to me to be oddly lacking in all mementos of the short life of Dorothy, the firstborn child of Mommaw and Poppaw. Unlike photographs of the rest of us holding place on a wall, or a page in a photograph album, or ranging the top of a table, there was no faded photograph of Dorothy. There were no baby clothes carefully preserved in a cedar chest or a drawer, nor was there a lock of her hair tied up in a ribbon and tucked between pages in the family Bible, as far as I know. Of course, if she died at birth or shortly thereafter it is doubtful that any photographs of her were ever taken, and maybe she hadn't yet grown any hair. There must have been a small article of clothing, or maybe even her birth certificate put away somewhere that over the years has gotten misplaced. My grandmother, one of the great mourners of all time, a legacy she passed on to me during our many months together in that old rocking chair when I was a toddler, one I have faithfully upheld in all of the ensuing years, would have been compelled by her very nature to put something away belonging to Dorothy, something she could look at and hold and cry over during her long and frequent periods of grieving. Although among her parents and siblings, the firstborn status of Dorothy, and the place of Bussy as the most-favored child, were faithfully preserved in the family, "Poor little Dorothy," or "Poor Little Bussy," were the only words Mommaw seemed able to articulate to me regarding her fallen children, when, as a teenager, I first chanced exposing myself to her grief again, and asked her about my dead aunt and uncle. Her pain-filled eyes took on a faraway look, brimmed with tears, and darkened to that pit of hollow sorrow that as a child had been so very frightening to me. It was a look I remembered all too well, and although I loved my grandmother, and felt great sympathy for her, I had

212 LINDA LEE GREENE

to turn my face away from her eyes. I was afraid I would get lost in her sad eyes again, as I had so long ago. I was afraid I would be engulfed in her quivering arms, and the rocking and crying in that old rocking chair would begin all over again.

Strongly recalling the mystery of the life of my dead aunt to me, in addition to the sad eyes of Mommaw, and her reluctance to talk about Dorothy, was the regrettable absence of what should be by now her pitted and moss-clad tombstone at the head of a small grave in the burial plot of our family, a tombstone prominently placed to the left of that of my grandmother's—the appropriate side—the side of her heart, like that of Uncle Bussy. Having died in a distant part of the state, where, for a short time, my young grandparents had moved for my grandfather's work, Dorothy must have been buried there. Nobody seems to know anymore. It is a terrible thing to be interred in a place alone, separated from ones kin. Although it is doubtful it will ever happen now that nearly a century has passed since her birth and simultaneous death, it seems appropriate, as well as a means of closing a prickly gap in the saga of our family, to find her, and to have her moved to the place where she belongs.

We were a family reliably dedicated to the visiting of our relatives both alive and dead when I was a child, the dead ones on every holiday and birthday and the days marking the transitions of the seasons in between, if not oftener, those visits requiring appropriately decorating and maintaining their graves. In warmer months, we thinned, then supplemented the old-fashioned lilies of the valley and irises with geraniums and petunias, and on each Memorial Day and 4th of July, we added wreaths and miniature American flags waving perkily from wooden pegs. As the weather turned brisk again, we placed pumpkin-colored chrysanthemums on each grave, their ebullient faces reflecting the last rays of the sun, their drooping heads at the end of the season recalling to us the need for the removing of the Christmas decorations from their midst, and the placing of new grave blankets of hay over them before the January freezes blew in on the frigid north winds.

There exists a legend that birds shun other neighboring trees, preferring to gather en masse instead among the leaves on the branches of an ancient pipal tree in a shimmering land across the sea, the pipal a direct descendant of the holy tree the Buddha sat beneath while attaining enlightenment during his long days of contemplation there. It might be my prolific imagination at work, but I swear a similar phenomenon occurs in a venerable oak tree arching above the burial plot of our family, where, in the old cemetery among Civil War and other war veterans, upper-crust titans, and lower-caste farmers of the area, my grandparents, my mother and father, and most of my nearest, deceased kin now lie.

Back when my mother and her siblings were young, their old car of the day being too small to accommodate the whole of their large brood, their team of broad-backed workhorses, Roger and Smoky by name, straining against their leather harnesses, pulled their heavy flatbed wagon on their visits to the graveyard. Mommaw and Poppaw, taking a rare break from the demanding duties of their farm, were at the helm of the wagon. Dean, the baby of the family, sat between his parents on the high seat of the buckboard, a vantage point overlooking the ample rumps of the horses. In the back, the seven other children sat on bound bundles of hay perched vicariously on the gaping floorboards forming the bed of the conveyance. The group of them, in perfect harmony at the tops of their lungs, accompanied by Uncle Bob and Uncle Bussy on their mandolins, sang the old song, "On Top of Old Smoky," while the groaning wagon appeared in danger of imploding from the weight of its human cargo and the strain of the rough terrain suffering its challenged wheels and chassis. As the first grandchildren born to that family, my brother and I also rode on that wagon on some of those excursions, singing that old song in unison with our aunts and uncles at the tops of our voices. As the newest youngsters in the family, it was we who then got to ride between Mommaw and Poppaw on the high seat overlooking the broad backs of Roger and Smoky. I was a grown woman and married, with children of my own when suddenly one day it dawned on me for the very first time that the song was about the Smoky Mountains rather than a horse named Smoky. My Uncle Dean and I, during every gloriously long and adventure-filled summer of my young life on our farm, rode bare back together on top of our own old Smoky many times, often singing the song. In my young mind, it was natural that the theme of the song took on the meaning of horseback riding on our own Old Smoky.

I still can see in my mind's eye the wobbly wheels of the buckboard and the iron-shod hooves of the horses kicking up clouds of dust on the deeply-rutted mud-caked lane leading to that hillside cemetery, the accumulated clamor of buckboard, horses, and human beings setting in motion the flight of the collected birds in the old, oak tree, their overlapped and snapping black wings, for those brief moments in time, blotting out the sun.

One of my prized possessions is the old, earthenware jug that contained the grease Poppaw used to lubricate those screeching wheels, the interior of its fissured walls coated to this day with black and slick remnants of the grease. During those journeys, every once in a while, he would yell, "Whoa, Roger…Whoa Smoky," and the buckboard would come to a grating halt. While the horses snorted from their huge nostrils and pawed the ground with their heavy hooves, their hot bodies steaming and making auras of their perspiration all around them, down from the high seat on his long legs Poppaw would jump, pulling that jug from beneath the seat, a stick jutting from its open top. The working end of the stick wrapped in a grease-blackened cloth, he would smear the axles of the wheels with it.

Not long ago, a psychic, supposedly consulting messages pertaining to me emanating from the realm of the spirits where, I presume, such things are known, and scripted within her crystal ball, told me that I should make a habit of visiting cemeteries on a regular basis again. I am yet to figure out how she was privy to the habits of my family of old, and it wasn't until my writing of this book that I understood her counsel to me.

At the entrance to the road looping the community of Cedar Fork, although several new homesteads have sprung up over the years, still it feels to me as if I am entering an evolutionary backwater, a safe-haven cut off from the rest of the world. These days I come to call in my car rather than on the old buckboard. I take the left turn in the loop that leads me past "Greene Acres," the location of the fallen log cabin built by my paternal grandfather A. E., my father Lee, and his brother Bill so long ago. Just across the road our shelter house now stands. I pull my car into the area where many of the remaining members of the Greene family occasionally congregate for camping weekends.

I walk to the edge of the property, its border high above Cedar Fork Creek. In the canyon below, sunlight filters through the trees, winking gaily upon the water. I stretch my eyes to get a glimpse of the footbridge by the ancient, mountain spring, and a bright ray of sun, as if switched on for my benefit by the Hand of God, isolates it and sets it aglow. I take it as a "token" message, a greeting to me from the spirit of my paternal grandmother Eva Love, and I smile and wave at her as if she were actually standing there. Satisfied that my presence has been acknowledged and welcomed, I return to my car.

Further along the looping, gravel road, I drive across the bridge spanning the creek, now of concrete and steel, but in the young days of my father and his kin, and even the youthful days of my siblings and me, the bridge was of native timber and indigenous stones. I recall the washboard rumble of the log floorboards of the bridge, rumbling on the tires of my father's car when we returned to the log cabin to visit his mother and his younger brothers and sisters. I travel on to the cemetery.

Over the years, the markers of my deceased, maternal relatives have accumulated there in the graveyard in Cedar Fork much too early in our collective story. I am shocked, as always, at the number of them as beneath the tires of my car the gravel on the lane leading up to the small, country cemetery loudly pops and crunches. And yes, as if in testimony to my childhood memories of such a phenomenon, while its abutting trees appear to me to be empty, huddled within the gnarled branches of the same wizened, oak tree, the gathered birds are perched. The noisy flight of the birds as I approach the graves briefly blankets the sun, those graves now almost exclusively under the care of my Uncle Dean.

GUARDIANS AND OTHER ANGELS 215

I have read somewhere that birds are manifest angels on earth, but I am less wise about such things than when a child. Knowing it will not be confirmed to me until I return to my source, I leave it to the humming wheel of the universe, and to my elders, almost all of whom, on my mother's side of my family, are already there.

Today again, the day of my birthday, as when a child, more than any other, I am drawn to the tombstone of Bussy, a simple flat-topped rectangle. Like me, it has grown old and pitted. I am alone in the cemetery, except for the birds, and as usual they have resettled in the old, oak tree, keeping a wary eye on me, I suspect. A huge bumblebee is taken with the bundle of flowers I hold in my hand, its sun-struck, yellow stripes phosphorescent, so bold the stripes jump out at me. It is heavy with heat, this midday, and heady with the gray smell of clay comprising the soil. My face is washed with my sweat, and my worn-to-thin denim jeans rolled up to my knees and my thin cotton shirt covering my upper torso are too hot for this sojourn in the cemetery. My stomach lurches with guilt yet again, as it does with each visit, guilt at the certain knowledge that my mother has been turning over in her grave at my neglect of the burial plot of my relatives. I acknowledge her with a gentle brush of my hand across her name incised in the granite, and then I turn my back to the graves of my parents, as my mood draws me to reflect on other members of our family today.

I bend at my waist, for kneeling is difficult for me now, to place the small bundle of flowers across the face of the tombstone of Bussy, flowers for him to celebrate my birthday. It is difficult for me not to think of him, and especially on my birthdays, for I have always had the feeling that he has looked over my life, that envelope marked *Tadpole* in his handwriting, and the five-dollar bill tucked inside of it, his ticket to go along on the ride with me. Now, however, as never before, the mystery of the missing tombstone of Dorothy tugs at my consciousness. I wonder about her. Would she have been a toe-head like Uncle Bussy and Uncle Bob and Aunt Re, or a redhead like my mother and Aunt Bette and Uncle Dale and Uncle Dean? Or would she have been a brunette like Uncle Dick? To even things out, I pronounce Dorothy to have been dark-haired like Uncle Dick, with his brown eyes, eyes flaming with an inner passion unfamiliar to most of the other members of my family, a passion while intriguing and motivating, was by contrast as well, perplexing and frustrating to him, and like an unscrupulous master, one, too often, leading him astray. Dorothy, as Dick, I decreed further, would have been enigmatic and charismatic, where so many of us were and are elementary and transparent, and yes, rather bland by comparison, I'm afraid.

It had been a revelation to me, after the photograph on the wall of my bedroom when a child, to see Uncle Bob home and in street clothes, the whole of him intact although changed immeasurably by the war and the loss of Dorothy, the girl he had left behind. In no time at all it seemed, he was married to Louise, and becoming the father of five children. I walk to the shared tombstone of Uncle Bob and Aunt Louise, Uncle Bob's side perpetually decorated with an American flag and military mementos. Next to their grave are those of three of their children: Marcie, Joe, and Anita. Aunt Re and her stillborn firstborn child Nita; Uncle Dick and his wife Betty; Uncle Dale and his wife Patty; Aunt Nellie, the wife of Uncle Dean; my mother and father, all of them are there—all but Aunt Dorothy and Aunt Bette and her husband Ray and their son Ernie, and daughter Connie, all of whom are buried somewhere else. Of the generations of my grandparents and parents, only my Uncle Dean remains with us, but his place is waiting there, the empty spaces on the shared tombstone of his wife still blank and in that blankness a stark and jolting reminder that all of us must die.

There is so much about this silent place that bewitches me, the way I am bewitched when I cross the threshold of a great library. All of these stories, these remnants of the past scrolled in the living universes within the outwardly lifeless rectangles of granite gravestones, and in the cases of those first inhabitants of this site, moss-glazed, natural stones, stories tugging at my imagination, stories tempting me to unearth them and tell them. My Muse reminds me, however, to keep to the narrow path set down for me by my soul when it embarked upon this journey embodied as Linda Lee Greene. I walk to the shared gravestone of Mommaw and Poppaw, the real reason I am here, after all. Lying there side-by-side are Mary Evalena Caplinger Gaffin and Joseph Elmer Gaffin, Lena and Elmer, Mommaw and Poppaw to me, and to my many cousins. I feel the eyes of Mommaw staring out at me, burning eyes replete with our story, calling me to tell it. This is why the psychic sent me here—to remember, and to tell! "All right!" I say to my grandmother. "But not today—tomorrow!" I submit emphatically, and I turn and walk to my car.

Twenty-three

My back and forth childhood is revisited with each milestone of my family, in the marriages and deaths of my aunts and uncles, of cousins born and cousins dying, of the deaths of both of my grandfathers not long after the births of my own two children Frank and Elizabeth. During their long marriage, Mommaw and Poppaw Gaffin had prospered. At the time of his developing the emphysema responsible for the taking of the life of Poppaw, he and Mommaw owned two adjoining farms, the German Hill and the Brush Creek farms. At the onset of the ill-health of Poppaw, plans were set in motion to relocate Mommaw and Poppaw to town where they would be closer to their doctor and the hospital. After selling the German Hill farm to Uncle Dean, and the Brush Creek farm to Uncle Dale, Mommaw and Poppaw moved into the first home of Uncle Bob and Aunt Louise, a tiny two-bedroom house on Fifth Avenue within the town limits of Peebles, Mommaw living there alone for many years after the death of Poppaw.

There comes a time, if we live long enough, when so much of life exchanges itself for memory. I recently heard a story about a man, who because of his heart disease, can no longer eat red meat. To indulge himself vicariously in his former great pleasure, he reads reviews of steakhouses in newspapers and magazines. It was the same for Mommaw after the passing of Poppaw.

"These old bones jist don't want ta git me out o' bed no more," Mommaw said to the vacant spot beside her on the ancient, past-its-prime mattress, the musty, feather-filled mattress having long escaped replacement due to extenuating circumstances having injected themselves, stirring up trouble and messing up the usual routine of her long life, a peaceful life she preferred it to be, a goal she pursued several times a day with the lament, "Lordy, Lordy, give my life some peace."

218   LINDA LEE GREENE

Her middle daughter Reva, her ornery, jokester-child, liked to tease her mother with the taunt, "You would be better off, Mother, if you asked the Lord to put some life in your piece."

The still visible indentation of Mary Evalena Caplinger Gaffin's dearly departed husband's form, her husband of over fifty years, one Joseph Elmer Gaffin, still lingered in the broken-down mattress, his scent still just as plain as day, his presence still as real as if he actually sat on the side of the bed.

"Land, how many eggs an' biscuits an' pots o' coffee do ye reckon I cooked in my time, Dad?" the old woman asked the still visible imprint of her passed-on husband's head in his pillow. "Land, it seems like only yisterdy that our little Linnie stood at the bottom o' them stairs when she was only a little tot, an' yelled ta the boys, 'Up, up, becky time – toatie in da pate and milk in da guyash.' Now Linnie is all grow'd with grow'd children of her own. Land, how time flies. Lordy, how many mornings do ye reckon we got up with them chickens, Dad?" Mommaw questioned Poppaw's empty imprint on the bed.

"I don't reckon I know, Mother," she insisted she heard him counter, the sound emanating from the empty spot in his sunken-in-at-its-center-feather-pillow where, during all of the years of their marriage, and before his death, he had lain his russet-haired head, the sound still tainted with what she swore on a stack of Bibles to be his tobacco-tainted breath scrolling up from his compromised lungs. When still alive, when still robust and active, never a sound exhorted from him during actual slumber, never a snore, nor a snort, nor a whimper, nor a whistle, nor a cry, nor a word had passed his lips, a silent unmoving sleeper was he, "sleeping the sleep o' the dead," Mommaw used to say. "Dalie and Deany is takin' me ta that new place over at West Union tuhday, Dad. They say it's a nice facility fer old folks like me. Don't rightly know if I'll like it there er not. With all o' them old people afoot all the time, how does a body breathe, I ask ye?"

Mommaw died on January 6, 2001, eight months shy of her 100th birthday. I was too ill to attend her funeral. For many years I had been afflicted with Crohns Disease, having grown so ill by then that it had been decided I would undergo major surgery to save my life, surgery whereupon my large intestine, including my lower bowel, would be removed, and a permanent ileostomy constructed to take its place. My surgery occurred three weeks after the death of Mommaw. I had last seen her on the occasion of her 99th birthday, my sister Sherri, her daughter Samantha, my daughter Elizabeth, her son Alixander, and I having gone to see Mommaw in the nursing home where she had been a resident for several years. Upon her bed, her fragile body permanently twisted into a fetal position from osteoporosis, her face sweet, her demeanor content in a way as never before, her aura was as luminous as an angel's. Lost to dementia, although she smiled sweetly when we walked in the door, for she had been told of our coming, she hadn't the faintest notion of who we were. "We're Roma's daughters, Mommaw, and Roma's granddaughter and her great grandson. You remember who Roma is, don't you?" I inquired of her hopefully.

"My land, o' course I do. Roma's my oldest girl. I don't 'spect I've saw my girl for a good while," Mommaw responded, a disconcerted look entering her milky eyes. Mommaw, having been lost to dementia even then, was unaware of the death of her eldest daughter eight years before. Mommaw took the opportunity to begin to reminisce briefly. It was apparent that in her mind, she was there, still living in the happiest time of her life, the time when she was on the farm with Poppaw, when all of her children were youngsters. She was completely unaware that she had outlived all of them: Poppaw, Bob, Roma, Bussy, Reva, Dick, Bette, Dale, all of them except for her youngest Dean.

I reached down to her, taking her hand in my own. She raised her glowing face, her eyes searching mine. "And I'm Linnie, Mommaw," I told her, my face alight with anticipation of her acknowledgment of me.

Her eyebrows wrinkling in dismay, she half-turned her face away from me, her eyes aslant with suspicion, studying my face intently. "Nah, you ain't my Linnie. My Linnie's got blonde hair," she informed me emphatically, failing to recall that upon my entering puberty, my hair had grown darker. As with her own children, she remembered me as I was in my toe-headed childhood. Those were the last words Mommaw ever said to me.

During the summer of 2007, for the first time since my late adolescence, I took to spending some time with my Uncle Dean on his farm, the same German Hill farm Poppaw bought after the death of Bussy. Recently, both Uncle Dean and I celebrated another birthday, both of us having birthdates in August. The evening of my birthday, we sat out on the front porch of the farmhouse and reminisced—we talked politics and lamented the state of the world—we complained about the aches and pains in our old bones.

Uncle Dean, my first playmate, and in my mind anyway, the relative most like me—a moderate Democrat, content with his solitude, his duties, his role as witness to the journeys of his kin and kind, the receptacle of their stories now passed down to me as with my pad and pen I recorded his words, even down to the sound of his countrified dialect—still undiluted and pure in spite of the influences of the satellite TV in his front room and the cell phone hanging from his belt.

As it was with Bussy, this life I have lived is so very unlike the one I had imagined, the one I set into place in the beginning. Sometimes I am still amazed that the boy I married at the age of nineteen is no longer my companion, as has been the case for three decades or more—that instead of that early love at my side, on a fairly regular basis I find myself sitting on the front porch with my first companion: my Uncle Dean. We seem to be given our roles rather than choosing them, and now I am certain that the writing of this book was part of my soul's assignment—one that couldn't have been accomplished had I stayed on that other path. Does it make up for the loss of that earlier life with that boy I married so long ago? I don't know. What I do know is that this journey of the heart I have taken while writing this history of my family and their times, has engendered in me a new sense of proportion—has closed the curtain on my former sense of the past, a past far too tragic and far too absent of wonderment. It has been good for me to remember it—it has led me home again.

After Uncle Dean went to bed, I stayed up for awhile, lingering on the porch. It was a dark night—moonless and still—silver with glistening and wandering stars. I thought of Uncle Dick and imagined him harnessed to one of those stars and racing it along the topknots of the blue-black foothills spanning the broad horizon. And I tried to envision Bussy in some ongoing endeavor, perhaps in another galaxy, that one, young boy who in incalculable ways had become the conscience of those who were, and would continue to be now, witnesses to his short life while here in Adams County, Ohio, USA, planet Earth. Surely, wherever evolution has sent him, his role is to continue to lead other souls back home.

A fire glow in the clear and silent night sky pointed to the rim of the star-wound where I was born, and in my mind's eye I transformed into an archaeologist whose job it was to unearth the secrets of that early Indian civilization, the bits and pieces of their lives contained within the great mound of the serpent lying there in the cradle of the debris of that long ago meteor strike. With the delicate tools of the trade in hand, I imagine myself beginning to dig. *Will I find her?* I wondered. *Will I find that other woman, that Indian woman who like me was born on the rim of this star-wound?* Among arrow heads and shards of pottery, I imagined I found a small bone—a section of one of her fingers, then remnants of her jawbone lying beside a rock that revealed itself to me to be a pillow for her head. A group of four small and nearly matching stones fairly tumbled into my hand when my trowel scraped away a knot of finger roots of a tree. Each one of the stones was punctured with a little hole at its center, the jewelry for her necklace, I realized. *Yes, four stones...the sacred number of these early people...the number four symbolizing the four directions of the world...the four seasons. Did she have her own Mommaw and Poppaw, an Uncle Dean, her own Bussy?* I inquired of the mantle of stars lighting my way. I declared kinship with that Indian woman, and in that new sisterhood, I felt buoyant and lifted, taken above and beyond this material world as our joined spirits floated on the silver mist blanketing the panorama before me. My transcendence was short-lived and I quickly became earthbound again, however, as at my back, emitting through the open door to the front room, I swear I heard the voices of my grandparents. I swear I heard Mommaw say, "Linnie told our story, Dad, an' a goodly piece o' it's about Bussy. Thisaway

GUARDIANS AND OTHER ANGELS 221

he'll git to live a nice long life like the rest of us only in the pages of Linnie's book."

Poppaw replied, "Ain't too many common folks git ta live a life thataway, Mother. The differentness of it is jist right fer Bussy. Ye know how he was always hankerin' fer something new an' different. Remember the time he took a shine to that new cowboy hat Bobby brought home from CCC camp an' Bussy wanted it so bad he....."

These fleeting birthdays of our dotages, rolling in softly on calm waves of gentle tides, stay for a few hours then mistily swoop back out toward a future far less panoramic in depth and breadth than that of our pasts, that is, unless there really are ongoing journeys of our souls. If the universe follows the orderly progression humankind would have it do, my Uncle Dean will be the next to go, and then me.

If there is some designated meeting place, all of them will be there with arms outstretched to welcome me in. And having gathered Dorothy and Bussy to her bosom again, Mommaw, past grieving—well, she'll be right there in the middle of all of them, right in the central place where she belongs, gaily rocking in her old, rocking chair—and recognizing who I am once more, she'll pull me onto her lap, and she'll rock me.

222   LINDA LEE GREENE

Author's Note

I wrote the first draft of *GUARDIANS AND OTHER ANGELS* in 2001 during a lull in my work on the manuscript of my first novel, the Amazon best-seller *Jesus Gandhi Oma Mae Adams,* co-authored with my maternal first cousin Debra Shiveley Welch. The working title of the piece at that time was *These Old Bones,* but with each revisit to the manuscript, a much larger and much changed story evolved, and I realized a new title was required.

Four years later, on the occasion of the sixtieth birthday of my brother David, the writing of this book about our parents and their origins became a full commitment on my part. We spoke by telephone, he, in Northcentral Florida where he had made his residence for four decades; I, in Columbus, Ohio. Other than spending the tumultuous sixties in New York and the early seventies in South Florida, I have resided in Columbus, the city where we grew up. My brother and I were discussing my having reached the long-sought milestone of publishing *Jesus Gandhi Oma Mae Adams.* He was struggling with forced and permanent retirement due to his having developed a serious illness of his lungs, and I suggested to him that he might fill his time by writing a book of his own. He responded hesitantly, but also with a hint of curiosity. "I've thought about it, but the only thing I could write is a story about Mom and Dad," were his words. Seven years later, with *Guardians and Other Angels,* I fulfilled that goal for him.

GUARDIANS AND OTHER ANGELS chronicles a significant era in the lives of my maternal and paternal families, the bulk of it spanning the Great Depression and the Second World War, the culmination of my extensive six-year study of those historical eras. Inspired by tales passed down through four generations of my family, at its core, it is a true story, one evocative of porch swings and farm houses, of barnyards and rural roads, and of people atuned to raw, pure soul. However, I chose to write it as fiction to accommodate interesting and important historical events of the first half of

GUARDIANS AND OTHER ANGELS 223

the Twentieth Century, tandem events of the hard economic times and the war, events that in all likelihood did impact my ancestors directly, but have not been substantiated through family lore. In addition, writing it as fiction allowed me to showcase the complexities of the principles of the story by placing them in imaginary situations.

Since there are so many more stories than I could work into this book, and conflicting versions of some of the ones I did use, I chose the stories and the versions of them I concluded to be most compatible with the story I wanted to tell. Often, I exercised literary license in presenting them in a manner conducive to a novel, meaning I sometimes used them as launching points for my own imagination where there are gaps or differences in the oral legends. Ours is not a precise family history, therefore at times, I found it necessary to manipulate and enlarge the tales, and/or to couch the lives of the characters in this book in experiences of my own invention.

All but a few of the letters included in *GUARDIANS AND OTHER ANGELS* are transcriptions of actual letters initially preserved in a collection by my maternal grandmother Mary Evalena "Lena" Caplinger Gaffin, and currently by my maternal first cousin Mary Rosalie "Rosie" Gaffin Brown, this volume containing those written from 1936 to 1941. To accommodate the story I wanted to write, in a handful of cases, I supplemented the authentic letters with ones I composed expressly for the book, and although credited to the various characters in my story, the letters I wrote are identified at the signature lines with (llg), the code I devised to separate the unreal from the real letters.

Just as it is important to separate the authentic letters from those I wrote for this book, it is also imperative that I identify fact from fiction in the legends I have herein depicted. All of the principle characters in the book are real, other than Arthur Billings, who appeared in my imagination through a phenomenon of the Great Depression about which I learned in my research of that period of history, and as described in this story

In addition, to simplify the story, I eliminated the Neal Place Farm in the town of Peebles that was the actual residence of my maternal grandparents at the time of my birth, and was therefore the real place of my birth, as well as that of my brother. The remaining backdrop of the story as I have described it in Chapter Two is factual.

It is true that I spent many months of my toddlerhood with my maternal grandparents as recommended by our country doctor, a sojourn designed to help Mommaw through her grieving time over the loss of Bussy. My reference to the frequent episodes of rocking in the lap of my grandmother as she cried is also true. Visiting the photos is a story I designed around the fact that the photos of Bussy and of Bob in his military uniform always were prominently displayed in the farmhouse, their presence eliciting questions by me through the years. The incident of my getting up in the middle of the night and Mommaw finding me in the kitchen with a knife in my hand is my much enlarged version of a true story. Legend has it that due to my despondency over missing my mother, I got hold of the knife and threatened to kill myself if she didn't come and get me.

Many of my other renditions of the tales are symbolic in nature, however. An example is my fictionalized account of A.E.'s actual difficulty with a neighbor over his profiting from a purchase of timber land from the man. I have no idea of the real details of that story. Even though my description of the family of origin of Lena in Chapter Four is fairly accurate, and it is true that when a girl she did wish to be a carpenter, my little story about it is fictional. Mommaw's relationship with the person I identify as Otto Burley (a fictionalized name) is essentially true, and there has long been speculation as to whether or not she carried a torch for him all the days of her life.

My account of the loss of vision in an eye of Aunt Re is a manipulation of that true incident. My depiction of it initiates and supports the bittersweet relationship between my maternal grandmother Lena and my mother Roma, as well as my mother and Bussy's conflicting feelings toward their little sister. On the other hand, my story about the circumstances leading up to, and including, the death of Aunt Re, and my ministering to her after her death, is absolutely true in every detail. Another story I invented is the one where Mommaw insists that my mother go to the henhouse and get the chicken. Again, I wrote it as a way of illustrating the factual misgivings Mommaw had about the romance between my mother and my father, and the steps Mommaw actually took in sabotaging their courtship. The story of my father Lee milking the cow and walking to school in the snow when a young boy is a fictional story, one based on the very real and unfortunate circumstances of his childhood. My depiction of the character and behavior of A. E. is my very conservative estimate of my enigmatic, paternal grandfather. The exchange between Lee and Bussy at the schoolhouse is an imaginary tale, as well, created by this author to depict the beginnings, and the flavor, of their actual friendship. In every other instance, the details of the lives of Roma and Lee, the two people who are my parents, are true.

As mentioned above, Arthur Billings is a fictional character. My maternal grandfather never had any hired hands on his farms. He did all of the work himself, other than the help he received from his sons when possible. I added Arthur for several reasons: Since the backdrop of this story is the Great Depression and World War II, while conducting my research on those subjects, I came across the phenomenon of the quarter of a million teenagers of both genders who had lived as hobos on the roads of America during the Great Depression. I was so taken with that aspect of my country's history that I wanted to include it somehow in this book. Arthur became my teenage hobo. He was a good device for creating imaginary scenarios in which I placed the Gaffin family, episodes such as my involving the family in the great snowstorm and the flood of the late 1930's. It is safe to deduce

GUARDIANS AND OTHER ANGELS 225

that the family was caught up in those historical events, but nothing in the historical record indicates the form of their involvements. My stories of those two historical events as they relate to my family are wholly products of my imagination.

In addition, Arthur evolved as a way of placing Bussy in one of the central roles in the story, an example being my invention of Bussy's coaching of Arthur in the art of tobacco chewing in Chapter Six. In actuality, Bussy did contract the measles virus and went out to play "hoops" too soon, which was the source of his lingering illness and eventual death. However, the story in which I couched those facts is fictional. Since Bussy died a few months before I was born, and as such I didn't know him in reality, I fashioned a personality for him in this book, one I believe to be highly representational of him based on family lore, but especially on descriptions of him as related to me by Uncle Dean and my father. In addition, I do feel a special connection to Bussy, one that I believe gives me exceptional insight into his soul. Bussy's relationship with the radio as related herein is fictional, as is his interest in baseball, but the little poultry kingdom he developed is true. The story of Tarzan, the fighting rooster, is my fictionalized version of a true, but sketchy story, and is the source of my little book for juvenile readers titled *ROOSTER TALE*. Arthur's giving his mandolin to Bussy provided me with a way of dramatizing the natural musical talent of Bussy. Although Bussy did play the mandolin and other instruments, and music did take the place for him of normal childhood play due to his compromised health, I have no idea of how he actually came by his mandolin. The story of Mommaw's reluctance to allow Bussy to get his driver's license also is my completely fictionalized characterization of what I believe must have been her fear of loosening the ties of the symbiotic relationship between her and her sick child.

In fact, Bussy did want to go to Arizona, and he and Aunt Reva were all packed and ready to go. Mommaw and Poppaw were preparing to sell out, the entire family to follow. Even my mother and father had decided to join the family in Arizona. But for some obscure reason, the Wards rescinded their offer. Bussy wouldn't have survived the trip anyway. The death scene was also invented by this author, but it is true that Bussy did give Dean several pennies and a knife just prior to his death. Dean did break the point of the knife, and Bussy did caution his little brother to be careful not to put out his eye. They were the last words Uncle Dean remembers Bussy saying to him. Bussy did not maintain a map for the purpose of tracking Bob's movements in the war. I came up with that idea as a way of including Dale in Bussy's last hours of life. The scene between Bussy and my mother near the time of his death when he wanted to listen to the "Tadpole" in her abdomen is as near to the true incident as I was able to accomplish. He did, in fact, leave an envelope with a five dollar bill in it for me. It is true that Mommaw spent night after night crying over the grave of

226   LINDA LEE GREENE

Bussy, and as a consequence, Poppaw did move his family away from their Cedar Fork Farm.

Arthur Billings also became my way of presenting the character of Uncle Bob in all of his legitimately fine and noble aspects. In reality, Uncle Bob did not run away to join the CCC, and he did not leave a letter for his mother and the kids. He did lie about his age to get in the CCC, and his primary motivations for joining were to get money for the medical care of his brother, for the repair of the farm equipment, as well as to contribute to the financial requirements in the building of a new house for his family of birth. In real life, this person was a great writer of letters, and sending him off to CCC camp the way I did opened up for me the opportunity of depicting him through his letters in this book. His opening sentiment, "My Dearest Darling Mother" is based on the literary contents of his actual letters to his mother. Most assuredly, he was born to be a writer, but did not follow through with it, as far as I know. It is my fervent hope that in depicting him through his letters in this book, I have been instrumental in satisfying that requirement of his soul.

Uncle Dick did get in some hot water for making amorous advances toward his teacher, but the form of his advances and his penalty are unknown to me. Again, my account of that legend is fictional. My characterizations of the personalities of Uncle Dick and Uncle Dale fit them to a tee, and together they did vandalize the hardware store, and Uncle Dick did go to BIS for a short stay. But his going on the run and Bussy's appearing to him and saving him from drowning as I have portrayed it, is purely a product of my imagination. I created the ingredients of that narrative as a way of bringing the story to a climax. The letter to Dick from Bob in that chapter is fictional, as are others of the letters herein included, especially those I credit from Bussy to Bob. Even though I dated it near the time of the surrender of Germany, still the letter I wrote to Dick from Bob wouldn't have survived the censors of the letters the G. I.'s sent back home. It is simply too descriptive of key military positions. For the purpose of eliminating redundancies, I did condense a few of the actual letters.

I chose not to change the names of any of the members of my family herein included, although not in every case, nor in every detail, are my characterizations complete or accurate. To insure anonymity, I did change the names of many other persons mentioned in the authentic letters.

This novel is written from my own perspective, but I hope the consensus among the members of both my maternal and paternal families of origin will be that although I may have taken some liberties with sacred memories, and in places may have made some outright errors in facts and judgment, the result is an acceptable approximation of my family's specific histories preserved within a larger story.

In this pulling back of the curtain of time, my initial intention was to preserve in written form these pivotal years in the lives of my great grandparents and their descendants. Over time, however, I recognized that in this warm, sweet, and deeply emotional human story of ordinary people living big lives spawned from the very soil from which they were spawned, I was also authoring a qualified submission to the vast body of work devoted to the conservation of stories centered on the fundamental way of life herein depicted, narratives to which so many modern-day people turn for solace, times too often cold and lonely and bitter.

In this piece of Americana at its most personal and profound, I have presented a sort of Hillbilly Eden as its backdrop. In many ways, it was just that, but it is also an uneasy history in some ways—any straight talk about the past must be uneasy—for, as in all histories, not only does this one tell of life and light and triumphs, it also includes death and darkness and devastating loss. It is a tenet of good writing that it should avoid rank sentimentality. I had no desire whatsoever to follow that rule in this book. Therefore, it is my hope that this story comes across to its readers to be as heart-wrenchingly sentimental as a good old lump-in-your-throat country song.

GUARDIANS AND OTHER ANGELS was a joy to write. I hope it is a joy to read. I will welcome your comments and inquiries about this book, or any other subject, at my
email address:

lindaleegreene.author.artist@gmail.com

Linda Lee Greene – Columbus, Ohio, USA – 2012, 2015

Author Biography

Linda Lee Greene was born in a farmhouse bedroom of her maternal grandparents located on the rim of the famous star-wound in Peebles, Adams County, Ohio known the world over as the Great Serpent Mount Crater. Mother of a son and a daughter, and grandmother of two grandsons, Greene resides in Columbus, Ohio. An award-winning artist, an online exhibition of some of her artwork can be viewed at www.gallery-llgreene.com. The cover of *GUARDIANS AND OTHER ANGELS* is printed from one of her paintings of a Southern Ohio forest.

In the year of 2000, Greene wrote the original draft of the murder mystery/historical novel, *"Jesus Gandhi Oma Mae Adams,"* a manuscript that evolved into a co-authorship with Debra Shiveley Welch. Upon its release, it was an Amazon best-seller.

GUARDIANS AND OTHER ANGELS has inspired a book for young readers titled *ROOSTER TALE*. It will be released in 2015. Greene plans to publish her new novel *Cradle of the Serpent* in early 2016. A story of love, passion, infidelity, intrigue, tragedy, and more, in it, the commitment of a married team of archaelogists is tested greatly. Further information about Greene's books are at: www.booksbylindaleegreene-llgreene.com.

eBooks for your Kindle, your laptop, your PC, and smart phones for Greene's books are available at www.Amazon.com.
Blog: http://Ingoodcompanyohio.blogspot.com
Email: lindaleegreene.author.artist@gmail.com
Book Website: www.booksbylindaleegreene.gallery-llgreene.com
Art Website: www.gallery-llgreene.com
Amazon Author Page: https://www.amazon.com/author/lindaleegreene
Facebook Author Page: https://www.facebook.com/#!/LindaLeeGreeneAuthor
Twitter Username: @LLGreeneAuthor

Made in the USA
Lexington, KY
25 April 2016